The
Independent

Also by Art Burton

For Hire, Messenger of God
A murder mystery

Caught in the Line of Fire
A murder mystery

Concealed From Sight
A murder mystery

The Bag of Money
A murder mystery

The Poker Game
A murder mystery

Hobos I Have Known
A collection of short stories

More Hobo Stories
A collection of short stories

Check out: artburton.ca

The Independent

ART BURTON

Cover photos by Flame

Published by Art Burton

Printed by CreateSpace

3 5 7 9 10 8 6 4 2

Contact Art Burton at art@artburton.ca

For Peter

ACKNOWLEDGMENTS

First of all, I must thank my son, Peter, for the idea for this story, although he may not recognize his suggestion in the final product. Unlike my other books, this one is set in the United States of America. I had to do this because I needed their political system. The Canadian parliamentary system would not work for my purposes.

Bev Dauphinee once again stepped up as my editor and once again did a masterful job of making it look like I am an English scholar. Thank you, Bev, for your patience and persistence.

Sandy Boutillier made some great catches of some typos and other errors. Thanks, Sandy.

Google proved to be invaluable as I worked my way through the intricacies of the American political system. I hope it makes more sense to the people who live there. Google maps turned me into a knowledgeable traveller of the country to our south.

And as always, I must acknowledge my wife, Flame, who allowed me time to drift off into this make-believe world of political intrigue and terrorism.

◀1▶

"A SCHOOL IS going to blow up? Where? When?"

Governor Peter Weston searched the face of his chief-of-staff for some hint of a prank. Malcolm Truex looked deadly serious.

"There's a YouTube page we must check out. It may be a hoax, but—"

Malcolm Truex served as the consummate political aide. He had the CYA, cover your ass, principle down to a science. More accurately, Malcolm saw his position as protecting the governor's ass, PGA. Malcolm's avowed goal in life was to advance the career of Peter Weston, current governor of Georgia. Not because of some blind loyalty, but because Malcolm believed Peter Weston stood out as a leader among men who deserved to be governor and eventually even president. "—if it's not a hoax, then we want to get out in front of this thing right away."

"Come on, Malcolm. I have better things to do than surfing the social video sites on the Internet looking at man-eating spiders and the lost city of Atlantis and so do you. Where'd you get this wild idea?"

The concerned look on Malcolm's face indicated to the governor this wasn't some giant-sized spider stalking the highrises of New York. He swung his luxurious, black leather executive chair around to face the screen.

The governor knew Malcolm was the hardest working person on his staff, and everyone on his staff worked hard. The governor only surrounded himself with the best men and women he could find. Not everyone liked Peter Weston's politics; he served as an Independent in a staunchly two-party political system. No one could deny his dedication to moving Georgia up the ladder from a backwoods state to one of leadership in the nation. His enemies believed Peter Weston looked at the governorship as a stepping stone to the office of the president.

He watched as Malcolm leaned across his desk and turned the keyboard towards himself. Malcolm referred to a scribbled note placed on the desk and tapped a few keys.

"I didn't discover this myself," he said as he walked through the menus appearing before him. "I received several calls from concerned constituents. Heavy traffic popping up on people's news feeds for the last hour demand people stand by for some major event about to take place. The teaser ads indicated it could be catastrophic.

"'Politicians and businessmen ignore this at your peril,' the messages read. 'This school could be anywhere, even in your backyard.' Memories of 9-11 still lurk in the backs of everyone's minds. I could hear the panic in the voices of those I talked to."

He stood back as a picture materialized on the screen.

The high-definition picture sprang to life. "This isn't a YouTube site; this is a live feed from somewhere."

Several children in colourful party clothes—boys in button shirts, girls in puffy dresses—were munching on french fries and hamburgers, washing them down with Coke and milkshakes. Squeals of delight formed the basic soundtrack. Despite the formal clothing, bedlam seemed to be the rule of the day. The sugar-charged kids bounced from one seat to another, crawling wildly over each other, oblivious to gender in a way only small children can be. Here and there, spills on the tables, chairs and floor went unnoticed by everyone except the adults who gingerly stepped around them. The easily recognizable setting was a BurgerCircus fast-food restaurant. The image of their clown lurked everywhere. Just as obviously, a birthday party was underway.

The governor looked at his aide with a perplexed expression. He held out his hands searching for some explanation. Malcolm's face remained glued to the screen. "Whatever is supposed to take place is going to happen at the top of the hour," he said. He pointed to the clock in the bottom corner of the screen as it ticked away the seconds towards noon.

The camera started to close in on one of the children's faces. Presumably, the governor thought, the birthday boy. The governor squinted to see if he recognized the little tyke. Blond-haired, blue-eyed, he looked like hundreds of kids everywhere. The smiling, young face slipped from the centre of the frame. Beyond the boy's left ear, the camera focused on a view outside the large, picture window. The zoom continued to enlarge the background, centring on a brick building across the street. *Alexandra School District* was inscribed over the main doors.

The governor gave Malcolm another confused look. "Are you saying this school is going to blow up? Where is—"

The governor lurched back in his seat as the brick building exploded into thousands of pieces of flying debris before the men's eyes. Flames poured through every window and shot out of the roof like a Saturn rocket launching. Seconds later, the picture jolted as the percussion from the explosion rocked the restaurant. The sudden jerking of the camera showed spilt drinks and kids tumbling to the floor before it steadied and resumed its outside viewpoint. A black mushroom cloud slowly rose over the building and disappeared out of the top of the shot. Fine particles of dust, all that remained of the pulverized building, filled the air, turning the scene through the window into a white haze of nothingness.

"Holy shit, what happened?" the governor asked in a

rhetorical exclamation as he regained his proper position in the wheeled chair that had flown almost to his office window.

Malcolm remained silent as he studied the words filling the screen.

"This Is Only The First" appeared in tall Franklin Gothic letters. That image faded away to what could only be another school, then another and another and another. The images were coming and going faster and faster until they were simply a blur of changing buildings, some large, some small, flickering on the screen.

More words formed on the screen, coming in wide and then scrolling into a narrowing image reminiscent of the original Star Wars movies. A deep bass voice resembling Darth Vader or James Earl Jones did a voice-over reading the text. "No one was injured or killed in this explosion. You were lucky. What about the next time? Starting tomorrow at midnight one school will be blown up every night unless you pay us one hundred million dollars. That's a one followed by eight zeros before the decimal point. The second school disappears at 1:00 a.m., the third at 2:00 a.m., etc. You do the math while you still have schools to teach you how to do it. These schools could be anywhere in the country. We have placed the bombs already. One hundred million is a lot of money, even for your free-spending government. We suggest all the fast-food companies band together to raise it. They have, after all, made their fortunes on the backs of the very children who use these schools. We shot this video in a very recognizable building. Mr. CEO, you and your clown are in charge of raising the money. BurgerCircus's new goal and slogan will be $100,000,000 raised. You, Ray Tutty, are responsible for overseeing this endeavour. Do not fail. The safety and education of our children depend on you."

The picture returned to the opening shot of the happy

kids and played through to the point of the explosion. The frame froze as the building exploded, capturing the debris as it fanned out from the epicentre. A small insert in the bottom of the picture showed the company clown with an exaggerated shocked look on his face. He then faced the camera and gave an equally exaggerated laugh. There was no sound for the insert. You had to make your own interpretation of the sound of the laughter. Ghoulish sprang to mind.

Then a fast-talking announcer spit out the words, "This message was brought to you by the Society to Save the World" followed by an email address and a website.

The governor said nothing for several seconds. Then he looked at Malcolm who was still standing beside the screen, his cellphone in his hand. "This is a joke, right?"

"There is an Alexandra School District in our state, sir. We'll know in minutes if this was a hoax or not." Malcolm was already dialling the number of the staff security chief.

The governor turned up the volume of the TV hanging on one wall. An all-news station displayed a talking head sitting behind the desk. The anchorman looked to his right instead of into the camera. Nothing was being reported yet, but something had the newsroom in an uproar. The dead air lingered.

Malcolm covered the mouthpiece of the telephone. "Herb confirms an explosion in Alexandra that rocked the city."

Herb Solstace was the governor's capable security chief. He had his fingers on the pulses of every part of the state and feelers out into the national arena as well.

"I'm going down to Herb's office to see what information he has. You'll have to make a statement reassuring the people. I'll have something ready when I come back." Malcolm hung up the phone and rushed from the office. The governor kept his eyes on the news show, waiting for the talking heads to start to spin the story. He acknowledged Malcolm's statement with a slight wave of his fingers.

Less than one-half hour later the two men resumed their meeting in the governor's office.

"I have a call in to Ray Tutty. He's the CEO of BurgerCircus. So far, he hasn't gotten back to me. His staff has seen the video. They expressed shock. They didn't know if Mr. Tutty was aware of it yet. He's out of the country," Malcolm reported..

"Jesus," Peter Weston said. "They can't honestly think anyone is going to pay them that much money. I've been talking to the mayor of the Alexandra. There is a general feeling of panic down there. He wants us to send in the National Guard."

Malcolm replayed the message that followed the explosion. He paused the computer with the frozen image still on the screen. "I don't think that would serve any purpose. We may have to activate them to search other schools in the state, but I think Alexandra has had its moment in the sun. These guys, whoever they are, have given the timing of this thing a great deal of thought."

"Damn right they have." The venom in the governor's voice sent a chill through Malcolm. "Two and a half months until election day. There's no way any politician will be able to ignore this issue."

That fact startled Malcolm. The upcoming presidential election had not occurred to him.

"Yeah, that too. That's not the real problem. It's nine days until school goes back in after the summer vacation. If this plays out all the way, the 8 a.m. explosion will coincide with the first day of school. We'll have no choice but to delay the opening."

Storm clouds filled Peter Weston's molten, grey eyes. His head involuntarily shook back and forth. "It will never get that far. We can't let them blow up nine more schools. We will catch them long before that." The governor paused to reflect on that statement. "Do you have a press statement prepared for me. I'll have to assure the people these criminals will be caught," he paused, "quickly."

"I'm working on it," Malcolm said. "We should at least find out who we're dealing with first. It may shape the tone of our message. The press is as eager as you are for a statement."

The governor swung his chair back to centre himself behind his desk. The resolve on his face said he was ready to tackle this issue head on. *"Carpe diem,* Malcolm. Seize the day. We must stop them. What do we know about the Society to Save the World?"

Malcolm shook his head. "Nobody has ever heard of them except in this video. I've Googled the name. Nothing. I've called the FBI. Nothing. They promised to check with the CIA and Homeland Security. We don't know if they are foreign terrorists, local militia or simply run of the mill extortionists. I expect to have this information imminently."

"What about the website? That must tell us something."

"It goes into more details about how the money is to be delivered and gives a pretty complete listing of the fast-food restaurants in this country. Otherwise, the message is pretty much what you see in the video. One hundred million or they keep blowing up a school a day until they get it."

"Can't we trace the URL?"

"The FBI is working on it. You know as well as I do it probably won't lead to anything concrete. The bombers have used an anonymizer with daisy chaining and onion routing. All the standard anti-detection stuff. Even when we get back to the source computer, we'll probably discover it has been set up at some cyber cafe somewhere in the world where we can't get access to the company's records. It's a long shot at best, but the FBI is doing its thing."

Malcolm tapped a few more keys. He watched the screen as the 404 error message came up. "They've already taken the site down."

"But it's on YouTube now?"

"It was, briefly. Once I contacted the administrators, they took it down immediately. I downloaded the copy you have here."

The governor let out a gruff laugh. "You, and how many others? Once it's out there, it's out there. Nothing disappears in cyberspace. You can't put the genie back in the bottle, Malcolm. You know that."

Malcolm nodded. He was aware he would be one of the thousands who had downloaded a copy of the video. It would soon be popping up all over the Internet. Tracing those copies would be a waste of time and resources. The extortionists would let the Internet thrill seekers get their message out to the world at no risk to themselves. Already some of the copies of the message had gone viral. Half of America would have viewed the demise of Alexandra School before this day was over.

"You're right, Governor, you can't."

"I want to talk to the CEO of BurgerCircus. Whether he wants to be involved or not, he is. Make an appointment for him to come and see me as soon as possible. By that, I mean today."

"I think the FBI will be taking the lead on this, not us."

The governor did a slow turn and his eyes burned into Malcolm's.

"This happened in Georgia. Georgia will take care of it. Those bastards picked the wrong state to start blowing up schools."

Malcolm grinned. "Keep that intensity for the television cameras, Governor. But this is going to be bigger than both of us."

◀2▶

THE ZING OF the nylon fishing line losing its slack rang up the Upsalquitch River as Ray Tutty hooked into a gleaming silver salmon. It was late in the season to be catching the big game fish. Late, that is, unless you were rich enough to afford to have a few salmon released from a holding pond each day before you boarded your canoe and started upriver. As the chief executive officer of BurgerCircus, Ray Tutty fell into that class of people.

The salmon made one high leap into the air, its body vibrating as if a charge of electricity flowed through it, and then disappeared under the crystal clear waters of the river. Line peeled off Ray's reel like cable on a runaway express elevator. A boiling split in the river traced the big fish's progress towards the headwater.

"Keep your tip up. Keep your tip up." Pierre Bouchard, Ray's guide, said in a soft, but urgent voice. Pierre stood in the bow of the boat, his eyes, hidden behind Polaroid glasses, concentrated on a moving spot in the river. At the same time, he was trying to manoeuvre the canoe into shore to give Ray a more secure footing.

As soon as the boat touched land, Pierre jumped onto the shore and held the rod. Ray leapt from the canoe into knee-deep water. His feet were still ankle deep in the river when his hands eagerly grabbed for the rod, blue eyes sparkling with excitement. Pierre pulled the canoe up on land out of the way, snatched up his net and killing stick and returned to the water's edge.

The salmon showed no signs of stopping its mad swim

up river. The line, whistling off Ray's reel, was now into its backing. Pierre did a quick mental calculation of how much further the fish could go before being jerked to a stop by the fully extended line. Or, if luck was not with them, before the line snapped from the reel and the trophy fish disappeared forever.

"Let him run, but keep your tip up." Pierre gave a running litany of instructions. At the same time, he was unconsciously reaching out towards the end of the rod, prepared to push it higher into the blue, cloudless sky if Ray failed to follow his orders. The pitch of the unwinding reel dropped a tone. Immediately, Pierre's well-tuned ears detected the difference.

"Now! Reel!" he ordered. "Wind that son of a bitch in."

Ray cranked hard on the handle of his quality Shakespeare reel. For what he had paid for the rod and reel combination, he could have fed salmon to a small nation for several weeks. His gaze dropped to the spot in the river where the line was cutting through the water. The tip of his rod followed his line of sight.

"Keep up your tip, *tabernac*," Pierre pleaded, his hand pointed skyward. It was too late. The line went slack. The salmon disappeared from his view up the river.

"Damn," Ray said. "I thought I had him hooked."

Pierre sat down on the edge of the canoe and pulled the slack line towards himself. He lifted the fly from the water and examined it. He gave it a shake to dry it and watched the line disappear as Ray dejectedly wound the handle of the reel. "Don't worry, Mr. Tutty, there will be other fish to kill. Maybe this evening."

Ray forced a smile at the guide's ever-optimistic outlook. "I hope so. I have to head back to the real world tomorrow morning. I thought I had this one hooked."

Pierre gave him a knowing smile as he tamped a bowl full of tobacco into his well-worn pipe. "We catch one before you leave. Don't worry."

Ray smiled as the cloud of sweet smelling smoke drifted around his head. He gave Pierre an envious look as the man drew in a puff of tobacco smoke. Here was someone doing exactly what he wanted, working in one of the most beautiful locations in the world, nobody telling him he couldn't smoke, nobody telling him to pick up his pace, and he was being paid for it, well paid.

"I never worry when you're my guide, Pierre. You've never disappointed me."

"A good guide is important, yes," Pierre said, "but it takes a good fisherman handling the rod and reel to make for success. Together, we are a team."

Ray smiled as the man gave a yank on the white cord attached to the small outboard motor. It instantly puffed to life. Ray knew bullshit when he stepped in it, but still, the words had a nice ring to them coming from a guide as capable as Pierre.

He had already told Pierre he would release any fish he caught or Pierre, himself, could keep it if he wanted. Pierre thanked him for the offer but declined. Ray understood Pierre didn't need any American businessman to catch fish for him. At the same time, he knew Pierre had made sure the fish released in the river on this occasion were the larger Atlantic salmon. Anything over 25 inches had to be put back into the river for spawning. Between 12 and 25, the sport could take the trophy home for his consumption. The fish Pierre let loose were nearly as long as a yard stick and almost a foot deep.

Ray recognized the importance to Pierre of having a picture hanging in Ray Tutty's office of Ray posing with a 35-or 40-pound salmon. A photo like this would generate more business than any advertising Pierre's outfitting company could do in magazines or newspapers. Pierre would make every effort to take that picture, even if he had to reel the fish into the edge of the shore himself before passing the rod to Ray.

Unfortunately, there are events that take place far away from the Upsalquitch River over which Pierre had no control. A radical bunch of militants blowing up schools is one such happening. Demanding that the CEO of BurgerCircus be in charge of the fundraising of the ransom was another. So, while the two men contentedly lay back in the late morning sun, the beauty of the wilderness of northern New Brunswick slowly drifting by the motorized canoe as the river twisted and turned back to the fishing lodge, life was conspiring against the plans of both men for a successful culmination of this fishing adventure.

When Ray climbed from the canoe, a uniformed delivery man from the nearby town of Campbellton stood waiting for him. Ray had turned in his BlackBerry and pager when he signed in at the fishing camp. This was not the luxurious Hilton Hotel. The buildings were rough-hewn and sparse of furnishings. There were no phones in the rooms. No computer jacks. No television. The outside world didn't exist as long as the fishers were on this property. It was not the fish they were paying for, or even the chance to catch them. It was the solitude and opportunity to forget about everything for three or four days. As a bonus, the home-cooked meals eclipsed the food served in the finest restaurants back in Atlanta.

Ray scowled at the messenger. "What's this?"

"I'm sorry, sir, but I believe this is extremely important. My orders were to make sure you got it as soon as possible and to wait for a reply."

Ray snatched the envelope from his hand, tore it open and scanned the message. Then, he read it again, slowly. He gave the messenger a fierce scowl. "Is this some sick joke?"

The messenger blanched at the comment and the

intensity of the stare. He had no idea what message the envelope held.

"Not on my part, sir. I'm only the delivery man. Is there any reply?"

Ray gave the man a half smile. He didn't believe the message was real. "No, no answer. I'll take care of this myself." He patted his pockets. "We don't carry money up here, but tipping is overrated anyway. My people get by without it quite well."

The messenger crawled back up the bank to the lodge. One of the other guides was standing there watching the events unfold. He had heard the line about the tip. He knew the tip depended on the service delivered. His client had landed himself a keeper salmon that morning. His tip was assured. He patted the messenger on the shoulder.

"You can't expect to be rewarded for delivering bad news."

The messenger looked back down at Ray. "I don't think the content of the news mattered. Some people have to have their money wrestled away from them."

A third canoe pulled into shore. They had been close enough to hear the by-play between Ray and the messenger. Out here in the wilderness, sounds carried far. The vice-president of operations for BurgerCircus, Paul Johnson, stepped from the boat.

"What's up, Ray? Bad news?"

"Someone must have found out we are here. This is their idea of a joke." He passed the slip of paper to Paul as he crawled from his canoe.

"You must contact Georgia Governor Peter Weston immediately. This situation is beyond urgent." Paul looked up from the message to Ray's withering glare. "I didn't even know you knew the governor."

"Only superficially. He invited himself to one of my parties. He was looking for campaign contributions from my guests. I put the run to him."

"Haven't you ever heard about having friends in high places?"

Ray's look turned to a half grin. "Let him call me when he becomes president."

"From what I hear, that could be soon. What are you going to do?"

"Give Barbara a call. She's the only one who knows we're here. See what the hell is going on."

Barbara Bishop functioned as Ray's executive assistant, Girl Friday, and all round expediter of things Ray wanted to have done. She had come up through the ranks with him. At one time they both stood shoulder to shoulder at the front counter of one of the burger restaurants and asked: "Do you want fries with that?"

When Ray graduated with his business degree from Saint Francis Xavier University in Nova Scotia and came back as manager of that store, he sent Barbara to the same school at the company's expense, wages included. They sported matching black and gold X rings. He still considered that the best decision he had made in his entire career. If he ever forgot, Barbara would quickly point it out to him.

A worried look crossed Paul's face. "Not quite the only one. I had to tell my wife where I was going."

"Your wife? Why? If she's behind this, I'll bust you down to a fry cook at one of our outlets in Alaska. You'll start next month with the coming of the cold season."

"The governor is probably planning a birthday party for one of his grandkids. Delegating everything to the best man available is his governing style. He didn't know how to get in touch with me, so he had to settle for you."

Ray offered his vice-president a one-finger salute. Both men laughed. Their last shared laugh for a long time to come.

◀3▶

MALCOLM TRUEX HAD worry written over his face as he laid the blue-jacketed report on the governor's desk.

"Fertilizer and diesel fuel. Just like the Oklahoma City bombing. I don't like the look of this. I was hoping for something more exotic. Something from overseas."

"You think it's one of the local militia groups?" Governor Weston asked. "It's a little ambitious for them, don't you think?"

"I don't know what to think. If it were the militia, they'd be coming after the government for the money, not private enterprise."

"You think the fast-food industry can come up with that kind of money? One hundred million dollars. Not that we're going to pay, we don't negotiate with terrorists, but money like that could only come from the federal treasury."

"That's another problem. I called back my FBI contact to see how they're making out finding the Society to Save the World group. They've had no luck with any of their sources. That's the bad news. The really bad news is unless there's another bombing in some other state, they can't become involved. Like you said, it's not a federal issue."

The governor stopped scanning the report. "Not a federal issue? I might have been caught up in the passion of the moment when I said that. These are terrorists. They're extorting the government out of millions of dollars. Surely, Homeland Security is at least involved."

"Technically, they're not after government money. They are extorting the fast-food industry." Malcolm held up a hand. "Don't go ballistic on the feds yet. Unofficially, there are several agents working on the case. They want to hit the ground running if another school blows up tomorrow night. That will make it a terrorist threat. The FBI has informed the president of what is happening. He's been shown the video, but is not commenting on anything at this time."

Malcolm understood the conundrum his friends in the FBI struggled with. In his former life, he had been an agent himself. He still maintained strong friendships within the local office.

The governor scoffed at the mention of the president. "He's waiting for someone to tell him what he thinks, you mean. We can't sit around on our thumbs waiting for another school to be destroyed. We've got to find these assholes before that." The governor's eyes took on a look that would freeze water in the hot desert sun.

"You've activated the national guard. They are searching all the schools in the state for any sign of bombs. We've put in calls to all the local police units to be on the lookout, as well. You've also sent out a communiqué to all the other governors in the nation warning them of the threat." Malcolm clicked off the things he had done in the governor's name on his fingers.

"Good. I'm glad to see I'm taking some concrete action." The governor smiled at his aide. "When are we going to tell the people what we're doing?"

"You already made that brief, general statement earlier, and Herb Solstace, as head of security, has added several statements suggesting that we are on top of the situation.

"Tonight, you will be the lead item on the local six o'clock news. All the local stations have given us five minutes. They've been covering the bombing live throughout the day. I've already finished the first draft of your speech. You are going to be concerned, but not worried. We are putting the full resources of the state on this matter and will contain it quickly. We will catch and punish the culprits to the full extent of the law."

"The local news? What about the networks? This is a matter of national interest."

"We both know that, and the local news managers agree. It's not their call. Some suit in New York has to decide it is of national interest. So far they don't think so. An isolated school blowing up in Georgia can't compete with the federal election issues like whether the president should appear while campaigning in a three-piece suit or in more casual apparel that could appeal to the average voter."

"Jesus, we're losing valuable time." The governor looked at his watch. "We've only got a little over 30 hours to keep another school from blowing up. Somebody higher up has to start taking this thing seriously. Have you heard back from Ray Tutty?"

"He's fishing in Canada. His secretary has a call out to him, and she tells me he has his private plane at a nearby airport. She expects to hear from him any minute now."

"We need him back here by six o'clock. I want him standing beside me when I go on television. That will show the terrorists we are taking their threat seriously. That's an important step in the negotiation process."

Malcolm shifted back and forth from one foot to another. "Governor, despite their current lack of movement, I don't think they're going to let you lead these negotiations."

Sparks shot from the governor's eyes. "Who's not going to let me? I'm the only one showing any interest in this damn thing."

"If another school blows up, the FBI will be all over it like sand on a beach. The president will appoint one of his people to be in charge."

The governor made a fake spitting motion. "The election is in a little over two months. The president will be too busy campaigning to do anything else. I, personally, don't think he has a chance in hell of winning a new mandate. As you said, next week all his attention will be wrapped up in what to wear when he heads out to California."

"That's all the more reason for him to look like he's handling things. This disaster could be the break he needs, especially if he catches the bad guys before any more schools are destroyed. That could turn this election on its ear."

"Oh Lord, spare us. That could end up costing the country more than the hundred million the terrorists want. I don't see him making a major statement until he sees which way the wind is blowing. If this is foreign terrorists, he will be all over it like dog shit on the sole of your shoe. If it looks like domestic terrorists or just people in it for the money, he will ignore it. He wants to protect America from some radical outside force. That's where the votes are, and with him, everything is about votes."

Malcolm smiled. "You still think you should have thrown your hat in the ring. Even though the good people of Georgia elected an Indepentent governor, I don't think the rest of the country is ready for an Indepentent president. They still have fears of Indepentent candidate Ross Perrot, and no one has forgotten the former Georgia governor, Jimmy Carter."

The smile on Peter Weston's face appeared forced. "You could be right. Maybe in another four years, the electorate will be tired of the old two-party system where nothing gets done unless both sides can dip a hand into the old pork barrel and pay somebody off." He gave his hand a dismissive wave.

"Maybe next time one of the major parties will try to recruit you, but that's a discussion for another time."

"Right now we have to find out everything there is to know about these crazy bombers and chop them off at the knees. How far are we from where that school was blown up? I want to tour the site in person. I want to see the damage up close."

"You can be there is less than an hour. Should I tip off the news media?"

"Don't be crass, Malcolm. Just call the local chief of police and tell him I'm coming."

Malcolm winked. "Small town like Alexandra, that should be all it takes."

◀4▶

RAY TUTTY, PAUL Johnson, and a third member of their fishing party, Derek Saunders, the CEO of a rival fast-food restaurant being considered for takeover by BurgerCircus, were crowded around the small screen in the back of Ray's rented limo. Barbara had downloaded the video from YouTube to Ray's BlackBerry. Ray fed the image to the limo's TV.

This was the third time the trio had watched the school evaporate into nothingness and listened to the droning message that accompanied it.

"Jesus Christ on a crutch. Where in hell do they think we can come up with that kind of cash?" Ray's anger increased with each watching of the video. "Owning a fast-food chain doesn't give us a licence to print money. We squeeze every penny until it screams."

Derek Saunders looked at Ray. "You could always cash one of your personal bonus cheques. The money doesn't have to come from BurgerCircus."

"Don't be a smart-ass, Saunders. Your company is as much on the hook as mine. They said to collect from the fast-food industry." Ray pushed the replay button to watch the video one more time.

"Not if you take over my company," Derek answered, tension obvious in his voice. "You want to own all the toys in the toy box; you're responsible for looking after them."

"I could buy your outlets, resell them and still not have enough money to pay off these extortionists." Ray didn't look at Derek. He was studying the image of the little boy.

"We won't come that cheap," Derek said. As an afterthought, he added, "Remember, I'm the only one who caught any fish on this trip." He gave the other two men a triumphant smile.

"Yeah," Ray said. "Pierre will never forgive himself for that." He gave a half-hearted smile and pointed to the screen.

"Is that a reflection of someone in that kid's glasses?"

Paul and Derek leaned in closer.

"Maybe," Derek said. "Someone must have noticed whoever had the camera. They had to be sitting right there in the restaurant. It wasn't a cheap camcorder that captured these images."

Paul shook his head. "It was a birthday party. The place was probably full of cameras. All the aunts and uncles would be recording this moment for posterity."

"Including us," Ray said. "We will have images of everyone who passed through the door that day."

"I'm sure the cops have those in their possession by now along with every other camera that was in there," Derek said. "They wouldn't have to wait to see this video to know they had a problem. They had bricks raining down all around them."

"Maybe," Ray said. "Once that building blew, everyone in town would be out of whatever building they were in to see what happened. It's not like they'd be waiting for the police to come and tell them to leave. Anyone with any decent footage would be hiding his camera hoping he could sell the recording to some news network or reality show."

Paul nodded in agreement. "Case in point, the cops didn't get this version, and it has the whole show in it. They are live streaming to YouTube."

"All the toys," Ray said. "He stopped shooting before the dust settled. You can bet he was getting the hell out of there before any cops arrived. We need our security tapes."

The BurgerCircus private jet was already warming up on the runway at the small airport outside Campbellton. The pilot opened the limo door as the car came to an abrupt halt.

"We are cleared for takeoff whenever you're ready," he told Ray. "Ms. Bishop called me and said we've been rerouted to Macon from Atlanta."

"Macon? Why?" Ray's look demanded an answer. The look on the pilot's face transmitted that he couldn't provide it.

"She didn't say. She wants to talk to you as soon as we're airborne."

Ray's face changed to a resigned image. "That would be right now," he said. "Sorry to have snapped at you. Let me talk to Barbara before you set your final destination. Load up our luggage and Derek's fish." He smirked at the rival restaurateur. "He's going to add a new item to his menu. He has just about enough to supply all his restaurants."

The pilot nodded. "The fishing was good, sir. I caught two myself." The crew had been assigned to another fishing camp further down the river.

He recoiled from the look his boss gave him, not understanding what he had said wrong. Some days you were better off keeping your mouth shut.

In less than five minutes, the party was in the air and heading for Georgia. Ray was on the phone getting an update from Barbara. His face was grim.

"I'm not going to be a stooge in any dog and pony show the governor is putting on. Tell him to get his photo ops out of the way before I arrive and I want a full report on who this group is and what the government is doing about it."

He listened for a few minutes, his facial muscles reacting to whatever Barbara was telling him. Finally, that familiar look of resignation came back to his face.

"Only if you're sure, Barbara. I don't want this blowing

up in our face, no pun intended." He returned the phone to the slot in the arm of his seat where it blended in so well it almost disappeared.

Paul raised his eyebrows. "What's up?"

"Barbara thinks I should appear on camera with the governor. Makes it look as if BurgerCircus is on top of the situation and a willing participant in the solution. Otherwise, she says, it looks like we're shirking our responsibility."

"Makes sense."

"Not to me. What makes this our responsibility? Hell, we've got franchises all over the world. BurgerCircus is as widely recognized as Coca-Cola. No one is mad at us, at home or abroad. It's the goddamn government that has pissed off everyone. They are the ones responsible for both homegrown and imported terrorism. Let them handle this."

Paul shook his head. He was the other of only two people who could openly disagree with Ray on any subject. "Barbara's right. Get out there in front of the camera and look like a solid world citizen. Behind the scenes, fight tooth and nail with the government to either come up with the cash or capture these renegades. Image is everything. Don't forget that."

"What if they don't catch them? Every morning, when a new school explodes all over their TV screen, our image takes a hit. It won't take too many newscasts like that before we become the villains in this little show." He pointed a finger at Paul. "Mr. Vice-President of Operations, you had better start working on how you are going to put a positive spin on that scenario."

Derek slowly shook his head. "What we should be trying to figure out is where we are going to come up with the money. This could be a public relations disaster for everyone in the industry, not just BurgerCircus. If we get the blame and people boycott our stores, it won't take too many days before we won't be able to find any money anywhere. We could all become bankrupt in the blink of any eye or the explosion of a school."

"Maybe you guys, but not us." Ray's look was defiant.

"Why not? You think your clown is so lovable people won't boycott you?"

"No," Ray said. "Our international business will carry us. There will be no boycott in Asia or South America. I bet Canada wouldn't even join in. We've got an over inflated image of how much the rest of the world cares about what happens inside our borders. I've toured these other countries. They don't give a damn about our internal problems unless it involves some entertainment icon. Some blond bimbo exposing her crotch to the world catches everybody's attention. Our internal problems don't even make their newscasts. Barbara and I attended university in Canada. I know."

He held up a hand before Derek had a chance to answer. "Don't get me wrong. We will bleed, but we won't die."

Paul had avoided getting involved in this dialogue. Now he spoke up again. "When you look at it that way, one hundred million is not that much."

Ray's face flushed red. "We're not going to be extorted. Nobody pays. Pay these guys once, and it never ends. The terrorists will be lining up to take a number to see who gets the next handout. We have to find them and crush them," he paused, "on live TV if possible."

On that note, all three men fell silent. A minute later the door to the cockpit opened. "Anyone care for a beverage?" the co-pilot/steward asked.

For once they were all in agreement. Doubles all the way around.

◀5▶

THE ROAR OF motorcycles announced the arrival of Governor Peter Weston in Alexandra. His white Lincoln limo had raced down Interstate 75 escorted by four Harley Davidsons, two in the front, two bringing up the rear, sirens screaming all the way.

On the advice of Malcolm Truex, the escorts turned off their sirens as they wound their way around the exit ramp leading into the small town outside Macon. Malcolm reasoned the good people of Alexandra would already be on edge from the morning's explosion. Another round of sirens in the air would only increase their anxiety.

The governor reluctantly agreed but insisted they radio ahead to alert the police chief of their arrival. As a result, a green Ford sedan with the words Alexandra Police Dept. stencilled on the side awaited their arrival at the end of the ramp. Inside they could see the gold-bedecked shoulder boards of the driver indicating the chief himself would guide them to the scene of the destruction.

News cameras rushed up to the governor's car as they pulled to a stop in the dust-and-debris-covered parking lot of the former school. Malcolm watched as the governor tried a series of serious faces behind the tinted glass before stepping from the vehicle.

You should have been an actor, Malcolm thought as he disembarked unnoticed from the opposite side of the vehicle. Malcolm could hear the governor mouthing the list of platitudes Malcolm had written for him on the trip down. Not only did he look the part, but he could remember his lines with little effort. He was a natural for the job.

The dust-covered forensic workers sifting through the building's remains looked up briefly to see what all the excitement was about, grunted their disgust and then returned to their unrewarding task. Finding clues in this mess would be impossible. Still, they had to look.

Malcolm ducked under the yellow tape surrounding the scene and walked over to where one coverall-clad man appeared to be in charge.

"Malcolm Truex, the governor's aide," he said and extended his hand.

The man gave him a hard, cold stare. "You're contaminating my crime scene," he said, his voice exuding anything but the hospitality the South was famous for.

Malcolm looked down at the white dust covering everything in the area. "How can you tell?" he asked. "It all looks the same to me." His voice wasn't threatening, but at the same time, it carried the message Malcolm wasn't intimidated by this supernumerary suddenly thrust into a position of power by happenstance.

The man's glare softened. "It sure as hell does. Now that the governor is here, I imagine he'll be expecting immediate answers as to what took place. Answers we don't have."

"Answers you don't have yet. We'll give you the time you need to do your work, up to a point. You have heard about the video on the Internet."

"Hasn't everybody? Midnight doesn't give us much time to figure out this mess."

Malcolm reached out a hand and grasped the man's shoulder. "Midnight tomorrow." He smiled. "Already it's not as bad as you think."

"Tomorrow? Are you serious? Hell, we can pause and take a coffee break."

"Up to ten minutes, anyway. Seriously, have you found anything of value to the investigation?"

The man looked at Malcolm again. "Who did you say you were?"

"The governor's chief of staff. I'll be heading up the investigation for the state. Authorizing overtime, paying the bills."

Enlightenment showed in the man's eyes. He realized this was not an enemy he wanted to make. "Lester Cleary, head of forensics for the Macon area." He extended his hand. "Call me Les."

"OK, Les. Call me Malcolm." His southern drawl became more pronounced. "Can you give me anything yet?"

Les looked down at the highly polished brown shoes on Malcolm's feet. He reached into a pack on his belt and produced a pair of paper booties. "Put these on. You *are* contaminating my crime scene."

"Sorry." Malcolm slipped on the footwear and tied them at his ankles.

"One of two things has come to light so far," Les said as he started walking towards the wreckage of the school. "Either these people were trying to make a really loud statement, or they don't have a clue what they are doing."

Malcolm followed along, gingerly getting used to his new footwear that tended to slide under his leather soles. Unbalanced broken bricks and unseen crunching glass made walking a tricky exercise. He waited for Les to continue.

Les stopped at the edge of a huge crater gouged into the earth. "Way too much explosive," he said. "A quarter as much would have done the job quite adequately."

"Holy shit," Malcolm said, awe in his voice. "Fertilizer and diesel fuel did this?"

"It's a deadly combination when it's mixed right."

"How did they deliver it?"

"There would have been a truck involved at some point. We haven't found anything we can recognize as truck parts.

From the plans of the school, this area would have been a subterranean delivery bay leading to the school cafeteria in the basement. That's what contained the explosion. Otherwise, half the town would have disappeared. We don't know if the truck was part of the bomb or if the bombers dumped its contents here. At this time of year, the schools are pretty much vacant."

Malcolm looked around at the surrounding area. "Do any of these local businesses have video cameras that could have picked up activity on the street?"

"You're in Alexandra, not Atlanta. Video cameras here record birthday parties and Christmas morning. BurgerCircus is the only place I know that have them. Investigators are studying them now in Macon."

"Whoever shot that video was sitting in BurgerCircus. He should be on their videos. I guess that's where the investigation will have to start. There's not much here that will help. What do you think? Were they destroying the crime scene or were they incompetent?"

"I guess we'll have to wait and see what happens the next time. See if they learned any lesson from this one. Then, I'll be able to answer that question."

Malcolm gave him a queer look as the significance of that answer sunk in. "Great. Keep in touch. Remember, if you need anything, call."

"Sure." Les pointed over to where the limo was parked. "Looks like your boss is through explaining everything to the press. I wish he could tell us what is going on."

"Yeah, well I'll bring him over, and he can try. I want him to see this hole. I think the overkill is significant."

"Here are some booties for him. It's a shame about his suit. It will probably get covered in dust."

"Don't worry about that. He has coveralls and a hard hat in the trunk. You might want to do something about your hair. You're going to be on the local news tonight."

◀6▶

THE MAKEUP TRAILER provided by the TV studio was small. Ray Tutty stood 6-foot-three. Paul Johnson towered over Ray by an inch. Les Cleary looked Ray straight in the eye, and both the governor and Malcolm Truex hovered around the six-foot mark.

Ray, Les and the governor were all being prepared to appear live on the air at the site of the devastation. Paul and Malcolm were giving last-minute instructions to their charges about what to say and what not to say.

Paul's instructions came from corporate headquarters via his BlackBerry where Barbara had taken charge of the company's involvement. As far as Barbara was concerned, Ray was just the face the public would see. He couldn't be relied on to make the decisions. He was too gung-ho in his manner. This approach would not work in these early stages of negotiation. Maybe, if all else failed, she would turn him lose to handle things his way.

The plan was to have Les and the governor walk the site with Les explaining how the explosion had occurred and the governor asking him intelligent, clarifying questions to get all the points out. The two men would end up at the site of the crater, where they would meet up with Ray who would make the corporate pitch about shock, concern and cooperation. That was the plan.

The three men took their positions along with a cameraman, two men on the sound boom mike, a person to drag the cable and the director.

"Roll sound," the director said and as if on cue two

military jets appeared on the horizon and made a beeline for the destruction site. The low pass vibrated the trailers, rose gusts of dust in the air and made the sound man whip off his earphones.

"Holy fuck," he said and covered his ears with both hands. "Who ordered them in?"

"We're live on the air." An icy voice from the studio barked.

The camera zoomed in on the face of a visibly shaken Les Cleary. He was watching a couple of bricks toppling into the hole near where Ray Tutty stood. "This area's not safe. Burger man, get your ass out of there."

"We're live on the air," the voice from studio screamed. "Cut to commercial."

"Places, everyone," the director said. "We're going to try it again." He was not watching the live action but instead was focused on a small monitor showing only the shot.

"Like hell." Ray ran towards the other men. "That hole is collapsing in on itself."

The camera man started picking his way across the field of debris. Finally, he was going to get something worth shooting. He had been out here all day shooting dust. Now, he had something that at least moved.

"Stop," the director said. "We're back on the air live in two minutes."

The studio voice crackled in his ear. "Not on a bet is that going to happen. Try to get some footage for the 11:00 p.m. time slot."

The camera man's eyes asked the question. He too was wearing earphones that picked up the voices from the studio. "Go ahead," the director said. "But be careful. We only have the one camera here."

"No," the governor said. "You can't cancel me. I've got to speak to the people, to reassure them."

"We do news breaks all night long to promo the

newscast. We'll put you on those. It will be a better show if we put it on tape and then edit it. We'll make you look a lot better, I promise."

"Malcolm. They can't do this. The people are expecting to hear from me."

Paul and Malcolm had been back at the make-up trailer watching on a monitor as one screw-up after another occurred. They opted to watch the monitor because they wanted to see what the people out in TV land would see. In short, they wanted to rate the performances of their star actors. Both men shook their heads at the same time.

"Whose idea was it to do this live?" Paul asked. "They should be shot."

"Talk like that could land you in jail," Malcolm said. "Shooting a governor is called an assassination. It's like treason."

"It was the governor's idea?"

Malcolm rolled his eyes. "His reasoning was that if he did it live, they couldn't cut out anything he had to say or take it out of context. It sounded good at the time."

Paul looked skyward at the cerulean sky. "So who ordered in the National Guard?"

"Had to be the president. The governor wouldn't do it without my knowledge."

"Makes sense, I guess. The planes had wing-mounted cameras. They were getting some overhead shots of the scene."

"You could see cameras?" Malcolm made no attempt to hide his disbelief.

"Used to fly jets myself. Know what to look for." Paul gave him a self-satisfied smile that only pilots can give when it comes to talking about jet fighters.

"Malcolm. Handle this, will you? They've cut our spot. And who in hell ordered in those airplanes?" the governor's voice shouted.

"Duty calls," Malcolm said to Paul.

The director held one hand to his earphone and listened intently. "They are replaying the earlier spot of you exploring the site, Governor. The desk man is explaining why they delayed your live appearance. Incidentally, the network has aired that initial piece as well."

"That explains the jets," Paul said. "The president will be able to say they are taking the matter seriously and are conducting their own investigation."

"The jets carried cameras," Malcolm explained. "Paul is an ex-fighter pilot."

"I prefer inactive fighter pilot. I still maintain my accreditation."

Malcolm looked over to where Les and the camera man were watching the bricks slide into the bomb crater. The vibrations from the jet flypast had unbalanced some of the debris, and it was now finding a new equilibrium.

"That footage they are getting now shows how unstable the area is. It would make a good backdrop for the two of you to make your cases on camera."

"Not me," Ray said. "I'm no coward, but I don't take foolish chances just for good television. I'm a food industry worker."

The governor said nothing. The look on his face showed he was glad Ray had put his sentiments into words before he had to.

"No," Malcolm said, "we want you safely in a studio in front of a green screen. We will add the falling bricks later. One fiasco is enough for today."

"Good idea," the director said. "If you get tired of public life, we can find a spot for you in television. We're always looking for innovative thinkers."

"Thanks, I'll keep that in mind." Malcolm looked at Ray and the governor. "Your message will be the same as it was going to be during the live broadcast. You'll assure the bombers we are taking this matter seriously, and we are ready to negotiate at any time. We want both of you singing from the same song sheet. That way they can't work one side against the other. We don't want to be making any concessions everyone hasn't agreed to. We must present a united front."

"From my point of view, we don't want to be making any concession at all." Ray Tutty gave Malcolm a look defying him to argue with that statement.

"Amen to that, brother," the governor said. "Find them and crush them."

"I guess we're all on the same page," Ray said and reached out and tapped the governor on the shoulder with a closed fist.

The governor's principal security agent stepped forward and gave Ray a look that transmitted a clear message. "Don't do that again."

Malcolm let out a heavy sigh and looked over Ray's shoulder to where Paul was standing. Malcolm had taken the governor's limo to the Macon airport to meet the BurgerCircus private jet.

During the ride to the bombing site in Alexandra, Malcolm spelled out what the governor expected from Ray, BurgerCircus and the other fast-food outlets. At the same time, he told them what kind of support the government was prepared to offer in return. The negotiations had not been easy. Ray declared there would be no negotiations and nothing would change his mind. It wasn't until Malcolm found out about Barbara and got to talk to her on the phone that things made a slight change for the better.

In effect, the school system was being held hostage by the terrorists. Unlike ordinary hostage situations, there was no face to negotiate with, no one to offer concessions to in exchange for hostages, no single location to surround. Like all hostage situations, Malcolm's ploy, supported by

Barbara, was to negotiate for more time before the terrorists took any further action.

Paul stepped forward. "All we are trying to get from this first contact is an agreement that they won't blow up any more schools until we talk. We have to appear willing to negotiate. Do we all understand that?"

"We know that Paul," Ray said. "As long as we don't lose sight of the big picture. We are not going to give in."

The four men then sat down to hammer out a script to use in the five-minute spot the station had granted them. They were aware sound bites would be lifted from this piece and used on the networks. Until the bombers destroyed another school, they would be lucky to get thirty seconds of air time across the country.

Once again, Ray displayed his obstinacy. He wanted to appear to be the strong one, the one who wouldn't back down. Once again, Paul put in a call to Barbara. He held out the phone to Ray, who simply scowled at Paul.

"She wants to talk to you." Paul gave the phone a flick in Ray's direction.

"Women. Can't live with them; can't shoot them," Ray said. "There's no sense talking to her. What does she want me to say?"

By the time Les and the cameraman came back from the crumbling crater, everything was worked out. Each man had a task assigned. The governor was to reassure the people everything was being done to protect them; Ray Tutty's job was to persuade the terrorists to set up a dialogue so things could be discussed and resolved. Together, they wanted to create the impression that the Georgia government and BurgerCircus were working in concert to resolve this issue in the best possible way.

The director promised the first promo would be on the air in less than an hour. It would last a full minute. Audience reaction would dictate if the whole piece aired before the 11:00 p.m. news slot. Not everyone wanted to miss out on five minutes of *Survivor.*

In the end, the whole piece played at 7:55 and again at 8:55 as teasers for the late-night news show.

◀7▶

THE NEXT MORNING the phones rang endlessly. The email box was jammed full. None of the communications was from the terrorists. Reporters—print, TV, and radio—from across the nation tried to set up interviews. All wanted the inside track on how negotiations were going.

The governor had a state to run. He cancelled as many duties as possible, but in the end, he realized sitting around waiting for the desired phone call was a waste of time. Malcolm would contact him as soon as he heard anything concrete.

Malcolm, on the other hand, devoted his time to nothing else but the bombing. Despite promising Les the time he needed to fully investigate the site, Malcolm kept harassing him for updates and offering more resources if they were needed.

Les appreciated the offers of help. He didn't need them. The devastation at the school had been to such a point that no clues remained. He was spinning his wheels with the help he had. Any more would make a dangerous situation critical. He had lowered a couple of people into the blast hole suspended from cables from a crane. They gingerly searched for any remaining clues. Les's next most important job was to keep everyone else away from the location. Any vibration could collapse the hole completely.

As an afterthought, Les reported they had found the twisted wreckage of what appeared to be a truck in a farmer's field about a half-mile from the school. They believed it had once been a GMC, but further investigation would be required to confirm that.

The doorway and counter videos from BurgerCircus came up cold. Although the live feeds displayed the inside of the building and showed what took place moment to moment, none of the recording devices captured any of this. Powerful magnets, attached to the bottom of the machine, distorted any recorded images beyond recognition. Further investigation showed this had been taking place for days. No one checked the tapes unless there was a problem. In Alexandra, there were seldom the kinds of problems requiring a video replay.

Police rounded up as many personally owned camcorders as they could. None of them showed anything useful. Depending on the owner, various kids starred in the recordings, but none captured the view outside the party area. Why would they? Who cared who spent their afternoons at BurgerCircus. The party was the thing.

Malcolm utilized the best IT minds he could access to trace the YouTube video and the WordPress website. These experts found themselves exploring the inside operations of a cyber cafe in Indonesia. Going further back from that point proved impossible. They all promised to keep trying.

Every hour, Malcolm showed up at the governor's office to give him an update on proceedings and to answer a bevy of questions from the governor about day to day operations of the state. Things people believed the governor normally handled, but in reality fell under Malcolm's job description. Still, the governor handled the increased workload with aplomb.

"They're not going to call," Malcolm said at the four o'clock meeting. If money doesn't show up in their offshore account by midnight, another school is going to be history."

The governor said nothing but continued tapping on the keys of his computer. He gave Malcolm a weary look. The pressure of the day was catching up with him.

Malcolm collapsed on a blue, leather chesterfield against the wall of the governor's office. He rubbed his eyes with the tips of his fingers and let out a long sigh.

"I've set up a meeting with BurgerCircus for five. They haven't had any more success than we have. In fact, their day has been worse than ours. They've been fielding calls telling them to pay up. One hundred million is a drop in the bucket for all the fast-food stores in the country is the consensus.

"We've been tracking those calls."

The governor looked up.

"Tracking the calls? Why?"

"We think some of them may be from the terrorists themselves. If necessary, we'll have police visit everyone on the list." Malcolm shrugged. "So far we have nothing else."

"You say we're meeting BurgerCircus at five. It's not a supper meeting, is it? Hamburgers and french fries are not my idea of an evening meal."

"It will be a supper meeting. The menu will be a little more exotic. There will be representatives of the other food chains there, and one of them is supplying an Atlantic salmon he caught on a recent fishing trip up north."

"How recent? I like my fish fresh."

"He was with Ray Tutty in Canada when the school exploded. Fresh enough?"

"I look forward to it. Is it just you and me against the fast-food crew? They may try to overwhelm us with their numbers."

A sly smile crossed Malcolm's lips. "Not from what I hear. Getting them to show up in the same room has been a major accomplishment. They are not a united front on this. Paul Johnson tells me most of them are washing their hands of the issue. In fact, most of them think it is a non-issue. They don't think it involves them at all."

"They are only coming for the salmon is what you're

saying."

"That's what they think. They are in for a surprise. The message from the terrorists was very clear. All fast-food companies should pay. I don't know what the terrorists have in mind except blowing up schools, but I suspect there will be bad publicity if the money doesn't materialize. They seem to be able to put up messages on the Internet at will."

Just then the governor's BlackBerry beeped. He had an urgent email message waiting. He opened the folder, and a look of shock popped into his eyes.

"It's them. How did they get this address? This is for intergovernmental communications only. Less than a half-dozen people have it."

"What does it say?" Malcolm was more interested in the message than the messenger.

"Enjoy your supper and make sure the fast-food people pick up the tab."

Malcolm shrugged. "It was never intended to be a secret meeting. Still..." He let the thought drift off into nothingness. The terrorists may not have been communicating with the authorities, but they were certainly on top of events.

The governor slipped the electronic device back into his pocket. "I'll look into this breach personally," he said.

A half-hour later, the governor's white limo roared out the front gate of the governor's mansion with its usual Harley escort. Many press vehicles were lined up in the streets and took up the pursuit. Five minutes after that, a nondescript, light grey Toyota drove out through one of the side gates. Only the driver, apparently one of the mansion's gardeners, could be seen through the tinted windows. The press snapped a few pictures, but no one gave chase. It was knock-off time. Several cars owned by staff members were leaving through the various exits and heading for home.

The grey Toyota ambled out to the Atlanta airport.

Ray Tutty, when he was in Georgia, lived on a multi-acre estate that made the governor's mansion look like a suburban tract house. Among its accoutrements was a fully operational airfield. Many of the incoming CEOs from the other companies landed in Ray's backyard. The others were met at the Atlanta airport and ferried in aboard a company helicopter. Passengers boarded the chopper inside the hangar before the aircraft rolled out on the field for liftoff. The press had no idea who all was there. The governor and Malcolm Truex came aboard one of the helicopter flights along with one security person. The gardener's Toyota found itself in a parking spot in a secure area of the Atlanta airport.

Eight representatives of the fast-food industry made the trip to Ray's mansion. Some, like Ray, headed up their companies. Others were, like Paul Johnson, vice-presidents. One company had sent their regional sales manager. He quickly realized he would have no meaningful input into this meeting. He was strictly here for the food. His bosses would soon be getting a scorching phone call from Ray Tutty himself.

The meeting started with the replaying of the video from YouTube. Everyone had already seen it, but it did establish the sombre tone of the gathering. Despite the promise of an exciting meal, this was not a social gathering.

Malcolm took the floor and spelled out the efforts of law enforcement to date. Scowls and groans greeted his litany of dead ends. He made no effort to gloss over the lack of success. One by one, he engaged each person sitting around the table.

"Gentlemen, we have six hours," he looked at his watch, "and eighteen minutes to stop this insanity."

"The insanity is in this room," Gustav Delano said. "These people are not going to blow up a school a day. They know we are soft. They know if they make a threat severe enough, we will pay. In my country, we knew how to deal with scoundrels like these. Terrorists were sentenced and executed on the same day."

Malcolm and Paul exchanged glances. Paul had warned Malcolm about Gustav. Gustav owned the only non-North American chain in the room. His restaurants served a variety of spicy meat and vegetable products catering to the burgeoning immigrant population. He located his franchises in the major cities along the East Coast where these people made their homes while getting established in the land of opportunity. Although Gustav never took out American citizenship, he spent much of his time in this country.

"Not only that, my restaurants cater to an adult clientele. I am not included in their threat because I don't make my living off the back of the poor eating habits of American children."

"Perhaps you didn't see their website, Gustav," Ray said. "You would need modern things like a computer for that. The guest list for this meeting didn't come from me. It came right from the source of the problem. I am only sorry to see such a pitiful turnout. If you had visited the site of that former school yesterday, like I did, you would have no doubt about how serious these terrorists are. Those that aren't here are involved whether they know it or not, whether they like it or not. And," he looked around the room with steely blue eyes at each participant, "any decisions we make here are equally binding on them."

Paul Johnson, who was sitting beside Ray, looked down at his chest. He fished his BlackBerry out of his shirt pocket and read the message on the screen. He then hit a few buttons, and the others watched his face go pale.

"What is it?" Malcolm asked. Malcolm was sitting across the table from Paul.

"It's a message from Barbara." Paul leaned forward and

slid the laptop connected to the overhead screen closer to him. His fingers deftly danced over the screen, and a Facebook page opened up.

"BurgerCircus Should Pay" screamed the banner-sized headline. Paul's email address flashed on the screen. "Be my friend," the message read.

A counter on one side of the screen showed the people logging on and joining the page's friend list. The number was over a thousand and climbing as fast as the server could process the requests.

"There," Gustav said, "the people have spoken. BurgerCircus are the ones who should pay, not struggling little companies like mine." He looked around the room for support. Nobody expressed disagreement with him.

Ray Tutty slammed his hand on the table, causing the laptop to jump. "Nobody is going to pay. You don't pay terrorists." His eyes centred on Gustav. "We know how to deal with terrorists in this country as well," he paused for a moment before continuing, his eyes never leaving those of the foreign businessman. "We also know how to deal with infiltrators and spies."

Gustav's dark faced turned ashen. His hands were shaking as he stood up at the table and leaned towards Ray Tutty. "I am no infiltrator." There was a tremble in his voice. "I am a businessman like yourself. My goal is to provide decent food to the people from my country who have settled in America and to save them from the deep-fried crap you use to kill your own citizens. I am at this meeting to provide you with advice because I know how to deal with terrorists first hand. Don't insult me with your wild accusations."

Ray pointed his first two fingers at his own eyes and then at Gustav. A sly grin snuck onto his lips. "I'll be watching you; that's all I'm saying."

Gustav abruptly raised his right fist while placing his left hand on his biceps. Without further comment, he resumed his seat.

Meanwhile, Malcolm had his cellphone in his hand placing a call back to his IT crew.

"We're on it," they told him. "It's only been up for a little over five minutes. I've never seen anything like it. I'm betting we end up in Southeast Asia again. Want a piece of the action."

"Can you analyze the friend's list? See where they are coming from and if there is a group that seems disproportionately large?"

"It's only data. We can slice it, dice it, do anything you want with it."

Malcolm watched the counter continue its climb. "That's going too fast. Someone must be streaming a data file into it. I think the whole thing is contrived. Try and trace that source as well."

"My money's still on Southeast Asia. I'll get back to you."

◀8▶

THE MEETING AT Ray Tutty's house had long since been adjourned, but nobody had left the building. It was now five minutes to midnight and the tension in the air was so thick you felt walking across the room would be more than you could handle. People were noticeably lower in their chairs as they kept glancing up at the ancient grandfather clock dominating one end of Ray's library.

"Is there supposed to be some sort of warning?" Gustav asked. "Some way for us to know what is happening?" He and Ray Tutty had put aside their earlier differences as heat-of-the-moment comments. Both had apologized, sort of.

The other men turned to the governor for an answer.

"The last one went up on YouTube as it happened," Malcolm answered. "Presumably something similar will happen with this one. Getting the message out is as important as doing the deed."

"Are you taking any steps to protect the schools?" Paul asked.

"The National Guard has searched as many as they could. Local police are keeping a watch on the buildings in their jurisdiction. We have advised no one to enter any of the buildings after 2300 hours. According to the first message, the bombs are already in place. We are not looking for dead guardsmen. We've advised all the other governors across the country of our actions and recommended they do the same." He paused. "Some have."

The implication was not wasted on those in the room.

Like some of the fast-food owners, not everyone was taking this threat seriously.

At that point, BlackBerrys, pagers and cellphones started ringing around the room. Everyone made a grab for their respective devices. The text messages gave the address of the state's website.

"What is this?" the governor asked. He looked at his aide. "Malcolm, what is going on?"

The men had long ago abandoned the formal chairs surrounding the boardroom-type table where the meeting had taken place in favour of the more comfortable easy chairs clustered in little groups around the room.

Paul Johnson went over to the laptop that was still hooked up and entered the website address. The governor's seal appeared on the screen.

"Any idea which link I should follow?" he asked. Malcolm started over to assist him when the picture changed to a brick building set back from the road. It was still daylight in this setting. The camera started to zoom in closer, slowly filling the screen with the image of the building. It was déjà vu all over again.

Richard Nixon Junior High said the sign above the main door. Then the camera started to fade back, allowing a view of the surrounding area again.

"California?" Paul asked of no one in particular.

Everyone in the room jumped as the old clock bonged out the first chime on its way to midnight. Eleven more followed. The suspense built with each fading echo. Five seconds of silence followed. No one moved. Their attention was devoted to the web image. Just as they started to relax, smoke started to pour out of one of the school windows. The tension in the room increased as they all leaned forward to observe the expected blast.

Nothing happened. The picture faded back to the governor's seal.

After a minute, Gustav was the first to speak. "It was a dud."

Malcolm grabbed his phone and rapidly punched in some numbers. Instead of the expected "hello", a voice said: "We've been hacked."

"Find out how."

"Working on it."

Malcolm broke the connection. His next call was to his FBI contact, already listed on his speed dial. He identified himself and listened, nodding his head every couple of seconds. The others watched, waiting for some sort of report. Malcolm's face remained serious but gave no other indications of what was being said.

"Can you let me know as soon as you find out something?" he finally said. Apparently, the answer was in the affirmative. Malcolm said "thanks" and hung up.

"The FBI watched the same video we did. They have identified the school. It is in California and they have agents on their way."

"How did they know?" Ray asked. "Was this on more than the state government site?"

Malcolm shook his head. "They received the same advisory text message as we did. Even though they weren't officially working on the case yet, the terrorists knew who to contact."

"I guess this means they are onside now," the governor said.

"So," Ray said, "Gustav was right. They were only kidding about blowing up more schools. It was all a bluff. I knew the bastards didn't have the guts to follow through on their threat."

"I wouldn't jump to that conclusion too quickly," Malcolm said. "They did have a bomb in another school. They have proved they can do it."

"A smoke bomb. They can talk the talk, but they can't

walk the walk. True terrorists would have blown up that school, too."

Malcolm's phone rang. It was the FBI calling back already. He answered and his face went white.

"Now what?" Paul asked.

"The feds tipped off the local police department to go out and secure the scene. The first officer to arrive followed the smoke to a closet full of undetonated pipe bombs. For some reason, they hadn't gone off, yet. He hightailed it out of the building and now they're waiting for the bomb squad."

"A double whammy." Gustav took out his handkerchief and wiped his brow. "The first bomb brings in the first responders; the second one kills them. I have seen this in my country many times. This is more dangerous than we thought. It is spiralling out of control."

"No," the governor said. "I can't believe that was their intention. They seem to be trying to avoid casualties. The schools appear to be isolated from the surrounding population."

Paul sat down at the keyboard of the laptop and started typing. The image of the governor's seal disappeared and a list of addresses popped up in its place. Paul did a quick copy of one of them and then waited as a Yahoo page opened. "We have a BurgerCircus near that school."

He pasted the address into the map page and watched as a satellite picture appeared on the screen. He moved the cursor to increase the magnification. The roof of the school could be seen up the road from what was obviously a fast-food restaurant surrounded by a large parking lot. The school was set back from the main road and surrounding buildings.

"I'm impressed," Malcolm said. "You know the location of all your BurgerCircus outlets?"

Paul smiled. "Not really. If there is a school that size, there is probably a BurgerCircus nearby. This is not a real-time image. The governor is right. The school does appear to have been selected because the damage would be contained to its own area. Killing the first responders doesn't seem to fall into line with that caution."

"Who the hell are we dealing with?" Malcolm asked, his growing frustration becoming evident. "On the first school, they used way too much destructive power. The second one fails to go off at all. Are they incompetent? Are we dealing with a bunch of rank amateurs?"

The question hung in the air.

"Their technical expertise suggests otherwise," Paul said. "How difficult would it be to hack the governor's web page?" He looked at Malcolm for an answer.

"Not that easy. We have several layers of security. We've never had our firewall breached to my knowledge and I would know." He looked over at the governor for confirmation.

"I've never heard of it happening." The governor got up from his easy chair and took his seat at the head of the table again. "Gentlemen, we appear to have dodged a bullet. But, as I see it, we have less than twenty-four hours before another bomb is detonated. What are we going to do?"

◄9►

THE SILENCE IN the room was palpable. All the men had rejoined the governor at the boardroom table. Each man tried to think of a solution. You could see in their eyes as they came up with ideas and then rejected them. Ray Tutty was the first to speak.

"All I know is we can't pay. That will open a floodgate we will never be able to close. Somehow we have to find these bombs before they can go off and more importantly, we have to find the assholes who are planting them."

"We keep saying that," Malcolm said, "but now the problem is 50 times bigger. The first school was in Georgia; the second was in California. The third could be anywhere in the nation. We don't have the manpower to search every school in the country."

"Of course we do. Each principal gets a team together to search his school." Ray's look defied Malcolm to disagree with him.

"No, Ray. That's the last thing we want. A bunch of non-professionals who don't know anything about bombs. We could have schools blowing up everywhere with the loss of life in each case. Professionals must be the ones doing the searches."

"Bah, professionals. A professional is just someone who gets paid for doing what others do for free. On really busy days, I've grabbed a kid off cash and put them to work flipping burgers. In a couple of hours, they were doing it almost as well as the permanent cooks. You just make sure you pick someone who can follow directions. Tell the principals not to touch anything. Just look."

Malcolm shook his head. "Worst-case scenario in your restaurant, someone gets an undercooked burger. They bring it back and get another one for free. In our scenario, the worst case destroys a school and kills innocent searchers. We can't mess with people's lives."

"You're not suggesting we pay these bastards?"

Malcolm studied a sheet of paper in front of him. Columns of figures were scratched in pencil. A heavy, dark line underscored one of the figures.

"We may have to make a good-faith offering to buy us some time. Maybe five million. It will cost more than that to replace a school the size of that one in California."

"No." Red flushed into Ray's face. "I'm not paying."

Malcolm looked at his watch. "It's late. It's been a long, stressful day for all of us. Let's get some sleep and meet back here at nine tomorrow morning."

Paul glanced over at the grandfather clock. "That's in a little less than seven hours. What will have changed?"

"I don't know," Malcolm said. "The FBI will have studied the pipe bombs. Them not exploding may be the break we need. If they can track the components, they may find the bombers. Someone had to be in that area with a camera. They may have captured him by then. By now Homeland Security should be involved. They have unlimited powers. Things will start to happen soon." He hesitated. "We may just need to give them a little more time."

"Not five million dollars worth of time," Ray said. "Anyone who wants to stay the night, there are guest cottages available. If not, my pilots are standing by to helicopter you back to the city. Good night, gentlemen." He turned and walked from the room.

Paul waited for the door to close before addressing the others.

"He's right, you know. We can't be seen to be weak in

this."

"Weakness is one thing; stupidity is something else entirely." Malcolm closed the folder with his scribbled notes and started to get up.

Paul held up his hand. "Governor, they've communicated with you once, correct?"

The governor expressed surprise at that knowledge.

"I told him," Malcolm said, still half standing and half sitting. "We've got to do this as a team. We can't be withholding information from each other. That seems to be the favourite tactic of our esteemed president and we know that doesn't work." He looked at Paul. "What do you have in mind?"

"Like I said, I agree with Ray about the money. Maybe we can offer them some other kinds of concessions. Free air time to get out their message, free burgers for life. I don't know, something we both can live with."

"We could offer to set them up in franchises in their own country," Derek Saunders said. The scornful looks from the others would have wilted the plants in the centre of the table if they hadn't been made out of plastic. An indignant look darkened his face. "Wait, hear me out."

"I don't think that's what they want," the governor said.

Derek held up his hand to suppress the comments from the others. "Nobody has been killed. These are not truly fanatical terrorists. They want to save the world according to their name. If we set up jobs in their country and supply them with a source of income," he shrugged, "who knows, they might go for it."

"We don't know that their country is not the United States," Paul said. "That is part of the frustration. We don't have a clue with whom we are dealing."

Malcolm resumed his seat and opened his folder. On a clean piece of paper, he wrote down Derek's idea. "I doubt they would go for that, but at least we are thinking outside the box." He looked around the table. "That's what we need, gentlemen. Ideas."

The governor pushed back his chair and stood up. "I'm sorry, Malcolm. All this talk and speculation has fried my brain. I need to get some sleep. You can stay if you want. I'm going back to the mansion."

"Let's all give this some thought," Paul said. "Remember when we meet back here at 9:00, we will be down to sixteen hours until the next scheduled blast. You can see what their plan is. By making each blast an hour later, they are depriving us of sleep. They are trying to reduce our ability to make sound decisions. We must all take care of ourselves."

"In that case," Malcolm said, "let's not meet until supper time unless someone comes up with a definite plan. Sitting here looking at each other for twelve more hours will accomplish nothing. I'll send you bulletins from the FBI as I get them. Agreed?"

Several men yawned. None objected.

◀10▶

NINE O'CLOCK FOUND both Malcolm and the governor in the governor's office. The affairs of state had to go on. The second bombing in California had awoken the country's news media to the immensity of the story. Successfully blowing the school to smithereens would have been a more effective wake-up call, but the reporters did hear the alarm and resisted the urge to hit the snooze button. An onslaught of calls from the national media replaced the previous day's onslaught from the local media.

The suits in New York had to answer to their bosses as to why the networks were a day behind on a story of this importance. The higher priced suits were less concerned with the news content of the story and more concerned with the howls of protest coming from California. Californians were demanding to know why they weren't informed their schools were at risk.

The California governor assured his people everything possible was being done to protect them from these acts of terrorism.

"We will catch these terrorists," he assured them. His script sounded like it had been written in Georgia. Only the accent was different.

Malcolm was bringing the governor up to speed on the overnight findings of the FBI before a scheduled call with the president took place at 9:30.

"The bombs themselves were not defective. It was the fuse that failed to function." Malcolm slowly shook his head as he read the report. "There were enough explosives packed into that closet to level the building and rattle windows for miles around."

"What happened to the fuse?" the governor asked.

"Too complicated or too simple. I'm not sure which," Malcolm said. "Two canisters of chemicals, one containing nitric acid and the other holding hydrazine, were designed to spill and mix. This would result in an explosion which in turn would set off a chain reaction igniting all the pipe bombs. The frequency of ringing cellphones would release the covers.

"Only the nitric acid was released, and all it did was react with the wax on the closet floor. It ran out into the hallway, burning a trail of melted wax and linoleum, and created the smoke we saw in the video. The technicians discovered the battery on the second phone was dead. The school district dodged a bullet. A school that size would have cost millions to replace."

Malcolm paused while the governor visualized the effect.

"The phones were triggered by a call from a pay phone in Islamabad."

"Pakistan?"

"That's what it says."

"How much help can we expect from officials there?"

"I don't think it makes much difference. A person at a bus station made the call. The pay phone is in almost constant use by incoming and outgoing passengers. There's no video surveillance in the area. It would be impossible to find out who was using the phone at exactly that time."

"Couldn't we trace who the next caller was? He must have seen who was ahead of him."

"They did. It was a woman, and as is their custom, she didn't look at the man in front of her. She averted her eyes from the stranger and could describe nothing other than his footwear. Sandals. She could give us no other description. She couldn't even give us a nationality. She said the man dialled a number, waited a few seconds, said nothing, then hung up. Dialled again and repeated the process. She was just happy he hadn't made a long, chatty call. She was anxious to contact her family so they could come pick her up. She was returning from a meeting at her mosque."

"That would be our man," the governor said. "The phone was never answered."

The button on the governor's intercom flashed. He touched a switch, and the voice of his secretary came across the line. "NBC is on line one. Are you ready to talk to them?"

Malcolm shook his head. "No," he mouthed.

The governor hit the mute button. "Why not?"

"This is a federal case now. All calls should be referred to the FBI."

"We did have one of our schools destroyed, and BurgerCircus is headquartered in our state. As governor, that makes me still involved."

"The FBI is handling the investigation now. They will want to control any information that is released. At least talk to them before you agree to any interviews. We don't want to jeopardize any of their efforts."

The governor pushed the talk button once again. "Tell them I'll get back to them. Get a contact number."

He screwed up his nose at Malcolm in a childish gesture. "Satisfied? You've thwarted the freedom of the press."

"You know I'm not against keeping the people informed. The thing is, we don't have anything to tell them that you didn't say yesterday. Telling them we don't know anything new is not good politics."

"Yesterday, I was talking to the local media. This is the networks, Malcolm. This is the big time."

"And you don't have anything new to say to them."

"Governor Ramsay from California was already on the *Today Show,* and it's the middle of the night out there. I know more than he does."

"Governor, I'm telling you. Stay out of the public eye on this. It will come back and bite your ass. Things are going to get out of control. Every time a school blows up, the people are going to get closer and closer to panic. They are going to demand results."

"Results is what we will give them. The president is not stepping up to the plate. Someone has to."

"And you think that someone is you? Besides, what results? If that school in California had blown up last night, there would have been panic in the streets. By now, just about everyone in the country has at least heard about the threat to our schools. I hate to be the first one to say this out loud, but we may have to pay them off."

The governor's eyes turned steely cold. "Don't ever say that outside this office, Malcolm. We are nowhere near that stage yet. You'd be surprised what the FBI can find out. Give them time."

"That's what I'm telling you. Before you go on network TV, you have to give them time to track these guys down."

"No, Malcolm. You don't understand. If this plays out the way you predict, no one is going to be interested in talking to the governor of Georgia. They will want the president or nothing. Unless," the governor held up a finger and pointed it at Malcolm, "I can become the face of this disaster in the eyes of the people. They must see me as the one who is going to solve the mystery of who these bombers are. I have to convince everyone I've been on top of this from the start and am actively seeking a solution."

Malcolm gave the governor a silent stare.

"Me, you and the FBI. We are going to get to the bottom of this. Our IT experts are second to none, Malcolm. You know that. You only hired the best.

"The terrorists are running their campaign on the Internet. They are spitting in our face by using our website. We will set some digital traps for them and follow them back to their real-life location. I have to appear on TV so that they won't move on to some other less-prepared server. Do you understand?"

Reluctantly Malcolm nodded his head. "That might work, but it will take time. We're going to lose a school a day while we set it up."

"I've been up all night. When I came back to the mansion last night, I started writing code for the trap. It is still a little crude, but we can polish it up and make it work. I know we can. We will catch these bastards. We'll show them they made a mistake by attacking Georgia first."

A kaleidoscope of expressions danced across Malcolm's face—surprise, disbelief, incredulity. "You've been writing code, Governor? It's been a long time since you tried your hand at writing code. Coding has changed a lot in recent years."

The governor returned the expressions with a sardonic look of his own. "Computers don't use the binary language anymore? Switch open, switch closed? That's not the principle they operate under these days?"

Malcolm realized the governor was serious. He also realized he had insulted his boss by challenging his abilities. "Yes, all that is true at the basic level." He struggled to find the right words to redeem himself. "But now there are libraries of pre-written code programmers utilize. Instead of knowing how to write the code, you have to know where to look for it."

The governor's stare was unyielding. "That, my friend, is exactly the problem. We need a program the hackers can't access. They've built in defences against all the standard library stuff. We have to get beneath that layer of programming. Don't forget, I made a large contribution to building those libraries. I haven't spent my entire life as a politician."

Malcolm shrugged. On a superficial level, this plan might make sense. "Let me see what you've written. I'll help you debug it."

Malcolm's knowledge of programming came from his days at Langley. He had learned from the best. Now all he had to do was remember it.

◀11▶

MALCOLM MARVELLED AT the simplicity and tightness of the program the governor had put together in such a short time.

"This code is amazing, Governor. I have to admit I'm not sure how it works."

"It's quite simple. When they hack into our system, each bundle of code they send does a simple mathematical check of itself to make sure it is complete. If it checks out, it sends the next bundle. If not, it sends that bundle again. Happens millions of times a second."

"I understand all that. Basic network protocol." Malcolm pointed to a subroutine in the code. "This is what I can't figure out."

"Ah, that's the heart of the program. We alter the incoming bundle to give a false reading and then attach our little program to the returning code. It doesn't matter how many hoops and loops it jumps through, we follow it back. Just like that, we've hacked into their computer. At this point, if our program carried a virus, it would become destructive. That is not our intent. We simply want to monitor keystrokes. Everything they do, we will see here in Georgia." The governor beamed.

Malcolm studied the screen, marvelling at the simplicity. "No offence, but this archaic code might just work."

The governor smiled. "I'm not offended, Malcolm. You underestimate my many abilities. The secret of being a good leader is to surround yourself with good people, people like yourself. But just because I delegate a lot of my tasks doesn't mean I can't do them equally as well. I simply have too much to do to get caught up in the minutia of some small tasks."

"Forgive me, Governor, I am properly chastised. Let's get this program over to IT and have them install it on our server."

"No." The governor's retort was sharp and harsh. "We don't want to do that."

"Why not? That was the intention of writing the trapping program."

"We'll install it ourselves. Someone hacked into our state-of-the-art mainframe. I trust all our IT guys with my life, but I can't believe we were hacked without inside help. Let's take no chances."

Malcolm started to object but stopped. The governor may have been over-reacting, but he did have a point. Their computer system was designed to be fail-safe. It had proven to be anything but. Somehow their firewalls were breached.

"And Malcolm, we don't mention this plan to anyone at the meeting tonight. Not the BurgerCircus people, not the FBI, no one. The terrorists can't know we are tracking them. We can't risk any leaks."

Malcolm stared intently into the governor's eyes before nodding his head. His contacts at the FBI would not like being left out of the loop, it was true. But the governor was also right. Somehow the terrorists seemed to have an inside track on what was going on at these meetings. Until they found out how, everyone had to be suspect.

The cast of characters at Ray Tutty's home that night had altered. No longer were there any district sales managers. Executive level personnel, people who could make decisions without consulting anyone else, had replaced these lower-level minions. They represented every company on the list. The FBI had been asked to provide a report on the investigation. To everyone's surprise, they had agreed to the request and showed up in person to deliver it. To no one's surprise, they expected to run the meeting when they got there.

The late August temperatures in Georgia had gone up several degrees as a tropical storm ground its way along the coastline of South Carolina. At this point, there was no rain in the forecast, but the winds were freshening and massive storm clouds hung in the eastern sky. Suit coats and ties had been discarded and glasses of spiked peach punch filled everyone's hand. If one hadn't known the serious nature of the discussion, one would assume this was a typical suburban barbecue.

The CEO himself treated the gathering to BurgerCircus burgers cooked on the patio barbecue. Ray was trying to emphasize his business catered to working-class Americans. They did not have millions of dollars to pay off any terrorists. Most present were in full agreement. Their companies took in considerably less revenue on a weekly basis than BurgerCircus took in daily. Despite the sizzle of beef emanating from the grill, burgers of this quality had never crossed the counter of any fast-food outlet anywhere in the world. The ground meat had started out as premium cuts of steaks. Ray liked the idea of the symbolic gesture, but this was going to be his supper.

In one corner of the patio, a 60" screen television dropped down from an overhanging balcony. This served two purposes. One, it kept the sun from diminishing the high-quality digital image and two, it protected the set from the weather. The early NBC news was about to begin. To just about everyone's surprise, the opening shot was of Governor Peter Weston sitting in his office with Ted Shires, the network's current golden boy on the interview circuit.

Leading questions from Ted allowed the governor to spell out the story of how the first school blew up in

Georgia, followed by the dud in California. Until they paid the huge ransom, an additional school would blow up every night somewhere in the country.

"Governor," Ted said, "I understand it is the fast-food companies who are on the hook for this ransom, most notably BurgerCircus."

All eyes on the patio focussed on the image of the governor on the screen, ears straining to catch his answer. Malcolm rubbed his forehead with both hands and looked at the live person sitting to his right. He had not been present for this interview and didn't know what the governor had said. To refer to Peter Weston as candid would be like calling the Atlantic Ocean a small pond. Malcolm feared those present in this room wouldn't like the answer. The governor seemed to be waiting with the others with equal anticipation to see what he was going to say.

"Well, the initial message from the terrorists demanded the money come from the profits these companies, not just BurgerCircus, make on the backs of the children of the nation. Of course, we all know—"

The screen went blank. Great flashes of lightning, in the direction of the Atlantic Ocean 250 miles to the east, cracked through the sky. Tropical storms were notoriously fickle. This one had chosen this time not to follow the coast as predicted, but to make a path directly over Columbia, sending the outer bands of its winds and rain in a circulatory path over Atlanta.

Suddenly, flood sized drops of rain pounded down on the patio. The men sprang to their feet and beelined it towards the eight-foot patio doors, crowding through, pushing and shoving. Laughter permeated the air. Ray dropped the cover of the barbecue closed and joined the others. A white-jacketed man with a large umbrella battled the winds to rescue the evening meal. He rolled the barbecue under cover and continued the cooking.

Ray squared himself on the governor. "What the hell were you saying to that TV guy?"

Governor Weston's face flushed red. "The power went off before I explained our position. I was cut off."

"Well, now you're back on. What did you say?"

Malcolm joined the two men. What kind of spin control was he going to have to put into effect here? He waited to hear the governor's answer.

The governor pulled his wet shirt away from his body and gave it a shake. "I said we all know that's not the truth. Fast-food restaurants feed millions of everyday people in this country on a daily basis. You are all good corporate citizens and contribute a lot to the economy."

Malcolm relaxed a little. This wasn't as bad as he thought it would be.

"It is not our policy to negotiate with terrorists. We are taking every step possible to trace these people, but if we must make concessions, I will sure–"

The ringing telephone of one of the FBI agents interrupted his comments. Ray turned and glared at the agent, who gave an apologetic wave and turned to take the call as privately as one could in a room of almost a dozen people.

"He said what?" the agent exclaimed. He wheeled on the governor. "He's right here in front of me. I'll ask him."

Christ, what now? Malcolm thought.

"Did you say the Pakistanis were behind this plot? Where did you get information like that?" The agent elbowed his way to where the governor was standing. Malcolm tried to step between them, but the FBI agent would have none of that. He swept Malcolm to one side as easily as if Malcolm had been on roller skates.

"Jesus." Ray Tutty turned away in disgust. "This guy is a loose cannon."

"I may have said the call that set off the bomb in

California originated in Pakistan. That's the truth, isn't it?" The governor leaned towards the agent.

"That's not the point. It was not the Pakistani government that did it. You've created an international incident." He looked at Malcolm. "Did you tell him this?" He thumped Malcolm in the chest with two pointed fingers. "You're out of the loop, buddy boy."

Malcolm raised his hands in protest. Before he could defend himself, the white-coated cook pulled open the patio door and shouted to be heard above the wind now whistling outside the house. "The burgers are ready." His face showed surprise at the lack of reaction from the assemblage.

◀12▶

AFTER FIVE MINUTES, the generators deep in the basement of Ray Tutty's house automatically kicked in and restored power. By then, NBC had moved on. An Amtrak train derailment in California had replaced the terrorist threat as the item of interest. Despite the threat of a school a day blowing up, attention spans of the average viewer were limited. They had heard the story; now they were ready to be tantalized by something else. Train wreck, plane crash, hurricanes in the Caribbean, anything new to entertain them for a few seconds. If it hadn't happened on their street, a brief mention on the newscast was all that interested them. More details would be available on the Internet or in the daily paper to those few news junkies who wanted more.

Governor Peter Weston hadn't entered politics for nothing. In less time than it took the power to come back on, he had spun the stories to his advantage. He satisfied Ray Tutty with his defence of the fast-food industry. He convinced The FBI that he had simply pointed out to the people of the nation that an overseas agency might be at work here. Despite Peter's affiliation as an Indepentent governor, the Republican president would encourage talk that the threat was from foreign nationals. The FBI should be thankful to Peter for bringing it up. All indications led to an agency outside of America as being the culprits—Internet cafes in Thailand, phone calls from Islamabad. The people had a right to know this.

The cook brought in the generous supply of

hamburgers. BurgerCircus containers held the condiments. At first, there was some surprise at the quality of the food. After one or two bites, no one was fooled into thinking this was everyday fare at any BurgerCircus outlet anywhere in the nation. Everyone ate heartily.

After the meal, the meeting began in earnest. Tom Burke, the FBI agent in charge, gave lessons in spin-doctoring to one and all. He talked steadily for thirty minutes. His voice was engaging. His Power Point presentation included national maps, international maps and local maps showing city schools. He talked about the efforts to track the Internet messages and the bomb parts. He gave a discourse on bomb-makers' signature styles and how that might lead to a capture. He explained what steps were being taken to find other bombs that might be planted, which schools might be targeted. Then, he smiled at everybody and sat down. He didn't ask for questions.

At first blush, the report was comprehensive. Those around the table nodded their heads in understanding. Then, Malcolm leaned forward and spoke.

"Excuse me, Tom. Did you say you knew where this group originated?"

Tom stared daggers at Malcolm. "No, I didn't say."

"Do you know?"

"At this point, we're keeping that information confidential."

"What is it they stand for?"

Tom hesitated before answering. "We're not sure."

"But you do think you have a lead on which schools might become targets?"

"We have some schools under close watch."

"To date have you found any explosives?"

"We'd rather not say. We don't want to cause a panic anywhere."

"So you have found something?"

"Malcolm, I've given my report. Weren't you paying attention?"

The line wasn't as condescending as it appeared to the others present. The two men were former partners in the agency. Bickering between them was old hat.

"Sorry, Tom. I'm just trying to get some clarification on where we stand. To find out exactly what it is we know."

Ray Tutty's voice boomed across the table. "What the man is asking is if a bomb is going to go off at 1:00 a.m. and where?"

Tom looked over at Ray. "We're hoping for the best."

Ray gave a dissatisfied grunt. "Hoping? That and a buck will get you a cup of coffee at any of my restaurants."

"What about the men who took the video?" Derek Saunders asked. "Any leads there?"

"Not yet. The schools chosen so far have been isolated from the businesses around them. With that information, we are narrowing our search to similar school locations." Tom held up his hands. "You have my report, gentlemen. I'm not entertaining questions."

The room became silent.

"Governor, do you have any more to add?" Ray Tutty asked.

Malcolm said a silent prayer and gave the governor a pleading look.

"No, Ray. The FBI is heading up the investigation. Any support the state of Georgia can offer is available to them. We are cooperating in every way possible. I have placed our full resources at their disposal and, as you know, Malcolm is working full time on this."

Malcolm heaved a sigh of relief, prematurely, as it turned out.

"We are doing a few things on our own," the governor added as an afterthought. "But for the present, we wish to keep them close to our chest."

"What things?" Tom asked, a sharp edge in his voice.

"Nothing that will get in your way, Agent. These criminals destroyed one of our schools. We do have a special interest in finding them."

"Governor, I implore you, keep us fully informed of anything you are doing. We don't want to be working at cross purposes."

"That will not happen. Be assured you have our full cooperation. Unlike the president, the state of Georgia is devoting its full resources to this predicament."

"Ray," Malcolm said, "has your organization given any thought to raising money if that becomes necessary?" The question was strictly a diversionary measure to get the governor out of the spotlight.

The set of Ray's face tensed. The wrinkles around his eyes hardened into deep trenches. "You know my position on that. Nothing has changed. We will not pay."

"I heard some talk in one of my stores today," Gustav said. "Some people think we should pay."

Ray made no attempt to hide his contempt for that statement. "Why doesn't that surprise me?" he said. "I'm talking about real Americans."

"The Facebook site, BurgerCircusShouldPay, has had hundreds of thousands of people sign up," Derek said before Gustav had a chance to respond. "I've checked it a few times today. The list keeps growing and growing."

"We are monitoring that as well," Tom said. "We believe the first few thousand names were fake. Some of the latest ones are real. Ordinary citizens are signing on. That's not a good sign. It's a follow-the-herd instinct. These people don't believe they are supporting terrorism, but" he nodded his head at Ray in a moment of agreement, "there is no other way to look at it."

"We could look at it as democracy in action," Malcolm said. "The people do have a right to express themselves. I think it might even come under the First Amendment."

"Not when they are encouraging our enemies," Ray said. "That's treason."

The debate was on. Hard-liners on both sides expressed their views. No minds were going to be changed. The middle-of-the-road people who could see both points of view soon decided it was better to keep their mouths shut. They were being ganged up on by both sides.

Forty minutes into the discussion, everyone realized nothing new was being said. The same things were not even being said in more creative ways. The debate fizzled.

"Time to open the bar," Ray said. "What would everybody like?"

Again the white-jacketed man who had evolved into a cook materialized. This time he was in the guise of a bartender. The storm outside continued to rage. The wind whistled through the palm trees surrounding the estate. Rain continued to beat against the windows. No one was eager to board their planes or Ray's helicopters for a trip home or anywhere else. They hunkered down and waited for one o'clock to roll around to see what would unfold.

This time no warning message was required. The computer monitor on the library wall was showing the governor's logo from the state's website. As the top of the hour approached, everyone slid their big, heavy chairs a little closer to the screen, then leaned forward to be closer still. They were not disappointed.

As the timer at the bottom of the screen showed the time as 12:59:30 a.m. the logo disappeared just like the previous night. The governor looked at Malcolm sitting in the chair beside him. His head gave a barely perceivable nod. Malcolm responded with the same motion. None of the others in the room observed this. Their attention was locked completely on the greenish hued image that appeared to be slowly zooming over some grassland. Here and there the darker glow of what could only be steers passed under the lens.

"That's a night -vision camera," Tom said. "We're not in California tonight."

"That looks like hamburgers on the hoof," Ray said. "We're on ranch land somewhere."

The speed of the zoom picked up, blurring the image in the outer part of the screen but centring on a brighter light at the screen's focal point. To no one's surprise, the rectangular shape of a building developed in the lit-up area. The night-vision image disappeared and what had to be a large school commanded most of the screen.

As the clock rolled from 12:59:59 to 1:00:00, the whole screen erupted in massive flames and debris. There were no screw-ups on night two. Stunned silence in the room matched the lack of soundtrack on the monitor. As the afterglow from the explosion faded from the backs of their retinas, the image on the screen disappeared into blackness. The massive lights that had surrounded the building were no longer in existence.

The greenish image returned, showing only a pile of rubble.

Red letters formed from all parts of the screen tumbled into place like an overdone Power Point demonstration:

DO WE HAVE TO DO THIS AGAIN TOMORROW NIGHT? $100,000,000.00. PAY UP!!!

BURGERCIRCUS, GET YOUR ACT TOGETHER

A new web address followed the message.

◀13▶

RAY TUTTY SPOKE first.

"Texas or Oklahoma, that's my guess."

Tom Burke held up the screen of his BlackBerry. "Texas. A small town near Laredo. The cameraman shot the video from the Mexican side of the border. The bombers are getting more careful. We've got agents already on their way to the site."

"To do what?" Peter Weston asked. "Verify the school is gone? I'd say the video speaks for itself."

"No, Governor, to try and catch these bastards before they do it again tomorrow night."

"Paul." Malcolm looked over at Paul Johnson, "Do you folks have a BurgerCircus in the area?"

Paul checked the location obtained by Tom Burke from FBI headquarters. He typed the address into his own BlackBerry. "Just down the street."

Malcolm gave his head a firm nod. "That may be our first lead. We want to concentrate on remote schools near a BurgerCircus Restaurant."

Ray Tutty shook his head. "Don't you think that's just coincidence? We have outlets everywhere."

"No, Ray," Malcolm said. "You are the target. I think this is a vendetta against you."

"Against me? Why the hell would anyone target me? Hell, if it's money they want, go after GM or GE or Microsoft. They make more money than BurgerCircus."

"They're too obscure. You've seen the Facebook site. Tomorrow, there will be protesters in front of your restaurants all across the nation. Mark my words. Your profits might be nickels and dimes per item, but you can be cut off in a flash." Malcolm swung his gaze to Gustav, Derek and the other CEOs. "You guys as well. You've said it yourself. You're everywhere. The protests will be highly visible across the country."

"Malcolm," the governor interrupted. "I think you've misspoken. You said the vendetta is against BurgerCircus. It's against all the fast-food restaurants. Even at that, I think they are just a highly visible part of corporate America."

Malcolm turned on his boss. "No, it's not. The others are a smokescreen. BurgerCircus is the target. These guys are trying to pass themselves off as terrorists. You, yourself, think they are operating out of Pakistan. I think they are after BurgerCircus specifically and Ray in particular."

Tom Burke stepped to the forefront. "It's an interesting theory, Malcolm, especially about a BurgerCircus always being in the vicinity. But that could be a coincidence. Let's face it; there are BurgerCircuses everywhere. Part of Paul's marketing strategy is to put these things wherever kids congregate. I think there are international implications. I must agree with the governor on this one."

Ray laughed a brusque, non-humorous laugh. "Why me, Malcolm? Where would I come up with a hundred million if I was the target? That's ludicrous."

Malcolm shook his head. "No, it's not. Your net worth is in the billions. That's pretty common knowledge. If push came to shove, you could cough up the money if you had to."

"Those are fairy-tale figures you read about, not real money. If I sold everything I owned, I might reach those figures. This is a lose-lose situation for BurgerCircus. Unlike you civil servants, we have to answer to our shareholders."

Governor Weston's head snapped up at that comment. "Bullshit. I have to answer to the taxpayers. I don't own shares in Georgia. I can't keep myself in power simply by being the richest man in the state like you do."

"That's where you're wrong, Governor. Voters have little choice. If it's not you, it will be someone like you. They have to vote for somebody. There will always be a governor. There's no concrete way of telling if you are doing a good job. Some people vote for you because they like your stance on the environment; others because they like your tax policies; and still others because they like your handsome, good looks. It's all arbitrary.

"My shareholders have only one scale. Is the company paying dividends that make owning the shares worthwhile? If not, they can, and will, move on. They don't even have to move on to another fast-food company. They can buy shares in companies that make guns like Remington or Rapid Fire. This terrorist threat will increase their sales, making them a better investment."

"Except you'll still be CEO. You own more shares than anyone else. You could liquidate enough to hit the $100,000,000 mark without breaking a sweat."

Ray shook his head. He fought to suppress the anger in his voice. "Like I said, it's a lose-lose situation. I sell off enough shares to pay off; the price tumbles to nothing. We can't pay our dividends. I refuse to pay, and we get boycotted. We can't pay our dividends. The share value tumbles. Our company could go out of existence. There is no upside to this for us." He looked around the room at the other fast-food people for support. They were all nodding their heads.

He turned to the FBI agent. "You guys have to get this thing under control. You have to catch those sons of bitches, or it's the government that has to pay. One industry can't shoulder this responsibility."

"I still don't think it's one industry. It's you, Ray. You are the target." Malcolm held up his hands to end the conversation. "That's an argument for another day. That's not really why we're here. We all agree we have one common enemy. What we have to do is find out who is behind these bombings, where they are, and how we are going to shut them down."

"We learned a great deal with last night's failed attempt," Tom said. "With what we discover down in Texas, we are going to move forward. We will interview the people around these locations to see if they saw anything out of the ordinary. The fact there is always a BurgerCircus in the vicinity might be significant. If you could give us a corner in some of your restaurants all across the nation, we could have someone there collecting information from your regular customers. They may have seen something that could tip us off. These bombs didn't set themselves."

"That should bring out all the weirdos," Paul said. "If you think that will help, we'll give you the first booth inside the main door of every location in the country and throw in free coffee for your agents to boot. Good luck."

"If they plan on doing the same thing over and over every night until someone pays them off, there will have to be a pattern. You can't keep doing the same things without developing one. Eyes on the street, ears wide open. That's what we have to do. After 9-11, there were people everywhere who claimed to have been forewarned of the event and ignored by the government. We want to hear from those people. We will not ignore them."

"Hindsight is twenty-twenty," Malcolm said. "It's easy to look back and see all kinds of things that led up to an event. Putting them together beforehand is a one-shot-in-a-million happening. The same bunch of random events can produce thousands of different outcomes with just the slightest divergence anywhere along the line."

Tom looked at Malcolm and a small smile formed on his lips. "You, of all people, should know how good we are at this. The people never hear about most of what we stop from happening. We don't idly boast about these things. It's hard to take credit for something that didn't happen. When we take out a terrorist cell, we don't announce it to other cells. We leave them guessing." Tom gave his head a firm nod. "But *we* know what we've done. It keeps us going from day to day. We will stop these guys, as well."

"It was the same thing in the old country," Gustav said. "The police over there did many things without telling the people what they were doing. Every so often, someone you were doing business with on a day-to-day basis would simply disappear. The police would show up and tell you not to worry about it. Everything was under control. You moved on and didn't ask any questions."

Tom started to speak, to defend the FBI's actions. Then he realized what Gustav was saying could be attributed to his actions even though the reasoning was different. The FBI were removing criminals and terrorists from circulation who were about to commit unsavoury acts, not ordinary businessmen who disagreed with the government.

"Gentlemen, it's late," the governor said. "Tomorrow, if this happens again, it will be even later. I think we should coordinate our activities with Tom. If he sees a need for a further meeting, he will arrange it. Otherwise, let's all keep our eyes sharp and pursue our individual paths in this investigation. I trust by morning the president will make a statement. Our involvement may become secondary to that of the federal authorities, but our efforts won't diminish. We must bring these thugs to justice."

He looked at Malcolm to see if his aide had anything to offer. Malcolm didn't. Both men walked to the huge patio doors and looked out. To their surprise, the storm had passed. Thousands of stars twinkled down on them in the area devoid of outside lights.

The storm had moved north, but the power outage still gripped the area. Ray's generating system had made them forget the rest of Atlanta was sleeping in darkness and quiet. Most would be unaware another school had been wiped off the map until the power came back on. With luck, they would catch up to the rest of the country with the early news reports when daylight broke. Georgia Electric would have done their thing by then.

However, with each school destroyed, more and more people would be staying up later and later or soon getting up earlier and earlier to have first-hand knowledge of what evil lurked in their country. An evil the authorities seemed unable to stop without throwing a pocketful of money at it.

If the people had been privy to this million-dollar view of the stars from Ray Tutty's patio, they would have been thinking Ray could easily afford to stop the destruction. Ray's place was not ostentatious, but Ray did not go without. His helicopters, his private jets, his Olympic-sized pool, even his gas-fired power generation plant all reeked of someone living in the lap of luxury.

At the same time, taxpayer-built schools were being blown to kingdom come. Everyone knew it wasn't Ray Tutty's money that would replace these schools. In their minds, people like Ray didn't even pay taxes. It would be their hard-earned paycheques that fueled yet another demand.

◀14▶

"HO, HO, HEY, hey. BurgerCircus has to pay.

"Ho, ho, hey, hey. BurgerCircus has to pay.

"Ho, ho, hey, hey. BurgerCircus has to pay."

The senseless chant rang out along the sidewalk outside the fast-food outlet as a long line of placard-carrying protesters marched back and forth in front of the main entrance.

Malcolm looked out the tinted windows from the back of the state-owned vehicle that whisked him to his office each morning. He shook his head in surprise at the size of the demonstrations that had already formed along the strip leading to the governor's mansion. The largest crowds converged on the three BurgerCircus outlets marking his route. Boycotters blocked the drive-in entrances. This action caused traffic to back up into the streets as commuters hungry to grab a bite on the way to their work locations refused to drive on without getting their morning fix of fried egg with sausage on an English muffin and black coffee.

Staff members lined the windows wondering why they were being victimized and almost imprisoned by these radical protesters. It wasn't BurgerCircus's executives who were blowing up the schools. They were trying to help catch the bombers. The first thing they had done on entering their stores that morning was designate a place for the FBI to conduct their interviews. These unsmiling men, dressed in dark suits, had been waiting when the early staffers arrived to unlock the doors. Now, no customers could get in these doors to face the federal representatives. The protesters refused to let them pass.

"Are these protests just here on the way to the governor's mansion?" Malcolm asked his driver. "They seem pretty well organized."

"No, sir. From what I hear they are popping up spontaneously all across the country. It kept me from getting my morning caffeine fix. I couldn't find anyplace to get into a drive through." Robert Pettala worked for the state but was assigned full time to Malcolm Truex. He was a combined driver, messenger, researcher. Anything Malcolm needed.

Malcolm surveyed the scene as they left that strip of businesses behind and entered a more upscale neighbourhood. Here BurgerCircus had yet to establish any roots although there was a sit-down steakhouse whose profits eventually ended up in Ray Tutty's wallet.

"Stop by my office when we get to the mansion. I'll have coffee ready for you."

"And a couple of those peach crullers I see being made in the kitchen every morning?" Robert looked into the rearview mirror and smiled.

Malcolm laughed. "They'll be there, too. I want to get your thoughts on these school bombings. Who do you think is behind it and why?"

"Hell, that's easy. You don't have to bribe me with coffee and doughnuts to find that out. It's the Pakistanis. The governor said so on the news last night. I was watching the TV in the car while you were hobnobbing with the fast-food elite. I hear you had hamburgers. Big fancy joint like that and they serve you hamburgers." Robert shook his head in disgust. "I'd have expected something better."

Before Malcolm could respond, Robert dialled the car into the long curving driveway of the governor's mansion. Robert pulled to a stop in front of the impressive front door.

Malcolm let himself out and ran up the steps. His office was on the second floor next to the governor's, within easy shouting distance. He wanted to find out how successful the trap that had been set on the mainframe computer had been.

He didn't have to wait for an answer. When he poked his head in through the governor's door, Peter Weston was fully involved with his laptop computer. Row after row of numbers and letters were streaming by the governor's intense scrutiny.

Malcolm stood in the doorway for a full minute waiting to be acknowledged. Finally, he cleared his throat.

"Ahem. How's it looking, Governor?"

Weston looked up, surprise registered on his face. He hit one of the function keys, and the flow of data on the screen halted. "Malcolm. I didn't see you there. We're making progress. The program backtracked to the home computer, but it didn't lock on. Somewhere, there's a bug. I'm searching for it now."

"Back to Indonesia?"

"No. This time it came from New Delhi. At least, that's where I lost the connection. Our terrorists seem to be citizens of the world. Of course, it could have just as easily been initiated down the street and got routed around the world. That's why it's so important to lock on to the originating computer itself. The waypoints are of little interest to us."

Malcolm walked into the office and closed the door.

"Put it up on the big screen, and I'll help you," he said.

"Uh, uh," the governor said, shaking his head. "This baby only gets compiled on this laptop. All that goes on the mainframe is the .exe file, and we will bury that in code." He looked up at Malcolm with an earnest look in his eyes. "This stays between you and me, buddy. We can't afford any leaks."

"I understand that. If the bad guys find out, they'll cover their tracks and make it that much harder to find them."

The governor gave a short, curt laugh. "That scenario is the lesser of the two evils. They could also pretend they don't know we're on to them and feed us all sorts of useless information that would waste our resources and have us searching in all the wrong places. Their bombing techniques may be a little shaky, but we can't underestimate them; they are tech savvy. There are some highly intelligent minds running this operation."

Malcolm smiled. "There are equally intelligent minds tracking them down."

"Hopefully, more intelligent." The governor returned the smile. "What's the latest from your FBI friends?"

"Like the bombing here in Alexandra, there wasn't much left at the scene. They have found traces of C4 plastique. Military issue by the looks of things. Our military."

The governor rubbed his chin in a thoughtful gesture. "Three bombs, three different agents. That's interesting."

"Tom Burke didn't use those words to describe it. Bombers are tracked down by their signature techniques. This guy doesn't seem to have one."

"Or this guy is these guys."

"You mean someone different is setting each of these bombs? That could explain the uneven level of competence. It also makes tracking them down much more difficult. Each investigation is like starting over from the beginning. Things learned from one attack can't be used in the other attacks to trace a pattern."

The governor leaned back in his chair. "There's no room for naysayers on the team, Malcolm. To put a positive spin on this, the more people involved, the better the chances of one of them slipping up. Murphy's Law could be on our side on this one. Also, the more of them there are, the more they have to communicate with each other. That's why this program is so important. If we can tap into their computers, it will be like having a man on the inside."

He sat forward again and released the pause button holding back the flow of data on his screen. "I'm going to work on this. You take over running the state for the rest of the day."

Malcolm watched for a minute or two longer as the governor got lost in the stream of numbers. He knew he had been zoned out. He knew his chauffeur was waiting in his office and eating all the fresh peach crullers that were supplied each morning for his enjoyment and sustenance. He got up from his chair and walked to the door. The governor was not even aware he was still in the room. Malcolm gave a slight wave and closed the door on his way out.

Robert Pettala was sitting in Malcolm's outer office chatting with the receptionist when Malcolm made the short trip from one door to the next. A mug of steaming coffee filled Robert's hand, barely touched. He hadn't been waiting long.

Margaret Murphy, Malcolm's long-time executive assistant, looked up as Malcolm came through the door. She nodded her head in Robert's direction. "Claims he has an appointment and I'm supposed to be feeding him peach crullers." She smiled at Robert. During the run of a week, Robert and Margaret spent a lot of time working together. Malcolm didn't have a great division of labour in his work schedule. He grabbed whoever was available to carry out his wishes. He could do this because he only surrounded himself with competent people.

"Well, the first part is true, he does have an appointment. I'll have to count the crullers before we see if there are any to spare." Malcolm walked across the room and entered his inner office. He motioned for Robert to follow him.

Malcolm walked directly to a tray of fruit and pastries on a dark, walnut side table. A silver coffee carafe was plugged in beside it. His busy schedule did not allow him the luxury of a leisurely breakfast at home. Despite being the most important meal of the day, Malcolm always had breakfast at his desk, usually several hours earlier than this. But, usually, he was in bed before 4 a.m. The kitchen staff brought up the food when Malcolm came through the front gate.

He lifted the plastic cover off the tray and made an offering gesture to Robert. "If this is what it takes to get you to talk, dig in."

Robert stepped forward. He needed no further encouragement. The kitchen staff at the governor's mansion was second to none. Peter Weston justified their expense by hiring them out to cater major events in the state. Any profits they made were turned over to medical research at the University of Atlanta. Dissenters ran the risk of appearing to oppose this research if they criticized the arrangement. There was no upside for them in nitpicking. The governor used his best spin doctors to quickly and brutally attack his dissenters. For him, it was a win-win situation. He ate only the best of meals and at the same time appeared to be a humanitarian in support of finding cures for the major scourges of the world.

The two men placed pastries onto plates; Malcolm filled a coffee cup, and they sat in the less-formal leather chairs surrounding a small coffee table to the right of the working desk area.

Malcolm got right to the point. "What are your thoughts on this school bombing issue? Should the fast-food companies pony up the demanded hundred million?"

Instead of answering, Robert bit the corner of one of the crullers. A little peach filling stuck to the corner of his mouth. His tongue darted out to bring it home with the rest of the bite. A few flakes of pastry spilled onto his tie. He quickly brushed them off into his other hand and pocketed them.

"Man, those pastry chefs are worth their weight in gold," he said and took another bite.

Malcolm reached across the table and pulled the plate away. "This is a working breakfast. Work first, eat when it's not your turn to talk. Right now, it's your turn. So talk."

Robert finished chewing his bite and smiled. "You want to know what the great unwashed think, is that it?"

"Yeah, something like that. The man in the street."

"BurgerCircus could probably come up with the money. Not the local one here, but worldwide I bet they could." The expression on Robert's face darkened. His eyes narrowed. "But you can't give in to terrorism, man. It just can't be done."

"Nobody is going to argue with that sentiment." Malcolm paused and looked at his watch. "Except in about fourteen hours, another school is going to blow up somewhere in this country. And then another one, and another one, and another one."

Robert held up his hand to stop Malcolm's litany. He shook his head from side to side. "You can't give in to terrorism, man. It's that simple."

"So, we just keep losing schools?"

"No. We stop the bombers."

Malcolm stared across the top of his coffee cup at his Man Friday. He finally took a sip and returned the cup to its saucer. "How do we do that, Robert? How? The next one could be anywhere in the country. From Maine to Washington state. From California to Florida. How do we stop that?"

Robert leaned forward in his chair. All thoughts of crullers faded from his mind. "That's true, but we do know where they've been. They were here in Georgia. They were in

California. They were in Texas. They had to leave some trail. To stop them, you have to find out who they are. To do that, you have to find that trail, track where they've been and then catch up to them and hammer them from behind."

Robert brought his fist down onto the coffee table causing the dishes to rattle. He grabbed the plate containing his crullers and smiled. "Your turn to talk." He stuffed a big bite of peach sauce-covered pastry into his mouth.

"Even though you think they can afford it, you don't think BurgerCircus should pay?"

The hardness returned to Robert's eyes.

"No one pays. That would be like opening a floodgate." He slowly shook his head. "No one pays."

Malcolm nodded in agreement and at an emotional level, he agreed with that assessment. The discussion continued, but the sentiment never changed.

After Robert had left, Malcolm sat for a long time in his swivel, black leather executive chair. He still had a cup of coffee in his hands that he unconsciously sipped. His chair faced the window overlooking the manicured front lawns.

Robert's words and the demonstrations at all the BurgerCircus restaurants observed on the drive in didn't seem to jive with each other. Malcolm had always trusted that Robert had his fingers on the pulse of what the common man was thinking. Often he used Robert's words to offset the words of the bottom-line driven businessmen who advised the governor.

Robert had been adamant. There had been no room for intellectual reasoning. His view was simple and to the point. *No one pays.*

Malcolm swung back behind his desk and tapped his intercom. "Margaret. Get me Herb Solstace up here at once."

"Pardon me," an icy voice crackled back at him.

A smile popped onto Malcolm's face. Malcolm was an excellent administrator, dealt with people well most of the times and had the ability to get things done. Sometimes he could be a little too abrupt, which didn't always foster cooperation. Margaret had taken on the task of correcting that bad habit.

"Margaret. Would you be so kind as to contact Herb Solstace and request he come to my office, ASAP?"

"Yes, Mr. Truex. I would be glad to do that for you." She paused. "I know you're under a great deal of stress, but that is all the more reason to treat people appropriately. The results will be worth the effort." Robert could sense the smirk on her face through the intercom wires.

"Thank you, Margaret. You're right as usual. Tell me, who do you think should pay off these school bombers? The government or the fast-food people?"

There was a moment of silence on the line. "I can't believe you're asking me that." There was no sense of a smile in her voice now. "You can't allow terrorists to extort us. No one pays."

A smile crept across Malcolm's face. Margaret's sincerity easily came across the wires.

"Thanks. Send Herb in as soon as he gets here."

That line seemed so simplistic. No one pays. Malcolm knew they were right. In South America, a few years back, a foreign national was kidnapped by extremists. The man's company paid the ransom to get their executive back. Now kidnapping was a growth industry in that part of the world. Nobody with even a remote relationship with money travelled without heavy security. If you couldn't afford the security, you had better stay home or at the very least, have a blank cheque in your pocket.

Off the coast of Somalia in Northeast Africa, pirates were now capturing supertankers filled with oil. The ransoms being demanded, and paid, were in the hundreds of thousands of dollars. Each ransom paid made the area less safe for oceangoing vessels, not more secure.

On the upside, the world's navies were getting live-fire practice while pursuing these criminals without fear of starting a war. Somalia had no real government to speak of and no other nation claimed the pirates as their own.

Malcolm knew no one should pay. Malcolm's staff knew no one should pay. That didn't explain the thousands of people demonstrating outside all the fast-food outlets across the country. Surely, these people must understand no one pays.

Malcolm took another sip of his coffee. A scowl crept onto his face. It wasn't the coffee. It was as good as ever. He had to face reality. He knew that sentiment wasn't always true. Even though he hated to admit it, even to himself, he knew you had to make concessions sometimes. Sometimes, you simply had to put a stop to the madness anyway you could. Sometimes, even though you didn't want to, you had to pay.

There was a tap at the open door. Herb Solstace, head of security for the governor, entered the office. Dark circles around his eyes gave him the look of a tall, well-built racoon in need of a few hours of sleep. His blond hair had a greasy look about it, suggesting the shower and Herb had been strangers for a few days.

"You look like shit," Malcolm said as Herb slid into a seat across the desk from him.

"Thanks, I needed that. I hope you've called me in here to tell me you've solved this bombing thing. I'm not finding anything useful about them, and I've looked under every stone, behind every door. Nothing."

"We're working on it." Malcolm pointed towards the coffee pot and pastry tray. "Help yourself. I want to run a couple of things by you."

"You don't have to twist my arm. All I've had to drink

lately is five-hour old mud. No one has had time to make a fresh pot."

Malcolm waited for Herb to fill a plate and slip back into his chair. He allowed Herb to take a couple of bites of the cruller before he started talking again.

"Why do you think the terrorists are getting so much support from the general public about making BurgerCircus pay? Protesters clogged every restaurant I passed on the way here. It doesn't seem to make any sense."

Herb nodded in agreement. "Sometime after the school in Texas was blown to hell, a blog appeared on the BurgerCircus Must Pay Facebook page ranting about the obscene profits BurgerCircus and its ilk make. It progressed to how obese our children are becoming and placed the blame for that squarely on the shoulders of the fast-food diet most of them follow. To read the blog, you would think every kid in America is at least 20 pounds overweight, and our sports programs are all played on a computer screen. Blame everything wrong in this country on the fast-food corporations.

"From there it exhorted the people to get out and boycott these restaurants if not to protest the school bombings, which it somehow blamed on the fast-food chains, then to at least protect the health of our youth. I'm not sure most of these protesters even know what they are protesting."

Herb savoured a sip of the fresh coffee before continuing.

"Most of those parading up and down in front of the stores think it has to do with saving their children from a life of heart disease and diabetes and has nothing to do with who should be paying off these terrorists. The message was not a spur-of-the-moment rambling of some blogger. It was carefully thought out and designed to hit all the major hot-button issues of what is bothering people these days. It was extremely manipulative. No offence, Malcolm, but it was like something you might have written. It's not the work of an amateur."

Malcolm laughed a deep-throated laugh. "I'll take that as a compliment, I think. You believe this is all part of the original plan?"

"Without a doubt. Those signs they are carrying were all made and ready when the people started showing up around 5 a.m. We have video surveillance of some of those who were handing them out. A lot of them are professional rabble rousers. Show up to protest everything from the war in Iraq to the price of tea in China. A lot of the faces are familiar from G8 protests all across North America and Europe."

"Professional? You mean they are being paid."

"That's what I think."

"That would be a large payroll."

"Not so big. It only takes a few to fire up the masses. It's a learned skill just like anything else."

"Can we pick them up?"

"We have grabbed some of them. They know nothing of value. They don't know who is paying them. It's all cash, upfront. The extortionists contacted them, sold them a bill of goods and offered enough money to arouse their interest. I lean more towards extortionists than terrorists. Money is the driving factor here, nothing else."

Malcolm slowly sipped his second cup of coffee while he let this new information churn around in his mind. Herb's view was not foreign to him. The entire operation had the earmarks of an offshore operation. Still, Malcolm thought it went deeper than just a money grab. There seemed to be a bit of a vendetta attached, a vendetta against Ray Tutty and BurgerCircus. If you wanted to get Ray Tutty's attention, in Malcolm's opinion, you had to go after his money. Nothing else mattered as much to him as that. Attacking his business kept him interested.

"I'd like to talk to the ones you've picked up," he said to Herb.

Herb shrugged like that was no big deal. "You'll have to be quick. They are down at police headquarters, but the authorities can't keep them for long. They haven't broken any laws. They are simply exercising their rights to free speech. You know, the First Amendment and all that. If you aren't familiar with it, they will gladly bring you up to speed. They can quote it verbatim and then throw in a thousand ways about how we are violating their God-given rights."

"I didn't know the constitution was a religious document. I thought a bunch of men in Philadelphia dreamed it up. If it had come from God, surely it wouldn't have needed so many amendments attached to it."

Herb fought back a smile. He could detect the strain Malcolm was trying to hide. "It is to them," he said. "It's their Bible, to be twisted to mean anything they need it to mean."

"Well, I don't want to argue with them. If someone is paying them, there is a money trail. This may be our best lead to date. God knows the others haven't led us anywhere."

"FBI agents conducted the interviews I listened to, not the local cops. I don't believe these kids know who hired them. They're just dupes."

"I'm sure they don't," Malcolm agreed. "I'm hoping to figure out if the source is big business, organized crime, local militia or perhaps even offshore terrorists. They all have their signature ways of operating. Maybe I'll give Tom Burke a call. He's the lead FBI agent on the case. His men should have been probing for the same thing. I'll see what he can tell me."

Herb reached out and took a cruller from the nearby plate. "Good luck. Sharing isn't one of the strong points of the agents I have been talking to."

Malcolm nodded. "Yeah. The governor ticked them off with his Pakistani remarks. If Tom is still tight-lipped, I'll form my opinions when I talk to the protesters. Then I can share my thoughts with Tom. We go back a ways. I may have nothing new to offer, but at least I'll be seen to be sharing. Tom may open up. If not, it's another avenue for us to pursue on our own. Anything leading us back to the people behind this crap is all that matters."

Sean Rhyno — Morning Commentary

In other news:

The president said yesterday that the U.S. will take punitive action against the African nation of Surroto. "Their leader is getting too big for his boots," the president said, "and is a threat to the nations boarding the small, mountainous country."

You will recall our government is the one which stepped up to supply Surroto with modern planes and armaments only two years ago. At the time Surroto's president said they needed the arms to protect their struggling diamond mining industry from invaders. American backers also stepped in with funding to revitalize the mines.

Surroto may be small in land area but they are rich in resources. Their diamond mines are the envy of their neighbours. As a result, supplying arms from the U.S. proved to be a lucrative deal for some of our major arms traders, many of whom are said to have links to the current administration as do the companies which took over the diamond mines.

It now appears Surroto intends to nationalize these mines and throw out their "imperialist masters." Washington is listening to the calls to prevent Surroto, a sovereign nation, from acting in its own best interests by overthrowing the current government and setting up its own puppet regime.

Now, it appears, we will be the invaders the arms were designed to protect against.

◀15▶

RAY TUTTY, PAUL Johnson and Barbara Bishop were hunkered down in Ray's twenty-first-floor executive office at BurgerCircus's headquarters building in downtown Atlanta. Outside the sweltering late summer heat beat down on the city. Not so in Ray's hideaway. Here the temperature was a comfortable 68 degrees. That did not mean the office occupants were cool.

"Say that once more, and I'm going to smack you silly." Barbara pointed a well-manicured, red-tipped finger at Ray.

"I'll say it as often as I have to until you start hearing me," Ray shot back. "We-Don't- Give-In-To-Terrorists. There will be no ransom paid out of this office."

"And I'm not arguing with you about that—"

"Well, someone in this room sure as hell is, and it's not Paul. He's uncharacteristically keeping his mouth shut." Ray's eyes turned to his vice-president. "That's because he knows you're wrong and hasn't got enough guts to tell you to your face." Both people looked at Paul for acknowledgement of that statement. Paul's face remained stoic. At least until Barbara turned her attention back to Ray. Then Paul gave a quick wink to Ray.

Before Ray could respond to the gesture, Barbara started up again:

"What I'm trying to say, if you'll get down off your goddamn soapbox, is, in theory, I agree with you. In real life, we have to prepare for other eventualities. Sales across the nation were down fifty per cent for this morning's breakfast run. That's only anecdotal information. We're still waiting for the real numbers to come in." She paused to let the two executives digest what she had told them. "We can't stay in business if these boycotts keep barring our doors for even a short time.

"And that's not all. We've been getting a steady stream of calls from our competition asking what we are going to do. They weren't hurt as badly as we were because we were the main targets today. But they still took a hit. They are looking to you for leadership. With your giant ego, you should be flattered by that. However, you saying over and over you're not going to negotiate with terrorists is not leadership. Some of these smaller franchises are in real trouble just from today's actions."

She threw another sheet of paper onto the table. "That's not all that's happening. The price of our stock took a severe hit in late trading today. You two are both a lot poorer than you were when you got up this morning."

Paul shook his head and spoke for the first time. "Today's figures are meaningless. A blip at best. If it happens again tomorrow and the next day, then we've got a problem on our hands."

"Meaningless?" Barbara turned on him, her usually calm face full of fury. If this had come from Ray, it wouldn't have bothered her. But, coming from Paul, she was shocked. Paul was in charge of marketing. He knew how small a fluctuation it took to affect the company's bottom line. He was known for his calmness at all times, but he was too calm in Barbara's opinion. Either he didn't understand the situation, or he was totally unrealistic.

Paul held up his hands in a placating manner. "Don't blow a gasket, Barbara. I'm not saying this is not a serious issue. It could be fatally serious. I'm saying one battle does not lose a war. We have to define our enemy, and then we have to come out fighting. We need to counterattack, fast and hard." He turned to Ray. "You have to get on prime-time television, even if we have to buy the space, and expose the people behind this boycott." He held up a finger for silence. "Not the boycotters. No one wants to be told they were wrong in their actions, but the extortionists who are blowing up our schools. Those people blocking our driveways are being manipulated by the real enemy. We have to get them back on our side without making them look like fools. There's a very fine line here, and we have to be careful we stay on the right side of it."

"Now somebody is making some sense," Ray said. He gave Barbara a childish screwed-up nose to show how wrong she was. "I'll damn well tell them."

Paul put a hand on Barbara's shoulder to keep her from responding. He continued to look at Ray. "This speech may be the most important thing you've ever said in your entire career. I don't want you venturing off extraneously and off the cuff. It has to be carefully prepared and delivered with the right degree of intensity and conciliation. The message has to be the country is under attack from outsiders, and we all have to fight back shoulder to shoulder to preserve our way of life. I'm not sure you're up to something like this. It's going to require a Churchillian effort. Maybe it would be better if I do it myself."

"Like hell. No one outside the business even knows who you are. It has to be the face of BurgerCircus, and that face belongs to me. Remember that advertising campaign you made me suffer through a couple of years ago. At the time I thought it was demeaning, hawking hamburgers during some silly sitcom; now it may pay off."

Barbara got up from her chair and walked over to the sideboard at the back of the office. An elaborate, stainless-steel coffee machine sat on one end of the bar. She placed a ceramic mug under the spigot, pushed a couple of buttons and waited for a freshly brewed latte to appear in the slot. The two men watched and waited for her to speak. Neither man assumed the coffee would be for them. They both know how to operate the machine. Barbara was no one's coffee girl.

"We tightly scripted those commercials, and they worked. Ray can be persuasive."

"I'm not sure if I'm being complimented or insulted."

Barbara looked up at him. "Neither. I'm simply stating facts as I see them."

Paul nodded in agreement. "The key thing is they were tightly scripted. We have to get this message out in the next couple of hours. It has to be right the first time. There can be no do-overs. We want it on every network, on every station and," he looked into Ray's deep blue eyes, "we want to have it right. I can't over emphasize that point, Ray. You can't go off on any tangents of your own."

"You two make me sound like an idiot. I can make a goddamn speech on my own."

"Not this one," Paul said. "It's not going to be your own. I say we go to the experts in people manipulation. I'm going to ask Malcolm Truex to write it for us. I've seen his work, and he's good. He got that clown, Peter Weston, elected and keeps him looking good. You can tell when Weston is speaking from prepared notes and when he is speaking extemporaneously, which is not very often. Malcolm keeps a tight leash on his public utterances."

"And you're putting me in that same class?" The disgust dripped in Ray's tone.

"Not at all. We became the biggest player in the fast-food market by being the best in everything we did. In this instance, I'm telling you that Malcolm Truex is the best."

"What do you think, Barbara?" Ray *would* make this decision, but not until he consulted the people he trusted the most. They were both in this room with him.

"I have to admit I'm not an expert on political speeches and on who writes what for whom. I have been impressed by the governor. I did vote for him in the last election. It never occurred to me the words he was speaking were someone else's words. But, if we can get that guy, let's go for it."

Ray got up from his chair and walked to the tinted window overlooking the city. Down below he noticed the ant-like cars wending their way up and down Moreland Avenue. Heat waves shimmered in the air. Their occupants may have wondered what all the fuss was about as they drove through the fast-food section of the city. No more. Now they focused on their concerns. They had businesses of their own to run or employers to satisfy. Their worlds revolved around themselves. Most had heard about the school bombings, but as of yet, they weren't a major concern in their lives. It was still summer. School wouldn't be in for another week or so. It would take the destruction of a couple more of the nation's schools to get their full attention, perhaps the schools their children attended.

Ray looked up in the direction of the governor's mansion. He couldn't see it from his office tower, but he knew where it sat. On bad days, he often spewed his venom in that direction.

"There is one problem with this scenario. If we get Malcolm Truex, we are going to get the governor as part of the deal. The governor won't let me go on TV by myself. He will insist he be there and he has equal or more time than me."

Paul had walked over to the coffee machine. He was sipping from a cup of rich, black coffee. He shook his head at Ray's remarks.

"That's not a problem," he said. "We want this whole thing to be the government's baby, not ours. We never want the people to forget it is not up to BurgerCircus to solve this dilemma. The authorities are the people responsible for bringing this whole sad situation to an end, hopefully by catching the bad guys, but if not, any solution is up to them. Having the governor with you will drive that point home without us having to say it. Saying it out loud makes us sound like whiners. The governor stepping up and taking the lead role will put him and his administration in the forefront. The next logical step from there will be for the president to step in. There is no love lost between the president and Peter Weston. The president will do his best to pre-empt him."

Ray looked as if he was about to object. Paul held up his hand. "There is no upside to this for us, Ray. None. We must give the appearance of helping the government, but we are only helping. We sell hamburgers. We don't track down criminal organizations. The bombing problem is not ours." Paul pointed a finger at Ray to emphasize his next point. "And we want the boycotts of our stores to stop. Remember, that's why you are there. That's to be the focus of your message. The boycotters are only helping the terrorists' cause. We want to convince everyone that loyal Americans don't side with terrorists. Ever."

"Amen to that," Barbara said.

◀16▶

MALCOLM TRUEX ROTATED his chair towards the window behind his desk and let the late morning sun wash over him. He had just returned from the Atlanta FBI offices where Tom Burke had allowed him to sit in on the questioning of the lead protesters from the morning's boycott. At first, Tom had refused to let Malcolm get involved, but when Malcolm said that was no problem, he would conduct his own interviews, Tom had changed his mind. Tom didn't want the governor's office branching out on its own investigation. He wanted to keep everything under his control.

The governor had already come close to causing one international incident. Malcolm was not to ask any questions on his own. If he felt the need, really felt the need, Tom emphasized, Malcolm could pass written questions to the lead agent who would decide whether or not to ask on his beehalf.

This method, as it turned out, posed no problems. Malcolm had no desire to ask any questions. It took him less than two minutes to realize these iconoclasts believed in dissension for the sake of dissension. The actual cause meant nothing to them. The sad part was they sold themselves cheap. The bombers would have paid them much more for the services they offered. The fools failed to realize the criminals had manipulated them.

Malcolm didn't have time to waste and soon dismissed himself from the interview. When he explained to Tom why he was leaving so quickly, the FBI agent didn't even comment. His body language spoke volumes, however. Tom knew these fools were a waste of valuable time and resources. Still, he had to do it. They had no other leads to pursue.

The buzz of his intercom brought Malcolm out of his reverie.

"Paul Johnson on line one," Margaret's mellow voice informed him.

Malcolm reached out and picked up the phone. "What's up, Paul?"

He listened for several seconds. "You want me to write a speech for Ray Tutty? And you want it later this afternoon?" Malcolm chuckled. "Sorry, I don't freelance my services."

Again he listened. His eyes narrowed. This new information was having an influence on him. He opened the bottom drawer of his desk and pulled out a yellow, legal pad and started to take notes.

"You're sure this is a good idea, Paul?" Another short pause before he continued. "Let me run this by Tom Burke at the FBI. We want to keep our efforts coordinated. We can't have anyone branching out on their own. I'll have to check with the governor. I am on his paid staff."

He scratched a few more notes on his pad and heavily underlined one point.

"I realize time is at a premium. Give me ten minutes, and I'll call you back."

He hung up the phone and massaged his temples. Paul was right. It was time to take the offensive away from the bombers. It was time for the good guys to start controlling the message. In the back of his mind, there was a lingering doubt. The bombers had attacked three schools already. Could antagonizing them make things worse? Probably not, he concluded. He dialled Tom Burke's number.

Tom listened to Malcolm's explanation without interruption. When Malcolm wrapped up his comments,

Tom said: "Mom's apple pie and waving the flag can never be wrong. If BurgerCircus wants to pick up the tab to spread that message across the nation, let's do it."

Malcolm looked at his notes as he made the short trip down the hall to the governor's office. "BurgerCircus will pay," was what he had underlined in his notes. It was true the governor could probably get television time with something as important as terrorists destroying the nation's schools. Both the amount of time and when it occurred would be up for discussion. There was no time for that. BurgerCircus could walk in with its chequebook, point out it already did millions of dollars in advertising and come to some understanding in a hurry. Money still talked and with each new school that was blown up, these speeches would attract more viewers than the usual summer repeats. It was win-win for everyone.

The governor looked up as Malcolm tapped at his door and then walked in. His eyes were bloodshot and bleary. Strings of computer code still covered his screen.

Malcolm smiled. "Making any headway?"

The governor tapped a couple of keys, bringing up a screen saver. He rolled back his chair, stretched towards the ceiling and then glanced at his watch.

"Time flies when you're having fun," he said. "I can't believe how late it is. What's up?"

"BurgerCircus is getting concerned about the effects of the boycotts on their bottom line. They want to buy some TV time to combat it and convince the protesters they are siding with the wrong people in this battle."

"Sounds right to me. I'm not a fan of Ray Tutty, but if it's a battle between American business and destructive, terrorist scum bags, there's not much of a choice."

"So you would think." Malcolm hesitated. "He wants me to write his speech."

"You? Why would he want you to be pitching a

commercial message?"

"That's not the message he's after. I'm to sell the red, white and blue, the American way, and Mom's apple pie. He wants an us-against-them message."

The governor did not answer right away. He walked over to the coffee bar and brewed himself a cup of black coffee. Malcolm could almost see the wheels spinning behind his eyes. He waited.

"Ray Tutty wants you to write him a speech letting BurgerCircus off the hook. Is that it?"

Malcolm shrugged. "It's not BurgerCircus's problem. These guys aren't blowing up restaurants. They are blowing up publicly-owned schools. It's only the extortionists who are making BurgerCircus responsible. And we don't want to let them be calling the shots."

"Sounds like you've already started working on the speech."

"Maybe I have. I've already got the blessing of the FBI."

The governor looked surprised. "The FBI has signed off on this? What's their rationale?"

"We've got to appear to be in charge," Malcolm said as he, too, made himself a coffee. "We don't want the general population in the street supporting terrorism. Our spin doctors have to out-spin their spin doctors. With the Internet and a knowledge of how these social interconnections work, anyone can appear to be pushing the populist view. Facebook and YouTube are replacing Fox News as the leading source of misinformation."

The governor pointed a finger at Malcolm. "Be very careful where you make that statement, my friend. Even if it is true. Write two speeches. I'm going to get in on this as well. Make sure the people realize it is their government seeking their cooperation, not BurgerCircus. Not only don't we want the people to be supporting terrorism, but we also don't want them to think big business is running the show.

Spin your magic, Malcolm. Tell Tutty we're doing this together."

"That's what Tutty is hoping you'll say, Governor. This time I agree with both him and you. We have to be seen to be the ones in charge. I'll have the first drafts ready in less than an hour. This is going to be pretty basic Mom's apple pie, wave Old Glory, salute the flag type of stuff. More of a wake-up call of who the enemy is than anything else."

The governor smiled at the simplification of the problem. "No one waves Old Glory as well as you, Malcolm. Don't be modest. That's not why I hired you."

A slight amount of pink slipped onto Malcolm's face. He let the remark slide and instead looked at the screen of the computer monitor. A picture of the governor's mansion with the flag of Georgia blowing gently in the wind filled the screen. Every few seconds it dissolved to a shot of the White House and the American flag providing the action. Unknown to most people who observed this screen saver on the governor's computer, if you look at both pictures really, really closely, you would see the image of Peter Weston standing on the front steps. In both he made the houses look like his own. Malcolm was one of the few aware of this feature of the photos.

"How is the programming going?" he asked. "Any luck in finding your bug?"

The governor glanced at the computer. "It's not a glitch on my part. Their defences are a little more advanced than I had anticipated. It kicks me out before my code can latch on to their locations. I'll solve it. There's always a workaround."

Malcolm smiled. That was one of the reasons why he had thrown his hat into Peter Weston's camp. "There's always a workaround" was one of the tenets of the governor's life. He never quit on a problem, no matter how impossible it seemed. Often he would throw it to a group of experts to come up with a solution and demand they produce one. In really difficult cases, he would often work through it himself.

A committee can take the possible and make it impossible was another of his sayings. Malcolm knew only too well how true that could be.

"If you need some help, I'm always ready to lend a pair of fresh eyes."

The governor nodded his thanks. Malcolm knew the offer wouldn't be taken up. The man did have his faults. Sometimes stubbornness was one of them.

◀ 17 ▶

"LET US BE very clear about one thing."

Governor Peter Watson peered intently into the lens of the camera. His right hand was slightly extended, pointing with the thumb instead of a finger as politicians were trained to do. Behind him, those in the know could recognize the front steps of the governor's mansion. Despite the fact BurgerCircus was footing the bill for this pseudo news conference, the government had taken centre stage in its production. Paul Johnson had been right in his prediction. The governor would not let Ray Tutty overshadow him. This outcome pleased Paul.

The camera zoomed in to capture only the governor's face and the emphasizing fist.

"It is these madmen who are blowing up our children's schools, blowing our tax dollars into the wind, and making us afraid to turn our televisions on in the morning for fear the latest explosion may be in our neighbourhood. They are the enemy. Worse than an enemy. Our enemies acknowledge who they are and openly fight us. These cowards perform their craven deeds under the cover of darkness. They don't attack us because of fundamental differences in our ways of life, because we differ on how we govern our countries, or because we do not share the same religious beliefs." He paused for effect. "And don't get me wrong. I don't condone these as legitimate reasons to attack and kill other people.

"But, my friends, these extortionists, I won't even dignify what they do by calling them terrorists. Terrorists at least have a political agenda. These scum bags have only one driving force: Greed. You heard me correctly. Greed. They do these acts for one purpose only: to extort money from you, me, and our hard-working neighbours.

"These schools will have to be rebuilt and quickly. In Alexandra, kids are wondering where they will start school in less than two weeks. Californians and Texans ask the same question. School staff and others are frantically trying to come up with answers. New schools will be built and built with your taxpayer dollars. Dollars are coming out of budgets that did not include the millions these new schools will cost. They must divert money from other worthwhile causes because not educating our children is not an option. In the meantime, there will be doubling up at other schools in the area. This overcrowding can only reduce the quality of the education these children will receive. We can never counteract these effects. Any shortcomings will live with these children forever."

A look of regret washed over the governor's face as if this detail deeply disturbed him and he was powerless to prevent it from happening. Sparks emanated from his eyes as he started to speak again.

"That is not all. On top of the costs of rebuilding our education system, they want us to fork over another one hundred million dollars."

He popped both his hands up in front of his body, palms facing out. "But wait, you say. It is not the taxpayer who has to pay that ransom. It is the fast-food industry. That's what the extortionists are demanding."

The governor stole a sideward glance at Malcolm, a slight glint in his eye. He was going off-script.

"They are like Captain Picard on the Starship Enterprise saying 'make it so, Number One' and it happens. But real life does not work that way. Companies don't have hundreds of millions of dollars lying around idle. They plow their money back into their business. They invest in our communities.

"Remember, it was not the fast-food industry that destroyed these schools." He was on-script again. "They are not the enemy. They are your neighbours."

He paused and looked over at Ray Tutty who was standing beside him. He then gestured with his hand.

"Ray Tutty is not *your* neighbour. That is what you are thinking. Many of you probably said that aloud to the person with whom you are watching. Ray Tutty is some millionaire fat cat."

The governor nodded his head as if he and the watchers at home were sharing a moment of honesty.

"Ray Tutty is a successful business man. There is no denying that. But the kids who serve your burgers and fries when you stop in at one of these establishments, they are your neighbours. They may be working their way through college supplemented by the wages they pick up doing this. In fact, these kids may be going to university on scholarships Ray Tutty has set up for his employees. A scholarship that comes from the money these terrorists are trying to extort from BurgerCircus."

The camera zoomed in to display Ray's nodding head in the picture.

Then back to the governor. "That money comes from the pay packet of the single mother who can work in her neighbourhood while her kids are in school. Her flexible hours allow her to be home to take care of these children when school is out. Someone else takes her place in the middle of the afternoon. Having two people fill one position is not the most efficient way to run a business. It doubles the paperwork. But BurgerCircus gives their employees the flexibility to have an income and still enjoy a home life as their children are growing up. "

The governor picked up a baseball bat hidden beside the

podium. He did not grip it like a ball player but instead clutched it in the middle, offering it to the camera as a display item in a court case.

"When you go by our playgrounds just about any day of the week in the summer, you see hundreds, no thousands, of kids proudly wearing uniforms just like the big leaguers do. Those uniforms sport the logo of BurgerCircus, McDonald's, Wendy's, Burger King and many other fast-food outlets. The kids are using equipment like this." He shook the bat for emphasis. "Paid for by these sponsoring companies along with the many other expenses involved in running a sporting adventure for our kids.

"This is the money these extortionists are trying to steal from us."

He held his free hand out to Ray again as the camera faded back to include both men in the picture.

"So Ray Tutty and the CEOs of these other companies are at work in your neighbourhoods. They are your neighbours. Don't turn on them for the lowest of low. People who want to steal the money that helps your kids; that educates your kids; people who care absolutely nothing about you and your family."

He gave an emphatic nod of his head to indicate he had said everything he had to say and turned to look at Ray. The camera followed his gaze and filled the monitor with the image of Ray Tutty. For a second, Ray didn't realize the governor had finished his speech. Ray was too busy working on his presentation in his mind to listen to the governor's words. He had heard them before during their one quick rehearsal designed to familiarize the camera man with what shots both men wanted.

When the governor realized Ray was not about to speak, he quickly jumped in to cover the awkward silence. "Now, Ray Tutty, president and CEO of BurgerCircus, would like to say a few words. Ray."

In the wings, Paul Johnson realized the error he had made in having Ray follow the governor. Ray was a powerful CEO, a good businessman, and an able public speaker, but he was no Peter Weston. The camera loved Peter Weston, and Peter Weston loved the camera. The most important thing a public speaker can do is fake sincerity. The governor had that feat down to a science. When he spoke, he swallowed you whole. He brought you kicking and screaming into his reality. This ability explained how he, an Indepentent candidate, was able to defeat the two much better-funded leaders of the two national parties and how he had hung on to power for a second term once elected.

Paul tried to catch his boss's eyes and transmit the message: "Keep it short, stay on message." He could see the competitive look coming across Ray's face. He knew that wasn't going to happen. Ray was going to try to outdazzle the dazzler. Paul would have to intervene.

"Hurump," Ray cleared his throat and stepped closer to the microphone.

"Thank you, Governor. You have pretty well summed up the situation we find ourselves in. There can be no confusion about who the bad guys are here. Our American way of life is under attack. We have got to defend that way of life."

Ray looked over at Paul. He was already striking out on his own, Paul thought.

"Stay on message," Paul mouthed. He put his hands together in front of himself in a praying motion. "Please."

"As the governor pointed out, I am a rich man. I make no apologies. But, as many of you may know, I started out working behind the counter at a BurgerCircus in the exact fashion that thousands of kids across the country are doing today. I have worked my way from that position to be the CEO and principal shareholder in the company. That is what America is all about, my friends. Work hard, and you will achieve your dreams. It's the so-called American dream, but it is more than a dream. Any of us can achieve this vision."

He looked over at the governor. "Peter, here, has done the same thing. Look where hard work and dedication have brought him."

The camera panned briefly to the other man. The governor smiled to acknowledge what Ray was saying, and then Ray's face filled the screen again. The cameraman was ad-libbing as well. None of this was in his working script.

"But these scum bags, I believe that is what Peter called them, are trying to shatter that part of the American dream. They want the money with no effort on their part. No legal effort, at least. Blow up a school. Make a demand. 'Give us one hundred million or else.'

"That, my friends, is not the American way. It treats all hard-working Americans as chumps. In America, we treat those who take shortcuts like that harshly. It is not us, the fast-food industry, against them, the extortionists. It is us, the people of America, against them, people who are trying to destroy our way of life. We must stay strong. We must stay united. We must find these creeps and bring them to justice. That is the American way."

A smile lit up Paul's face. Ray had come through on his own. He gave him the thumbs-up signal, then pointed to his watch and twirled his finger in a circle. Wrap it up, was the message.

"BurgerCircus is throwing all its resources into making this happen. We are cooperating with the police; we are cooperating with the government. We have set up information kiosks at all of our locations across this great nation of ours. Anything you may have seen, no matter how obscure, should be reported at one of these sites or call 555-1234 to report it anonymously. We ask you to join us at this difficult time in the life of our nation. Together we can capture these punks. Together we can bring this situation to a successful conclusion. Together we can keep America great. Thank you."

The camera faded back to a two-shot. Both the governor and Ray raised a fist to shoulder height and gave it a firm shake in a show of solidarity. The camera went dead as the face of a news anchor replaced the two men. It was his job to tell the people what they had just heard. Malcolm Truex smiled. He had also written the anchor's script in case anyone missed the point of the speeches.

He gave the governor and Ray a firm thumbs-up. Both had come through admirably. Malcolm had rewritten Ray's speech at the last minute and given it to him just before air time. He wanted Ray to sound spontaneous. He denied him the opportunity to rehearse and make changes. The plan worked. Ray delivered the words as if they had been his own.

Now all they could do was wait until morning. BurgerCircus paid for the first spot. All the evening newscasts repeated it for free. Malcolm would upload a copy to YouTube. He knew people would want to re-watch it and discuss it with their friends. Everyone secretly believed in the American dream. They all believed they were just a break or two away from being like Ray Tutty. Deep down, they too believed they could achieve this dream.

The lack of boycotts in the morning would be the real test. A bonus would see the FBI hotlines light up with tips from everyday Americans. Somebody had to have seen these men in the vicinity of the schools planting their bombs. They were not invisible. Malcolm's intent was to make every person in the country feel like they were part of the team trying to squash these enemy bombers. Get the people thinking of anything suspicious they had seen and most importantly, to call it in. For now, they could only wait.

◄18►

THE EUPHORIA OVER the speeches was short-lived. After receiving the effusive praise of everyone in the room, Malcolm snapped everyone back to the here and now.

"We're eight hours from the next explosion. We can pray that the FBI gets a tip on their hotline that will prevent it, but I think that is pie-in-the-sky dreaming."

"Thank you, Malcolm, for that reality check," the governor said. "I, for one, think Ray and I did a good job of getting the message out. Let's at least hope for some positive results."

"I am, Governor, but this is no time to lose sight of the reality of the situation."

Malcolm felt a tingle in his left breast. He reached into an inside pocket and pulled out his cellphone. The call was from the FBI. Even in his wildest dreams, he hadn't expected results this fast.

"Good job stirring up the nation," Tom Burke said as a response to Malcolm's hello. "We've got two promising hits already, one in Kentucky and one in Nevada. In both incidences, men were seen taking large boxes into the schools early in the morning. At the time, no one suspected anything. Schools are reopening in the next couple of weeks. Now, the people are not so sure it was that innocent.

"We've got calls into the school administrators, and bomb squad teams are on the way to each location. These calls could be the break we're looking for. Pass along my regards to the governor and the fast-food guy."

"Will do. When will you know something for sure?"

"The Kentucky call came from Hodgenville, a little town just south of Louisville. If it pans out, I'm going to fly up myself. I've got a helicopter on standby. Wanta come?"

"Hodgenville?" Malcolm said. "That could be significant. That's the birthplace of Abraham Lincoln."

There was a hesitation on Tom Burke's end of the line. "Lincoln's birthplace? Good catch," he said. "There might be some significance to that. We'll have to revisit the other locations and see if they have any historical reference. I'll get an agent on that right away."

"OK. Yeah, I'd like to come along. It might help to see what the site looked like before someone blew it to hell. See how careful these guys have been. How well hidden the bombs might be."

"My thinking exactly. Can you be ready in 15 minutes? We should know if it's a go by then. Hodgenville is about 300 miles north of here."

"I'll be ready."

A little over two hours later the helicopter sat down in the parking lot of the Lincoln High School. Flashing red and blue lights of emergency vehicles lit up the yard. Two big yellow fire trucks were standing by at the outer edge of the perimeter set up by the police. Despite the air of excitement that surrounded the place, most people were standing around doing nothing.

A tall, well-built man in a black suit, white shirt and highly polished shoes waited for the doors of the helicopter to pop open. He then rushed up and shook Tom Burke's hand.

"Special Agent Barry Brother," he introduced himself. "We've found the boxes in a closet just inside the cafeteria. A night watchman showed up shortly after we got here and showed us where they were. He had signed for them last week."

"Anything unusual about them?" Tom asked.

"We've talked to the school principal and the cafeteria superintendent. Neither were expecting any deliveries. The boxes say ACME Manufacturing. Neither has any records of ever dealing with that company."

"And what do they look like?"

The agent shrugged. "Ordinary boxes. They're in a closet so it's hard to get a visual all the way around and we don't want to be touching them until the bomb squad gets here. Apparently, they are tied up at another call in Louisville."

"Another call?" Malcolm stepped forward. "Is it another school?"

"No. A suspicious package in the arrivals area of the airport. Came in just before our call. They are in a crowded building; we are in an empty school. That gave the airport priority. So we wait."

"There's only one bomb squad in the state?" Tom shook his head. "What about the off-duty guys?"

"These are the off-duty guys. It's after 6 o'clock."

Tom looked around at all the emergency vehicles in the parking lot. No wonder everyone was standing around looking bored. "The military must have bomb experts. They deal with them all the time."

The on-site agent nodded his head in agreement. "If you have the power, bring them in ..."

"I have the power," Tom said. He looked at Malcolm. "Do you know who I have to call to do this as quickly as possible?"

"I'll call the governor of Kentucky. We're friends. I'm sure he can expedite things."

Tom handed him his cellphone.

Malcolm reached into his jacket pocket. "Mine has the number in its directory." He pulled out his phone and quickly made the call.

"There's a team at Fort Knox. They'll be here within the

hour."

Tom nodded. His gaze had shifted to the school building on the far side of the parking lot. "Where did the airport call originate, Barry? Who spotted the suspicious package or whatever it is?"

"Bomb-sniffing dog. That's why the airport staff are taking it so seriously. We have some agents there going over the video tapes. Whoever dropped off that package will have been captured on camera. The place is full of them."

Tom turned his attention back to Malcolm. Tight wrinkles radiated from the corners of his eyes. "I know we have focused our attention on these school bombings, but we don't want to get too deeply into a tunnel-vision situation here."

Malcolm gave his head a little shake. Confusion registered on his face.

"Bomb call at the airport. Tip of a bomb here. Bomb squad from Fort Knox dispatched to here. Is this part of a bigger conspiracy?"

The local agent smiled. "As secure as Fort Knox is not a cliché. Taking one bomb unit out of the mix over there is not going to affect security."

"It does raise an interesting point," Malcolm said. "Our resources for fighting this thing are extremely thin. Two calls in one area and we have to bring in the military. Instead of calling on the army for help, I think we had better get the president to mobilize them as our first call. They have the experience. They have the numbers. We don't want to be wasting time when we don't have it to waste."

He looked at his watch. "We're five hours away from the next scheduled detonation. That allows us to loaf around with our hands in our pockets looking at each other. If this time frame were tightened up by three or four hours, we would have a higher stress level. We want to eliminate any in-between steps and have the military be the first ones out of the gate when we need action."

Tom scrunched up his face. "That sounds good, Malcolm, in theory. In real life, there are all sorts of jurisdictional issues. There's the question of deploying fighting troops on our own soil. When these guys pull in from Fort Knox, you know they are going to be armed to the teeth."

He pointed across the lot to two TV trucks that had set up operations on the street directly in front of the school. The cameramen trained their cameras on the front door. Reporters were vying for their piece of the sidewalk that had the best background shot.

"Those cameras have been filming boredom since we got here and probably for an hour or so before that. When the high-tech army equipment rolls in, that's what's going to lead off any newscasts, unless the place blows up in the meantime."

Again, Malcolm shook his head. "I don't see your point. The enemy is here on our soil. That is where we should deploy the army."

"And ninety-five per cent of America agrees with that. The quiet ninety-five per cent. But for the last hundred years or so we've been pretty good at confronting our enemies on their front doorsteps, overseas, in South America, anywhere but on our streets. Local police have dealt with the few that broke through. Now you want to make the army the first line of defence. The noisy five per cent will have a field day. Anarchy conspirators will be claiming it's all a ploy by the government to take control of the country.

"People get nervous when they see armed troops in the streets, even the onside ninety-five per cent. There's a sense of betrayal that our local police forces can't protect us anymore. The words 'To Serve and Protect' are written across the sides of all their cars. People expect that to be true. They want it to be true. We're only two months away from an election. Optics are important right now."

Even as darkness was settling in, the red creeping into Malcolm's face could be seen by the other two men. He made like he was spitting on the ground in disgust. "In five hours we are going to have another school blown to kingdom come. Do you think I care what a bunch of conspiracy wingnuts is complaining about or who feels betrayed?

"Besides, we deploy the National Guard all the time in emergency situations. What's the difference?'

"The National Guard? Civilian soldiers? These troops we're bringing in tonight are the real deal. These are professionals."

"I'm a captain in the Guard. We know what we're doing. Most of our members have overseas experience. We were professional soldiers."

Tom held up his hands in a conciliatory gesture. "That's not what I'm saying, Malcolm. I'm talking perception. The National Guard handles local emergencies. The news wires are flooded with bad press when they are called out. The army protects us from our enemies. We don't expect to see them carrying out this role on our streets or in our school yards."

Malcolm gave his head a weary shake. "You, of all people Tom, understand this is not a political issue, no matter how hard these extortionists try to make it one. We have to use any resources we have available and use them to their fullest extent. The message we want to send out to the world is that we will protect our citizens, anytime, anywhere, anyway."

"Hey, you're preaching to the choir here. I'm just telling you what's going to happen when the sun comes up tomorrow. You're the politician here. You know I'm right."

Malcolm took a couple of deep breaths and forced

himself back into control. "This is bigger than politics, Tom. We can't let the vocal minority run this show. There's too much at stake. For now, we have to do the right thing and worry about the consequences when we've captured these bastards. No one will feel betrayed when they are in custody or even better: dead."

Tom reached out and put a hand on Malcolm's shoulder. "If you were the power behind the throne in Washington instead of Augusta, I'd have more faith in that happening. As I said, the election is only two months away. Rational thought is not going to be the dominant force among our leaders during this period. Optics will rule the day."

◀19▶

"I SHOULD RUN for political office," Ray Tutty said, a huge smile smeared across his face. "Within minutes of my speech, we have our first positive results."

Paul Johnson laughed a brief, harsh grunt. The two men and Barbara Bishop had returned to BurgerCircus's downtown office tower after leaving the governor's mansion. The speech was a major first step in taking control from the extortionists, but they still had an empire to salvage. The sales results from the previous day had finally come in, and they had been brutal,

"You don't think your running mate may have anything to do with those results?"

"No, Weston was just my opening act. Malcolm gave me the power role. You simply can't beat waving Old Glory and talking about warm apple pie. In fact, I think to thank the public for their response, we should give away a free apple turnover with every full meal ordered tomorrow."

Barbara's head snapped up from the pile of reports she was studying. "Whoa, let's not do anything too hasty. Let's consider the optics of a move like that as well as the financial ramifications."

"The optics are perfect." Ray thrust out his chin, defying Barbara to argue with him. "The speech was about it being us against them. A gesture like that helps up bond as a team. We'll have to come up with a patriotic name for the promotion.

"As for the financial aspect. Sure, it will cut into our bottom line, but not as much as it would if people continue boycotting our stores. We're not giving these things away. We are making them part of a complete meal package. The important thing is to get bodies back into our restaurants. We don't want even a little bit of residual blame falling on our shoulders."

Barbara didn't answer right away. As far as Ray was concerned that was a bad thing. He couldn't argue with silence, although she was challenging him to do so.

He looked over at Paul for support. Paul was looking out the big picture window at the panorama of the city below.

Ray knew he had two people studying his proposal, looking for loopholes. The idea had simply popped into his head. He had not given it the thought it deserved. Still, it seemed sound to him. The secret would be volume. It had to generate enough extra sales to cover the reduction in profits that would result from the giveaway. It also had to convince the general population that BurgerCircus was not the enemy, that they were all in this together.

Paul was the first to break the silence. "Here's the deal. Your speech was all about waving the flag and appealing to everyone's patriotic instincts. There was nothing subtle about it. Malcolm made sure that no one missed the point. Our way of life is under attack."

Both Barbara and Ray nodded their heads.

"I have nothing against the apple turnover giveaway. The costs will easily be absorbed. But from a marketing point of view, how do we approach it?

"Do we have a picture of Beaver's mother standing in front of an open oven offering a hot apple pie? That would get the motherhood image across. Or do we try the more subtle approach? Here's a special promotion to thank the people of the nation for their support. Let the apple pie part of it be subliminal. Most people will subconsciously make the patriotic connection."

"This is no time to be subtle," Barbara said. "We want to

be as blatant as possible. Malcolm's speech was us against them. Let's hammer that point home. The people blowing up our schools are the enemy, not us.

"We have to get that message out to the people in the street. In turn, that will get the message out to the Wall Street people.

"They are as bad as the extortionists. The hit that our stock price took today sends out a very bad message. It almost amounts to treason. It reinforces the extortionist point of view that BurgerCircus is responsible.

"I'd like to find a way to punish those sons of bitches as well."

Paul put a hand on Barbara's shoulder. "Calm down, now. Don't blow a blood vessel. A couple of calls to the tip line tonight with actual information is a good sign.

"What we want to see is a rebound in the market when it opens tomorrow. That will be the true sign that we're all on the same side again. We will punish anyone who sold their shares at the lower price when they try to buy back their stocks again. There may be a God in heaven after all. We'll see."

Barbara knocked his hand away. "Don't try to calm me down. I'm mad, and I want to stay mad until we resolve this situation. I want those bastards caught and sent away for the rest of their lives."

Paul could see that the fire had gone out of her eyes a little bit. He smiled and gave her a friendly pat on the arm. "OK, tiger. You stay mad."

Barbara returned the smile. "Why are you still standing around here? Marketing is your department. Get hold of your graphics people. We need some promotional material ready for the morning. We have to strike right now. Make if fast and dirty. We'll clean it up later."

She turned to Ray. "If you're going to be giving away apple turnovers, you had better make sure the restaurants have them on hand to give away. Get someone working on that tonight."

She clapped her hands sharply together. "Let's get moving people. We've got a war to fight."

◀20▶

TOM BURKE WAS right.

The vehicle driven by the bomb squad was right out of some science fiction movie, and the news cameras had eyes for nothing else. Protruding from the front, a solid, six-inch thick, five-foot high wall of a new synthetic material that resembled glass but was stronger than iron protected the vehicle from any explosive impact.

The clarity of the substance allowed the operator an unrestricted view of the progress of the vehicle. The vehicle itself sat low to the ground and showed no flat surfaces towards the front. All surfaces were angled in such a way that anything projected towards the vehicle would slide off to one side or the other. As you looked at it, there seemed to be a shimmering quality along the surface. The cameramen kept focusing and refocusing their equipment, trying unsuccessfully to get clear pictures of the machine. Despite this sleek appearance, there was also a sense of unbending strength.

Robotic arms, made from the same crystalline material, extended from the blade, giving the operator a total hands-on feel to his work.

Nothing of this nature had been filmed by the news people before and to their surprise, they were not getting clear pictures this time. In their excitement to capture the images, they almost seemed to forget why they were there. To forget that a powerful bomb may be in a closet in the building in front of them could be fatal.

This lack of judgment did not extend to the military

personnel. These were Middle East veterans. They had seen fellow soldiers blown up in the streets of Iraq and Afghanistan by rudimentary bombs such as were being used in the school explosions.

"Everyone move back to the next block."

The voice seemed to have no source. It seemed to emanate from everywhere. With the very slightest hesitation, most people obeyed the command.

News people were the exception. They exuded a sense of entitlement. The ordinary rules did not apply to them.

Suddenly sound men started whipping off their headsets. Dials on their monitor boards shot into the red. All the microphones in the area emitted feedback squeals. Armed soldiers, in full swat-like gear, started pushing the stragglers back to a safer distance. The network people resisted at first, but then, fearing for the safety of their equipment, they too fell back.

Three soldiers approached the assembled FBI agents. One of them handed out earphones while the second checked their ID. The third stared intently over their heads at the receding crowd. When the other two finished their tasks, his gaze fell to Tom Burke.

"Follow me," he said, then turned on his heel and marched towards the second truck in the collection of army vehicles. He didn't look back. Tom, Malcolm and Barry Brother snapped the headphones into place and hustled to catch the retreating soldier. The other two members of the squad fell in behind them, their automatic weapons at the ready. Their eyes concentrated solely on the diminishing crowd.

A lieutenant rose from his seat behind a computer terminal as they were escorted into the office-like setting in the back of the army truck. He extended his hand to Tom Burke.

"I have good news and bad news, sir. I've just been in contact with authorities in Nevada. Their bomb is a hoax. Nonetheless, we will proceed as if ours is the real thing." He looked directly at Tom. "I believe you are the agent-in-charge of this exercise."

Tom nodded as he accepted the outstretched hand. A vibration in his inside coat pocket diverted his attention.

"Excuse me. I have to take this."

He extracted his cellphone from his pocket, swiped the screen and listened.

"That's our agent on the scene in Nevada confirming your information. Your sources are fast. How did you know before we did?"

"Our men were supplying your people with technical support. We have live cameras on location. We've been studying their scene ever since they arrived. We don't want to reinvent the wheel every time we go to a bomb site."

Malcolm stepped forward. "You say the bomb is a hoax. Don't you mean it's simply not a bomb? I'm sure the people who called in were sincere in their information. We asked for people to call if they saw anything suspicious. We don't want to discourage them by referring to their misinformation as hoaxes."

"Point taken," the lieutenant said to Malcolm. "You are from the governor's office in Georgia, I believe?"

"Yes," Malcolm said. "The results are disappointing, but they don't qualify as a hoax."

"Actually, they do." The soldier turned his monitor towards the FBI men. The screen showed Windows media player. The officer hit the play icon.

All four men watched as a less-sophisticated robot on the Nevada scene folded back the cover of a similarly shaped ACME box. Almost immediately, a red flag with the word "Boom" embroidered on it, popped from the opening. It was visible for less than a second before the robot slammed a metal box over the entire cardboard container in the cupboard, snuffing out any opportunity for further damage.

"See, the lieutenant said. "A hoax."

"Dammit," Malcolm said, disgust in his voice. "They are playing with us." He turned to Tom Burke. "When did you say these boxes were delivered."

Tom consulted a notebook from his pocket. "Last week. Nobody suspected anything until the governor and the fast-food guy went on TV asking for help."

"That means they anticipated that we would appeal to the public. They had these dummy boxes in place waiting for the opportunity to use them." He pointed to the image on the screen. "Look at that. 'ACME.' That's the company that supplies bombs in the Roadrunner cartoon. Bombs that never work as they should. They are still one move ahead of us on anything we do."

"Well, let's not jump to any conclusions," the lieutenant said. "We haven't dismantled our box yet. The team is moving the X-ray machine into place, as we speak. Until we thoroughly examine the box, we can only act on the assumption that it contains a bomb."

He hit a key on his monitor, and the image changed from the events in Nevada to the events taking place across the parking lot from the command unit. The robotic unit moved towards the school. Treads supplied the propulsion, not wheels. Stairs presented no problem to the machine. The blade folded back slightly, allowing easy access through the school doors. A squeegee-like device at the bottom of the blade scraped along the hall floor. Even liquids would not get under this device.

The robotic arm reached out and pulled the closet door in the cafeteria open. There sat the box. "ACME" emblazoned across its full width. Malcolm was right. It looked like something right out of a Roadrunner cartoon.

He looked over at Tom. Tom leaned towards the monitor, his attention riveted on the screen.

"Do they know about the Roadrunner in the Middle East? Do they think we are like Wile E.Coyote?"

Malcolm's eyes broke away from the action on the screen. "They're the ones buying from ACME, not us. This whole fiasco is going to blow up in their faces just like it did to the stupid coyote every Saturday morning."

Now Tom looked confused. "In what way?"

"It's giving up a live test of what happens when a bomb is spotted." He glanced over at the army officer sitting at the desk. "No offence, but this is not going as well as it could have. We have, however, seen our shortfalls. The next time we will do better. The next time may be real."

"I think this is going pretty smoothly," the soldier said. "It would have been better if we had the floor plans for the school a little faster, but outside of that..."

His voice drifted off as an X-ray image of the contents of the box was displayed on the screen in front of him. There appeared to be nothing solid except for a spring-like device near the top of the box.

"Exactly," Malcolm said. "Let's have school authorities finding out where their building floor plans are right now, not when we need them in an emergency. Let's not wait for an hour to call in the army if we have to.

"That thing looks like the Nevada bomb. We're not opening it in front of any news cameras. I don't want the lead story on tonight's news starting off with the word 'BOOM' dancing around on a piece of cardboard at the end of a little spring."

"No problem. We're still treating this as real. The device will be contained in a metal box and examined more closely at a safer location. There will be no non-military eyes viewing that investigation."

"So the news cameras in Nevada didn't capture the hoax

explosion out there either?"

The lieutenant shook his head. "What you saw was a replay of our live feed from their robotic camera. Secure eyes only." He hesitated and looked from Malcolm to Tom. A touch of red crept slowly into his cheeks. "Maybe I shouldn't have shown that video to you."

Tom reached out and tapped his shoulder. "Don't worry, soldier. I'm running this show for the FBI. I have all the clearance there is to have. Malcolm is the government liaison. He brought you into the game. You're safe."

Tom realized those titles might have been a bit of an exaggeration, but he didn't want to lose this vantage point to see what was taking place. The soldier grinned at him and looked relieved.

"I knew that," he said.

◀21▶

MIDNIGHT HAD COME and gone before Tom and Malcolm got back to Atlanta. To everyone's relief, the Kentucky bomb proved to be a hoax. Thirty-two additional leads had come into the hotlines. Of those, twenty-seven turned out to be legitimate deliveries. Schools were gearing up for the upcoming season. The remaining five contained ACME duds. These five were scattered throughout the country from coast to coast.

The fake bombs were identical. The boxes contained Styrofoam plates manufactured in China. The boxes had come from the same printing press, but there was no indication of where that press lived. ACME was the only thing on the container. The spring mechanism at first glance appeared to come from the same piece of metal. Further investigation would confirm that in the morning. A lot of work had gone into this phoney production.

It also gave them their first real chance at coming up with a concrete lead. The more people involved in this operation, the better the prospect that someone would come forward and spill the beans. They may not have signed on for the destruction of schools that was taking place in the early morning hours of every day now.

"Seven fakes," Malcolm said. "That's a lot of work for nothing. What do you think they hope to achieve from this? The news impact diminished with each new one found. It lessens the resolve that people think we should pay their demanded ransom; it doesn't increase it."

Tom swung his office chair around to face Malcolm. His

computer showed the locations of the fakes with green stars. The three actual explosions glowed red. None were near the others.

"Only until the next real bomb explodes. That will put everyone on edge again. Did you see the people from the neighbourhood? None of them looked too complacent. But what I think is happening is the bombers are doing the same thing we are, collecting data. We need film of all the spectators at each of those sites."

"Collecting data? Do you think they are studying our response at each of these locations?"

"Why not? With each bomb they explode, we are going after them harder and harder. They will exploit our weaknesses. Assuming they don't have a master plan all laid out, they will pick locations where we are least effective in our response. What better way to determine that than by planting fake bombs? They can study our response time. They can see if we would have effectively defused the bomb. I disagree with you about the effectiveness of these fakes. Each one of them increased the anxiety level in that local community. It increases people's fear, even if it is only a subtle increase. Local TV covered all seven of these events. Even the ones with nothing in them got a few seconds on the local newscasts. When the demolition teams arrived, the people in the background looked worried and concerned."

Tom turned back to his computer screen, his face a mask of concentration.

"If we can find and destroy one of their real bombs before it goes off, it will be a great psychological lift for us. People will see us making progress. Every time they explode a bomb successfully, we look worse in the eyes of the people. They get the impression we can't protect them.

"What we are fighting for here is the minds of the citizens of America. We have to persuade them to maintain their faith in our ability to look after them. There's much more at stake here than a few school buildings. We will rebuild the schools. Once fear works its way into your mind, into your psyche, it's hard to get rid of it. I've seen it too often in other countries where the governments change on a whim. Every time some strongman gets a little power, he tries to take control. If he succeeds, he kills off his perceived enemies. The people live in constant fear. We can't let that happen here."

"Hey, you're preaching to the choir. I'm behind you one hundred per cent."

A little red tinged Tom's cheeks. No one doubted that Tom was a good agent. His rise through the ranks of the FBI attested to that fact. Not everyone was aware of the evangelic dedication he had to not only fighting crime but to maintaining the American way of life. He had been a marine officer. He had seen the rest of the world and knew what America offered its citizens was worth the fight. He also knew how tenuous the shield protecting those citizens was, how easily it could be penetrated if society became complacent. He would not allow that to happen. Nothing would destroy that way of life on his watch.

A shy grin stretched his mouth a little. "Yeah, pal, I know you are. I just get so pissed off at those protesters, those spoilede namby-pambies, who have no idea who or what they are supporting in the name of keeping the establishment responsible to the people. They have no idea how fragile the line between democracy and dictatorship is."

Tom's face seemed to lose some of its elasticity. "I've been privy to what takes place at some of those back-room meetings among the people in power. I know that's what you do now, Malcolm, but some of these characters are scary. They have no concept of the expression 'government by the people, for the people.' For some of them, it's all about power. These kids who think they are protecting us are playing right into their hands."

Malcolm nodded. "They've grabbed on to the wrong coattail this time. These extortionists are in it for the money and nothing else. I can feel that right to the marrow of my bones. This fiasco is not political. These are not enemies of the state. I've dealt with those extremists. These are thugs out trying to make a massive money grab and using the passions of our citizens to help them do it. They are con men of the worst sort."

"I'm amazed at the breadth of their coverage," Tom said with a sweeping gesture towards his monitor. "How many men do you think are involved in this?"

Malcolm took in the scope of the red and green stars on the screen. Dots covered the entire nation. "They do seem to be everywhere." He hesitated, leaning in closer to the screen. "But if you look close, the coverage is not as great as it appears at first glance. They are actually in small bunches in Georgia and Kentucky; they're not that far apart. Nevada and California, just a car trip away from each other. Even closer if they take commuter planes. The others are also reasonably close to each other. One or two men could cover a lot of these sites without too much trouble. They allow themselves a full day between each event. They set the fakes up days ago. One or two people could have done them all."

"It's early in the game to confirm anyone's stories, but the deliveries of the fake bombs all seem to have been done by legitimate delivery companies. Purolator, FedEx, whoever. There was always someone on hand to receive them. Everyone involved followed normal procedures. No one was suspicious until the calls came into our hotline.

"We traced two of them to concerned citizens who were reminded of the deliveries when they saw the governor on TV. One of them received an email refreshing her memory of what she had seen. It appears she mentioned it at a card party or something. She wasn't sure where or even when she had told anyone what she had seen. Still, when reminded, she thought it best to call it in. Her neighbours would expect her to. She considers herself the 'eyes and ears of the neighbourhood,' She is always helping out law enforcement with tips on people they should be watching out for."

Malcolm rotated his chair away from the computer. "I bet she does, and to make the bet more interesting, I'll add a rider. None of the people she calls in about is a short-haired, clean-shaven, white Anglo-Saxon Protestant."

Tom consulted his notes. His eyes twinkled. "The FedEx delivery man had dark hair and a swarthy complexion. Her words."

Malcolm raised his eyebrows.

"No," Tom added. "The man does work for the company, has for years. Well-tanned is how the agent conducting the interview described him."

Malcolm looked at Tom with an astounded look on his face. "Is that a coincidence? Someone had to be watching this delivery being made and observed that the 'eyes and ears of the neighbourhood' had observed him. Now, that's what I call planning. I want to talk to these people, Tom. I want to know why they even remember seeing a delivery truck in their area. That is not something so uncommon that people remember it. Something else has to be at play here, something that may lead us to the brains behind this scheme. And I don't say that lightly. The person behind this operation is a brain. We must be sure we don't underestimate him."

Malcolm got up from his chair and started to pace around the room. With each step, he became a little more excited.

"I had asked you why they would go to all the trouble of planting these fake bombs. I was wrong when I suggested that they would diminish the people's resolve. All these fakes were in more populated areas than the real bombs. Hundreds of people have been evacuated today, even for a short period. Hundreds of people have felt the fear of having a bomb in their backyard. This is genius. Real bombs are expensive. These fakes create almost as much terror as the real thing at a fraction of the cost, and there is no risk of loss of life. I honestly don't believe these guys are killers. I think it's strictly about the money."

Tom looked at his watch. He then slipped in behind his keyboard and tapped a few keys. The State of Georgia website popped up on his screen. Vignettes of the governor appearing at various events along with the financial value to those communities played on the screen. Tom held out an upturned palm to the screen as he turned to face Malcolm who was now all the way across the room with his pacing.

"What's this?" he asked.

Malcolm walked over to the desk and studied the screen. He stood quietly for a few moments before giving his head a shake and stifling a small chuckle.

"Son of a bitch," he said. "That's a promotion we put together for the last election. Looks like the governor has dusted it off for re-showing. The hits on our site are through the roof," he looked at his watch, "especially at times like this when the next explosion is imminent."

"It's in poor taste," Tom said. "It smacks of opportunism."

"Welcome to the world of politics. Those two things don't fit in the same sentence." He looked back at the screen. "Besides, all he has done is replace the state crest that usually sits on the home page. All the links are still there if our constituents are looking for something in particular. Besides, I produced that piece. Everything in it is true. It wouldn't hurt for the rest of America to see how well we are doing in the state of Georgia with an Indepentent governor."

"Yeah, well I still think it's in poor taste."

"Maybe so, but I find something else much more disturbing about this situation."

Tom looked up waiting for Malcolm to continue.

"We still haven't figured out how they've hacked our site. We have some of the best IT minds in the industry on our staff. Our firewalls are the best available, but someone is still getting through. It doesn't make sense."

Tom nodded. "The FBI doesn't understand it either."

Malcolm's eyes narrowed. "What doesn't the FBI understand?"

Tom immediately looked defensive. " How they've breached your firewalls. This is our biggest lead to date. Of course, we are trying to track them through your site. Our staff is working with your staff; you must realize that."

"Yeah, I knew." Malcolm gave the FBI agent a wary look. "I'm sorry. I read more into your statement."

Tom shook his head. "No. There should be no secrets between us. We are in this together. We have been trying to hack your site from the first day. Even with all our resources, we can't do it." He hesitated for a few seconds. "I'll be honest. We're leaning towards an inside job. We're running background checks on all of your IT staff."

Malcolm lowered his eyes and slowly rubbed his chin. After a few seconds, he captured Tom's eyes with his own. "I hired every one of those men, personally. I'd almost stake my life on their honesty."

"Almost?"

"I've got Herb Solstace, our security chief, going over our background checks again. Somehow, the extortionists have gained access to our Internet servers. What if they have gotten onto our main frame? We have a lot of classified information residing there. We are monitoring every keystroke in our whole system."

"Just so you know, buddy, we are checking you out too. You seem to have an intimate relationship with the IT department at the mansion." Tom waited for Malcolm's reaction.

"I'm glad to hear that. It means you're thorough."

There were a few seconds of silence while both men reconciled the ramifications of what Tom had revealed. Then Tom broke the silence with a serious question.

"Have you thought about taking your Internet server down in the interim?"

"We've discussed it. The governor thinks it's more important to maintain contact with them. They've got to slip up sometime. If we cut off communications, we may miss that slip-up. Besides if they can hack us, they can hack anybody. They would simply move on, and we'd lose the link we have with them."

"True. So far, they've been either really good or really lucky. Let's hope for the latter."

Malcolm looked at the clock on Tom's wall. "We're fifteen minutes from the top of the hour. Do you think all the publicity from these fake bombs will wipe out the necessity of destroying anther school? They may have changed their tactics."

"We can only hope, but I doubt it. They can't be seen to be waffling."

◀22▶

THAT TURNED OUT to be wishful thinking on Malcolm's part. No one waffled. Fourteen and a half minutes later, the governor's good works disappeared from Tom's computer monitor. In its place came a dark image with a reddish hue. Both men leaned closer to try to understand what they were seeing.

Tom spoke first. "It's the inside of a building looking through an internal doorway. The focus is getting a little better. Whatever is recording it must have just been turned on."

Malcolm pointed to the top right-hand corner of the screen where the red glow shone brightly. "I think the light source is an exit light. We are inside the building. Those look like boxes in a hallway."

"I think the word on the side is ACME," said Tom. "These are just like the boxes we saw earlier this evening that were hoaxes."

Both men jumped back as the telephone on the desk let out a sharp ring.

"What?" Tom said as he snapped up the receiver. He covered the mouthpiece with one hand. "It's the governor. He wants to know if we're catching this."

Malcolm took the phone. Before he could speak, the screen flared with a bright, blinding light, momentarily went blank and was replaced with an image of the governor, himself, standing behind a podium.

"It is time to stop mollycoddling criminals."

His voice rang out loud and clear. They were back

watching the promotional video on the state's website.

"Amen to that," Malcolm said into the phone.

Before the governor could respond, control of the computer reverted to the hackers. A new message appeared:

The time for rhetoric is over. BurgerCircus and its band of junk food purveyors MUST PAY. Only they can save your schools. Make them do it. $100,000,000.00 NOW.

The message faded to a distant shot of a night-time scene with the glow of a burning building in the centre. Details were too sparse to identify the area. It seemed to encompass a wide open space with little in the way of buildings. Then this blinked out and the governor was back on the screen extolling his good works. Somehow, the words seemed to ring hollow.

"That's different," Malcolm said. "Why didn't they zoom in like they did on every other occasion?"

"Where is that, Malcolm?" the governor asked. "Do you recognize anything?"

"I don't know, Governor. Somewhere in the Midwest, maybe. It looks pretty open. Tom is calling Washington to see if they know. All the police forces in the country know enough to call the FBI if there is trouble at any of their schools."

"That first bit? Was that inside the building? Did we see the actual bomb before it exploded?"

"So it seems. Some program must have sparked a computer to life with its webcam aimed at the bomb. It would be interesting to examine that bit of software. It might give us some clue of whom we are working with, their level of sophistication."

"Don't hold your breath waiting for that. I measure the distance between the computer and the bomb at ten, twelve feet at the most. It's history."

"I agree. It would still be interesting to see what programming language they are using: Basic, C++, G4 or simple internal settings. It might help us figure out how they are getting into our system."

"What is your agent-friend finding out? Any word on the location yet?"

Malcolm looked over at Tom. The frustrated look on his face suggested he was unhappy with the answers he was receiving. Malcolm raised his eyebrows. Tom gave a shake of his head. The two men were getting back to the point that they no longer had to talk to communicate. This camaraderie was like a revival of their former days as partners when they were both young agents.

"Nothing yet," Malcolm told the governor. "It's only been a couple of minutes."

"That's true, and despite the FBI demanding they be immediately informed, the locals may think trying to save their school from the ravages of fire takes precedence."

"The area did look pretty remote. Despite our intense involvement over the last few days, it is possible that some parts of the country aren't in panic mode yet. There's nothing like having one of their schools blown to hell to bring them up to speed with the rest of us."

Malcolm watched as Tom gently returned the telephone receiver to its cradle. The continued destruction of school property and his inability to prevent it raised his frustration level. Malcolm noticed Tom was making a conscious effort to rein in his emotions. Tom understood that a dispassionate examination of all the facts was the key to success. He smiled wanly in Malcolm's direction.

"My sister is a principal in one of these rural schools," Tom said. "The same place I got my educational start. It's hard to step back, but I'm working on it."

Malcolm gave him a thumbs up and returned his

attention to the voice on the telephone.

"I'm replaying the fire on my big screen. By playing with the contrast, I can make out a few more details. There does seem to be a town close by and if I blow up the image, no pun intended, I think I can see a BurgerCircus clown mounted outside one of the nearby buildings. Whether Ray Tutty wants to admit it or not, his company plays a big role in the choice of targets. Maybe the extortionists are right about him making his fortune on the backs of our children."

Malcolm let that statement hang in the air for several seconds. "Governor, I know you are stating an opinion and would never, I repeat, never express that opinion out loud to anyone but me and never, I repeat again, never make it within earshot of anyone else."

The governor chose this time to remain silent for several seconds. "It's not an opinion, Malcolm; it's an observation. There is a difference."

"Maybe so. But, let's keep it a private observation. There are two sides here, Governor. The bad guys. That's the extortionists who are blowing up schools all across this country of ours. And the good guys. That's everyone else. Everyone. There are no grey areas."

"It's late, Malcolm. I'm going to bed. Call me when you find out where the school bombing took place."

"Can it wait until morning? There's not much you can do."

"No, call me. I'll let my brain grind away at it while I sleep. I may come up with something new that will give us a different perspective."

"Good night, Governor."

Malcolm hung up. "He's sharing your frustrations. He had hoped for some results by now just by the brute force that we are throwing at this problem. To be honest, we are no further ahead than we were on day one. The lack of sleep is wearing away at all of us."

"Go home and go to bed. I'll call when I know something. The locals don't seem to be going to inform us. We may have to use our satellites to spot the fire." Tom smiled. "How would that be for brute force?"

"It will have to come out of your budget. Mine couldn't cover it."

◀23▶

THE JANGLING PHONE yanked Malcolm back from the land of nod. His fingers clutched an untouched glass of whisky balanced on his knee. His suit coat lay on the sofa beside where he sat. His bed proved to be a destination beyond where his legs could carry him. A quick glance at his watch told him he had been home for a little over an hour. He set down the drink in exchange for the phone.

"Yeah, Tom. What did you find out?"

Montana proved to be lucky number four on the extortionist's list. A call from a reporter to Langley looking for a comment on the latest bombing provided the long-sought information. The authorities in Busby were still concentrating their efforts on fighting the flaming building.

Whatever the bombers used this time contained an accelerant that kept the building burning long into the morning. Instead of the Internet, amateur video graced the TV screens of the network stations. Although shaky and lacking definition, it got to the point that anyone, anywhere could be the target. Multiple points of view gave the impression of a small budget film. Cameras caught the action from all angles. It brought back memories of *The Blair Witch Project.*

Malcolm tapped the speed-dial button to the governor's residence. The governor picked up on the first ring. Sleeping soundly seemed to be a thing of the past for everyone.

"Busby, Montana," Malcolm said upon hearing the governor's voice. "Ring any bells?

"Busby?" The governor sounded alert. Tom doubted he had been sleeping. "Not exactly a major city."

"Didn't you speak at their commencement exercises last spring?"

Speaking engagements outside his state were rare for Peter Weston. Anyone who had ties to the two major parties in the country shunned having the governor appear at their events. That included just about everyone who hired guest speakers. The few exceptions were some forward-thinking universities and the odd high school run by graduates of those centres of learning. People in areas like Montana prided themselves in not being tied to a political party system. They liked to believe they still had the independence of the old west running through their veins. When offered, Peter jumped at opportunities to spread the word that the two-party system was corrupted by cronyism and squelched free thinking.

"Little high school off I-90 in the middle of nowhere. I remember that. Same place?"

"I'm still checking," Malcolm said, "but I'm pretty sure it is. Do you think that's a coincidence?"

"You think they attacked the place because I spoke there? Hell, Malcolm, you wrote the speech. Was it that bad?"

Malcolm chuckled. "No. It was damn good. Maybe too good. You did get national attention." The tone of his voice became serious. "I'm clutching at straws. Our state does seem to play a prominent role in this whole screw-up."

"Not in the choice of targets. This is the first connection, and it's remote. I think it may have more to do with the headquarters of BurgerCircus. What has the FBI found out?"

"Still too early to say. Their agents are on the way to lead the investigation. Busby has another distinction. It's near Little Bighorn battlefield. It has historical significance.

Remember, you made mention of that in your speech. History seems to be becoming a factor. One of the false alarms was the birthplace of Abe Lincoln. Tom has an agent looking into this, as well."

"Everywhere in the country has some historical significance, Malcolm. Our history is not that long."

"True, but any port in a storm. We're still looking for an edge."

"Don't discount the BurgerCircus connection. We have to concentrate on schools in sight of those restaurants."

"Tom is. He's just keeping that tidbit of information quiet for now. Paul Johnson told me one round of demonstrations at their locations sent the stock market prices into a frenzy. We don't want to encourage a repeat occurrence."

"Malcolm, BurgerCircus's bottom line is not our concern. We have bigger fish to fry. We must keep the public as up to date as possible on what we know. Ray Tutty can be damned."

"Go to bed, Governor. You need to get some sleep. We all do. I'll see you in the morning when we know more."

"Malcolm, you're not holding anything back from me, are you?"

The question caught Malcolm off guard.

"Holding back? Hell no. You're as entrenched into the loop as deeply as anyone involved in the case. Why do you ask?"

Several seconds of silence ensued. "What about you? Are you deeply in the loop as well or are your FBI friends holding things back from you?"

"Why the questions, Governor? What do you suspect?"

"Nothing, Malcolm. Just keep me informed, okay?"

"Sure, Governor; you know I will. Get some sleep."

That morning meeting was not to be. Malcolm poured

the whisky down the kitchen drain, untouched. He discarded his shirt, tie and pants and collapsed on top of his bed where he fell instantly to sleep. All thoughts of school bombings, extortionists and fast-food empires erased themselves from his mind as it sought a much-needed reprieve from the recent events.

The much-needed respite eluded him once again. Alexander Graham Bell's vile invention plunged into the depths of his sleep-starved brain and dragged him back with its incessant ringing. He fumbled for the bedside receiver, and the words on the other end brought him instantly awake.

"We've got one of them," Tom Burke said before Malcolm said the customary hello. "Our agents picked him up in Montana about two miles from the school."

Malcolm's feet swung onto the floor. A hundred questions swept through his mind. "Do we know who he is?" won out. "Is he an American or from some other country?" The real question: Is he a terrorist or an extortionist? was implied.

"I don't know anything yet," Tom answered. "He's unconscious. Apparently, he suffered a heart attack just after the explosion. That's why the demonstration was cut short. Our agents spotted him while they were flying into Busby by helicopter. It was pure luck that he was on their flight path. Fortunately, there was a full moon that completely illuminated him. I think the lens of his camera reflected the moonlight into the pilot's line of sight."

"Is he going to live?"

Tom detected the trepidation in Malcolm's voice. He shared the concern that an interview might not take place.

"We're doing everything we can. We airlifted him to Nellis Air Force Base in Nevada where we've assembled a top-notch trauma team. If he can be saved, they will do it."

"We'll pray for his survival." Malcolm made no attempt

to hide the sarcasm in his voice.

"I have a car on its way to pick you up. If you want to come, grab a toothbrush. We're going to conduct any interviews ourselves. I have a jet warming up as we stand here gabbing."

"Damn, I like the way you do business. I'll call the governor while I'm waiting."

"Don't. This is strictly on a need-to-know basis. No one is to know we have him or where we are keeping him. That's why we took him to Nellis. We can lock up security there tighter than a constipated asshole. There's too much money on the line to take any chances."

"But, the governor?"

"Need to know."

A knock on the condo door ended the conversation. Malcolm guessed that refusing to come was not an option. The car had obviously been dispatched to pick him up long before Tom had called. Tom knew that Malcolm's desire to run down these criminals was his highest priority at the moment. Nothing would stand in the way of Malcolm being on that jet heading west.

The two men would have lots of time to resume their discussion about the security of the mission on the flight. Malcolm grabbed his pre-packed travel case and headed for the door. This kit had all the components for a quick getaway: toothbrush, socks underwear, clean shirt.

◄24►

THE TRIP PROVED to be an exercise in frustration. Despite the efficiency of the evacuation team and the expertise of the trauma team, the unknown suspect would never offer any insights into who or what was behind this endeavour. It remained unknown if he held a position of importance in the criminal organization behind the bombings or if he merely handled the cameras and Internet uplink.

The highest quality equipment recorded the events. High-speed satellite connections broadcast the information around the world. The portal into the Georgia state computers consisted of a few lines of encrypted code, another challenge for Malcolm and his IT compatriots.

During the three-hour trip flying west, Tom Burke justified his position on keeping the lid on who knew about this suspect's capture.

"No one knows why this operative suddenly went dark," Tom explained to Malcolm. "There is a multitude of explanations: equipment failure, evading possible discovery, lost communications link and finally, heart attack. The latter would be so far down the list that in most cases it would not even be considered. The suspect looked to be in good shape. A guess at his age would put him in his thirties, possibly early forties. He did not present the appearance of a cardiac-arrest candidate except for one undeniable fact: he lay on an operating room table with the muscles of his heart turned to mush.

"So far as we know, we are the only ones who know where he is and that his condition is critical. Our hope is to get enough information about him that we may be able to infiltrate the operation. We have his computer on its way back to Washington to be stripped of information. With luck, we will be able to build a profile that will allow us to get inside his head and then extract the additional information we need."

At this point, Tom believed the man was still alive and struggling to breathe. He would soon discover that even the man's nationality would elude their investigations. He would be a cipher in the underbelly of crime.

Security staff from Nellis Air Force Base greeted Tom and Malcolm as soon as their jet touched down. They reported the unpromising prognosis from the operating team. Ever the optimist, Tom requested to be whisked to the Trauma Centre. When he penetrated the ring of security on the top-floor operating theatre, the looks on the other agents' faces broadcast the bad news to him.

"We have transmitted his fingerprints to agencies around the world," Oscar Parks, the special agent in charge, reported to Tom. "So far there are no hits."

"What else do we know about him?" Tom asked.

"Not much. He's a pretty nondescript looking character. Could fit in almost anywhere in the Western world. His complexion is dark enough that few in Middle Eastern countries would question his origins. Could just as easily be a resident of New York City."

Oscar looked towards the operating theatre as if that would suddenly inspire him with new information. "Clothes are all typical of what can be purchased at mid-range stores anywhere in America. No jewelry."

"What killed him?"

Oscar barked out a short laugh. "The surgeon, who doesn't know anything about why we are here, blamed it on a fast-food diet. I guess BurgerCircus scored its first hit in the battle. Ironic or what?"

"So that means he probably lived in America," Tom said.

"BurgerCircus has outlets worldwide," Malcolm said. "Paul Johnson gave me some background on the size of the company. He postulates that the extortionists' beef might be somewhere else, but the corporate headquarters and thus the face of the company is here in America."

"Yeah," Tom said. "We've had that discussion. It doesn't make our job any easier."

Oscar stepped back into the conversation. "If I were a gambling man, and we are in Nevada, I'd say he's home-grown. Everything about him from the style of his clothes, hair cut and food choices cries out that he lives in America."

"But a foreign power would try to create that illusion," Tom argued.

"Not this well. His clothes are American, but they are mismatched. Some from Wal-Mart, some from Sears, high-end jeans. We've sent them all to the lab for further analysis. We might learn where else he has been."

Oscar turned to Malcolm. "You're the aide of the governor of Georgia?"

Malcolm nodded.

"We found your governor's card in his wallet along with a corporate credit card."

"A card issued by the state of Georgia?"

"No, ACME, but yes, to the governor's business card. Georgia State seal is embossed on it. Looks like the real thing."

"The cards are easy to come by," Malcolm said. "The governor passes them out like candy apples at Hallowe'en. And they have already contacted the governor by email. We know they have his email address. The ACME card sounds like a fraud. Have you checked?"

"We're checking."

"That may be our first break," Tom cut in. "Keep me

informed of any results. One other thing: Monitor missing-person reports from across the country. Someone will have to miss this man. His family may not even know what he does for a living."

Tom turned back to Malcolm. "Anything you want to add? If not, let's go up to the bombing site. We've come this far; we may as well have a look."

The site was reminiscent of the locations in Georgia, Texas and California. An isolated building stood back off the highway with a BurgerCircus restaurant serving as its nearest neighbour. No one knew yet how the ACME boxes ended up in the hallway. Maintenance staff said they appeared earlier in the week. They were waiting for an official notification about their final resting place. It was not unusual at this time of year just before school opening for materials to arrive before the people who had ordered them made an appearance at the school.

One of the maintenance men commented on how heavy the box was. His intention had been to slide it further down the hall, but being alone at the time, he opted to wait for help. In the end, he simply decided the box was not impeding traffic and would wait for its final destination before making an effort to move it.

When asked if he didn't find the delivery suspicious under the circumstances, his response shook the agent's belief that a quick resolution of the situation seemed possible.

"I never watch the news," the man said. "Find it too depressing. Never heard of schools being bombed."

The bomb components remained a mystery. Expert staff from Washington would soon be on the scene to take over that element of the investigation. At this point, all anyone knew was that the bomb had left one hell of a hole in the ground. The damage to the building, although extensive, lacked the destruction of the fertilizer bomb used at the Alexandra school in Georgia. With the description of the weight from the school employee and the blast pattern of the site, Tom concluded that old-fashioned dynamite fueled this attack. Dynamite would be readily available in this area of the state. He would have his men check for local thefts in the recent past.

Tom and Malcolm poked around the school as much as they could without disturbing any evidence. Finally, Tom suggested they head back to Atlanta. The bomb had been too powerful to leave any useful clues behind.

Tom's cellphone vibrated in his chest pocket as he climbed aboard the helicopter to take him back to Nellis. Their jet would be fully serviced and waiting for them when they reached the air force base. He paused as he brought the phone to his ear.

A look of disgust took over his features. Malcolm gave him an expectant look.

"The false alarms have started up again. We've had two already this morning, and a third call has just come in. This one is in Fargo, North Dakota. Want to have a look on the way back?"

"Why not? The more personal knowledge we learn about these thugs, the better."

"True, although as I said, I'm sure that is their reasoning behind these fakes. They are garnering intelligence as well."

By the time Tom and Malcolm reached Fargo, the incident there had been dealt with, and the bomb squad had returned to its base. The two men viewed the videos shot by the team and questioned them about what they had seen first-hand. It was pretty much a repeat of the previous day's operations. This time, the assembled crowd had gotten closer to the scene, and the local police force had to be deployed to hold back the curious. Their fear diminished with each report of a hoax, but their interest increased. A few protesters had shown up with placards demanding that BurgerCircus pay up and put an end to these threats. Unlike previous demonstrations, the bulk of the crowd ignored their antics or hurled insults at the protesters. Ray and the governor's pleas for support had carried the day.

Tom studied the video closely. He pointed out one of the protesters to Malcolm.

"Isn't that one of the people we interviewed back in Atlanta?"

Malcolm leaned closer to the screen. "I think you're right. That person right behind him was bouncing around passing out signs. She's not easy to forget. Neither one were from the Atlanta area, as I recall."

"This is not a coincidence." Tom turned to the local agent. "They had to have been flown in from Atlanta to take part in this demonstration today. Find those people and bring them in for questioning. We've got to find out who has hired these shills."

"This film was shot more than four hours ago. They arrested no one at the time. It was a peaceful protest. A bit of a dud. I wonder if they are still in the area."

Tom's scathing look left no room for questioning. "Use whatever means it takes. Check airports, train stations, bus terminals. They all have security cameras these days. Find these people and pick them up. We're going back to Atlanta. Call my office as soon as you have them."

◀25▶

THE PHONE ON Tom's desk let out a shrill ring startling Tom and Malcolm from a near sleep. At a quarter-to-three in the morning, the building was preternaturally quiet. A few other agents were still working on various cases, including this one. The normal daytime rush of activity had died down around midnight.

"This doesn't look good," Tom said as he reached for the receiver. "It's a call from Washington. They're waiting for the same thing we are."

He brought the phone to his ear. "Special Agent Thomas Burke."

He listened. His face grew a little paler in the computer monitor light. An expletive slipped from his lips as he continued to listen.

"OK," he finally said. "This may be the screw-up we've been waiting for. Get me the New York office on the line."

Malcolm raised his eyebrows. "Well?" He speculated that Tom was on hold.

"A new twist. A bomb threat has been called in to a school in downtown New York. They have less than fifteen minutes to evacuate the area at this time of morning."

"Fifteen minutes? How big an area?"

Tom gave a shrugging motion. "You've seen the other explosions. You tell me."

His attention returned to the telephone. He established with whom he was speaking and how far their knowledge of events extended. His frustration level seemed to grow.

"I want helicopters in the air and agents on the ground,"

he snapped into his telephone. "We've got less than fifteen minutes. The evacuation is not our concern. Our job is to catch and stop these sons of bitches. Let's not blow this opportunity."

Malcolm watched as Tom made a call to someone at the New York office of the FBI. By the look on Tom's face, he wasn't getting the response he wanted. In the New York agent's defence, he probably only had a fleeting idea of what Tom was talking about. Not every police person in the country was working on the school bombings. Crime had not taken a holiday while these events unfolded.

Tom fought down his frustration level and started speaking very slowly as if to a child. Malcolm could not see that manoeuvre increasing cooperation between the two men.

"Listen to me very carefully," Tom said. "They always film these explosions and broadcast them on the Internet. I want your men to pinpoint from where the filming is taking place and cordon off that area. We will then perform a sweep until we capture the perpetrators. You have to act fast. You have about ten minutes to put this whole thing into effect."

Again, Tom stopped and listened. Again, he did not hear what he wanted to hear. He turned to Malcolm.

"Malcolm. How long would it take you to get the governor's helicopter into the air?"

Malcolm was caught off guard by the question. He opened his hands in a gesture suggesting that he could only guess.

"Right now, in the middle of the night, probably at least half an hour, maybe more. We'd have to get pilots out of bed. Ground crew. Get to the hangar. Do a pre-flight check. It all takes time."

Tom's attention turned back to the phone. "You know what's on the line. Do your best." He hung up.

◄26►

CHAOS REIGNED ON 4th Street. Fire trucks and police cars, sirens screaming, lights flashing, raced up and down the streets in the three-block area surrounding Liberty School. Lady Liberty herself, from her post in Upper New York Bay, looked down at the scene of confusion.

Suddenly, everything went quiet. The silence attracted people's attention more than the noisy sirens had. The silence stretched out for a full fifteen seconds before a piercing high-pitched note spread throughout the neighbourhood followed by a crystal clear male voice barking out orders from the speakers of every police car and fire truck in the area.

"EVERYONE IN THE SOUND OF MY VOICE MUST IMMEDIATELY EVACUATE. TAKE NOTHING WITH YOU. HEAD IN ANY DIRECTION AWAY FROM LIBERTY SCHOOL AND AWAIT FURTHER INSTRUCTIONS."

There was a ten-second pause to let this information sink in, and then the procedure was repeated. Pause. Repeat. Pause. Repeat.

Doors along 4th Street popped open. People in pyjamas and nightgowns stepped out onto their stoops and looked around in confusion. Flashing red and blue lights were everywhere. Policemen and firefighters stood beside their rigs directing people. None of the uniformed people moved more than a couple of feet away from their vehicles. They did not permit cars on the street. People were told to evacuate on foot.

From a position on the Prospect Expressway, Captain

Leroy White of the NYPD turned to District Chief Elmer Johanson of the NYFD.

"You think this is the best way to do this?"

"In the time that we have, it is the only way to do it."

The chief looked at his wrist watch. "In three minutes, I'm giving the word for my rigs to get the hell out of Dodge. Bad enough losing a school. I don't intend to see any of my men or my gear go up with it."

"The bastards. They didn't give us much warning. That is if it's real. I've heard there have been false alarms called in all over the country in the last few hours. Bomb squads are finding boxes that pop open with a sign on a spring that says BOOM."

"I'd settle for that," the firefighter said. "A false alarm wouldn't bother me at all in this case. We're not going to get half the people out of that area in the next eight minutes. A lot of them have just rolled over and gone back to sleep. People are too complacent when it comes to terrorists. They don't think it can happen here. Even after the events of September 11."

The captain nodded in agreement. "That's fading from their memory. It's becoming more a political rhetoric talking point to justify taking more taxes from people. Despite all the talk, I haven't seen much of an increase in our department's budget. The money disappears into some federal waste hole called Homeland Security."

On the streets below them, movement was taking place. The flashing lights started moving like grease in a frying pan when attacked by a drop of soap. Everything receded away from the central point of the school building in all directions. The people on the street, many of whom were doing nothing up to that point, started running after the retreating police cars and fire trucks. If the first responders were pulling back, this must be serious. The first vestiges of panic started to appear.

People were knocked over if they went too slow. Children were almost having their arms wrenched from their sockets as parents suddenly became awake to the reality of the situation. Some people were jumping into their cars, finding the streets blocked with fleeing pedestrians. Their choice was to abandon the vehicle or run people down. Drivers exercised both options.

The sounds of mass confusion brought more people to the windows of their homes. They were having second thoughts about their initial indifference. After a few seconds of deliberation, they too were joining the mass exodus. Some carried water bottles; a few had photo albums, the more prepared had disaster packs on their backs. Those few would be able to sustain themselves for three days if necessary, according to the Red Cross advisories.

Prospect Park was less than a quarter mile from many of the evacuees' homes. That became the destination for those living on the east side of 4th Street. and the streets on that side of the school.

From his vantage point, Captain White could see the people pouring into the park. They didn't know what they were running from or why, but somehow, on reaching the park, they seemed to relax. They now felt safe surrounded by the greenery of the park instead of the brick and cement of the buildings. He rolled his wrist to bring his watch into sight.

"Less than a minute to go if the terrorists are on schedule." He continued to watch the seconds tick by. As the hand approached the top of the hour, he began to start counting down.

"Ten, nine, eight, seven, six, five..." He looked up towards the school building. "...four, three, two, one." He waited for a few more beats. "Nothing."

A look of disgust spread across his face. "Well, that was an exercise in futil–"

The night sky in front of him lit up. He and the chief instinctively ducked behind the railing along the expressway. The percussion of the explosion rocked them where they knelt. Screams and shouting filled the air.

The chief was the first one to his feet. His radio was already up to his mouth. "Fire trucks in first, followed by paramedics. Contain the fire and tend to the wounded."

The flashing lights converged on the blazing building at the centre of their circle. The big machines roughly shoved abandoned cars to the side of the streets. Pedestrians scattered to the sidewalks.

There had been no time to safely search for the explosive device, but at least they were on hand and at the ready to mitigate the damages. In less than a minute, water rained down on the flaming school as if Noah himself had told the Lord he was ready for the deluge and to turn on the taps.

◀27▶

BACK IN TOM Burke's office, a chime sounded from his computer causing both men to focus their attention on the monitor.

"Here it comes," Tom said. "This time we are working with a known location. We should be able to immediately pinpoint where the extortionist's cameras are set up. Even if we can't get helicopters there in time, we should be able to flood the area with agents. Technology is great, but you can't beat feet on the street."

Malcolm moved closer to Tom's desk. He was amazed at how little time had passed since the warning call had come in. "Christ, that was fast. They won't have been able to evacuate the area in that short a time. Are we about to see our first casualties?"

Instead of a picture appearing on the monitor of downtown New York, a message greeted them.

Tune in to your local network station.
You won't want to miss this.

The message filled the screen in large black type with a blue background. In smaller letters at the bottom of the screen was the tagline: *Brought to you by the Society to Save the World.*

"What the hell?" Tom said. He grabbed the remote from a holder on his desk and flashed up the TV hanging from the wall. "Do you think they are improvising because they've lost their camera man?"

A repeat newscast from earlier in the evening was showing on CNN.

"It looks that way. Try one of the New York-based networks," Malcolm suggested. "It will have to be someplace with fixed cameras already mounted with such short notice."

Tom punched in the numbers to change to the NBC news station. A scene of distant flashing red and blue lights filled the screen. The voice of an unfamiliar anchorman tried to describe what the men could see themselves.

The screen blanked out momentarily then came back on, showing a much closer picture. The camera continued to zoom in until they could see individuals fleeing down the street away from a central location.

"Thanks, Bob," the anchor said. "Bob Cromley, our engineer, has taken over the camera mounted on our roof. For those of you just tuning in, NBC received a tip about fifteen minutes ago that there was to be an explosion at the Liberty High School on 4th Street. Police and firefighters are evacu—Holy shit."

A massive fireball exploded into the air at the centre of the screen. The clock on Tom's wall bonged out the time. Bong, bong, bong.

"Right on time," Malcolm said.

"Oh my God. The humanity," a shaky voice came from the TV. "This is NBC bringing you live coverage of a bomb exploding at Liberty School on 4th Street. I can only let the pictures speak for themselves." The sound of someone vomiting into a garbage can followed.

"I don't think it's as bad as it looks," Tom said. "The explosive force seemed to go straight up. I'm willing to bet a shaped charge designed to create an impressive effect but do little damage outside the blast site triggered the explosion. I think you are right about them going out of their way to not hurt anyone."

Malcolm glanced over at the computer monitor. It still displayed the message sending people to network TV. Now it flashed on and off, the background changing from blue to red to yellow.

"I guess it doesn't matter that you didn't get any helicopters into the air on time. They don't seem to be covering this blast themselves. They've gone mainstream."

Tom changed channels to ABC. Similar pictures lit up their screen. Only the angle was different. The fire trucks had moved back in to battle the flames. Heavy black smoke rolled out from the remains of the school. Their commentator had already moved on from describing the scene to speculating about who had caused it.

The sleepy voice of an NYU professor explained how different acts of terrorism affected people differently. Tom flipped back to NBC. He'd rather have no commentary than wild speculation of people outside the loop.

"The professor has a point," Malcolm said.

Tom let out an audible sigh. "You want to go back and listen to him?"

Malcolm laughed. "No. He doesn't even realize what his point is."

"Illuminate me."

"The previous explosions took place in relatively isolated places. The hoaxes moved into more densely populated areas. That bomb blew a hole in the centre of the most highly populated city in the nation. The attacks are the same, but the perception of them has taken a major leap up the scale."

"How so?"

"A bomb explodes in your neighbourhood. You survive. Your mind revolves about what could have been. There are hundreds of stories about people's lives being saved by inches or by seconds. Good news stories to a degree.

"The ten minutes of terror those evacuees felt waiting for that bomb to explode were pure negative feelings. You saw the people running down the street before the explosion.

Anyone who got in their way found themselves smashed onto the pavement. It was strictly the survival of the fittest. That's not the American way. We are a caring and compassionate people. At least, we like to think so."

Tom sat quietly pondering Malcolm's description of events. On the TV screen, firefighters were quickly controlling the flames.

"Fifteen minutes in the middle of the night doesn't give you much time to organize an orderly evacuation."

"It was more than just that," Malcolm said. "Those false alarms all through the early hours of the evening set the people up to resist the authorities. Their mindset told them this was another hoax. They were too late reacting, and when they did, they reacted poorly."

Tom's dark eyes bore into Malcolm. "You're making these guys sound like geniuses. I think you're giving them too much credit."

"The worst thing we can do is underestimate them. We have to combat this new level of terror."

"Agreed. How?"

A sly smile came across Malcolm's face. "We take control of the story. We re-spin it with a positive result."

Confusion was evident in Tom's look. He shrugged. "I don't understand."

Malcolm put a reassuring hand on his shoulder. "You may not like this, Mr. Law and Order." He sat back in his chair, steepled his fingers and looked up at the ceiling. Slowly he started spinning his tale.

"Even as we speak, firefighters are rescuing two small children—a boy and a girl—right next to the site of the explosion. Large chunks of concrete surround them, but they are unscathed." He paused. "Their parents were both working the night shift, leaving the kids home alone, presumably safely in bed. Their small dog alerted them to the confusion outside. By the time they ventured out to see what all the excitement was about, everyone else had evacuated the area. Then, the explosion took place, knocking them to the sidewalk where a US government mailbox canted above them, protecting them from the falling debris. Unfortunately, Sparkie, the dog, died during his last heroic act for his faithful masters."

An amazed, but skeptical look took hold of Tom. "Are you serious?"

All traces of good humour fled from Malcolm's appearance. "Totally."

Tom shook his head in disbelief. "You want to lie to the American people. That story will never stand up. Where would we find two kids, and what about the firemen? Who are they? Give this some thought, Malcolm. It will never work."

Malcolm got up from his chair and started pacing. "The kids are no problem. They are too young to be exposed to reporters. They will have to remain anonymous to protect not only them but also their parents who had left them alone."

He pointed to the scene of the fire on the TV. "Look at the size of that school. It's big enough that it carves out a large chunk of the neighbourhood. You can bet the people on one street don't know the people on the opposite side. All they will be able to do is speculate about which house we are talking about. If we make the kids four or five years old, they won't have been involved in the school system yet. This will be the first year for one of them. It will be important not to put too much pressure on the tyke by making a spectacle of him or her."

By now, he had walked the full length of Tom's office. He turned back as an additional firefighting unit pulled into the picture on the TV screen. "One of your men will be the firefighter. I'll leave that up to you. I'm sure you can make it work. Have him just transfer in from another station or something."

Tom sat shaking his head. "I don't believe you. Why would we go to all this trouble?"

"Why?" Malcolm stopped pacing. "Why? We're battling terrorism here. We have to steal the spotlight. We have to make everyone forget that these extortionists blew up a school in the middle of one of our biggest cities and that we were powerless to stop them. We have to divert everybody's attention away from what happened and have them focus on something that has a positive outcome. It won't be that difficult. That's what the people want to hear: a good news aspect of this experience. That's what we are going to let them hear.

"Pick a man. You must know someone in your department with exceptional PR skills and who can work undercover. That's what this is. Undercover work. You guys do it all the time. Doing this is no more of a deception than what you practise on a regular basis. And believe me, this is for the greater good."

Tom had been impressed with Malcolm's abilities before. Now, he saw Malcolm in a whole new light. Now, he understood how an unknown Indepentent candidate had become governor of Georgia. He got to his feet. "I hope you know what you're doing, pal." He laughed a harsh, serious laugh. "I guess one hoax deserves another. Let's get to work."

Sean Rhyno — Morning commentary

In other news:

The unemployment figures for the second quarter have been released and they are not good. This will come as no surprise to many. Several major companies have pulled their manufacturing facilities out of the country and moved to third world countries where they can exploit the slack rules governing employment, health safety and the environment.

The president likes to point out that the products produced in these plants will come back to America and be cheaper to buy. He adds that the head offices of these companies are still in America and as a result the profits also come back to this country, just not to anyone in the middle class who, without their good-paying manufacturing jobs, won't even be able to afford the products at the new lower prices.

The rich get richer. Thank you, Mr. President.

◀28▶

AMERICANS WERE WAKING up with a whole grab bag of intellectual stimulation.

The bombers blew another school roof skyward, this time in downtown New York City. All the major networks had a video of the event, some better than others. Amazingly, the explosion produced no injuries or fatalities. Any trauma resulted from people being pushed down or run over in their headlong rush to vacate the area with such short notice.

Following closely on the heels of this story, they learned that a true miracle had blessed one family in the area. Two small children, left alone for the night, had narrowly escaped death at the hands of these criminals. A member of the NYFD had rushed to the scene of the explosion and plucked these two children from harm's way seconds after the school had been destroyed and while flaming debris still crashed to the sidewalk around them. His "aw shucks, I was only doing my job" demeanour plucked at the heartstrings of everyone watching. Deep down, they all wished that they could be equally heroic while only doing their jobs, whatever they may be.

Pictures of the crushed mailbox that had protected the children from the falling debris showed how close death had been. The consensus was: Those bastards must pay. This time the bastards were the extortionists and not the fast-food industry.

BurgerCircus sponsored the newscast. The serious, stern face of none other than the company CEO reminded everyone that we are all in this together. As a token of good faith, BurgerCircus planned to include a free apple turnover with every meal deal purchased until these criminals were captured or stopped. Ray did not elaborate on what he meant by stopped. He didn't have to. Everyone understood.

Nice touch, Malcolm thought as he dried his freshly showered hair. He had managed three hours of sleep and was now preparing for the office again, determined to get a handle on this mess before the terrorists actually killed someone. Despite the obvious efforts of the extortionists to prevent bloodshed, Malcolm knew it was just a matter of time. You couldn't play with toys this dangerous and not have someone get hurt.

A glance through his kitchen window showed Robert Pettala, his chauffeur, parked outside. Malcolm had assigned Robert a research task. He wanted to know if an extortion of this scale had ever taken place anywhere in the world before. He also wanted to know if the extortionists had been so careful as not to hurt anyone. This morning, he would have his report.

Malcolm waited until Robert had manoeuvred the car from the relative quiet of his subdivision and onto the main road leading to the governor's mansion. Their initial conversation covered the New York bombing. Robert admitted that he hadn't stayed up late enough to see it live. Instead, his information came from the edited versions he had seen on the early news. Seeing those two, small children spared had been the most exciting part. The protective hand of God preserved their lives.

Malcolm agreed. Someone had protected those children. God was as good a choice as any. Thank goodness the firefighters had reacted as quickly as they did. They were back on the scene before the initial explosion spawned any more damage. His press release would emphasize their heroic efforts when the governor commented on the situation.

Robert offered no arguments with that assessment. Men and women who made their living rushing into burning buildings were either fools or heroes. Robert opted for the hero designation.

Malcolm smiled inwardly. He hoped that was the consensus across the country. He hoped the attention was on the heroic efforts of the firefighters and not on the dastardly deeds of the extortionists. He would do his part to keep that aspect of the event in the forefront of everyone's mind.

"Any luck on finding other crimes of this magnitude?" he asked as they settled onto the freeway.

Robert glanced into the rear-view mirror. "Hundreds," he said. "Extortion is an industry unto itself."

Malcolm feared this would be the answer. The information would be too general to apply to this specific crime. He waited for Robert to continue.

"South America is the hotbed of activity. They are constantly shuffling money around from one crook to another. Blackmail, kidnapping, sexual indiscretions; any of those things can lead to extortion. The same holds true for the United States, but here most of it is kept quiet. It seems to be a rich man's sport. I guess it's not worth the risk unless the monetary value is high."

"What about violence associated with it?"

"Once again, the whole gambit. Some circles expect violence; in others, it seldom ever happens." He passed a bound report back to Malcolm. "It's all documented as best as I could discover. For obvious reasons, most people wanted to keep everything quiet. There's no sense paying up if the information is going to be released anyway."

Malcolm took the report and flipped through the pages. It contained charts, maps and lots of text. It was the thorough job he had expected from Robert.

"Anything of the magnitude of what we are currently facing?"

Robert smiled into the mirror. "Only one. I think the figure was $336 million."

In the back seat, Malcolm perked up. "Three hundred and thirty-six million? Now we're talking. Who was involved?"

Robert's smile evolved into a chuckle. "One of the largest criminal organizations in the world."

Malcolm observed the wide grin lighting up Robert's face. "Why do I think you're pulling my leg? Who are we talking about?"

Robert made an attempt to look serious. He failed miserably. The smile simply wouldn't leave his face.

"The United States government and the estate of Howard Hughes. The IRS levied that much tax on his estate."

Malcolm let out a low whistle. "Damn. Three hundred and thirty-six million. I wish he had lived in Georgia." Now it was Malcolm's turn to try on a serious face. "Just because it was the government doesn't mean they were all crooks. You can't judge everyone by the current administration."

◀29▶

GOVERNOR WESTON GREETED Malcolm at the door of the mansion with a look of contempt on his face.

"The great man is going to make a statement to the people in less than an hour."

With the combination of the facial sneer and the sarcasm dripping from the governor's voice, Malcolm deduced that the *great man* would be the president.

"He's going to jump on that brave firefighter's coattails to further his presidential ambitions," the governor continued. "What a dick head."

Malcolm was surprised at the vehemence being displayed by his boss. He knew there was no love lost between the two men, but this reaction seemed to be way over the top. He measured his response carefully.

"Without knowing what the president is going to say, I'm not sure this is a bad thing."

"It doesn't matter what he says. He's just jumping on the bandwagon. My speech the other day turned the people around. Now he's cashing in."

"That's a good thing, Governor. Catching these clowns is not a partisan issue. Having the president reinforce what you said drives the message home. We want the people on our side."

The governor stared into the eyes of his principal aide. Slowly, he started nodding his head. Some of the fire cleared from his eyes.

"Of course, Malcolm. You're right, as usual." The governor looked away for a second, then looked back. "It's just that that man rubs me the wrong way. You know that. Now, this issue could help him back into the White House for another four years. The whole thing makes my blood boil. He's an opportunist."

Malcolm placed a hand on the governor's shoulder. A smile seeped onto his face. "Your time will come, Peter. Four more years of this incompetence and the people will be begging you to run."

"It's not me, Malcolm; it's the country I worry about. It might not survive four more years." The steel came back into his expression. "It's imperative that we bring these terrorists to justice and be seen doing it. We must step up our efforts."

"Extortionists, Governor," Malcolm said. "I'm sure money is their only motive."

Meanwhile, at the downtown offices of BurgerCircus, a different discussion dissected the previous night's issue.

"Our stock prices rebounded yesterday as a result of your speeches," Barbara Bishop said. "This attack in the heart of New York City might bring them back down again."

Paul Johnson shook his head. "I don't think so. The bulk of the news coverage is on this firefighter who rescued those two kids. He is deflecting the people's attention from the real horror of what took place." Paul looked from Barbara to Ray Tutty and back to Barbara again. "In fact, he's almost too convenient. I wonder if he exists."

Ray had been studying the stock price figures that Barbara had provided. Paul's statement caused him to stop. "Of course he's real, Paul. Who could make something like that up? Besides, I saw him interviewed on TV. He looks like a firefighter from Central Casting. Exactly what you would expect a hero to look like."

"My point exactly," Paul said. "What are you studying so intently?" He gestured towards the papers Ray held.

Ray waved the papers. "It looks to me like someone is buying and selling large blocks of our stocks. Somebody is making a bundle on our misfortune."

Barbara nodded in agreement. "So I noticed. I've been trying to track down who it is, but I've had no luck to date. It's probably some opportunist who saw the opportunity to make some quick money. No one who understands the market could believe that our stock prices would stay down because of these events. A lot of people jumped in for a quick gain."

"I see that. Still, this one guy seems to be really cashing in."

Paul took the papers from Ray and quickly scanned them. He looked at his watch. "The markets are open now. What's happening today?"

"Not much," Barbara said. "They're down. I think everyone is waiting to see what the president has to say. He's going to be on television within the hour. If he steps up to the plate and takes responsibility, our prices should hold. If he is stupid enough to pass the blame back to us, they will take another dive."

"Politicians." Ray shook his head in disgust. "Why can't our prices be based on how we run our business?"

"They are," Paul said. "Your speech on network television followed up with the apple turnover promotion is responsible for our rebound. That is the way we do business. We take a leadership role in the industry."

"Don't spin me, Mr. Spin Doctor. You know what I mean. Our business has nothing to do with these kooks who are blowing up the nation's schools."

"It's not my spin doctoring you have to be concerned about. It's the people running the committee to re-elect the president. You can be sure his speech will have very little to do with the school bombings and a great deal to do with how he can best capitalize on this situation. Let's face it, his campaign to date is in the tank. The only thing he has going for him is that the other candidate is no better a choice."

"True," Barbara said. "It's not his campaign that's in the tank. It's what he is basing it on. He's trying to run on his record of the last four years. He should be doing everything in his power to wipe it from the minds of the people. The man is an incompetent ass."

Paul smiled at the executive assistant. "Don't hold back, Barbara. Tell us what you think."

"Don't get me started. Maybe Governor Weston should throw his hat into the ring."

Paul grimaced, threw the stock report on the desk and walked over to the window. "Let's face it, the bombers are winning this war. I'm sure the FBI, Homeland Security, even Malcolm Truex are doing their best to get a handle on this thing. They are running around in circles. The daily hoaxes aren't helping. I've heard from some of our managers that some schools have organized searches of their buildings. They are tearing open every box they come across, making a huge mess everywhere. One of these times, they will stumble across the real thing, and people will die."

The mood in the room became noticeably darker at that revelation. Even Ray Tutty held back any comments that popped into his head.

Paul continued: "These people are meeting in our restaurants either to organize their searches or to boast about their success, or lack of success, depending on how you look at finding nothing. If something goes horribly wrong, the will drag our name into the coverage."

Ray kicked the corner of his desk. "There's a classic lose-lose situation. We don't want to discourage people using our establishments as meeting places, but ..." He let his voice trail off. No explanation was necessary of the downside.

"Maybe something has been discovered after the New York bombing," Barbara said. "The president must have something new to offer to go on TV."

"You would think so," Paul said. "If he doesn't, the best thing he could do is rehash Ray's and the governor's speeches about waving Old Glory. Surely, their campaign is not so bereft of ideas that they would do that. That only works if you're the first one out of the gate." Paul shrugged. "Or he could jump on the back of that firefighter and the two kids. That's the only positive spin that has come out of the past week. It must be Malcolm's idea."

"That's real, Paul. I saw the destroyed mailbox on the morning news. *Good Morning America* interviewed the firefighter. They can't make stuff up that fast." Ray started pushing buttons on the coffee machine.

With Ray's back turned, Paul mouthed to Barbara. "Oh yes, they can."

◄30►

HERB SOLSTACE CAME down the hallway to where Malcolm and the governor were discussing the president's upcoming address to the nation.

"It's good to catch you two together," he said. "We've got a minor break in the Alexandra bombing."

This statement seized the men's attention. "Thank the Lord," the governor said. "How minor?"

"Les Cleary, head of forensics for the Macon area, called me this morning. They've found the front bumper of the truck that carried the explosives. Some kids came across it in a vacant field about fifteen hundred yards from the school site a few days ago. They've been playing with it ever since.

"This morning one of their mothers came looking for her kid to take him to a dental appointment. The sight of the bumper sticking out of the ground scared the shit out of her. The kids play in this field all the time. Fortunately, they were at the birthday party at BurgerCircus on the day of the explosion.

"She called the cops. The cops called Les and Les called me. I've been liaising with him every day since this started."

"OK," Malcolm said. "I'm excited by this breakthrough, but I'm not sure why. Is it of any value to the investigation? We already know they used enough explosives to wipe out an entire city block if Alexandra had been laid out in blocks. Didn't they find a chunk of the truck a few days ago?"

Herb grinned. "They did. It was unrecognizable. This

time we lucked out. The licence plate is still attached to the bumper. It comes in as stolen."

"No surprises there," the governor said.

"None, "Herb agreed. "But Les claims the Macon police department has a pretty good record of catching car thieves. They've been working this one since the day before the explosion. They do have some leads. Obviously, they'll never find the truck. You and I don't care about that. But the good news is: they do have some persons of interest in mind. Their auto theft suspects could become our bombing suspects."

Herb rolled his eyes to indicate the transition. "Just thought you'd like some positive news for a change. I'll keep you informed." He started to walk away.

"Wait." Governor Weston grabbed Herb's arm. "I want to pass this information on to the press. Will that jeopardize the investigation?"

"It might be a little premature. I'd have to check with Macon PD on that."

"Tell the chief that I will appear on stage with him when he makes the announcement that there's been a breakthrough in the case. We'll do it this morning."

The governor turned to his aide. "Malcolm, get the helicopter fired up and call Ted Shires at NBC."

Georgia didn't have its own helicopter. That would have been an ostentatious expense for a state of its size. Instead, Peter Weston had an understanding with a colonel in the National Guard who was always looking for an excuse to get air time. His pilots had to fly enough to stay qualified. There were hundreds of ways to justify those expenses, but ferrying the governor around the state caused the least amount of pushback when the bills were submitted.

Malcolm shook his head. "Governor, I know what you're trying to do. You want to pre-empt the president. Don't do it."

A shocked look occupied the head of state's face. "Malcolm. How could you accuse me of such an underhanded thing? The people need reassurance that we are fighting these criminals. They need to know we are making headway and are not being stymied by a bunch of extortionists, as you call them."

Malcolm chuckled. "You're forgetting who you are talking to, Governor. Don't try to spin the spin doctor." Then his look became more serious. "The one thing we don't want to do is build up a sense of false hope." He turned to the security chief. "Is this truly a breakthrough, Herb? Is it leading us any place promising?"

Herb hesitated. Few people intimidated him, but this was not a time to be taking sides between the two most powerful men in the state—the governor and the man who pulled the governor's strings. Both men were staring intently at him. They expected an answer, and as Malcolm had said, there was no sense in trying to spin the spin doctor.

"It may be premature, but I do think this is going to bring results. The cops down there have some definite leads. The problem was the truck had disappeared off the face of the earth, literally as it turned out. They were holding back waiting for that definitive piece of evidence to fall into place. Now, they may have it, even if it's only the bumper of the truck. Up to now, we had no face on the crime. An arrest here will give us a starting point dealing with real people."

"Will the governor's announcement jeopardize the investigation?"

"I'd have to check with Macon. It may work to our advantage. These guys think they are free and clear. This discovery may put some pressure on them which might lead to them doing something stupid. It never hurts to have the bad guys playing defence. They are usually not very good at it. They assume we know all kinds of things that we don't and end up giving themselves away."

The governor stood quietly, listening to both sides of this debate.

"Great," he said. "Set it up, Malcolm. I'm more than willing to do my part to capture these thugs."

"I'll check with the Macon PD first."

A sly grin slipped onto the governor's face. "You do that, Malcolm. Let's see if the chief of police turns down a chance to be seen on TV with the governor. How much time do we have before the president has his press conference?"

Malcolm checked his watch. "If we hurry, we'll be able to have you on immediately after him. I think it's important to let him go first. Otherwise, he'll be stealing your thunder. This way, you can steal his. Four years is not a very long time in the grand scheme of things. Regardless of who you are running against at that time, it won't hurt to build up points now."

The governor turned and looked out through the front windows of the mansion. "If we wait four years," he said in a low voice that the others couldn't quite hear.

◀31▶

"I'VE ORDERED PIZZA," Tom Burke reported to Malcolm Truex at two in the morning. "Come on over, and I'll bring you up to speed on Montana and New York."

Malcolm had been dozing on the couch in his living room in his east side condo. The call was not unexpected. Tom and Malcolm had tentatively prearranged the early morning meeting. Malcolm had been doing independent research as well as helping the governor with the day-to-day operation of the state. Tom had been deep into the investigation on several fronts. They agreed to meet if the situation warranted it.

"OK," Malcolm said. "First, I've got to change my tie. I have the days of the week embroidered on them. It's the only way I can keep track of what day it is."

"I hear you," Tom said, a note of laughter in his voice. "I've moved my wardrobe into my office. I send pictures to my wife and kids every day so that they won't forget what I look like."

"Good luck with that," came Malcolm's curt reply.

There was a brief period of silence on Tom's end of the phone. "Sorry, pal. I wasn't thinking."

Although still married, Malcolm had not seen his wife in over four years. She pursued her career independently in California. Occasionally, they would still talk on the telephone. Neither was dating anyone else. Malcolm didn't have the time; she didn't have the inclination.

The troubles had started when Malcolm was still an FBI agent. Like Tom, he threw himself into his cases at the expense of everything else in his existence. His wife finally convinced him that life was passing him by and persuaded him to throw it all in. Reluctantly he resigned from the FBI to spend more time with her. That lasted less than a month.

Malcolm met Peter Weston, the mayor in a nearby town. Life as an agent was a walk in the park compared to life in the political realm working for Peter Weston. Weston's rise to governor of Georgia was a rocket ride, in no small measure to the hours Malcolm devoted to the cause. In the beginning, there were only Malcolm, Peter Weston and a small cadre of local supporters. It could only be 24-7 because Malcolm couldn't stretch the time continuum. He had tried. His wife longed for the good old days of him being an agent. At least, there was sometimes a pause between cases.

Weston ran as an Independent. With no party structure to help him and the good old boys from both major parties fighting him tooth and nail every step of the way, nobody gave his team a realistic chance of cracking the two-party stranglehold on the people of the state. Weston worked for the prize equally as hard as Malcolm. The long hours paid off. Early on, both old-line parties spent most of their considerable budgets attacking each other. By the time they realized who their real opponent was, the battle was all but over.

Malcolm returned home late one night after a four-day excursion around the state to generate votes in the final days leading up to the election. He found a note on his kitchen table. She hadn't wanted to do it this way, she explained; she had no choice. Malcolm was never around to confront face to face. She had an offer to write for a television show in Los Angeles. An answer was needed immediately. She was going to pursue it.

The show turned out to be a success. On the rare

occasions that Malcolm viewed it, he recognized his wife's input. The jokes would bring a brief smile to his face. Other opportunities followed, demanding more of her time. That was the current status of their relationship; she on the west coast, he on the east. Was it on hold, or was it over? Malcolm wasn't sure.

The election had been a squeaker, but Peter Weston became the new governor. The people of the state were the winners. Peter had allegiances to no one. He could govern for the good of the people and not the whims of the party. The state of Georgia proved to be the big winner during Pwter Weston's first term. The next election was his for the taking. The people of Georgia still loved him as he approached the midpoint of his second term.

Both Malcolm and Peter had their eyes on the big prize: the White House. So far, their only disagreement was on the timing. Peter had wanted to run this time around because the incumbent was a joke and would be easy to beat. Malcolm insisted they still had things to accomplish in Georgia. It wasn't just about winning. There were things to accomplish along the way. Malcolm was persuasive. His view had won out, or so he thought. This school bombing fracas was disrupting his long-term plans. It was a distraction that Malcolm didn't need in his life.

"I'll send a car around to pick you up," Tom said. He knew Malcolm had no car of his own. He relied on either Robert Pettala or on taxis to get him around. Tom knew that Robert was working as hard on this case as he and Malcolm. The governor was treating the bombing as a crime against the state and consequently threw the full resources of Georgia into its investigation. Tom would allow the chauffeur to get a good night's sleep. Someone should be well rested.

Malcolm poured his first cup of coffee and settled onto

one of Tom's hard, wooden office chairs. It was best not to get too comfortable. He eyed the folder in Tom's hands, the studious expression on his face.

"Anything positive come out of this last round of bombings?"

Tom made a so-so motion with his hand.

"We think we've disrupted their agenda."

Malcolm perked up. "How so?"

"Last night's bombing in New York City wasn't as clean as the others. I think it was thrown together in a hurry. We've found traces of the bomb for the first time. We may have a video of someone delivering it. Our agents are still following up on that."

Now Malcolm was all ears.

Tom continued: "We think the cameraman was the one common thread in all the blasts. His sudden disappearance threw a monkey wrench into their well-oiled scheme. So far, we are the only ones who know what happened to him. The extortionists know he was in Montana when that bomb exploded. They don't know why the coverage was cut short. They don't know where their man suddenly disappeared to. They can only speculate."

"And if we can control that speculation ..." Malcolm's voice drifted off as a flood of thoughts entered his mind.

"Exactly." Tom smiled. He had already been working on some scenarios that would capitalize on this information.

Tom opened the folder on his desk, and Malcolm crowded closer to read the reports. After a few minutes of silence, he looked at Tom.

"Not a whole lot of useful information here."

The smile left Tom's face. "We had hoped for more. The computer used in the uplink was brand new. Powerful beyond belief, memory in the terabit scale. This machine did not come from the shelves of any Business Depot or even a high-end specialty computer store. It was custom built. Probably for the military or some secret government operation. We can only speculate on whether it was custom built for the terrorists or stolen.

"The only software we could see on it was to capture the video feed and upload it onto the Internet. Before we could examine it further, it executed a scrubbing program that wiped itself clean. We think it used a retina examination security system. Once it realized our technician wasn't an authorized user, it initiated the cleaning program. He shut it down at once, but as of yet, they haven't been able to come up with any useful information. We think the scrubber kept running even after the power was turned off."

"Bummer," Malcolm said.

"We have photos of the screen before the shutdown. It had only the one uplink icon on it. The itinerary of the planned bombings must either be in the man's head or stored somewhere else that he can access. We're speculating he used Internet cafes and the like to communicate with his bosses."

Tom flipped a few pages into the report. "Microscopic traces of sand on his boots indicate he was in both northern Mexico and California recently. The Texas bombing was filmed from the Mexican side of the border. This information leads us to believe he is the single cameraman for the endeavour."

Malcolm leaned back in his chair. "So, you think they had to improvise last night when they realized their boy was in the wind. They had to come up with a site that already had television coverage. New York was a natural choice. I've seen the outside shots of the city on the David Letterman show. Kelly and her flavour of the day frequently show the streets outside her studio. A tip to the networks had them doing their dirty work. A tip to the police gave them a chance to lessen the possibility of injuries to innocent people but gave them no time to intervene in the bombing.

It also greatly increased the anxiety level of everyone involved."

Tom walked over to the coffee machine at the side of his office and poured himself another cup of the black brew. "For a criminal organization, they seem unusually careful about anybody getting hurt. That rules out terrorists. They would relish a large death toll with each explosion."

"So far, they've been lucky. Their luck can't hold. You can't keep setting off explosions of this magnitude and not have someone get injured or killed. It's just a matter of time."

Tom's head nodded in unconscious agreement. "I know, and when that happens, the pressure to settle will be even greater. Material losses don't mean much to the average American when the material destroyed is not theirs. Even the fact that taxpayers will be on the hook to replace these schools doesn't carry much weight with anyone outside the actual districts where the destruction took place. So far the biggest losers are the fast-food joints and hell, it wouldn't hurt our kids to eat less of that stuff."

A slight smile crossed Malcolm's face. Neither man had an ounce of extra fat on their bodies. The fast-food industry had not corrupted either of these men. "You've heard me say it before and I'll say it again: Ray Tutty is the intended target here. Someone has a vendetta against BurgerCircus.'

Tom looked at Malcolm with a face that neither agreed nor disagreed. He did not want to get involved in that discussion at this time.

Malcolm let the silence stretch out for a few minutes. He sipped at the black poison that the FBI passed off as coffee and then he spoke again.

"When can I bring the governor back into the loop? I think he suspects that I'm holding out on him. His only interest at the moment is catching these criminals."

Tom stared intently into Malcolm's unwavering eyes. He

hesitated before speaking. "I know I could be way out in left field with this, but..." and he paused again seeming to be searching for the right words. "Is your boss taking a run for the presidency in November? If he is, the FBI can't be seen to be supporting him in any form, either real or implied."

Malcolm flashed a look of complete incredulity.

"Running for president? Don't be so damn crazy. The only thing on the governor's mind is bringing this extortionist threat to an end; he's not running for anything else."

Tom held up his hands in a placating manner. "I had to ask. I'm not the only one who thinks this. Are you sure you're not too close to the situation to see what is taking place?"

Malcolm shook his head. "No, I'm not too close. I'm close enough to know what is taking place. In four years, his name will be on the ballot, either as an established party candidate or as an Independent but not until then."

Tom gave Malcolm a friendly tap on the shoulder. "Good. Glad we got that out in the open. Still, I think we are going to stick to our need-to-know policy. That's just the way we operate. You understand?"

Malcolm said nothing. Then he reached out and punched the agent's shoulder in a little more than friendly gesture.

"You're the boss. You said you have some video footage of a possible suspect in New York?"

"Yeah, taken from a shop down the street. The explosion destroyed the school's cameras, but we lucked out on this video. In it, you can see a car pull up. A person jumps out, a sports bag over their shoulder. He or she calmly walks up to the door, blows the lock we later discovered and disappears inside. Less than five minutes later, they are back in their car minus the sports bag and on their way. That happened around 8 o'clock on the night of the blast."

"A stolen car I'm guessing."

"Bingo. You win the kewpie doll."

"Can you get a usable image of the bomber?"

"We're working on it. We have basics like height and weight."

"You're the FBI. Can't you tap into the talents of Penelope Garcia over at the BAU?"

Tom smiled. "I wish we could. If only she existed outside the world of TV."

The smile left Malcolm's face, his eyebrows furrowed. "You know, I know someone in real life who has that kind of talent. He's down in Florida, I think. He might be able to digitally trace these guys. I'll see if I can track him down."

"Anything I can do to help? We have resources all over the country for that sort of thing."

"No. And let's keep this hush, hush. Just between you and me."

Tom smiled. "Now, who is being secretive?"

"As you said, there might be people working on the inside against us. If not, no one wants to be thought of as being a suspect if they are innocent. Let's not take any chances This stays between you and me."

"Okay," Tom said. "This video suggests the New York bombing was not a part of their master plan. All the bombs are supposed to be in place already. Planting the bomb on the night of the explosion suggests they are ad-libbing. How much more have we disrupted their scheme?"

Malcolm flipped through the pages on Tom's desk and then casually tossed the entire folder to the centre of the desk.

"Our children rescue story usurped much of the propaganda value of this last bombing. Good job on your choice of agent playing the firefighter. I've watched the clip a few times myself, and he's got me believing he saved those kids from a major disaster if not a sure death. All the attention is being focused on that story."

"Yeah, and having the president come on TV and praise the heroic efforts of the NYFD didn't hurt our little ruse. Who would suspect the president would take part in deceiving the people of the nation?"

Malcolm looked into Tom's face. Sarcasm dripped from Tom's voice.

"He was a good opening act for the governor. The president mouthed platitudes while the governor implied we are finally making progress. There's no love lost between those two. The competition may free up extra resources to assist your investigation. I can't see the president denying you anything."

"That would be good if it were true. But, in reality, despite the governor's good words, even he was pre-empted by your hero firefighter. That was a stroke of genius. I can't believe we pulled it off in such a short time frame."

Despite the fact that the bombing took place in the heart of downtown New York, with no loss of life or multiple serious injuries, it didn't grasp its deserved position in the news cycle of the major networks. Two toddlers being rescued by a heroic firefighter trumped it on every occasion. The false story had taken on a life of its own. Not even anyone in the fire department questioned the authenticity of it.

A few members asked each other what battalion the guy worked with, but all agreed that in the chaos that ensued when the threatening call came in, they were lucky to have prevented a major loss of life. The call, after all, was not a false alarm. Units from different parts of the city had worked seamlessly together to keep the people of New York safe. All saved lives by expediting the quick and efficient evacuation. If one firefighter got more attention than the rest, it didn't matter. They were glad to have the man as one of their numbers.

Both men fell silent, lost in their thoughts.

Malcolm was the first to speak. "You know, we don't even have any idea how big this organization we are fighting against is. We now know for sure that it's not a one-man operation. At what point did the rest of the extortionists find out that one of their partners was missing? Do they have a backup camera operator available?" He paused, contemplated the question and continued. "It doesn't seem so. Do they even have the ability to tap into the state's network with another computer? They got a text message on the screen, but that was it."

"The bomb in New York was not up to the calibre of the other bombs," Tom said. "It didn't completely destroy itself. Whoever threw it together is probably not responsible for the other bombs."

Malcolm glanced at his watch. "We don't have long to wait to see if they are back on track or if the whole plan is going to be improvised from here on in. I'm not sure which one I'm hoping for. If they're making it up as they go along, catching them might be easier. At the same time, this increases the chance someone will get hurt, or worse."

"We've upset their apple cart. Everything had been running too smoothly for them. The true test of an operation of this magnitude is how they respond when things go off the tracks. We've given them a few glitches. Let's see how well they respond. Personally, I think, either way, it should make them easier to catch. They will have to increase their communications among their members, and that should give us a better chance to monitor them."

On the corner of Tom's desk, a beep sounded from his computer. Tonight's show was about to begin.

◀32▶

RAY TUTTY REACHED out and answered his phone on the first ring.

"Yeah, Paul, I'm up."

"Thought you might be. I had my alarm set for quarter-to-four, but I've been awake for at least an hour. Half the nation and I are suffering from pernoctation." He chuckled. "That means we're holding an all-night vigil. I looked it up when I couldn't sleep."

"I had a power nap earlier. I'm looking over yesterday's early sales reports. The breakfast crowd seemed to be back to normal, maybe up a little. There's not much room for improvement there anyway. We own a huge share of that market. The lunch-time numbers were up. I think the symbolism of the free apple pie has caught on. Of course, those posters you had made of everyone's mother passing them out with the flag flying over her left shoulder weren't exactly subtle. Where did you come up with that lady? She captured the mood perfectly."

Paul laughed. "That's my dear old Aunt Martha. She's mother to everyone in her neighbourhood. Runs a little confectionery store where the patrons all call her 'Mom,' and don't worry, there's no nepotism. She did it for free. Was glad to do her part to help the governor.

"As for being subtle, the posters weren't intended to be. Motherhood and freedom are what we are fighting for. This is war, Ray. Don't kid yourself that it's only about money. For the extortionists, it might be; for you, it might be; for the rest of us, it's about a way of life. We can't let thugs intimidate us."

Ray did not answer right away. He contemplated his role in this adventure. Finally, he spoke: "Got your computer turned on, Paul? Are you on the Georgia website? Now there's an annoying thug who is intimidating. Listen to that bullshit he's spewing. He's talking about creating jobs. He's never created a job in his life unless you're talking about feathering his own nest. It's people like you and me who create the jobs in this state, Paul. Every time we open a new restaurant, and that's not counting the spin-offs. And even your dear old Aunt Martha, who sounds to me like a down-to-earth, sensible woman, has fallen under his spell. How could you let that happen?"

"You're not an early-morning person, are you Ray?" Paul chuckled. "I've got to give the governor credit. He sees an opportunity, and he is capitalizing on it. That's not a bad thing in a leader."

"Leader?" You could hear the disgust in Ray's voice. "Now you're just baiting me. It's too early for this crap."

"Once a Republican, always a Republican," Paul said, a hint of mischief in his voice.

Before Ray could respond, the governor disappeared from the computer screen. A clock appeared on the bottom right-hand side reading 3:59:30 and was relentlessly clicking away the seconds towards the top of the hour. Somewhere, somehow, another school was about to be demolished.

Large blue letters flashed on the screen with the message: PLEASE STAND BY.

Before either man could comment on the redundancy of the message, the flashing stopped, and the so did the clock. 3:59:40 and holding.

A few seconds ticked by before Ray spoke. "What's going on, Paul? What happened? Is the countdown on hold?"

Paul did not reply right away. He was still anticipating a

school explosion. When nothing further happened, he answered Ray's query.

"I think the governor's server crashed. There would have been people logging on from all across the nation. It couldn't handle the load. It was designed for 10 million Georgians, not for 310 million Americans."

"Like I said: incompetent. The man can't do anything right."

Both men sat in their respective houses staring at their frozen computer screens. Somewhere, they knew, an explosive device blew another school to smithereens. They were sure of that. They accepted it on faith. It only took four days to convert them to this new religion of destruction.

"The networks have to be covering this," Paul said as he reached for his remote. "Turn on your TV."

The big screen flashed to life on the opposite side of the room. Paul was on the NBC affiliate, and Ted Shires joined him in his living room.

"They've got the big guns out in the middle of the night," Paul said. "I'm watching NBC, and their prime-time people are still there."

"Fox has the big guns hanging around as well," Ray said. "They've got a panel of their top reporters sitting around a table looking confused." Ray paused to listen. A red and yellow banner across the bottom of the screen declared this was "Countdown to Destruction."

"It looks like that left-wing iconoclastic governor of Georgia has taken down his website before we had a chance to see what part of the country received the brunt of the destruction this morning," one of the talking heads was saying. "He has a reputation for trying to control the news cycle."

"The president should have stepped in and taken over that site on the first day of this operation," another panel member interjected. "This is a national issue, not a state issue. His re-election depends on how he handles this crisis and to date, he is not stepping up to the plate. He must be getting bad advice from some of the moderates on his election committee. I've said before, and I'll say it again, he has to get rid of those clowns. He has to take the reins himself and show what a leader he can be."

Never would the president be accused of having liberal leanings; even Ray couldn't listen to this crap when important news was breaking somewhere in America. He clicked his remote to the NBC station.

Ted Shires had Governor Weston on the line. A still picture of the governor filled one-half of the screen as though he were actually in the studio.

"... my IT department is doing its best to get the server back online," he was saying. "We were overwhelmed by the volume of hits. At least the nation is now aware of what is going on. I'm reaching out to my contacts with the FBI to see what information they can provide us, Ted. I'll let you know as soon as we know. I expect to hear from my chief of staff at any moment."

"We've got our staff working on this as well," Ted Shires said, "I'm sure we will know something momentarily."

"Ted, I'm going to have to put you on hold. My private line is ringing."

"OK, Governor, but the entire nation is waiting to hear where the latest school bombing has taken place."

Ted Shires could be seen looking to his left as if something had distracted him. "We may not have to wait on the governor," he said, turning back to the camera. "We have some unconfirmed reports from Kalamazoo, Michigan, that one of their local high schools is ablaze."

Ted brought his right hand up to his ear and listened for a second. "It appears we have a native of Kalamazoo on the line who is watching the flames as we speak."

An insert map of Michigan appeared at the top right of the screen with a large star in the lower left-hand corner. The star started to flash as a new voice came on the air.

"Good morning, Ted. Bob Connors, mayor of Kalamazoo, Michigan."

"Good morning, Mr. Mayor. I understand you have had an explosion in your area and a school is burning as we speak."

"Ted, I can't believe the federal government has let this thing continue for so long. Right now, I'm watching a three-year-old building go up in flames. The explosion was so intense that it flipped me out of bed a few minutes ago. I live just down the street from the school. I can tell you this school is totally destroyed."

"Excuse me, Mr. Mayor. I believe we have a video of the explosion. Someone anonymously uploaded it to our website. Perhaps you can explain what we are seeing."

Ray leaned closer to his television. He had stayed up until the early morning hours to see these pictures. The presentation started with a far shot and slowly zoomed in on a building. As before, that building erupted into flames shooting into the night. In the background, a large building complex of some sort flickered in the shadows behind the flames. This explosion had taken place in a more populated area than the previous bombs, except the one in downtown New York. The bombers appeared to be becoming bolder or more foolhardy or both.

The voice of the mayor of Kalamazoo cracked as he watched what happened in his city a few short minutes ago. "Oh my God. A bomb like that detonated during the daytime could kill hundreds." He fell silent at the prospect.

"The initial blast seems smaller than previous explosions." Ted Shires' well-modulated voice broke the silence. "Is that part of the school that we see in the background?"

"No, Ted. That's the post office. The school is smaller than most. Less than 200 students are enrolled there."

Once again, large red letters filled the screen:

**How Many Schools
Do You Have To Lose?
$100,000,000 *NOW*.**

"Those bastards," said the mayor. "They should be found and shot. No questions asked."

"Thank you, Mayor Connors, for your input," Ted Shires quickly interjected. "We now take you to our studio where we have two experts on–"

Ray Tutty hit the mute button on his remote.

"Well, Ray, what do you think?" Paul was asking in his ear.

"I thought Kalamazoo only existed in kids' stories and limericks. Who knew?"

"We did, Ray. We have a restaurant just down the street. You can bet the protesters will be holding up our breakfast crowd in the morning. This move into the populated areas of the cities is going to increase the pressure on us. We need to come up with another offensive move."

"The Kalamazoo mayor was right. Shoot the bastards."

"No arguments from me on that front. First, we have to find them. Somehow, we have to lure them out into the open."

Ray walked across the room to where a coffee machine was perking away. He poured himself a cup of black brew, added a dollop of honey from a bear-shaped squeeze container and returned to his desk. One hand held a portable phone. He had been listening to Paul all during the trip. He took a sip of the coffee and smiled before responding to Paul. His restaurants were famous for the quality of the coffee they served. Going after this segment of the food market had been Ray's idea. He took pains to make it properly every time.

"We could offer a big reward for information leading to their capture and conviction, and I mean a big reward. Millions. They'd be falling over themselves to turn each other in."

He took another sip of coffee and waited for Paul to respond. The delay meant Paul was giving this thought serious consideration.

"Maybe. I'm not sure we're there yet. The FBI are still running down the leads from the appeal for help from you and the governor. We should let that work its way through first before adding the additional stress of thousands more phone calls. A reward like that will bring out the crazies."

Ray stared out his home office window while he pondered that statement. All he could see was his reflection in the glass. It was not a pretty sight. Dark rings circled his eyes. His face looked thin and gaunt in the dark image. These late nights were taking their toll.

"Those crazies might be needed to catch these bastards. To crash the governor's computer system means millions of people are finally sitting up and taking notice of what is going on. One of them must know something. Let's find that one person."

Paul chuckled.

"Governor Weston must be blowing a gasket. Being pre-empted by the mayor of Kalamazoo will not sit well with him. I wouldn't want to be in Malcolm's shoes right now."

Ray took another sip of his coffee. "It's good to see him taken down a peg or two. I'm not too sure he isn't thinking of taking advantage of this situation and all the publicity he is getting. I wouldn't put it past him to take a run for the presidency in November. Heaven help us if he is instrumental in capturing these thugs."

"Ray, I don't care who brings about the capture. The important thing is to get them off the streets and into prison, preferably for the rest of their lives."

"Why waste the money? Let's not capture them alive. Do the world a favour."

There was silence on the line for several seconds. Obviously, Paul was contemplating Ray's words. Even though he had flippantly agreed with the mayor of Kalamazoo earlier, he now believed Ray's statement was serious.

"No one has been killed or even injured to date, Ray. These guys are not killers. They just want money. Mostly yours, I should add."

"Well, they can't have it. And don't even think about suggesting otherwise."

◀33▶

"MALCOLM, WHAT THE hell is going on? Where has the latest bomb exploded?"

The governor still watched his television as he barked demands at his chief aide. He could see the map of Michigan appear on the screen and then heard the voice of Mayor Bob Connors.

"Dammit, Malcolm, I should be making that announcement. What information do you have?"

Malcolm's voice sounded distracted. He obviously was watching the same TV news as the governor.

"You know what we know, Governor. We have the same source of information right now. Wait." There were several seconds of silence. "The FBI have verified an explosion took place in Kalamazoo. Tom's talking to agents there now."

"Oh shit, here comes the video." The governor interrupted Malcolm and then fell silent. Neither man said anything while the events silently unfolded on their respective televisions.

Tom Burke had called up a satellite image of the school area in Kalamazoo. It was not real time, but it gave them an idea of the layout.

"That's I-94 going by to the south of the school. The camera man could have parked on Riverside Drive, shot his footage and hightailed it to 94 and out of town."

Malcolm looked at his watch. "This only happened minutes ago. If we get some troopers up on that highway, we might catch him. Set up roadblocks. How many cars can be on the road at this time of the morning?"

Tom smiled. "Thousands, Malcolm. As Dorothy commented to Toto in the Wizard of Oz: We're not in Nebraska anymore, or in your case, Michigan is not Georgia. They are approximately the same size, but your home state has only half as many people. With the amount of planning these guys do, they probably know exactly how far they can get before we have roadblocks in place. Once that happens, they will be either off the road or head in another direction. I think it's a waste of time, but I'll order it anyway. We don't want them to think we're giving them a free ride."

Tom turned his attention to contacting the appropriate authorities while Malcolm turned his attention back to the governor.

"You heard what we're planning?"

The governor yawned and then apologized.

"Tom's probably right. If there's nothing new you can tell me except what we've already seen on TV, there's no sense in me going back on the air to play second fiddle to the mayor of Kalamazoo. Let me know if the FBI comes up with anything."

"Why don't you get some sleep, Governor? These late nights are taking a toll on everybody."

"You're right about that, Malcolm. If enough people were up at four in the morning to crash our computer system, you know efficiency in the workplace will suffer in the morning. Not only will people not be at their best, but they will also waste hours of company time discussing the bombings. These events are costing the country more than one hundred million dollars every day in lost productivity."

"So true, Governor. Estimates say that on the Monday after the change to Daylight Savings Time, in the knowledge industry alone, the cost is over four hundred million dollars. Multiply that by every industry out there, and we are talking billions of dollars in lost revenue. We've got to put a stop to these guys."

Malcolm looked over at Tom who was deeply engrossed in a telephone conversation with one of his compatriots in Michigan. He was scribbling on a notepad on his desk. Malcolm turned away and lowered his voice.

"Did your little program have a chance to lock on before we lost the server?"

The governor hesitated before answering. "I'm not sure. I'm going to wait for our servers to come back up before I check it out. I don't want to risk losing any information I may have captured. We're going to have to increase our capacity for tomorrow night. We don't want another crash."

"Get some sleep, Governor. Leave the IT work to the IT experts. They're busy enough without you down there getting in the way. Trust me; everything will go smoother."

The advice was good. Malcolm knew it. The governor knew it. The question was, however, would the governor accept it. Malcolm waited for a response.

After a short pause, the governor responded. "Of course you're right, Malcolm."

Malcolm could hear the exasperation in his voice. The governor was not one to sit idly by when things that affected him were happening nearby. He needed something to occupy his mind while he waited.

"I know you think the mayor of Kalamazoo stole your thunder, but why don't you go back on the air and offer some insights as to how the investigation is going. Commiserate with another victim of this criminal gang. Just don't be saying anything that's going to upset the FBI or the federal government. Maybe you could push the lost productivity angle."

Malcolm knew that he was taking a chance with this suggestion. God only knew what kind of trouble the governor could get himself in when he was talking off the cuff. Malcolm also knew that if the governor got shoved to the sidelines in this investigation, so would he.

His only involvement was as a representative of the state of Georgia, the site of the first bombing. That link became more and more tenuous with each new attack in some distant part of the country. Malcolm also knew that he wanted to see this thing through to the end. He was too involved now to drop it and simply go back to the business of governing Georgia again. The FBI blood flowing through his system had staged a resurgence like a dormant seed bursting into full flower. He had to keep the governor involved.

"I could do that," the governor said. There was no enthusiasm in his voice.

"Put 'lost productivity due to Daylight Savings' into Google. That will give you enough information to start the discussion rolling. I'll have a press release ready for the morning news cycle with some hard facts that *you've* dug up on the subject. Once again, this will take the attention off the bombers and put it onto something we can control."

The idea had popped into Malcolm's mind as a spur-of-the-moment thought. At the time it seemed like a good one. But, with Governor Peter Weston, as brilliant a man as he was, risks loomed around every bend in the road. The governor never minced words. He believed in telling it like it is. Most of the time that was a good thing, even when he ruffled other people's feathers. Still, Malcolm thought, lost productivity seemed like a benign subject. What could go wrong?

"When you put it that way, it's worth a shot. See what you can dig up; I'll alert the nation to what is going on." And then, as though he had tapped into Malcolm's thoughts, the governor added: "Neither one of us wants to get bumped from this investigation. There's too much at stake."

◀34▶

"IN THE NAME of all that's holy, how can they let that wildly speculative claptrap on the air?"

Ray Tutty stood glaring at the television in the corner of his office in downtown Atlanta. A replay of the telephone interview with the mayor of Kalamazoo and Peter Weston had just aired. After watching the explosion the night before, Ray had turned off the television before the governor had come back on to talk about the loss of productivity caused by the bombers.

Paul and Barbara shared a quick glance with each other. There was some firefighting to do to contain the damage caused by the seemingly innocent comments made by the governor.

"I don't think he was casting blame on us," Paul said.

Ray's head snapped around; his eyes burned with fury. "He said we were the prime benefactors of these bombings." Ray pointed back at the TV as though the governor himself occupied the corner of the room. "The bastard said that while everyone else was losing sleep, losing money and living in fear, we were raking in the dough hand over fist serving breakfasts and coffee. We had become the unofficial meeting place for discussions on the previous night's events and practically charged admission to the citizens of the nation to hold these discussions."

Again, Paul and Barbara's eyes met. When Ray got off on a tangent like this, it was hard to bring him back to reality. His view became the only view.

"It was the Kalamazoo mayor who made the statement

about charging admission. The governor merely suggested that everyone was staying up too late, oversleeping and then grabbing some breakfast at a fast-food joint on the way to work. He didn't even mention BurgerCircus by name." Paul hesitated. "It is true, Ray. Productivity in the country is suffering because of this. People are tired, fearful and irritated. You can't blame that on Governor Weston. He is merely the messenger."

"And," Barbara interjected, "discussions of what happened the previous night dominate the first hour of every workday. Our coffee sales are up," she picked up a report that she had placed on Ray's desk when she came into his office, "but not that much.

"We, unfortunately, are not the benefactors of this sudden increase in business. It's the coffee and doughnut shops. Ironically they are not even included by the bombers in the list of businesses who should be paying their ransom. They are responsible for the fattening of the adult population, not the younger generation."

Paul snorted out a laugh. "You've got that right. The amount of sugar people are consuming in their coffee is a national tragedy. When we were in that coffee shop in Canada, the people even had a special code for ordering: Double-Double, two creams, two sugars. They don't even say the words anymore. Nobody mentions sugar; nobody mentions cream. It's boiled down to 'Double-Double,' as if that makes the drinks healthier."

Paul's face took on a more serious aspect. "These shops no longer serve simply coffee and doughnuts. They are in the breakfast business." He pointed at the report in Barbara's hand. "While we've experienced a slight increase in morning trade, cars lining up to get to their drive-through windows cause major traffic jams. They've got a reputation as a quick caffeine fix. We will lose future business to them if we allow this to continue unchecked."

Barbara studied Paul's face looking for a clue as to where he was going with this. "People are staying longer in our restaurants and," she shrugged her shoulders, "strangers are talking to strangers. Our productivity is down because of this but not like everyone else's. If they are in our restaurants, they are not doing any work at their place of business."

Ray showed no signs of being placated by the idea that it was someone else who was benefiting from the increased business. The veins in his temples were throbbing. "The talking heads are accusing us of profiting at everyone else's expense. Don't you get it? Suddenly, we're the bad guys here. Not only aren't we paying the money being demanded by these constipated assholes—" Ray waved a hand towards his executive assistant. "Excuse me, Barbara." He continued: "—but, they say we are cashing in on it. It doesn't matter that no one named us directly. Everyone knows who the extortionists expect to pay: BurgerCircus. This debacle is going to bite us in the ass. Mark my words." He dropped his body into his executive chair and spun it around to look out the window at nothing in particular.

The other two remained silent while they pondered their boss's rant. What he said could not be dismissed out of hand. There was a section of the population that would blame BurgerCircus. Many of these people already believed the fast-food chain should have coughed up the money to bring an end to this madness. The idle ramblings of the mayor of Kalamazoo and the governor of Georgia on a late-night pseudo newscast would fuel that fire. If they hadn't realized on their own that BurgerCircus and the other fast-food chains were having a surge of early morning business, they would know it now. In their minds, they wouldn't separate the coffee shops from the hamburger joints. Fast-food was fast-food, and that is who the bombers were demanding the ransom from to stop their future attacks.

"You are right, Ray," Paul said. There was calmness in his voice. "We are the face that people have put on these bombings. People expect us to somehow bring it to a stop. We can't change that. As you rightly point out, it's now a twofold attack: we're not paying, and we appear to be profiting. My concern is that in the long run, we are going to lose business to the coffee and doughnut people. Forgive me for being pragmatic, but we have to keep that long view in sight here."

He looked over at Barbara and took a deep breath. "I propose we give our coffee away for free for the duration of this event."

Paul looked back at Ray and waited for the explosion that was sure to follow. Instead, silence filled the room, a silence that grew thicker with each passing second.

Ray's chair slowly rotated the one hundred and eighty degrees to bring his attention back into the room. A sly smirk lit up his face.

"Provide coffee to the people and don't charge them. A capital idea."

Paul studied Ray's face trying to detect any sarcasm that might be lingering there. He wasn't sure. He turned his attention to Barbara. She looked shocked. He looked back at Ray.

"You think it's a good idea?" he asked.

The smirk left Ray's face. "No. As ideas go, it sucks." He looked down at his desk and slowly shook his head. Then, abruptly his gaze returned to Paul. "However, having said that, it's the only idea that makes any sense. We'll do it. We have to keep the people on our side until these extortionists slip up and make a mistake. They can't be lucky forever. Did you come up with this on the spur of the moment?"

"No. I stayed up last night and watched the interviews with the governor and the mayor. As soon as the words were out of their mouths, I knew we would have a problem.

Free coffee is the best solution I could come up with after racking my brain for the rest of the night."

"You're both crazy," Barbara spoke up. "We are operating on razor thin margins as it is. We start giving away coffee, we not only lose the profit from the product but have to cover the basic cost of it as well. That's a buck a cup we're losing." She held up the report in her hand. We can't do it. We are already losing on the free apple pies. Free coffee will compound the problem."

"OK," Ray said. "We'll only do it during the morning rush, not all day. It makes it look as if we are helping solve the problem caused by people not getting their regular sleep because they are lying awake all night worried about where the next bomb is going to explode. At the same time, we don't appear to be profiteering." Ray elaborated on the idea as if it had been his own. "Besides, we have the best coffee out there for the price. Your plan is an opportunity to introduce it to more patrons. Who knows, it may eventually cost us a hundred million in lost coffee revenue, but it will be money well spent if we maintain or even improve our customer base."

He looked at Paul. "Don't ever worry about being too pragmatic when it comes to looking after the interests of BurgerCircus. That's why we pay you the big bucks." Ray's face lit up into a genuine smile.

Barbara dropped the folder on Ray's desk. "I hope the shareholders are as excited about this plan as you two are. They might think we are financing it with their money. Many of them don't think long term. They may dump us during this promotion if they think it loses them money."

"Let 'em," Ray said. "In the long run, this is what is best for the company. I'll buy up their shares myself and hold on to them. They'll have to pay through their teeth to get back in when the stock prices rebound.

"Let's make this happen."

◄35►

MALCOLM BOUNDED UP the steps of the Capitol Building. He carried a preliminary report on the lost productivity of businesses, both private and public, caused by the lack of sleep of their employees. After talking to the governor the night before, Malcolm had called Robert Pettala, his chauffeur slash researcher, and got him working on the project. As always, Robert had come through with flying colours.

The results were scary. Malcolm had said the companies lost billions. In reality, it was tens of billions across the nation. The combination of tiredness and distraction was devastating. Traffic accidents were up; tardiness was up; productivity was down, way down.

Everyone in every office or factory had views on how to treat the situation. Everyone wanted to express his or her views to everyone he or she came in contact with. The first hour or two of the workday across the nation occupied this sharing of views. Most agreed that you couldn't give in to terrorists or extortionists. There was disagreement on what these people were. However, a strong contingent of let's end this any way we can grew each morning. If paying a ransom, no matter how repugnant their idea seemed, was required, then pay it by all means and let's get back to our normal lives. Our kids need a safe place to continue their education. School would be opening very soon. Others, especially those without school kids directly in their lives, insisted there was no backing down. You can't give in to terrorism, they exclaimed as their mantra.

In some places the holders of these two views came to blows with each other, adding to the loss of productivity in the workplace that would linger beyond this simple altercation. For some, the resentment would continue for weeks, maybe even months, possibly forever.

Accidents and freeway tie-ups were becoming so commonplace that the act of driving to work increased the stress levels of an already stressed-out nation. The combination of driver tiredness and driver distraction was making the roads unsafe. Tow-trucks and body shops enjoyed a big spin-off business as well as the coffee shops.

Something had to be done and soon.

Malcolm stopped at the governor's office. Jennifer McLeod, the governor's secretary, smiled and held up a hand.

"The big man is not in yet," she said. "Too many late nights must have finally caught up with him."

Malcolm looked at his watch. It had been only four and a half hours since the two men had talked. For the governor, that was more than enough sleep. Peter Weston was a cat-nap person who seemed to always be at his desk during daylight hours.

Malcolm hesitated. "Call the garage and see if his car is there." If the man was indeed trying to catch up on a string of sleepless nights, Malcolm didn't want to be the one to wake him. Still, he wanted to discuss this new problem before the press cycle spun it out of control.

Paul Johnson had already tipped Malcolm off about the negative interpretation of the governor's comments on the early morning talk shows. They were handling it, Paul had said, but Malcolm wanted to control the spin himself. This productivity problem was too big to let it take its course. He had to make sure it reflected badly on the criminals and no one else.

Malcolm watched Jennifer's blue eyes reflect surprise.

"The governor has left the building," she said. "He must have before I got in." Her finger was running down the morning schedule. "He has nothing scheduled until ten." She looked at Malcolm with a wry smile on her face. "You'll never guess where he is."

"Doing something not related to governing," Malcolm offered. "He is entitled to a little time of his own."

"I didn't know that." Sarcasm dripped from Jennifer's voice. The demands on the governor's time seemed never-ending to her. "Apparently, it is true. The governor is playing golf." Her voice rose at the end of the sentence. She couldn't contain her surprise.

"Golf? Who with?" Malcolm waved his hand at Jennifer. "That's not a real question. Of course, you don't know. Still, I wonder. The governor doesn't play golf for recreation. He must be meeting with someone. There is nothing in his appointment book?"

"Nothing."

"Who is he meeting at ten?"

"Russell Thompson."

"Right. Russell is supposed to bring him up to date on the hacking of our system. After last night, the focus of this meeting will change. Russell will be trying to beef up our servers. The governor doesn't know it yet, but he has a solution for Russell."

Russell Thompson headed the IT department for the state of Georgia. He had been working night and day trying to find the breach in the firewall that allowed the extortionists to use the state's computers at will. Malcolm wondered if there had been a breakthrough. With all the time he had been spending with the FBI, he was losing touch with what took place at the mansion.

Malcolm looked at his watch. "Well, I guess I have no choice. I'll have to wait. Call me when he gets in."

He started out the door, paused and turned back to

Jennifer. "What time did the governor go to the golf course? Did security say?"

"Daybreak. They saw him putting his clubs in the car. He was there before the course opened. Up with the sun."

"Thanks," Malcolm said as he turned to leave again.

The crack of dawn on this morning occurred within an hour or two of when Malcolm had last talked to the governor. Nothing had been mentioned of an early morning golf date or of meeting anyone. Was it a private meeting or had something come up that required immediate attention? The former was none of Malcolm's business; the latter might involve him.

A game first thing in the morning should only take a couple of hours to play. Nine holes would be pushing the governor's limit. Malcolm couldn't imagine it being stretched out to 18. He should have his answers very shortly.

In the meantime, he would work on a news release to take control of the lost production issue. The best bet was to encourage people to maintain their regular sleeping habits. People gained nothing staying up all night simply to watch an explosion as it happened. Wait until morning and catch it on the early news.

Good advice, even for himself. Malcolm knew the governor wouldn't follow it and neither would anyone else.

The east coast bombings were now up to 5:00 a.m. The west coast would begin getting into the wee hours of the morning. One a.m. would be the time of the next bomb out there. L.A. traffic was a nightmare at the best of times. If there wasn't a break in the case in the next day or two, the freeways would be a disaster.

As Malcolm walked the short distance to his office, the rumble of motorcycles grasped his attention. Two Harleys, red and blue lights flashing, drove by. The sun blinked off the windshield of a car pulling up in front of the mansion.

The governor's limo eased to a stop and discharged the man himself before anyone could make a move to open his door. Malcolm waited at the top of the steps.

"I see BurgerCircus is giving away coffee," the governor said in the way of greeting to the waiting Malcolm. "Bring me your weak; bring me your tired; bring me your sleep deprived; Ray Tutty will find a way to fleece them."

Malcolm laughed. "I don't think that's the image he's trying to project. Others will agree with you. This whole free coffee thing may backfire on him."

The governor looked at the folder in Malcolm's hand. "Is that the productivity report? What did you find out?"

"Come into my office. It's worse that we imagined. A lot worse."

The governor looked at this watch. "Have you got a summary page? I'm running late. The traffic is hell out there, even with a police escort."

Malcolm held up the folder but didn't open it. "I do, but I think traffic may be our top priority at the moment. We've got to control the message on this one. We must blame the extortionists for all this chaos. We want a message out on the next news cycle. As we speak the traffic lineups in California are probably grinding to a halt. As you said, traffic is still a bitch here in the east where the rush should have ended by now. Every one of those cars will have their radios on, and we want you to be telling them who is responsible for this mess."

The governor hesitated. He looked at his office door and then at Malcolm's. "Let's make this fast."

"Golf game went badly?" A wicked smirk occupied Malcolm's face. "Who beat you?"

"What?" The surprised response was genuine.

"You snuck out to the golf course this morning. There are no secrets here in the mansion. We know your every move. Was it government business or personal business?"

The governor gathered his wits. "How do you know it wasn't simple R&R? We've been working like dogs since this bombing thing started."

Malcolm let out a short, gruff bark. "This is Malcolm you're talking to. I'm going to go with it being personal. It's all right if you don't want to talk about it. You are entitled to some private time." Malcolm paused. "Not much, but some. We'll do our best to keep it quiet. Not everyone will think you should be out playing golf during this crisis." He winked at the governor and opened his office door.

A shrill tone sounded from the governor's pocket. He fished out his cellphone, took in the information on the small screen and shook his head.

"This is important. I've got to take it in my office."

Without any further explanation, he wheeled away and hustled down the hall, leaving Malcolm standing in the doorway with his handful of "priority" papers and a surprised look on his face.

◄36►

"LOOK AT THOSE goddamn stock prices. They're falling like shit from a seagull's ass."

Ray Tutty stormed around his office, glancing periodically at the computer screen. The action displayed showed BurgerCircus's latest transactions on the New York Stock Exchange. Barbara sat in front of the screen, her eyes glued to the events as they transpired.

"It started out with big block sales," she said. "Someone was trying to influence the market price. Now all kinds of small-time investors are jumping on the downward flowing slide. They have no idea what they're doing."

"No," Ray said. "The stockholders are listening to that clown we have as governor in this state. They're blaming us for what those extortionists are doing. When it levels out, buy as much as you can. We may as well make some gain from this mess."

A slight knock sounded on the door as Paul Johnson came into the room. "The free coffee is set up and running. I've arranged for ads on all the major networks." He looked at the dour expressions on the faces of his fellow executives. "What's up? Did somebody die?"

"You will when you check your portfolio." Ray indicated the computer screen.

Paul didn't even look. "We expected a dip in the prices. That's why we're giving the coffee away. Remember? It's nothing to worry about."

"I think someone is manipulating the market," Barbara said. She held her hand out, palm up towards her computer screen. "Have a look at this history of the morning sales."

Paul walked across the room and put a hand on Barbara's shoulder as he leaned in to look where she indicated. Slowly, she scrolled the figures down the screen. He watched for a while, then gave a squeeze with his hand.

"You're the expert, and it looks like you're right." He straightened up. "I'd have to study them in a little more depth to come to any conclusions. Anyway, now that we've taken action, they should rebound. It's a good time to buy."

"Whoa! What's this?"

Both men looked at where Barbara was pointing. "Someone is taking your advice. They're gobbling up the stocks faster than they can be listed. We're going to have to act fast if we want to get in on this."

Ray crowded Barbara from the screen. "Can we tell who the hell is buying?" He tapped some keys on the computer's pad. A new row of information filled the screen. "It looks like it's coming from overseas. Asia?"

Barbara crowded back. "Looks like it. Some small exchange over there. Do you believe me now?"

"Bastards. Who's doing this to us?" Ray pounded a fist on the desk.

Paul stood back and walked over to the coffee machine, poured himself a brew and smiled. "Relax, Ray. Nobody's done anything to us. We never sold anything. We never lost anything. In fact, when this little blip makes the news, we'll be able to drop our ads for the free coffee. It will be on all the news channels. Whoever did this did us a favour."

Ray gave Paul a scowl that would melt paint on a battleship. "There's a goddamn principle involved here. Someone is pissing in our backyard."

"And saving us money. To be honest, Ray, it's not really news. It's just the normal daily flow of the exchange. I'll have the PR department issue a statement that there is nothing to be concerned about. I'll make sure somebody out there notices this market action. Make sure they make the connection to the free coffee offer we've made. With luck, it'll get picked up by the big networks. We can't buy advertising like this." Paul held up his coffee cup towards Barbara. "Want a refill? It's free."

She smiled but declined. Her attention remained locked on the scrolling figures in front of her.

Paul turned towards Ray and held out his cup. "Ray?"

"Listen, bub." Ray was not prepared to be as blasé about this attack as Paul. "Somebody is attacking our company. We have to fight back."

Paul's eyes darkened. "Pick your battles, Ray. Right now, our concern is with the extortionists. For some reason, they have targeted us. We want to expend our energies on that fight, not with someone playing millionaire games on the stock market. We are under attack, but it's not on the stock market. It's right at the heart of our business. These clowns are trying to ruin our reputation and take down our company in the process. Malcolm Truex said it before, and I'm beginning to agree with him, Ray. The attacks are personal. You are the target here."

Paul hesitated and took a sip of his coffee. He took a step towards his boss. "If you go down, BurgerCircus goes down with you. Let's keep focused on what's really important here. It's not someone playing games on the stock market, and it's not Governor Weston. It's the goddamn extortionists who have picked you out to be the fall guy in all this."

Paul turned away from Ray and walked towards the window. His face and neck had become infused with blood during his little tirade. He took a few calming breaths before looking back at Ray.

"That's how I see it anyway."

Ray raised a finger and shook it towards Paul. His

mouth opened, but no words came out. Slowly the hand dropped to his side. His shoulders drooped a little.

"Yeah, you might be right. What's the latest on that front?"

"Same old, same old." Paul was back to his normal self. "We saw the school blow up in Michigan earlier today. The FBI have made no news releases. It seems to me that with each bombing, they are getting more and more secretive."

An abrupt laughing grunt emitted from Ray. He shook his head. "They don't want to tell the world they haven't a clue what is happening. They are no closer to solving this thing than they were on day one."

"I'm not so sure of that," Paul said. "They've got a lot of resources locked into this search. I think they realized that news releases were keeping the extortionists as up-to-date as the citizens of the country. Back on day one, they thought it would be a quick resolution. Now, I think they are in it for the long haul and are playing their cards very tightly to their chests. Even Malcolm is not as forthcoming as he once was."

"Believe that if you want to, Paul. I think they're stymied. As for Malcolm, I think he's trying an end run to get his boy elected as president. God help the country if he pulls that off." Ray gave a dismissive wave of his hand. "Let's find out who is making money on our stocks. There is nothing we can do on the extortion front."

He turned to Barbara. "Any leads? I know you've been looking."

Barbara looked up from her computer. She still wore the look of deep concentration. "Whoever did it covered their tracks well, but I don't think it was a deliberate attack. I think someone saw an opportunity to make a quick buck. Zipped into the market; encouraged the prices to drop; scooped up the bargains and got out. Most likely they spent the early morning hours glued to their TV just like half the country did. Rightly predicted the governor's statements would draw some reaction from the nervous nellies who have no business being in the stock market anyway and were ready at the sound of the opening bell. In, out, richer."

"Bastards. If they own that many shares, why don't we know about them?"

Barbara shrugged. "Could be some independent financial advisor who runs his trust fund with clients' money backing it. It's capitalism, Ray. The American way."

◄37►

WHEN MALCOLM STEPPED into his office, Margaret was talking on the phone. She smiled and held up a hand to stay his progress.

"One moment," she said to her caller, "I think he is somewhere in the mansion. I'll see if I can track him down." She put the call on hold.

In answer to Malcolm's raised eyebrows, she said: "Joe Fisher. Claims you have been trying to get hold of him and told him it was urgent."

Relief flooded onto Malcolm's face. "Thank God, I thought he was never going to reply. Get his number and tell him I'll call back in less than two minutes."

Margaret looked surprised, then shrugged. She took the phone off hold and passed on the message. Quickly she scribbled down a number and passed it to Malcolm, a look of confusion replacing her look of surprise. No explanation seemed to be forthcoming.

"I'm not even going to ask," she said.

"Good," Malcolm said. He took the paper, turned and left the office, went down the stairs and out onto the mansion lawn. He took a quick look up the driveway to the garage area where he could see Robert topping up his car with gas. He pulled out his cellphone and pushed a speed call button. In seconds, Robert pulled up beside him.

"Can you find me a pay phone, right away?"

Robert looked at the phone in Malcolm's hand, then at the one in the car console, then blankly out into the community. "Now that could be a challenge. I think there's a convenience store down the road about a mile that still has one."

Malcolm jumped in. "As fast as you can. There's an extra peach cruller in it for you if you can do it in less than two minutes."

"Joe Fisher, you old corn dog. Don't you ever return phone calls?" Malcolm seemed exuberant to be talking to the man.

"Just got back from hunting alligators back in the swamp land," Joe said. "Don't take a phone with me when I'm hunting alligators. Might startle a gator if it rings at the wrong moment."

"Right," Malcolm said with a laugh. "Don't tell me where you were. Some private job somewhere?"

"Huntin' gators" Joe deadpanned. "That's all I can tell ya."

"We've got some gators up here in Georgia that are causing us some problems."

"Yes, you have. I've been following it on the news. You suspect someone on your staff."

The statement caught Malcolm off guard. "My staff? No. I trust them all."

"So you say, but you're calling me from a Georgia Bell pay phone. You didn't tell your secretary where you were going. She probably thinks you're in the governor's office."

Malcolm was astounded at that theory. "Why do you say that?"

Joe paused for a few seconds before answering. "Well." He drew out the word. "You told her you would call me back in less than two minutes which would hardly give you time to leave the building. It took nearly five." Another pause. "And I'm sure there are still lots of phones in the governor's mansion you could be using. What's up exactly?"

Malcolm marvelled at Joe's logic.

Joe Fisher was a long-time friend of Malcolm's who was in Malcolm's opinion one of the best IT people in the world. A graduate of MIT where he intimidated as many professors as he dazzled with his command of computer skills, he now ran his own company and the world was his client base.

"We appear to have been hacked. You've seen those bombers using our website at will until they crashed the system last night."

"Nope. No one hacked you." The voice left no room for argument.

"Of course they did. How else are they using our servers?"

"Remember when you installed this system? You hired me to check it out. It was good, but there were two holes that allowed others to sneak in the back door. I installed fixes for both of them, and after that it was solid. I still check it every so often. Part of the service you bought from me."

Malcolm expressed surprise at that bit of information. "You do? Well someone must be better than you because someone is getting into our system."

"You don't believe that."

"Why don't I? There's always someone better coming along."

"You're calling me from a pay phone off-site from the mansion. There may be someone as good come along, but there is no one better. Your system is secure. The attacks are an inside job, and in your heart, you know that."

Now it was Malcolm's time to be silent. Joe let the silence stretch out. He had said his piece.

"OK," Malcolm finally said. "Maybe you're right. We've got to find that person. What time can you be here today?"

"Get with the times, Malcolm. I don't have to go up there. Why do you think I have a condo on the beach here in Florida? I love the weather. I've set myself up a little lab where I'm working on advanced remote-control technology. I'm living the good life. I'll have a look at your system and let you know what I find out."

"I thought you said no one could hack our system?"

"I said I closed all the back doors. I'm still able to walk in the front door. You made me a privileged guest the last time around. I still have my key."

"Jesus, Joe." The alarm was evident in Malcolm's voice. "You shouldn't have access to our computers. There is all kinds of classified information on them."

Joe laughed. "Malcolm, Malcolm, Malcolm. I think I have all the security clearances I need. Check with the president." He laughed again. "Don't bother. He wouldn't know. It's above his clearance rating. Check with the men who work for him."

"Never mind." Malcolm reminded himself whom he was talking to. "Let me know what you find out. Yesterday would not have been soon enough. The reputation of our country is at stake here, Joe. These extortionists have to be shut down."

Malcolm paused. "And Joe. Don't get caught. Only you and I know you're in there." Another pause. "And I guess I'd better tell the governor."

◄38►

"JOE FISHER? MALCOLM are you out of you ever-loving mind? We can't have unauthorized people freely roaming around our computer system."

This conversation was proceeding along expected lines. Malcolm knew how much the governor resented relinquishing any control to outsiders. He walked over to the coffee maker in the governor's office and slowly made himself a cup of coffee. He looked at the governor, held up his cup. "Want one?"

"Don't play games with me, Malcolm. You've overstepped your boundaries on this one. Joe Fisher may be a friend of yours, and he may be good with computers, but you can't give him free rein with our system."

Malcolm scoffed. "May be good? Governor, he is the best there is. Our guys, the FBI's guys, even you have been trying to track down this leak for almost a week. It's time to find these bastards. You're right about one thing. We can't have unauthorized people roaming freely throughout our system. Joe says no one can hack us. That leaves only one other option. The invasion is an inside job."

"No. I don't believe that."

Malcolm walked back to the governor's desk and sat in one of the two leather-covered chairs. "I hired all of those guys in IT. None of them is involved; I'll stake my reputation on it. It has to be someone else in the mansion, someone with enough clearance to get into the deeper layers of our security software."

He brought the coffee cup to his lips, took a sip and

leaned back. "Joe will find that person. You can depend on it."

Malcolm's features seemed to darken. He leaned forward again. "This is between you and me, Governor. No one else in the mansion knows. No one."

The governor was taken aback by the vehemence in Malcolm's voice. The veins in his forehead stood out. "I think that decision is mine, Malcolm." He strained to keep his voice controlled. "I am still in charge around here."

"No, Governor. These attacks are not about you. Our country is under attack by a handful of extortionists. The greater good is at stake here." Malcolm's voice showed no signs of backing down. "We must let Joe do his work his way with no interference. Don't worry. Joe is a patriot. Country comes first with him."

Peter Weston's face took on an unhealthy, reddish hue. The cords stood out on his neck. "Well, he at least reports to me."

Malcolm shook his head. "No, Governor. He reports to me. I report to Tom Burke if I think it is relevant. There is no room for any extra links in this chain."

The governor jumped to his feet, sending his chair slamming back into the window behind him. He leaned towards Malcolm, his whole body shaking. "Dammit, Malcolm. There's a lot more riding on this than a bunch of terrorists. Solving this could be my path to the White House."

The words hung in the air. Malcolm's eyes became saucers as the shock of the declaration registered in his mind. The governor grabbed his chair and slumped back into it. His whole body became slack.

"That didn't come out right, Malcolm. You know that's not what I meant." He fell silent, searching for words. Then they started tumbling out.

"Of course, we have to catch these guys. We both

understand that. You know I'm devoting the full resources of the state to this project. I've refused you nothing up to this point." He shrugged and held up his hands in a resigned motion. "But if we can somehow spin this to our advantage without sacrificing any of our efforts, why not? Why wait another four years? We sure as hell don't want another four years of that clown who's in office now. What is the other party offering? No one." The governor became animated again. "The time is ripe for an Indepentent president. This is our chance, Malcolm. We both want it."

Malcolm got up and did a slow lap around the office, stopping to look out the window at the palatial grounds surrounding the building. He turned his gaze on the man behind the desk.

"Peter, I'm aghast," he said, using the governor's given name for the first time in months. "Don't you understand what is at stake here? These bombings aren't about us. They aren't about what we want. They are about a criminal organization trying to undermine our way of life. This is bigger than politics."

The governor held Malcolm's eyes for several seconds, saying nothing. He steepled his fingers and looked off into nothingness before slowly speaking. "Everything is about politics, Malcolm. You know that."

His eyes returned to Malcolm's. "We both know that it's all about timing. Maybe you're right. Maybe now is not the time. I don't know what I was thinking."

He took some sheets of paper lying on his desk; picked them up and jogged them into a neat pile which he set aside. "You had something important to talk to me about when I first came in. What was it?"

"No, Governor. We have to talk about this. We have to both be on the same page."

Malcolm sat down again. "I understand your desire to move to the next level. There's so much we could do from the Oval Office. Our country has so much potential. We could be the team that forces it to reach that destiny." He appeared to be in deep thought. "But this is not the time. The elections are only two months away, and quite frankly, we don't have the money to launch a campaign. Running for president can't be some half-assed effort, Governor. Running for president is the big time."

The spark of excitement returned to the governor's eye. "What if I could get the financial backing? I know some people."

Malcolm raised his eyebrows. "You know people that I don't know? Since when?"

"I know people, Malcolm."

"OK, you know people. I'll concede that point." Malcolm leaned forward in his chair. "That's not the way we do things. All our money for the gubernatorial races came from the grassroots. There were no major donations from anyone, none from big business, none from unions. We weren't beholden to anybody but the people of this state." He settled back into his chair, more relaxed. "That allowed us to make decisions that were good for the people, good for the economy, good for the state. No one had any sway or control over our method of governing. And it worked."

"It worked damn well," the governor agreed. "But, Malcolm, this is the big leagues. You said it yourself. It will cost millions just to run a low-key campaign. I can get those millions, but it has to be now."

Malcolm studied the governor's face for a few beats to see if anything more was forthcoming. The governor held his stare.

"Now? Why now, Governor? Why not in four years when we are prepared and have raised enough money?"

"Because these school bombings are giving us the national exposure we need. You are going to solve this thing. I've given you free rein to chase down these criminals. I know you, Malcolm. You will succeed, and when you do, when we do, the White House will be ours for the taking. You've said it yourself. There is so much good we could do from there. We have to cash in on this opportunity." He pounded his desk with his fist. "Now is our time."

The governor's eyes were flashing. Sweat beaded across his forehead. Malcolm could see the man's chest rising and falling as his heart rate accelerated.

"Governor, calm down. This is too important a decision to make without more thought. Let me think about it for a couple of days."

There was no doubt in Malcolm's mind what his decision would be. He needed a few days to figure out how to slow down Paul Weston. Running for president on the back of destroyed schools would be a career-ending move.

"OK, you think about it. We can't announce until we catch those bastards anyway. How close are we to that and what are we going to do about our servers? There's no way we can increase their capacity before tonight."

"Tom Burke and I have worked out a solution for the computers. The feds are going to boost our power." After the early morning server failure before the explosion in Michigan, Malcolm and Tom had brainstormed how to keep control of the bomber's computer connection. They had followed the KISS option. Keep It Simple, Stupid. It was Malcolm's job to put their solution into action.

"Jesus, Malcolm. First, you give Joe Fisher full run of our system; now you're letting the feds take us over. We can't do that."

Malcolm gave the governor a dismissive wave. "They're not taking over. They're going to handle our overflow. Contact Russell in IT and tell him I have a project for him. What I'm proposing should be a decision made by only you."

The governor gave a sardonic laugh. "Please, let me in on my decision. I don't want to look like a fool when he starts asking questions."

"You won't look like a fool. It's basic computer programming. We're going to use a password trap to transfer people to the federal site. The feds will be mirroring our site."

"A password trap? Explain."

"We're going to instigate a password to get onto our site. We'll tell people it's part of our new security system brought on by the extortionists. The password will be "welcome." The word will be on the screen. The first time they type it in, it will fail, or at least they will think it failed. They will assume they made a mistake. The second time it will transfer them from our servers to the federal servers thus reducing the load on us."

The governor shook his head. "I don't like this, Malcolm. We're giving up too much power to the feds."

"No, we're not. This system will only be in effect for a couple of hours around the expected time of the next bombing. They're not getting deep into our system anyway. They'll just be sitting on the surface watching a streamed video. It will work, Governor, and it leaves us as the ones in contact with the extortionists. That's what you want, isn't it?"

Reluctantly the governor nodded his head. "Most definitely, but you could have given me a little notice."

Now Malcolm laughed a deep-throated chuckle. "I tried to, Governor. First thing when I saw you this morning. You left me standing in the hall, hat in hand. Remember?"

The governor smiled back. "Yeah, I did. It was important."

"I would hope so." Malcolm picked up a blue folder from the chair. "Here, Governor. The figures about lost productivity. They're scary. We'll want to discuss this as soon as possible. It's important to make a follow-up statement to the press outlining some of the things our citizens can do to fight off this problem."

"You mean like going to bed and getting up at their normal time?"

"That's the crux of your message. It's all there. You want to be president? Convince everyone to do this for their country." Malcolm gave him a thumbs-up. "It's that simple."

◀39▶

MARGARET LOOKED UP as Malcolm re-entered his office.

"Here," she said and offered Malcolm the phone she had been holding to her ear. "Tom Burke, he says it's urgent."

A frown crossed Malcolm's face. The morning kept getting worse by the minute. "What now, Tom?"

As Malcolm listened, his features took on a slackness that brought a concerned look to Margaret's face. Malcolm only listened, giving Margaret no clue to what had happened now.

Finally, he said "OK, email me the website. I'll have a quick look, and then I'll head for your office. The governor should know about this as well. He's preparing to make a statement to the press anyway. He may as well include some comment on this and appeal for common sense to prevail."

He listened for a few more seconds, nodding his head in agreement to whatever Tom was telling him. Then he passed the phone back to Margaret. "There's a Facebook page out there encouraging everyone to get together and search schools in their districts. They recommend having someone on each team with a knowledge of bombs, but if you can't do that, they've posted a link to a website that tells you everything you need to know about defusing an explosive. How many people are going to die now?"

Before Margaret could respond, he pushed open the door to his office, sat at his desk and woke up his computer. Margaret could only stare through the open door. The foolishness of the plan appeared to leave her dumbfounded.

Malcolm looked up from his screen, slowly shaking his head in disbelief. "Get the governor in here right away. He has to see this."

"You're ordering him to come to your office?" Margaret looked uncertain. "I'm just making sure that's what you mean."

"Ask him to come in here right away. Word it any way you want, but get him in here. He has to see this crazy site." His attention had left Margaret and returned to his computer. She could see him scrolling down the page of comments, the disbelief becoming more evident with each posting he read.

"What's happened? Another explosion?" the governor asked as he burst into Malcolm's office. Margaret's request had brought him on the run. At first, he had been stunned when he answered his phone and heard her say "Governor, get your ass up here as fast as you can." But the demand left no room for doubt that something important had happened. He complied without question.

Malcolm continued studying the screen. "I can't believe the activity on this page. It's been up less than half-an-hour, and there are already hundreds of people signed in. Apparently, it started with an item on YouTube that has gone viral and now every nut case in the country is encouraging their neighbours to go search their own schools."

He turned the computer monitor so the governor could read the comments.

"Look at this one," Malcolm said. "'Which wire do we cut? The red one or the blue one? I want to get this straight before I find a bomb.' These people are bonkers. If you think the colour of the wire is important, you shouldn't be within a mile of a bomb. We've got to put a stop to this."

The governor plunked down into one of Malcolm's guest chairs, visibly shaken by what he was seeing.

"Oh my God," he said. "If they do this, people will die. They can't be allowed to do this."

He pulled his chair closer to Malcolm's computer, scanning the comments on the screen. "Are there any negative comments? Is anybody out there showing any signs of reason?"

Malcolm kept scrolling. "Not on this page. The frustration of seeing no positive results from the authorities has people scared. They want action, any action. We have to put a stop to this."

The governor sat back in his chair. Beads of sweat formed on his forehead. He took a white handkerchief from his pocket and wiped them away. "How many bombs do you think are still out there? We've had, what, five so far. I would think that at most there would only be five more. We can only hope they are in schools where no fools are clamouring around searching."

Malcolm gave the governor a penetrating look. "Five more? How did you come to that conclusion?"

"School starts in five more days. Surely they won't be setting off bombs when the kids are back in the classroom. That doesn't follow their *modus operandi* to date. They seem to be taking special care that no one gets hurt."

Malcolm shook his head. "You think if we wait them out for another week, they will go away. I don't think that's going to happen, Governor. I think as we get closer to when school starts, they are going to step up their destruction. I see people dying in the very near future. Maybe even kids.

"I can see some of these fools," he indicated his computer screen, "dying if they come across a live bomb. Stopping these searches has to be our number one priority. We can't let citizens run amok throughout our schools. We must squelch this plan right now." He hesitated for a few seconds. "But, we don't want to put it in exactly those words."

The governor leaned back in his chair and rubbed his forehead. "I don't care what words you put it in; we have to get the message to these people. They must not be searching the schools on their own. Defusing bombs is a specialized trade. There is absolutely no room for amateurs in this field."

Malcolm's fingers pounded away at the keyboard. "This probably won't do any good, but I've got to try to insert an element of common sense into this hoopla. People have seen too many bombs disarmed on TV. They think it's easy.

"I'm going to link it to an IED disarming gone bad from Afghanistan. I'll use a British site. We don't need any of our people seeing their sons blown to bits on the Internet."

The governor shook his head. "You don't think they have computers in England? Your link will go viral around the world."

Malcolm didn't hesitate. "They may have computers, but they don't have a bunch of whackos blowing up schools. We have to nip this thing in the bud, Governor. Lives are at stake. Besides, I'm getting this link from the Internet. It's not new material."

With a dramatic flair, he hit the enter key. "There. Done."

He swung the monitor towards the governor. "What do you think?"

The governor leaned in and chuckled.

"What's so funny? You didn't even have time to read my message."

Malcolm looked offended.

"It wasn't your message; it was the response to it." The governor swung the monitor back to Malcolm.

"Dont lissen to this goverment hack. hes just tryin to scare u." Malcolm shook his head.

"See what we're up against. That's four years of the president's educational reform," the governor said. "God save us."

Malcolm pushed back his chair and got up. "I've got to get over to FBI headquarters and talk to Tom. We have to take some more definite action on this."

He shut down his computer and headed for the door before stopping and looking back at the governor. "You don't need me to write you something about how stupid this plan is. Lead off your statement to the press with a plea for sanity. The rest of your statement about productivity is in your inbox. Try and stay on script."

With that, Malcolm turned and rushed from the office.

Within fifteen minutes, Malcolm was sitting in the office of Tom Burke.

"Shutting the site down will do no good," Tom said. "Another one will simply pop up to take its place. What we have to do is take over the site with a more common sense approach."

He read over Malcolm's comment and followed the link to the bomb defusing gone awry. He nodded his head, "Yeah, we need more stuff like this." He laughed as he read the other comments following Malcolm's. "But not from the likes of you. It's the government's lack of action these people are protesting. We need real bomb demolition experts to comment on this site. Someone whose words will carry weight."

"Hey, I served my hitch in the military," Malcolm said. "But you're right. Contact the army. They can give us a list of names."

"They can, but will they? They don't hand out those lists willy-nilly."

Malcolm's eyes darkened. "This is not willy-nilly. National security is at stake here. Find someone who can pull the right strings. Get the Office of Homeland Security involved. They don't seem to have any restrictions on them."

Tom picked up the phone, talked briefly to one of his fellow FBI members and turned back to Malcolm. "There, that's taken care of. Now, what about the big picture? What's our next line of action?"

Malcolm walked over to the window and looked out at downtown Atlanta. "The governor raised an interesting point while we were discussing this. What happens when school starts in five days time? Will the bombings continue?"

"Five days?" Tom scoffed. "We'll have them long before that."

Malcolm stared at his friend. "We said that four days ago. Are we any closer?"

"We've got one of them in cold storage in the morgue in Nevada. That's progress."

Malcolm gave a harsh grunt. "It might have been if we had caught him. He died on his own, remember. He was a gift." A short pause. "A gift that hardly slowed them down.

"We have to step up the pace. We have to get more aggressive."

Tom held up his hands in surrender. "No arguments here. What do you have in mind?"

◀40▶

"GOVERNOR, MARK SPITZ, Atlanta Guardian. Are you prohibiting people from entering and searching our schools?"

The governor gave a patronizing smile to the assembled group of reporters. "What I'm trying to do, Mark, is ask that common sense prevails. So far, these lunatics have used dynamite, C4, fertilizer and diesel bombs. Each requires a different expertise, and all are extremely dangerous. Only qualified and highly trained personnel should be attempting to defuse them."

"But, Governor, these people are only suggesting they search the schools. If they find something, they will call in the experts."

"That's not entirely true, Mark. The Facebook page is sending people to websites that purportedly tell you how to defuse a bomb. Also, some of these bombs are touch sensitive. All someone has to do to detonate them is simply touch them. The risks far outweigh the advantages of having untrained people roaming through these buildings."

Another hand shot up. "Gerald Savoy, Fox News. School opens in less than a week, Governor. Are there plans to delay the opening if you don't catch these terrorists by then?"

The governor studied the new questioner before answering. "We are very close to wrapping up this operation, Gerald. The opening of school should not be a matter of concern."

Hands shot up all over the room. Questions came in

rapid fire without waiting for any acknowledgment.

"What new information do you have?"

"Are you saying arrests are imminent?"

"Does anyone know about this but you, Governor?"

The room fell deathly silent. All eyes turned to the questioner in the back of the room. The governor's face turned bright red.

"What are you implying with that question?" he asked.

"Rod Sanderson, New York Daily News. We had a school blow up in our downtown area the other night. Are you saying the authorities had information that could have prevented that from happening? Are you sacrificing schools while you build a case?"

Like a flock of birds frolicking in the air, all heads turned as one towards the front of the room.

The governor smiled. *New York Daily News*, he thought, *now we're cooking.* He resumed his serious stance. "I'm saying nothing of the sort. I'm saying we have a new lead that we believe will bring us to these criminals in a rapid manner. I can't say any more on that topic at this point. I've probably said too much already."

He smiled. "But the people have a right to know that we are making progress. We are all in this together, and those in charge can't be seen to be keeping secrets. At the same time, we can't jeopardize our intense search efforts with loose talk."

Sanderson held up his hand once more. "A supplementary question, if I may."

The other reporters quieted down and looked at him. They were enjoying seeing the governor silenced at his own press conference.

Sanderson continued. "You say arrests are imminent. And yet you, a mere governor of a small insignificant state, seem to be the only one in possession of this information?"

The governor bristled at the charge. "Georgia is leading

the way in this investigation. We, as you know, were the first to have a school destroyed and have thrown all our resources into bringing these bombers to justice."

Sanderson held his position on the floor. His voice drowned out the other questioners. "Governor, on the subject of schools. Is it true the school in Alexandra was scheduled for demolition next year?

"I have information that a consolidated high school in the neighbouring town will replace it. My sources say the residents of Alexandra are up in arms about this. Didn't the bombers do you a favour by blowing up this school?"

Peter Weston's face turned a brilliant red. He looked over at his press secretary. She shrugged her shoulders. "Any destruction of a school is unacceptable. As for your charge, I am not in a position to answer that at this point. I will look into it and get back to you."

"It's a straightforward question," Sanderson persisted. "Was the school scheduled for demolition?"

The governor smiled at the smirking reporter. "Mr. Sanderson, I don't know how they do things in New York, but in Georgia, if we don't know the answer to a question, we don't try to shovel a load of bullshit on the questioner. We admit we don't know the answer and move on."

"Somebody up there with you must have a BlackBerry. Can't they check it out?"

"Relocation of schools is more complex than that. I will get back to you with an answer if you are interested. I do know some people are looking forward to getting a new, modern school for their children."

He held up his hand, indicating he was through taking questions. "Let me once more plead with the people of the nation to go back to your daily routines and get the productivity of our country back in gear again. Unfortunately for the people, the president is more worried about being re-elected than he is about this threat facing our nation, and let there be no mistake, this drop in productivity is a real threat. He has shown no real signs of leadership. He is letting our economic position in the world take a beating and is doing nothing to prevent it."

"Perhaps you should seek the office yourself," Rod offered.

The governor smiled. "President? Thank you, Rod. I couldn't do any worse."

The door to Tom Burke's office popped open. Kevin Desmond, the agency's second-in-command in Atlanta, looked at Malcolm. "I thought I'd find you here. You've let the monkey get separated from the organ grinder again."

Malcolm turned towards the agent. "What are you rambling on about now?"

Kevin had questioned Malcolm's participation in the investigation on a few earlier occasions. Their relationship could hardly be described as cordial.

"We have a source at the governor's mansion. He told us the governor is suggesting that he has new information about the case and an arrest is imminent. Care to share?"

Malcolm looked at the intruding agent. "I'm sorry, Kevin, I'm at a loss here. What specifically did the governor say and to whom?"

"He's holding a press conference and told the assembled reporters that the case would be wrapped up long before school starts in five days. You can see the press conference broadcast on CSPAN. I repeat. Care to share?"

Malcolm slowly shook his head. "I have no idea what you're talking about. I would have to hear the governor's words in context. He's a very smart man. We all know that, but he is a politician and politicians play with words. For what it's worth, your boss told me the same thing not five minutes ago."

Tom studied Malcolm before commenting. "What I say to

you and what the governor says to the press can hardly be compared. Are you sure this is just political boasting, Malcolm? These bombers are broadcasting through your computers, and we know you have brought in an outside expert to help track them down."

Shock registered on Malcolm's face. "What outside expert?" he finally got out.

"Come on, Malcolm, we're the FBI. You can't keep secrets from us. Besides, you told me you were bringing someone in, remember?"

Malcolm held up his hands in surrender. "You're right. We are using every resource available to us to crack this case. We have to find out how they are hacking our system. It's no secret."

"OK." Tom allowed a smile to creep onto his face. "What has this expert found out and why does the governor know about it before us? We are a team, right?"

"Honestly, Tom. I have no idea what Kevin is talking about. The computer expert deals only with me. The governor has no contact with him. We don't know where the leak is so the fewer people who know about our investigation, the better. Right now, those who need to know number two."

Malcolm rubbed the side of his face feeling the stubble that seemed to be there all the time now. "If you found out about him already and didn't find anything about the extortionists, that scares me. He is supposed to be the best. I thought he could walk around in any system without being discovered."

Tom put a reassuring hand on Malcolm's knee. "He's the very best. He came to us. I guess he figures he can trust me." He shrugged. "He wanted access to our computers once he discovered we were already running in parallel. Not that he couldn't simply have come in without telling us. However, getting caught hacking the FBI's computers can get you some serious jail time. Only Kevin and I know about him here. We are a team and share this kind of information." He gave Malcolm a meaningful look. "So he hasn't found anything that you know about?"

"Nothing." Malcolm got up. "I've got to talk to the governor. See what he is up to. I'll be in touch."

"One more thing, Malcolm," Kevin added. "One of the reporters suggested the governor should run for president in the November election. The governor seemed to like the idea. Our man thinks the question may have been a plant. Any comment?"

Malcolm blanched. "That's not going to happen."

With that, Malcolm grabbed his briefcase and headed for the door wondering what Peter Weston was up to now. As he reached for the door knob, his cellphone chimed with a familiar ring. He hesitated slightly and then snatched the phone from his pocket.

"What is it, Governor?" he asked with slightly more hostility that he had planned.

"I'm in, Malcolm. I've locked on to the bastards. Get over here right away." There was a hesitation before he continued. "Don't say a word to anyone just yet. We have to work a few details out before we go public."

Before Malcolm could respond, the line went dead. Malcolm looked at the two agents who were searching his eyes for some clue about what the governor might have said.

He hesitated. "I've got to go. "I'll be in touch."

◀41▶

PETER WESTON STOOD at the top of the mansion's stairway waiting for Malcolm to crawl out of the taxi.

"I got here as quickly as I could," Malcolm said as he ran up the steps two at a time. "What have you found? Do you have access to the extortionist's computer?"

"Better. I can see every keystroke, every movement of its mouse in real time. We're getting their email messages before they even send them."

The governor's eyes sparkled. Malcolm hadn't seen him this excited since the night they won their first gubernatorial election. "How long have you known this?"

The question took some of the smile from the governor's face. "I found out just before I was to have the press conference. I thought I had locked on and lost the connection again just like every other night." The sparkle amped up again. "That wasn't the case. I had locked on; the keystroke capture program wasn't showing up on my screen. It was an easy fix, and the data started flowing in.

"My first thought was to call you, but the press were waiting. I didn't think fifteen minutes would make any difference. I wanted to check it out before I said anything."

"But you announced it during the press conference." Malcolm couldn't keep the rebuke from his voice.

The governor looked shocked. "My mind was not really on what I was saying to those reporters, but I'm sure I didn't say anything like that. The possibilities of what we could do next were flowing through my mind. What do you think I said?"

"You said arrests were imminent."

The governor shook his head. "I don't think I said that, Malcolm. A reporter from New York asked me if arrests were imminent. I didn't say they were. I simply implied we were making progress." He smiled slightly. "Check the transcript. You know how these press guys can twist the truth."

Malcolm reluctantly agreed with that statement. His job was to make sure the true message got delivered and not some reporter's translation. Perhaps "true message" was a slight exaggeration. His job was to make sure the government's message got delivered. Sometimes truth lurked quite a ways in the background.

"OK, Governor. Let's not quibble over words. Show me."

The two men went into the governor's office, carefully closing the door behind them. The governor sat at his desk; his laptop was already fired up. Malcolm leaned in to have a closer look. An unfamiliar desktop lit up the screen.

"I called you as soon as I realized I had something, but I haven't had a chance to examine what we've got exactly. We see their desktop. Nobody seems to be using it at the moment, but while I was waiting for you, someone was writing an email. I could see every keystroke. I didn't want to do anything until you got here. We don't want to fuck this up."

Malcolm studied the screen. "Can we download the contents of the computer?" Excitement raised the pitch of his voice slightly. This was the break they had been hoping for since the school in Alexandra went up before their eyes. "Do you know where they are?" He reached for the keyboard.

"No!" the governor said. "Don't touch anything. We can control their keyboard, but they will see the mouse moving. We don't want to tip them off. Let me study this for a bit and then we should be able to do anything we want as long as they are not sitting at their keyboard."

Malcolm stood up straight and stroked his chin. "The first thing we want to do is turn on the computer's camera and send the image to one of our computers. That way we will know when it is unattended."

"Good idea. At a quick glance, this seems to be one of the latest and greatest computers on the market. It has all the bells and whistles. Let's make sure we know what operating system they are using and what features come with it. Then we can start turning them to our advantage."

Malcolm started pacing around the room. He stopped at the coffee machine, reached for a cup and then moved on without making anything. "I understand the need for caution, but another school is going to go sky high in a few hours. We have to find out where in time to get our people in to disable the bomb. The next important thing is to find out who and where they are. We don't want to arrest them until we know where the next bomb is."

"Our goal is to catch the bastards," the governor said. "We can worry about the other bombs once we have them in custody."

"No," Malcolm said. "It's not that simple. As long as they have armed bombs out there, they are in the driver's seat. They can use that knowledge as a bargaining chip. We want to hold all the chips ourselves."

He returned to the coffee machine. This time he made a cup. He made an offering gesture towards the governor. He shook his head and held up a cup of his own.

"This next bomb is the crucial one," Malcolm continued. "Time is not on our side with it. Hopefully, when we get into the guts of their machine, we will gather all the information we need about the others."

He paused and looked at the governor. "Did I tell you what a fantastic job you did? No, I didn't. Governor, the nation owes you a great debt of gratitude."

Peter Weston shook his head. "Not yet, they don't.

Maybe once we have these clowns behind bars, someone might think that." He raised his cup towards Malcolm. "I'm not doing this for the adulation I might receive, but thanks for saying that anyway. Coming from you, that means a lot."

Malcolm raised his mug in a return gesture. "Who are we going to bring in to help us with this? I should call Tom and get the FBI experts working on it. Did you call Russell Thompson? Our IT department is as good as any in the country."

"Slow down, Malcolm. I've called you. We still don't know how they are hacking our system. We still don't know all the players yet. We can't risk tipping anyone off. For now, we are going to keep this between ourselves."

Malcolm looked aghast. "I've got to inform Tom. The FBI has to be brought up to date."

"Not yet, Malcolm. We have these guys over a barrel as long as they don't know what we're up to. I'm not going to jeopardize this advantage. Only you and I know what we've got until we know for sure who they are. I know my laptop is clean. We can't be sure of any others, including the FBI's. When we find the bombs and are ready to make arrests, we call in the cavalry. Not one minute before that."

Malcolm started to protest. The governor held up his hands. "It's not the people I'm concerned about, Malcolm. It's their computer system. Theirs is not any more secure than the state's, and they've hacked us. So I repeat, not one minute before we need to tell them."

A look of resignation filled Malcolm's features as he faced this conundrum. "You're wrong, Governor. But, at the same time, what you say makes sense. We'll do it your way for now. Once we get the information we're after, I call Tom. Agreed?"

"I wouldn't have it any other way." The governor's television smile lit up his face.

◀42▶

WHEN MALCOLM RETURNED to his office, Margaret held up a stack of phone messages. "Tom Burke wants you to phone him. It must be important; he keeps calling. But he didn't want me to interrupt your meeting with the governor."

Malcolm reached out and took the handful of messages. "I bet he does. Thanks, I'll take care of it."

"Should I get him on the line?"

Malcolm shook his head. "Not yet." He had to decide how much information to pass on to the FBI and in what form. Malcolm found himself firmly between that proverbial rock and a hard place. Tom would be pissed if Malcolm kept him out of the loop. The governor would be equally pissed if Malcolm passed on the information about the computer trap prematurely and they lost their newfound advantage.

He stuffed the slips into his pocket and headed for the hallway instead of his office. Margaret expressed surprise at this change of direction.

"What should I tell Tom when he calls back in less than five minutes?"

Malcolm gave her a dismissive wave. "I'm going to call him. Tell him to be patient."

"His patience ran out five calls ago. That won't placate him."

"I'll call him."

The last thing Margaret saw was Malcolm's head disappearing down the steps towards the main entrance of the mansion.

Once outside, he headed for the garages. He tracked down Robert Pettala, his chauffeur and Man Friday, hunched over a keyboard in his office above the garage.

Robert reached for his jacket when he spotted Malcolm in the doorway.

"What's up? Did I miss an appointment?" He scanned the calendar on his desk.

"No, I needed the fresh air," Malcolm said. "How's the research coming?"

Robert relaxed and settled back into his chair. "We are a nation of habits. Staying up a few hours later than usual throws our whole lives into the blender. We can't think straight. We are less civil than usual. Our productivity falls into the category of a pre-school classroom writing classical music. Since this is nationwide, it is impossible to come up with an accurate figure for the loss of productivity. Let's say billions, although I'm not sure trillions would be too great an exaggeration. Every day it becomes worse. More and more people get sucked into the vortex of staying up late glued to their computers and TVs."

Robert held up a handful of newspaper clippings. "A lot of it is anecdotal. People have chosen sides and have the same belief in their convictions as if they were talking about a favourite sports team or whether smoking is harmful. There is no changing their minds, and they are willing to fight anyone who disagrees with them. There's no measuring the damage this will cause to relationships."

"You watched the governor's press conference? Will anyone listen to him and go back to their normal lives?"

"He made some good points," Robert smiled. "Or should I say you made some good points. But he seemed distracted. It didn't have his usual fervour and punch. I think the late hours are starting to take a toll on him as well. He should heed his own advice."

"That's not going to happen anytime soon."

"He did have an interesting skirmish with a reporter from New York. The guy was questioning whether our school down in Alexandra was scheduled for destruction anyway. Claimed the bombers did the governor a favour. The governor gave back as good as he got. I'd say he came out the winner."

Malcolm scowled at his chauffeur. "It was a press conference. There are no winners and losers. It is merely a tool for getting information to the people of the nation."

Robert looked around the room with a fake confused look on his face. "You talking to me? Come on Malcolm; you know there are always winners and losers. This guy from New York thought he had the governor on the ropes, but the governor did a rope-a-dope and slipped out of his clutches."

"Who was the New York reporter?"

"Rod Sanderson, *Daily News.* Ever heard of him?"

"Sanderson?" Malcolm expressed surprise. "We've shared a few lunches over the years."

"Well, he came looking for a fight. Trying to get a good quote, I guess."

Malcolm hesitated briefly. "I need you to drive me down to the mall. Can you spare a couple of minutes?"

"The mall?" Robert studied his boss for a second or two. "You really should get yourself an outside line."

Malcolm laughed. "Yeah. Maybe when this is over."

Malcolm stood at the bank of payphones and waited for the ringing to stop and someone to pick up. His frustration grew with each ring. An answering machine picked up his call. His message was brief and to the point.

"Dammit, Joe. Call me."

He slammed down the receiver. Two women, walking through the door at the same time as his comment, crowded away from him in the small entryway. Malcolm took a couple of calming breaths and smiled at them.

"Answering machines," he said. "A blessing or a curse? Sometimes I'm not sure which."

Neither woman replied. The pushed their way through the second set of doors and scurried into the mall.

Malcolm stood with the phone in his hand for several more seconds before fishing another quarter from his pocket and dropping it into the slot.

"Tom," he said. "Could you meet me at the food court in the mall for a coffee? I can't handle any more of that shit you guys serve."

He listened for a second then continued. "Right now would be a perfect time, but I can wait five minutes if that works for you. I can't discuss this on the phone, and I would like a neutral place to talk about it. It's important."

Again he listened. "I'll order you a mocha latte from Starbucks. The faster you get here, the hotter it will be."

Malcolm dropped the receiver back into the cradle and was startled when it instantly rang. He looked around and then picked it up again.

"Hello."

"Who do you think you are, Superman, hanging around in phone booths. What's up?"

"Joe? Thank god you called back. We've got a bit of a dilemma here."

He could hear Joe exhale a long sigh. Malcolm continued: "The governor has locked on to the computer of the bombers. What I'm wond ..."

"Locked on? How?" There was an out-of-character excitement in Joe's voice.

"He wrote a trace-back program that captured their signals when they cut into our website to make their broadcasts. It was old-fashioned. Simple. But it worked. Now we're afraid we'll either lose them, or they will discover we are on their computers."

Near silence answered him, but if he listened hard, he could hear the clicking of computer keys. He waited.

"Are you sure?" Joe finally asked. "I'm on the governor's computer, and I don't see anything suggesting he has another computer locked on."

"Shit," Malcolm said. "We must have lost them already." He hesitated, then asked, "How did you get on the governor's computer that quickly?"

"He's on the network. I can access any computer. You should know that."

Malcolm felt a sense of relief. "Are you on his desktop or his laptop?"

Again he heard the clicking of a keyboard.

"I don't see any laptop. Are you sure he has one?"

"Positive. I watched him compile his program on it."

A few more key clicks came across the line.

"I don't see any evidence of a laptop. He must have a private service provider."

"How can that be?" Malcolm sounded perplexed. "He captured their computer on his. He must be connected to our system."

"No mystery there. The bombers haven't hacked into your computer system."

"I know, I know. You think it's an inside job. We've been over that." The impatience in Malcolm's voice crackled through the line.

"No, Malcolm, I have a new theory. They haven't hijacked your computers, they've hijacked your web address. I'm still trying to figure out how they did it. They appear to be able to take over your IP address and broadcast their material at will. Their information appears to be coming from your system."

Malcolm said nothing for several seconds. "If that's true, why did our servers crash? They have to be on our system."

"They only pirate your signal when they want to

broadcast. Half of America logged into your site before the bombers took over and crashed your servers. That's the confusing part. If your servers are down, it takes down their broadcast. They are not totally independent. I'll figure it out soon."

"What about the governor? How did he find them if you can't?"

"He logged on last night after they hijacked your address. Ran his program and locked on to them. Don't tell him, but it was probably a fluke that it worked. It's something I'll look into."

"And you can't see where he did that?"

"Given enough time, I could find him. Half of America logged in at the same time. Unless you can give me his IP address, it will take some searching." Joe paused. "But that's not important. We've locked onto them without their knowledge. I'll fly up, and we'll see how this program works. We've got them now."

"No. No, you can't do that. The governor made me promise not to tell anyone about this until we get some definite information. He doesn't want to look like a fool if this doesn't work. Tell me what I have to do."

"Politicians. So hung up on their damn images. I'll send you a list of instructions, and you make them sound like your own. The procedure is pretty simple. It'll take me a couple of minutes."

Five minutes later Malcolm was sitting in the food court with two lattes in front of him. He had already violated the governor's confidence with Joe, doing it again with the FBI should be easier. He could see Tom Burke working his way through the crowd towards Malcolm's corner table. He appeared to be alone.

Malcolm stood as Tom arrived and indicated the seat opposite him. "Drink up," he said and pushed the fancy coffee towards him. Tom gave him an irritated look.

"What's up, Malcolm? I don't have time to be fooling around. What did you find out about the governor's claims?"

Malcolm looked around the room to make sure no one was paying any attention to them. "His remarks were taken out of context. You should school your guys to listen actively. It's bad enough that the press prints what they want to hear rather that what is said."

"The governor said a break is imminent."

"No. The press asked if a break was imminent. The governor never used those words."

Tom leaned back in his chair and looked away from Malcolm for a few seconds. He let out a heavy sigh. "What the hell is going on, Malcolm? I have more important things to do than sit here parsing sentences and dissecting political mumbo-jumbo. Why did you ask me to meet you? It had better be important."

Malcolm engaged the agent's eyes. He looked as tired as Malcolm felt. "We met in this public place because I don't want you making a scene. I don't want you to yell at me. You're not going to like what I'm about to tell you."

Tom looked around at all the people at the food court. He took a deep relaxing breath. "Tell me we are closer to capturing these guys than we were when you left my office an hour ago and I'll kiss you. That's all that counts. What does the governor know that I don't?"

"Good," Malcolm nodded. "We both understand what is important here, but keep your lips to yourself. I don't necessarily agree with what I'm about to tell you. Keep that in mind. I'm only the messenger."

"That's bullshit, Malcolm. The governor doesn't fart without you telling him what key it should be in. Every sensible word that comes out of his mouth comes from you. What are you two up to?"

Malcolm cautiously looked around the room. The tables

nearest to them remained empty. Everyone else seemed lost in their conversations.

"We have to do this the governor's way for the time being," he started. Tom tried unsuccessfully to hold back the revulsion he felt and transmitted with a hostile stare.

"The governor has locked on to the bombers' computers. We can see everything they are doing."

"Holy shit, Malcolm. That's what you didn't want to tell me? That's fantastic news." Tom took a quick look around. His excitement had overtaken him and made his voice louder than he planned. A few people had glanced his way and then returned to their own worlds. "When do I get to see this?"

"You don't."

"I don't. What do you mean?"

"The capture program is written in some archaic language from when the governor first got into IT. It's shaky at best, and he doesn't want to risk losing the connection. Joe Fisher thinks to make the connection at all was a fluke. It's a work in progress, and the governor adapts it to the situation on the fly. The fewer people playing with it, the safer the lock will be."

"That's bullshit, Malcolm, and you know it. He wants the glory for himself. He has to turn this over to the FBI. National security is at stake here. Let the experts take over."

"Experts. What experts? You've done a background check on the governor. I'm sure you have. He knows as much about programming as anyone on your staff, probably more. Graduated from MIT with honours. Helped write most of the standard library stuff that today's programmers use. That's why he could defeat it. He designed it in the first place."

"You're looking through rose-coloured glasses, Malcolm. If he is that good, why isn't he working in the field anymore?"

"Do you know why he got into politics?" Malcolm voice rose. A couple of people looked his way again. He paused to get himself under control. "He was working in IT for a small town here in Georgia called Bakers Siding. The name pretty accurately describes the size. The finances were a mess, so he designed a program from the ground up exclusively for that town. Took out all the inefficiencies in the system. Then he realized the problem wasn't with the technology, it was with the people running the town, a combination of greed and ineptitude. He ran for mayor and won and started to reform the local government.

"I had gone to MIT with him. When he heard I had stepped down from the Bureau, he called me. He wanted to run an operation to clean up corruption in the town and wanted me to head it up. Together we made Bakers Siding the envy of the state, financially and ethically. Then he set his aim at all of Georgia. The rest, as they say, is history. Now he's governor and still looking out for the common man. That's why he gave up IT."

"Yeah, Malcolm. That story sells in some places, I'm sure. Now his sights are set on the White House, and the glory of bringing in these bombers would be a big step towards that goal. Don't try and deny it."

"You're wrong, Tom. This is not about glory. This is about keeping a tenuous grasp on our first concrete break in the case. It doesn't matter who is running the computer. What matters is that we catch these fanatical bastards before they demolish another school."

Tom shook his head and leaned towards Malcolm. "We have to get this on a more secure computer system. I can assure you that's ours, not yours. Remember, they've hacked into you and you can't even find and block them."

Malcolm leaned back. "That may not be the case, but that's not important right now. What is important is that we track these guys and get ahead of them. Your boys couldn't do it. The governor has. He calls the shots." The finality in Malcolm's voice left no room for further argument.

"The FBI has to be on standby for when we give you a location anywhere in the country. The governor recognizes the importance of having you involved. Your guys are going to make the arrest. The operation is not a one-man show. Territorial fights can't be a part of this. We're all on the same side; let's get on the same page."

Tom's shoulders slumped slightly. "You're right about that. Getting the bombers is what this is all about. There is no room for showboating by anybody." He gave Malcolm a meaningful stare. "Nobody."

◄43►

AS MALCOLM DROVE back to the governor's mansion with Robert Pettala, he scrolled through the instructions Joe had sent to his BlackBerry. If Joe was right, and he always was, there would be no problem getting information from the bombers' computer without their knowledge. Now that the governor had connected, the rest was relatively easy.

They only had to make one big assumption: that the bombers didn't suspect that they had been hacked. Considering how surprised everyone was that the governor had been successful, this seemed to be a pretty simple supposition.

Given enough time, Malcolm and the governor would have figured out these steps. Time was not a luxury they possessed. Joe, on the other hand, spent most of his working time roaming undetected through other people's computers.

Discretion was second nature to him

None of the instructions was beyond Malcolm's knowledge and ability. The governor wouldn't suspect that he had violated his charge to Malcolm to tell no one. He had committed them to memory by the time Robert stopped the car in front of the mansion. To be safe, he made a list of the main points in his notebook.

He jumped from the limo into the bright mid-day sun. It's a beautiful day in the neighbourhood, he thought, and it will be a much better day when they take down this band of criminals. He hustled up the stairs and went directly to the governor's office.

The governor's secretary waved him through. "He's been looking for you," she said.

"Malcolm, where have you been?" The governor's face looked more relaxed than Malcolm had seen it since the first bomb exploded.

"Doing a little research on how to stroll through their machine undetected," Malcolm said. "Reminds me of our days back at MIT."

"Good," the governor said, although Malcolm doubted he had listened to what he said. "As soon as you left, they came back to their computer and started sending out emails. They're encoded, but the encryption is pretty basic. I've written down everything they've said. I think it will tell us where their next target is."

He pushed a pad towards Malcolm without taking his eyes off the computer screen. "It's time to bring in your buddies at the FBI."

Malcolm snatched up the pad and studied it. There was a garble of letters and numbers on the page.

Hry omyp [pdoyopm yp bofrp yjr npi;frt johj dvjpp; om vp;ptsfp d[tomhd yjrm yslr d svsfr,u n;bf yp o36 yjrm hp yp vjrurmmr ,pimysom dysyr [stl yp esoy gpt gityjrt omdytivyopmd/ "What's this?" he asked.

"Raw data," the governor said. "Go over to my desktop and type in that message by hitting the key to the right of the one on the notepad." He smiled. "If you're a good touch typist simply move your fingers one key to the left on the home keys. All will be revealed."

Malcolm lowered himself into a chair in front of the governor's desktop computer and started to type:

Get into position to video the boulder high school in colorado springs then take s academy blvd to i25 to the cheyenne mountain state park to wait for further instructions.

"Boulder High School in Colorado Springs. Fantastic.

How did you crack the code so quickly?"

The governor leaned over to look at the other screen. "My superior mathematical powers or just a lucky guess. I looked at the use of commas, semi-colons, and brackets and figured keyboard shifting was as good a place to start as any. Use of the bracket suggested they had gone to the right. They are buried deep in the so-called dark Internet; they don't think security is needed."

Malcolm slid his chair towards the governor. "What else do you have?"

The governor continued to scratch notes onto his pad. "Based on what you just read, this must be additional instructions about where to go or how to do it." He tore off another page and handed it to Malcolm.

Malcolm studied the hen scratching and sat in front of the desktop again. "It would appear that the videographer doesn't know what schools are next until the day of the explosion. Sounds like there is a small cabal at the top who knows what's going on and they keep everyone else in the dark."

The governor stopped writing and sat back in his chair. "Looks like they are finished for now. I didn't want to leave the screen in case he puts up something important again." He pushed his hair back out of his face. Despite the air-conditioned office, sweat ran down his face. "You're right. The 'need to know' principle seems to be firmly in effect. If we can cut off their head, we may bring the whole operation to a quick halt. Give your friends at the FBI a call and get them working on this. Tell them to get in and get out without being seen. As I said, we don't want to tip these guys off that we're on to them until we're ready to make the bust, but at the same time, we don't want to lose another school. Maybe their bomb guys can make it partially explode without doing any real damage. Then the bombers will think they've screwed up again."

Malcolm stood up and walked around to look over the governor's shoulder. The screen showed the message the governor had transcribed.

"If we act fast, we may get there before any of their people do. We are getting the message at the same time as the videographer. He can't be travelling by car because early this morning he was in Michigan. That has to be twelve or thirteen hundred miles. He would have to fly, get a car and get to his destination."

The governor nodded. "What resources do we have close by?"

"Fort Carson is just outside Colorado Springs. They should have the personnel we need. I'll get Tom working on this right away."

The governor pointed to the phone on his desk. "Call him from here."

Malcolm gave his head a little shake. "I don't want to sound paranoid, but I think I'll deliver this message to Tom in person. I don't want to use any digital or electronic methods of communication at this point. I'll get them in operational mode, and then I'll come back and help you crack the bomber's computer. I've got some ideas I'm sure will allow us to walk through their files without them knowing we are there."

"That's all right, Malcolm. You get moving. I've got some ideas of my own on hacking them. This isn't my first dance."

Malcolm reached into his pocket pulled and out his notepad. "I know that, Governor. You're one of the best." He tore out a page and handed it to the man. "Here are some ideas I scribbled down. They may help you."

The governor perused the list, a surprised look on his face. "These are good, Malcolm. I wouldn't have thought of this approach. I'll consider them." His eyes flashed down the page. Christ, do you do this often? You could be a suspect." He studied the list a little longer before looking up. "This is good. Now, get those agents in action and remember, discretion is the key word. We don't want to tip anyone off."

Ten minutes later, Malcolm jumped from the car driven by Robert Pettala in front of the FBI building. "Wait for me. I may not be long."

He ran into the building, looked at the elevator indicator, saw it was on an upper floor and headed for the steps. At this point, every second was crucial.

Tom looked up and scowled as Malcolm burst into his office. "Now what, amigo, more secrets?"

Malcolm stopped short. In his excitement, he forgot how the two men had departed their last meeting. Then a smile radiated across his face. "Saddle up the troops, bud. We have their next target."

◀44▶

TOM JUMPED UP from his desk. "Are you serious?"

"As a heart attack," Malcolm answered.

Tom sat down again. "The old bastard came through. Where? When? No, I know when. Five o'clock tomorrow morning."

Malcolm laughed. "Watch who you're calling old. He's our age. I went to MIT with him." Then Malcolm became serious again. He sat at Tom's desk and passed his copy of the email to the FBI agent.

"It's in Colorado Springs. We have to act fast and use our resources already on the ground out there. If it's at all possible, we don't want to tip the bad guys off that we're on to them. We're not looking to stop one school bombing; we're looking at bringing down their entire operation."

"No arguments here," Tom agreed. He studied the document in his hand. The information was limited, but already the wheels were spinning in his head. "Let's get busy."

The two men got down to some serious planning. Right off the bat, Tom phoned the commanding officer in Fort Collins, north of Denver, on a secure line and arranged for a bomb demolition team to be activated.

His next call was to the FBI in Colorado Springs. "We want to keep this hush-hush if we can," he told the agent-in-charge. "I don't intend to micro-manage. I'll leave the how up to you. Bring in as many agents from around the area as you need. From Denver, the surrounding states, wherever. Oscar Parks over in Nevada has worked with me on a previous bombing. He's already up to speed. The army at Fort Collins will help with the bomb.

"The last school blown to hell was in Michigan. We figure the videographer will be flying in from there."

As Malcolm and the governor had surmised, and now Tom concurred, the videographer would have to be en route to this new location from Michigan by air. It was the only way to get there on time.

"Step up surveillance at all points of entry into the city, but at the same time keep it low key. Create a diversion and then hold him as a witness. We want to detain the suspect without arousing suspicion we know he is involved with the extortions. That way he won't be tipping off his compatriots. Give him leeway to make any outside contacts he wants to and always give him the impression that he is free to leave at any time. Naturally, we will monitor all his calls and will eventually seize his phone."

Tom paused, ticking off the list of procedures in his mind. "All that, of course, assumes we can locate the person in the first place. We have no idea what he or she, I suppose, looks like. There can't be that many people booking at the last minute from Kalamazoo to Colorado Springs. I'd be amazed if there is more than one."

Malcolm listened to Tom's end of the conversation, occasionally nodding in agreement.

"We want to get the bomb team discreetly into the school to disarm the bomb." Tom continued. "That may turn into our major challenge. Citizens everywhere are on the alert. All activity around any school is resulting in phone calls to the local FBI offices. We have succeeded in getting this message out there. People across the country are highly attuned to any unusual activity and are keeping law enforcement phones ringing.

"Equally vigilant is the local press. Everyone wants to scoop the big story. While we've encouraged these activities in the past, now they will be an obstacle to overcome. Moving a fully equipped bomb destruction team onto any school property will stir up the locals and bring on the press. We can't have that happen."

Again Tom paused. "But I'm leaving that up to you. Work with the military. They have some experts on subterfuge."

The man in Colorado Springs laughed. "OK, Tom. I'm glad you're not going to try to micro-manage this event from across the country."

"It's hard to sit on our hands back here while you're out there having all the fun. Keep me informed on your progress. Good luck."

Tom hung up. "It's in their hands now. Tell me how the governor's key-trapping program works and when can we move it into our office."

Malcolm shook his head. "Not anytime soon. As I said before, it's written in some old, archaic language and it's not very stable. For now, we have to be happy to run it on his laptop. I've got Joe Fisher flying in. There's nothing he can't do with a computer. If anyone can stabilize the program, Joe will be able to. If not, I'm sure he will be able to get a feed off it into your computers. Be patient."

"Patient? Hell, man, I don't have time for patience. This discovery is the breakthrough we've been waiting for. I want action. The program is on a laptop. Have the governor bring his machine to our offices. We can work on it here."

Malcolm considered this for a few seconds. "That sounds like a feasible alternative. I'm not sure what network the computer is running on. Joe doesn't think it is an in-house connection. Let's go over to the mansion and see if there is anything new to report. The governor is sitting there monitoring it full-time. That's the best way to get on top of things. One of us should be looking after the business of the state."

"Right now the business of the state is capturing these extortionists. Nothing else matters." Tom picked up the copy of the email from his desk and reread it.

"This is pretty cryptic, but it tells us one thing."

Malcolm looked his way and raised his eyebrows.

"Information is doled out on a need to know basis. Only the people at the top know exactly what is happening when. If the videographer gets his information day-by-day, then he probably won't be able to tell us much when we bring him in. We have to be able to trace where this information comes from. No doubt, somewhere in the deep web. Those are the people we are after."

Malcolm nodded. "No one ever said they weren't smart. I wonder if he is going to meet someone in the state park or that is just some place to keep him out of sight."

"Good question. We start monitoring the park right away. See who is coming and who is going."

"Is there any point in picking up the videographer? He is no threat; he only takes pictures. We can put a loose tail on him, let him film and broadcast the failure, and then pick him up when he gets to the park. That gives us a chance to monitor his signal, and if he is going to meet someone there, he will lead us to that person."

Tom rubbed his chin as he thought this over. "Good idea. That will be after 5 a.m. our time. If we leave now, we can be there for the arrest. I'll arrange for a jet. Is your go-bag ready?"

"What about the governor? We should keep him in the loop so he can pass any new information on to us."

"We'll call him from the plane. At the same time, I'll inform the Colorado FBI of the change in plans. Let's get going."

Sean Rhyno — Morning commentary

In other news:

Once again the results of the contested convention of the party which should have been able to assume the presidency without even running a serious contest is coming back to haunt the country.

As you recall, the primaries were a brutal, take-no-prisoners battle between two men with extreme but opposite views and both had loyal supporters. They split the party down the middle and left little room for compromise or consensus. Both were convinced the presidency was theirs for the taking. They spent more time viciously attacking their fellow candidates than the current administration.

Neither had enough delegates to be declared winner coming into the convention. They chose to up the vitriol on the convention floor and what we ended up with is a candidate who slipped in through the back door who has no firm convictions about anything. The party is so fractured, she is too afraid to rock the boat and take a stand on the simplest questions. This lack of passion resonates with nobody including those in her own party who are still wondering what happened.

An opportunity squandered, I say. A downside of democracy.

◄45►

MALCOLM DROPPED THE receiver of the sky phone back into its cradle. Tom had listened to one side of the conversation.

"The governor wasn't happy with this trip?" he asked.

"He thinks we are wasting our time running around the country. He might not agree, but I think he expected it. He says you have enough agents out here to make a simple arrest."

Tom nodded in agreement. "Perhaps we do. I want to interrogate this guy myself. He may not know anything, but with our more intimate knowledge of the case than the local agents, we may be able to pick up something they would miss. Any tiny bit of information this guy can give us might be our big break."

"Our big break is the governor locking on to their computer, don't you think?"

Tom shook his head. "That's going to save one school in Colorado Springs. It's not going to catch these jerks unless he can lock onto a destination. So far, that hasn't happened. He's still being bounced around the world and ending up in Internet cafes. We have a couple of agents at the mansion working with him. They had reported to me before you talked to the governor. He refused to let us take his laptop to our headquarters."

Malcolm laughed. "Yeah, he told me. Needless to say, the governor is thrilled to have them 'helping' him." He used air quotes for emphasis.

"Three heads are better than one, and these guys know

their business. We're not worried about hurting anybody's feelings or wounding their pride. Not even a governor's. We want results."

Malcolm twisted the top off a bottle of water and took a long swig. He wiped his mouth with the back of his hand. "What's happening in Colorado Springs?" he asked. "They do know we are coming?"

"Yes. Stephen Spears is the special-agent-in-charge. He expected me to show up."

Tom looked out the window for several seconds. At thirty thousand feet, there wasn't much to see. "The governor did good work on this, Malcolm, but the president is not going to want to see him get any credit for it. This action is going to create a political shit storm. You're sure your man hasn't got any political aspirations for the upcoming election?"

Malcolm shook his head. "Hell, Tom, it's only two months away. He couldn't mount a campaign in that short time, even if he wanted to. These other guys have been campaigning for two years." Malcolm knew the statement was true. He only hoped the governor agreed with him.

"What if he brings in these extortionists? Could he ride that wave to the White House?"

Again, Malcolm shook his head, but with a lot less conviction. "Let's catch the bad guys, Tom. We'll worry about politics when the time comes."

"If only it were that easy, my friend. Politics is a fact of life that I always have to keep in mind. Surely you remember that. Always being aware of the political implications of every act is what made your transition to your new life in the governor's mansion so easy."

Malcolm took another long, slow sip of water before facing his friend. "Let's just catch the bad guys. We'll deal with the governor when the time comes."

Now it was Tom's turn to look pensive. "As long as

you're paying attention to what's happening in your backyard. We don't need any distractions along the way."

"This Special Agent Spears, will he be able to keep the lid on what's happening in Colorado Springs?"

"Don't worry about our agents. They are all focused on the task at hand. They have no hidden agendas."

Tom spread a map of the city out on the table in front of him. He placed Malcolm's water bottle on one corner and a glass on the other. With a red pen, he circled the high school in question.

"This school is in a pretty densely populated area. In similar circumstances in New York City, the bomber used C4 and shaped the charge to go straight up. Hopefully, they still are determined not to injure or kill anyone. The military bomb squad is going to be looking to see if this is still the case. They are bringing in a dog with special talents along those lines."

Malcolm studied the map before responding. "How far from the nearest BurgerCircus?"

Tom brought up a similar map on his iPad. He did a search for the fast-food restaurant. He then looked back at the map. "Right here. Three blocks away. Easily in sight."

"Might be a spot to look for the videographer if they don't pick him up at the airport. Regardless of how compact his equipment is, he should be easy to identify if we are looking for him."

"At three o'clock in the morning? I doubt if there will be many people out scarfing down hamburgers. Colorado is not known as the city that never sleeps."

"No, but it is a city that gets up early. Industries run round the clock out there. Shift workers will be having breakfast at that time of morning before reporting to shifts that start at 4 a.m. and go to noon. BurgerCircus starts serving breakfast at 2 in the morning. I've checked their website. We want to cover all the bases."

"OK. Good idea. We'll send a couple of agents in to bus tables. That will give them an excuse to be roaming around taking a close look at things."

"No suits, no ties, no shiny black shoes," Malcolm said, trying to look overly serious. "They should either look like a couple of high school kids or a couple of seniors trying to stretch their pension cheques to the end of the month."

"We don't all stand out in a crowd, but I do get your point. I'll call Spears and get him working on it right away. Any other helpful suggestions?" Malcolm smiled at the sarcasm evident in the question.

"Yeah, let's catch these bastards."

◀46▶

A LIGHT RAIN misted up the windows of the Lear 75 as it taxied down the runway at Petersen Air Force Base. The military shared runways with the Colorado Springs Municipal Airport where the suspected videographer would be landing. The Lear 75 had a faster airspeed than any of the commercial flights coming in. Tom deduced they would be there ahead of their suspect. If the local agents successfully located the man, Tom and Malcolm would go over for a private look before they started their interrogation the next morning.

Although only six minutes outside the city, both men agreed it was better if they stayed away from the school. They wanted to keep all activity there to a minimum. Special Agent Spears would meet them shortly for a special briefing. He had assured them everything was moving along according to plan.

A meeting room had been set up at the base for the FBI agents and supper had been laid on for the two men. Their internal clocks were still ticking away on Eastern Time while the local clocks reflected the current time as being two hours earlier. Agent Spears walked into the room as Malcolm dropped his napkin onto his plate.

The impromptu meal, consisting of barbecued steak, mashed potatoes and steamed vegetables smothered in butter, had been the most substantial meal he had had since this fiasco began four days previously. Being away from the mansion and Tom's office gave him a chance to relax for a few precious moments. The arrival of Agent

Spears ended that.

"The military came through big time," the agent said. "Apparently various bases across the country have been running mock exercises to increase their level of preparedness. They had a plan ready for action that surpassed what we thought we would do."

Tom looked up, surprised. "A plan of action. We are trying to keep this on the down-low. We're not looking for anything too spectacular."

Agent Spears shook his head. "Nothing to worry about there. Secrecy is the main element of their proposal. If everything works according to their plan, nobody will ever know they were involved." Spears spread an eleven-by-seventeen sheet of paper on the table. "This is an overhead view of the school. As you can see, there is an overhang above the main entrance which is off a curved driveway.

"They used an 18-wheeler advertising school supplies in big letters with pictures of pencils, school books and math sets on the side. It looks like the real thing, and the timing is perfect for a truck of that nature to be arriving at the school. They park in such a way that it obliterates the view from the road. The rain is picking up outside. There will be fewer people out on the streets to get curious in the first place.

"Instead of school supplies, the truck carried their high-tech bomb disposal gear, a trained sniffer dog and a crack team of experts. They were into the school in the blink of an eye and conducting their search in an orderly, efficient manner. In no time at all, the bomb had been found. As you suspected, it was C4.

"Ready for a little irony? We had to involve the school principal. He assured us his staff already searched the building and it is clean."

"For the love of God," Malcolm said. "Somebody is going to die before this is over even if it does not appear to be part of the extortionist's plan. Mishandle that C4, and you could blow off a hand, an arm or your goddamn head."

"Well," Spears said, "there was enough in that school that it would have killed all the searchers in a thirty-foot radius. They were lucky it was well hidden. The dog saved us a lot of time. When they're passing out medals, it should be at the top of the list."

He flipped over the sheet of paper. The word "CONFIDENTIAL" filled the top of the paper. "We had a little discussion about who is running this operation before I managed to get a copy of this. I had to emphasize the point that we all be on the same page as the scheme went forward. We didn't want any friendly-fire incidents."

"Friendly-fire?" Malcolm asked. "The extortionists are long-gone from the site. There should be no shooting of any kind, friendly or otherwise."

Spears shrugged. "You wanted to see a copy of their plans, right? I said what I had to say to make that happen. These soldier boys always think shooting is on the agenda."

Tom turned the page so he could read it better. Malcolm looked over his shoulder. Tom's head involuntarily nodded approval as he read the plan of action. "This is perfect," he said. "Better than what we had planned." He passed the paper to Malcolm.

Malcolm finished the last paragraph and looked at the other two men. "Was it General George Patton who said 'Don't tell people how to do things, tell them what to do and let them surprise you with their results'?"

"Looks like that is true in this case," Tom said and turned his attention back to Spears. "Is that truck still parked at the school? Won't that raise suspicions after working hours are over?"

"No, that was part of the plan. I left with the truck and the C4. I know it's supposed to be stable, but..." He let the sentence trail off. "They are putting up black-out curtains on the part of the school where they are working. They don't let the light out, but resemble natural windows from the outside. I've never seen anything like them."

"If I wanted to take a look for myself, how easy is it to get to the school from here?" Tom asked.

"Nothing to it. Take 24 to S. Academy Blvd, turn south on E. Platte Ave for a little over a mile and then north on N. Murray Blvd. Less than a mile and the school is on the left. Can't miss it." Spears hesitated. "I wouldn't recommend it though. We want to keep traffic to a minimum."

"You said they already removed the bomb from the building?"

"The did. If you want to see the bomb, it's at Fort Carson. Try flashing your badge, drop the president's name, they might let you in."

Tom laughed. "I talked to the general before we left Atlanta. Now I will have to explain why we are bunking at the air base instead of his fort, but even so, I think he will let us in."

"We can make that work," Malcolm said. "I'd like to see the bomb. I would like an assessment of how much damage it would have done. Moving into the downtown area of a city of this size might mean they are escalating things. There are schools on the outskirts of the city where it would have been safer if they were trying to cover a large geographical area of the country. The operation is becoming a psychological war, and we have to get into the minds of the men who are behind it.

"Their aim is to produce as much fear as possible and to force the government to move or more importantly, it seems, to get the fast-food industry to cough up the money. I'm hoping part of their plan is not to add civilian casualties to the mix before we bring them in."

Tom nodded in agreement and looked at Agent Spears. "Call the fort. Tell them we will be dropping in."

All three men turned to face the door to the room as a polite knock sounded.

They exchanged glances. "Enter," Tom said.

A steward in a white uniform pushed a metal table into the room with a covered container on it. "Dessert, gentlemen." He lifted the cover to reveal three large pieces of apple pie with ice cream melting down over the edges.

"I could eat," Malcolm said, speaking for all present. "The people at Fort Carson aren't going anywhere. I can think better if my sugar levels don't get too low."

"Make the call," Tom said to Spears as he reached for a fork. "It's going to be a long night of waiting anyway."

◀47▶

PAUL JOHNSON HUNG up the phone and turned to face Ray Tutty. "Malcolm's out of the office, and the governor is unavailable at the moment. I suppose they do have a state to run."

Ray shook his head in disgust. "I told you not to waste time with those political hacks. Call Tom Burke at the FBI. He will take our call."

"Already called him just like you said. He's out of the office as well, and nobody at the FBI could give us any information."

Ray's eyes blazed. "This school thing is the most important thing going on in the country right now, and they can't take our call. Did you tell them who it was?"

"Oh yeah, Ray. I dropped your name. No one jumped to attention." Paul smiled.

Barbara swung her chair away from the computer. "Considering the money is supposed to be coming from us, it is strange that someone couldn't take your call. I wonder if there is a break in the case."

"Break in the case." Ray looked over at his executive assistant, still fuming. "They have nothing new to report and are avoiding us. They are covering their incompetence."

Barbara refused to back down to her boss. "You know you're only the source of money. You have no part in the investigation."

"I want to tell them about the increased stock activity. I think it might be important." Ray took a calming breath. "You think it's important. You've been studying those figures ever since this morning."

Barbara glanced back at her computer screen. Rows of numbers flickered from the spreadsheet currently displayed. "There might be a pattern here," she said. "Some people look like they are making a lot of money from our predicament. I'm not sure it's the same person; there are a variety of untraceable addresses. But the blueprint is the same in every case. The prices start to drop. Big blocks are sold off, encouraging the prices to drop more quickly, and then someone buys even bigger blocks at the lower prices. I think it is one person, and if it is, he or she is increasing their holdings in our company exponentially. When everything goes back to normal, someone is going to make a fortune on this."

Ray walked over to the computer. "No way to trace anyone?"

"No, it's all dummy corporations."

"They know we'll never pay. Is this the real plan? If we pay out one hundred million dollars, our stocks will plummet. There will be no advantage to anyone in all this trading."

Now Paul joined the other two at the computer. "When you say it out loud, it makes a lot of sense. I'll call Tom again and express the urgency in him contacting us. This trading information could take their investigation along a whole new path."

Ray pulled up a chair and studied the figures more closely. "There must be some way of beating them at their own game. Monitor this, Barbara. The next time there is a run on our stocks, we want to jump in and buy before the prices bottom out. We can't stop them from what they've already made, but we can prevent them from making any more."

Paul ran his finger down the column of numbers. "The pattern is easy to figure out once you know it's there. We simply need to put in an automatic buy order at a price higher than the expected drop. We could do that right now, and it will trigger without any intervention on our part. We make a few dollars and as a bonus, we side-track the interloper who is cashing in on our misfortune."

Barbara pushed her chair back and engaged the eyes of both men. "That will work, but we have to be careful. It might look like insider trading. It won't be, but even if it looks that way, it could hurt our image." She raised her palms upward. "I don't have to tell you our image is a little tarnished right now."

"But we're giving away coffee every morning." Paul laughed, trying to lighten the mood. "That means more to most people than the value of our stocks."

◀48▶

MALCOLM AND TOM showed their ID to the soldier manning the gate at Fort Carson. Tom pointed out the general was expecting them. The soldier remained stoic, completely unimpressed by that statement. He spoke to another soldier inside the gatehouse, who passed him a clipboard. He ran his finger down the list of names, looked at the two ID cards again, then passed them to the man inside the building.

"Stop showboating," Tom said. "Our names have to be right at the top of the list. We made the appointment fifteen minutes ago."

"Sorry for the delay, sir. I'm simply following standard procedure. We take security very seriously at Fort Carson. Indeed your names are here and as you said, you are number one on the list. That doesn't mean we are not going to verify that you are who you claim to be. If you are, then I'm sure you understand our concerns."

Malcolm put a hand on Tom's shoulder before he had a chance to speak again. "Take your time soldier," he said, "but let me assure you, the general is waiting for us. He will personally be dealing with our concerns during his supper time."

A flush of red crept into the soldier's face. His partner poked the ID cards back out the window. "Looks like the real thing," he said. "Can never be too careful when the protection of the United States is on the line."

Malcolm nodded and smiled. "I think the company we work for recognizes that fact."

The inside guard gave him a blank look before the meaning behind the words sunk in. "Yes, sir. I'm sure the FBI has that thought uppermost on its mind."

Tom snatched the cards being offered to him and gave the borrowed FBI car a shot of gas. The tires chirped as it leapt forward.

"Easy," Malcolm said.

"I hope they take security this seriously all the time and weren't trying to impress us. We are getting too close to bringing this fiasco to a close to put up with any of that shit."

Malcolm studied his partner for several seconds. He could see the strain of the last week taking its toll. Black rings circled Tom's eyes, His complexion took on a sallow hue, and his shoulders had a dejected sag to them, possibly caused by his suit jacket not keeping up with the weight loss caused by missed or uneaten meals and irregular and interrupted sleep. When he thought about it, Malcolm figured he probably looked the same. He couldn't accept the extortionists were smart enough to have this as part of their plan.

The big breakthrough the governor's key-trapping program provided them served to emphasize how little they had accomplished in the last week. Now the hope was that Mr. Murphy and his law would keep the hell out of the operation.

"Hopefully, they are out of the actual loop, but they know something is up. I'm sure word spread quickly as the bomb squad assembled, disappeared, and reappeared without there being anything announced on the news. These guys at the gate know that fewer men came back than originally left. Somewhere there is an ongoing operation. That will be the true test of their security."

Tom eased back on the gas and studied the street names in the complex. The bomb squad had taken the captured C4 to an isolated part of the base. "The military everywhere is conscious of the need to keep alert in what they say to the civilian world. Here in Colorado Springs, I'm sure they have a heightened sense of awareness. They are sitting on one of the most secure sites in the country, almost literally."

"In the world," Malcolm corrected him. "And we come to visit and have the audacity to bunk down with the flyboys at Petersen. No wonder they are giving us the cold shoulder.

"Over there." He pointed to a sign saying Prussman Blvd.

Tom swung off Speclar Avenue and slowed down. "There it is."

Tom pulled into the parking lot and parked by the light brown Humvee outside the main building. A man with two stars on his shoulders stepped down from the truck. He reached out his hand to Tom as he climbed from his car. "Tom Burke, a pleasure to meet you face-to-face."

Tom shook the man's outstretched hand. "Thank you for seeing us on such short notice." He turned towards Malcolm who was coming around the front of the car.

"This is Malc—" he started to say before Malcolm cut him off.

"General Burns," Malcolm said. "Those stars look good on your shoulders."

To Tom's surprise, the two men embraced in a hug.

"Good to see you back doing what you were meant to do and not playing those silly political games," the general said as he stepped back and shook Malcolm's hand.

"Only on loan," Malcolm said. "The state of Georgia is still where my heart is."

"I'm going to go out on a limb," Tom said, "and assume you two have met before."

"We enlisted at the same time and spent two years defending our country together in the Gulf War," Malcolm said. "Roger stayed in, and it looks like he met with some career success." He brushed his hands over the general's stars. "Oh, the stories I could have told them if anyone had bothered to ask."

"Those same stories wouldn't help your political career either." Both men laughed and then the general turned serious.

"We've got that bomb in a safe location at the fort. We are going to explode it shortly so we can study the blow pattern. I assume that is what you are interested in as well."

Tom nodded. "We have to see if they are stepping up their threat to people's lives or if it is still property damage with a big bang."

The general indicated the Humvee. "Climb aboard. No sense standing here in the rain. We'll take this to the demolition site. Civilian cars don't travel on that part of the base." All three men stepped up into the high vehicle, and the driver immediately took off.

"We have sketches of the location in the school and are trying to duplicate the structure as much as we can. That way we'll have a better handle on the damage the bomb would have done and will be able to re-create the appearance as closely as possible."

"Your plan borders on genius, General. We were simply hoping for a little smoke and mirrors, but this is perfect. Don't you agree, Malcolm?"

"Definitely. It will give us another day to crack their computers without them being aware we're onto them."

The Humvee had turned off the paved highway five minutes earlier. Now the road seemed to exist only in the mind of the driver. Malcolm could see a couple of low buildings on the horizon as the sun set behind them. The cloud and the rain turned the distant sunset into a small ridge of yellow along the top of the mountains.

Once they reached their destination, the general quickly ushered them inside. "We want to get this phase of the operation done as quickly as possible so we can move on to re-creating what the explosion should look like. We are going to blow up the bomb in our lab. We have put up a few walls similar in construction to the school and added a roof made of the same materials as the real one."

He turned into a huge gymnasium-sized room open to the sky. The soldiers working on the project seemed oblivious to the rain falling around them. The general and the two agents stood behind a thick glass shield that protected them not only from the weather but from the explosion scheduled to take place in a matter of minutes.

"We get fourteen days of rain here in August. We had better than a 50-50 chance this wouldn't have been one of them. The gods are not with us tonight."

While they watched, everyone exited the room except one technician. He walked around the perimeter of the room flipping switches.

"We photograph everything," the general explained, "and we take measurements of the concussive force of the explosion."

He pointed to the devices all the way to the top of the walls. "Those sensors will give us an accurate reading of the general direction of the expended force." He paused, looked at the two men and continued. "I trust you realize you can tell no one of what you see here. If I didn't know Malcolm so well, you would have only read about this rather than observe it. It's not above your security clearance, but it is on a need to know basis that we even talk about it."

"Discretion is our religion, General," Tom said. "Your secrets are safe with us."

Alarms sounded throughout the building. More faces appeared in the glass walls around the room. White-coated lab techs, with laptop computers in their hands, came from the closed doors off this big room. Everything was ready. The room became deathly silent.

The general pointed to one of the techs with a cellphone. "It is triggered by the ring of a cellphone. I understand they used this technique on a previous bomb. Allows them to control the bomb from anywhere in the world."

Tom nodded. "Right. A phone call from Islamabad detonated the California bomb." He looked at Malcolm. "Nearly caused an international incident when Governor Weston blabbed to the press about it."

Malcolm scowled. "I think that is a slight exaggeration. The bomb turned out to be a dud." He turned his attention to the mock-up of the soon to be destroyed school rooms. The tech looked up from the cellphone with an expectant look on his face.

Suddenly the imitation walls shook, breaking the glass in the windows. Smoke filled the room. Then nothing.

"Another dud?" Malcolm said.

They waited. A block of C4 remained unexploded inside the room.

"Christ," the general said. "This is the worst possible outcome. Stay here."

The general hustled along the walkway to where a group of technicians was huddled. They opened a pathway to allow him to see the results on the computer screen. Another tech played with the keys and brought up a camera angle from inside the building. A bright spark had flashed before the smoke appeared. The explosion causing the spark also shook the walls and broke the windows. After a few more minutes of discussion, the general returned to the two agents.

"We think the C4 is defective. We have a man suiting up now to go in and check it out."

"In California, it was a defective battery in one of the phones," Tom said.

The general shook his head. "That's not the problem. The initial detonation that should have set off the C4 took place. You saw the results of that. It's unusual, but it looks like defective material in the bomb."

"Who knows where they get this stuff," Tom said. "It probably came from the black market somewhere. Someone might have scammed them and sold them something inferior."

Malcolm stood there with a pensive look on his face, saying nothing.

"What are you thinking?" Tom asked.

"We have a quandary," Malcolm said. "When we fake the explosion tonight, do we have it fail or do we put on a show as if it worked?"

Tom turned to the general. "Can you tell us definitively why the C4 failed?"

"Sure," the general answered, "but not in the time frame you want. We are geared up to measure explosions not to examine explosives. We would have to send it back to the east coast for that. The best we can do is tell you what should have happened from previous tests of this sort. We have seen the trigger mechanism and know how it should have worked."

The three men stood silently, each lost in their thoughts. Finally, Malcolm spoke up.

"They had a videographer on hand. I can't imagine anyone wanted to broadcast another failure. We already know that the explosives are their weak point. They have used too much power, too little power or had complete failures. To convince everyone we should be paying out one hundred million dollars, I would think they would want to put terror in our hearts."

"I agree," Tom said. "Proceed with the plan, General."

◄49►

AS THE GENERAL drove Tom and Malcolm back to their car, Tom's cellphone chirped. He glanced down at the text and nudged Malcolm. Malcolm read the message and nodded.

"Care to share?" the general asked from the front seat of the Humvee.

"Not sure you have the proper clearance level," Malcolm said. "This is official FBI business."

"Good one, *Captain* Truex. That was your rank when you left the army wasn't it?"

"The suspected videographer has arrived at the airport," Tom said, ignoring the by-play between the two friends. "If you could get us back to civilization, we might get a chance to look him over before he leaves."

"Son," the general said, "you're in a High Mobility Multipurpose Wheeled Vehicle with a 400 cubic-inch, 190-horse power turbo diesel engine. It can easily hit 70 mph, so hang on."

The driver looked at the general and smiled.

"Give-er, Sergeant," the general said.

The vehicle lurched as it left the pseudo-road and headed straight across the rocky terrain in the direction of their parked car. Malcolm and Tom hung on to anything they could get hold of to keep them in their seats. A steep hill separated them from their destination barely visible through the now intensified rain.

"Holy shit," Tom said. "I don't think he plans on going around that mountain."

"No need to," the general said. "Your car is on the other side."

"Let's do it," Malcolm said. "We have an extortionist who might not be waiting for us at the airport." It had been a while since he had experienced a ride like this, but the rollicking ride wasn't new to him. He had made similar trips in Iraq.

Within minutes, they pulled into the paved parking lot. Mud covered the vehicle from one end to the other.

"Thanks, General," Tom said. "In the future, I will choose my words more carefully."

Malcolm had already climbed into the car. He knew the scary part of the trip was about to start. Tom would waste no time getting back to the airfield.

As they drove down Highway 25, Tom's phone rang. He fished it out of his pocket, checked the caller ID and passed it over to Malcolm.

"It's Agent Spears," Tom said.

"What's up?" Malcolm asked.

He listened for a minute, periodically nodded his head in understanding. "We should be there in less than five minutes. Tip off air traffic control we are coming in for a landing."

"What?" Tom said. "We are in a hurry to get there." He eased back slightly on the gas pedal. "Three minutes, at this speed. I can see the airport."

"Keep stalling," Malcolm said into the phone. "We're almost there."

He clicked off the phone and slipped it into Tom's jacket pocket. "They're stalling him at the car rental kiosk. There are two agents in line ahead of him. The first one is giving the rental clerk a hard time; the second one is engaging the videographer in conversation to keep him occupied."

Tom pulled up in front of the airport doors. A uniformed man approached with a no-nonsense look on his face. "You can't park here," he started to say as Tom jumped out of the car.

Tom flashed his badge and flipped him the keys. "Park this somewhere close," he said as he zipped by him and into the building.

Malcolm glanced at the befuddled look on the man's face and followed Tom inside.

They stopped about thirty feet from the rental agency and studied the men in line. Their suspect stood about 5'10", had long blond hair and a fair complexion. He tipped the scales at about one hundred and eighty pounds. Hiking boots covered his feet below the relaxed blue jeans. He wore a brown sports coat over his pale yellow golf shirt. A light brown Tilley hat topped off his wardrobe. In his hand, he carried a leather case that could carry a laptop, a camera or both. In short, there was nothing remarkable about the man.

"If they're terrorists," said Tom, "they are the home-grown kind if he is a typical example."

"Resembles the one we captured in Minnesota," Malcolm agreed. "I think extortion is the crime. The whole thing smells like a money grab."

"In their dreams. No one is going to be coughing up a hundred million dollars to anyone. We don't negotiate with terrorists; that applies to extortionists as well."

Tom caught the attention of the lead agent. He covertly displayed his badge and indicated it was time to move on. The man acknowledged the instruction and smiled at the rental clerk.

"Let me think about this for a few minutes," he said. "I'll get back to you." Both men dropped out of line, and the videographer stepped up to the counter.

He tapped his credit card, paused, and picked up the keys to a waiting car. Everything had proceeded as arranged.

"That's interesting," Tom said. "This may be a lead back to whoever is running this show." He signalled the two agents from the line to come over.

"Once he's gone, see what you can find out about the source of that rental. Get a copy of the credit card number as well. Give any information you find to Special Agent Spears. We'll keep an eye on our boy until he gets settled in."

Malcolm looked surprised. "We're going to tail him in a strange city?"

Tom laughed. "Surveillance work is beneath you? Relax. Spears has a series of agents waiting to take over from us. We're taking the first shift. He can't be going far. The school is only five or ten minutes away. The bomb isn't going to explode for another four hours. We'll follow him for a bit, and then I want you to call the governor and see if he had any luck hacking into their computers. I thought he would have called you by now."

"Once the governor latches on to a project, he throws himself into it one hundred per cent. Time means nothing to him. I'll call him, but he won't be too pleased about it. He doesn't like me to hover."

"Hover is what you do, Malcolm. We all know who is the power behind the throne. Call him. We don't want him setting out on his own. That would be foreign territory for him."

Malcolm scowled at his friend but unconsciously nodded his head in agreement.

◀50▶

THE FOUR HOURS passed quickly. Malcolm contacted the governor, who reported he was making progress. As expected, he complained about the FBI agents who were holding him up by asking too many questions and making him explain how the program worked. Joe Fisher had called. He would be at the mansion before the bomb deadline. He wanted to see first-hand how they took over the state computer's signal. The governor complained about that as well. Malcolm assured all was going well at his end and the governor should contact him immediately if there were any breakthroughs.

After the call, Malcolm joined Tom in the officer's lounge at Petersen Air Base watching TV. Before long, both were snoring softly. The week's activity had caught up. Relaxing gave way to sleep.

At two-thirty local time, Agent Spears gently shook Tom's shoulder.

"It's almost time, Tom. Everything is in place."

Tom came awake and stared at the man standing over him. Almost immediately the lights came back on in his eyes. He looked at his watch. "Shit, I fell asleep."

He looked over at Malcolm who had awakened on his own at the sounds of voices in the room. Malcolm stretched his arms over his head. "I needed that," he said. He looked at his watch. "I guess zero hour is almost upon us. Is everything in place?"

"Ready to roll. You can freshen up in the restrooms over by the door." Spears handed both men a towel and facecloth. "Do you want to watch the explosion or head out for the National Forest and be there ahead of the cameraman?"

"We'll do both," Tom said. "We'll watch the action on our laptops as we head out of town. Malcolm's friend over at Fort Carson has laid on a helicopter for us. We'll meet one of your agents at the entrance to the park."

Spears rubbed his chin as if he were deep in thought. "Right, that's all set up. We have one camp site under observation. Some guy rented it yesterday, paid for two days, drove down to the site but hasn't spent any time there."

Again Spears consulted his well-used notebook. "Rented under the name of Mohammad Alzabar. He was driving a silver Honda CR-V. The vehicle has been recovered at the airport here in Colorado Springs. It was stolen in Denver the night before, and we have impounded it for examination.

"According to our agents on location, no one seems to be around the tent site, but there are other campers in the area. Anyone of them could be the man's contact. From what we observed at the airport, he has no tent, no sleeping gear. A camping park seems to be a strange choice of accommodation under those circumstances."

"It does sound strange," Malcolm said. "At least we will be able to pick him up away from the media. We want to keep this capture as quiet as possible."

"I wonder if this is a pickup point," Tom said. "Agents in Michigan traced him to a remote park in Kalamazoo where he received a laptop computer. Is this where he gets paid for this leg of the trip and gets his updated information for the next bombing?"

Tom vigorously rubbed his head with both hands trying to get the sleep from his mind. "He got this destination in an email, but cash in an envelope is harder to track than an e-money transfer. They seem to be mixing up new technology with old-fashioned hard drops."

"If that is the case, it serves the dual purpose of getting him paid and out of the area in a hurry, but with his handlers knowing exactly where he is. He has a car. The next destination may be within driving distance." Malcolm got up and started walking towards the bathroom. "Whatever is happening, we had better get on the road. Once that school goes up, he'll be on his way out of town. It's only about thirty-five miles down I-25 to the camping area."

He paused at the doorway. "Where is he anyway?"

Spears turned a page in his notebook. "About a half-hour ago he showed up at the BurgerCircus near the school. Went inside, ordered take-out and has been sitting in his car in the parking lot ever since. One of our agents took him a fresh burger soon after he went out under the pretence that his order had gotten mixed up and they had given him the wrong food. As expected, he took the new burger without questioning what had gone wrong. People are so damn predictable; it's scary. Just once I'd like someone to refuse the new burger or whatever because there was nothing wrong with the first one."

A sheepish smile crept across the agent's face. "Sorry, just a pet peeve. Anyway, our agent placed a small, magnetic tracking device on the roof of the car just in case the suspect strikes out on his own. We had a device planted at the rental location, but he declined that car in the parking lot at the last minute and upgraded to a bigger one."

Tom had already gotten to his feet. He gave Spears a thumbs-up. "Good thinking. Nothing has gone our way on this investigation up to now. Despite our lack of progress, they are taking steps to throw us off their trail."

Spears beamed at the praise. "So I've heard. We're doing

our best to cover all the angles."

"On that note," Malcolm said, "why don't we grab him as soon as the school goes up in flames? We could send an agent to the park to meet anyone who is there. They probably don't know each other anyway."

Tom stared at his friend for a few beats before answering. He seemed to be contemplating the idea. Then he shook his head. "Too risky. They might know each other. There might be some secret code word. There might be a definite pattern they follow on every occasion. We'll make the trip to the park, observe and capture."

Spears looked at the time readout on his cellphone. "You're going to be able to watch the explosion from the air if you hurry. It's only ten minutes away."

"I hear you," Tom said and followed Malcolm into the washroom.

◀51▶

AT THREE MINUTES to three, Mountain Time, the army helicopter, an MH-6, commonly called Little Bird, carrying Tom and Malcolm lifted off the tarmac at Petersen Air Force Base. In less than a minute the pilot took the machine straight up, hovered briefly at two thousand feet, aimed south and said: "Head for the park, or wait for the action?"

"What action is that, Captain?" Tom asked.

A hesitant smile flickered across the pilot's face. "It's three o'clock in the morning. I've got two FBI agents in my bird, and I'm flying to a camping park, part of the National Forest. Believe me, Agent, I've been fully briefed. I'm responsible for this aircraft in every sense of the word. We don't blindly follow orders."

"Head for the park, Captain," Malcolm said in a voice designed to quell any discussion about who was in charge of what. "We've seen enough of the 'action' to last us a lifetime. Besides, even with this overcast sky, we'll be able to see what happens."

"Yes, sir. ETA about fifteen minutes." The nose of the copter dipped, the noise increased, and they roared off to their destination expecting to arrive about twenty minutes ahead of their prey. Both men had their eyes glued to the north.

As they cleared the edge of the city, they could see the glow in the sky behind them. Flames shot straight up into the air followed seconds later by a muffled humph. All the raindrops in the area took on a reddish hue looking like a beautiful sunrise.

"Looks like the real thing," Tom said. "A heck of a lot more impressive than the test they ran at Carson."

"Yeah," Malcolm said. "I hope we didn't overplay our hand."

Confusion covered Tom's face. "Overplayed our hand? In what way?"

Malcolm stared back over the city as the bright flash faded to an after-image in his eyes. "What if it was an intentional dud?"

"Too late to be second-guessing ourselves now, my friend. We had that discussion back at the fort. All those arguments we had there still apply."

"You're right." He leaned forward and tapped the pilot on the shoulder. "Tell your guys they did a great job. Looked exactly like the real thing. Better actually. They are using a higher grade of explosives than our extortionists."

The pilot took the compliment as if he had taken part in the deception. "We aim to please, and we never accept second rate at Fort Carson."

***

Sitting in an overstuffed easy chair in Ray Tutty's spacious living room, coffee in hand, Paul Johnson watched yet another school fill his screen with fiery debris. He cringed as the flames lit up the night sky. The low clouds flattened out the top end of the explosion giving a reddish hue to the whole picture.

"Another one bites the dust," he said to Ray Tutty. "I had hoped when I couldn't get hold of Malcolm that they might have made a break-through." He nodded towards the 72-inch TV dominating one end of the room. "Doesn't look like it now."

Ray walked over to the big picture window and pulled back the drapes allowing the early morning sun to flood the room. "Those clowns don't have a clue what they're doing. Our clown could do a better job of solving this fiasco. Call the FBI and tell them we'll send him over to their headquarters so he can take over."

He took a drink from his cup of coffee. "At least we don't have to stay up all night to see the show anymore. Let's get into the office and see if our stocks are taking another hit. Barbara is probably there already. She's really into tracking whoever is leading the buying and selling. I hope your plan works and we capitalize this time. It will pay for the coffee you're giving away."

Paul tipped his cup towards his boss. "This free coffee is a brilliant idea if I do say so myself. I bet customers have already filled our shops, both watching the news and buying breakfast to go with their coffee. That's not why we're doing it, but we'll take the good with the bad."

He took another sip of the brew. "Malcolm said he would keep us in the loop. I hope to hear from him today, and I don't think I'll make the clown offer. Those guys are working themselves into the ground trying to get a handle on this. Cut them some slack."

Ray slammed his cup down on the coffee table beside the window. "Cut them some slack? People have dragged my name through the mud. There's still a large part of the population out there who thinks I should be paying these bastards off. No amount of free coffee is going to convince them otherwise. They don't grasp the idea that you don't negotiate with terrorists. Never. We have to catch them and crush them."

His face had taken on a dangerous red turning-to-purple colour as the emotion in his voice exploded into the room. The stress would appear to be taking a toll on him as well.

Paul got up; concern was written all over his face. "Settle down, Ray. You're going to talk yourself into a heart attack." He put his hand on Ray's shoulder, gently forcing him into a nearby chair. "I'm sure a breakthrough is imminent. With both Malcolm and Tom Burke off the radar, something big must be in the works."

Ray brushed Paul's hand away. "I'm sorry, Paul. These attacks leave me feeling helpless. There must be something more we can do. Where's Homeland Security? Where's all this expert surveillance we hear so much about?"

"You are doing something. You're out there in the public eye keeping everyone as upbeat as possible. You're not hiding in an office somewhere. People feel comforted that you are tackling these guys head on. Don't underestimate the effect these TV appearances have on people."

Ray's eyes suddenly twinkled, leading to a complete smile. "That asshole of a governor and I do make a good team. You're right. Keeping the troops rallied is important." The smile faded. "But it's time for the talk to end and for the action to begin. We have to end this once and for all."

Paul punched him lightly on the shoulder. "No arguments from me on that."

◀52▶

MALCOLM AND TOM jumped down from the "Little Bird", hunched over and ran from under the twenty-seven-foot spinning rotors. They turned and gave the pilot a thumbs-up. He had dropped them onto a playing field in the park and would come back in an hour to wait for them unless he heard differently. Neither agent expected to spend much time in the camping park. Sunrise was a distant three hours away. The earlier rain had turned into a fine mist. Any serious searching would have to wait.

A set of headlights flashed on at the far edge of the field. Their reception party awaited their arrival. Pulling their overcoats tight, they headed towards the illumination.

"I'm Special Agent Maurice LeBlanc," said one of the two men standing beside the car. Their clothes were more casual than the men from the east; both were already soaking wet. "This is Special Agent Rodney Archibald."

Tom handled the introductions for his side of the meeting. Everyone shook hands.

"Let's cut the formality," Malcolm said. "I'm getting wet. Can we talk in your car, Maurice?"

Maurice smiled. "Hop in."

Once seated, Tom got right to the point. "Did you find anything of value here?"

"We were assigned to this location as soon as we received your information that the photographer would be spending time here in the park. We have his location under surveillance. There are two more agents in a tent two sites away from the suspect's. Nothing of interest has taken place yet, but we didn't want to risk being seen searching the place.

"I had a chat with the ranger who rented out the camping spot. Despite the man's Arabic sounding name, he looked as American as Dan Aykroyd. Dark hair, round face, a little on the heavy side. *White.*"

He placed extra emphasis on the final word. "Aykroyd is Canadian," Malcolm said. "The Arabic name could be designed to throw us off, or he could be a home-grown convert. I trust you checked him out."

"Tried to. The man doesn't exist in any of our records."

Tom shifted in the back seat and leaned forward a little. "Strange that they went to this effort to deceive us. I wonder if they have been doing this all along and we have been missing the clues. Any thoughts, Malcolm?"

Malcolm leaned back in his seat and looked out into the night air. He waited a long time before answering. "I don't think we would have missed anything this obvious. We've thoroughly investigated every scene." He shook his head. "I don't know, Tom. I would hope we would have picked up something like this."

"If it hadn't been for the email the governor discovered, we wouldn't have found this place," Tom said. "Maybe they are covering tracks we have been missing. Jesus, that raises the level of their expertise even higher. Who are these sons-of-bitches?"

He turned to the agents in the front seat again. "Did you find anything else?"

"Rodney and I had a quick look around under the pretence of gathering firewood. With this constant drizzle, having an outdoor fire seemed ill-advised. We did go through the motions. Lit the fire, had a few non-alcoholic beers, appeared friendly, but no one dropped over to talk with us. With the rain, the camping area is not too crowded tonight.

"Short of setting up high-powered spotlights, it's hard to do an investigation in the dark."

He paused and studied the two men sitting in the back seat. "No offence, but you don't look the part of campers."

"We're from Georgia," Tom said with a twinkle in his eye. "We don't camp when the temperature is in the fifties."

"Sooks," Maurice said. His demeanour changed. "What is the plan?"

"You boys will make the arrest," Tom said. "Malcolm and I will hang back and observe. We don't think he will spend much time here. He has no camping gear. We think it's either a drop-point where he will pick up his payment and perhaps more information or a meeting spot where someone else will give him his payment and more information. We're hoping for the latter because we could then have two suspects in custody."

"It's possible the next school is within driving distance," Malcolm said. "He may be heading out right away."

Maurice looked back at Tom. "Should we follow him if he takes off again?"

Tom shook his head. "No. Arrest him. We're not going through this charade again. We know the school wasn't damaged, but the general public thinks they blew it to bits. We're not doing that again. We're hoping today is the turning point, one way or another. We want to get hold of his computer before he has a chance to wipe the drive or destroy it in any way. Give one of your men the task of getting that right off the bat. That will be his sole mission."

Tom's cellphone vibrated in his pocket.

"He's about five minutes outside the park gate," Spears reported. "Drove as if someone shot him from a cannon down the Interstate. Good thing we had the tracking device on his car. There would have been no way to covertly follow him at those speeds."

"OK," Tom said. "We're still near the gate. We'll get into

position before he gets here."

Special Agent LeBlanc pulled out onto the campground road and turned down a secondary lane. "This comes in from the back of the site," he said. "If anyone is waiting, we don't want them to see us. We'll park a couple of hundred yards on the other side of his site and walk up." He looked in the rearview mirror, a wicked smile lighting up his face. "We'll be around a corner so that they won't see our lights. Sorry, gentlemen, you're going to get wet."

"Wetter," Malcolm corrected him. "We're already wet."

Five minutes later the four men slowly made their way up the trail towards the selected camping site, Special Agent LeBlanc in the lead. Suddenly they were lit up like a shadow puppet show in what had to be a million candle power flashlight.

"Damn," Malcolm said. One hand shielded his eyes; the other held his nine-millimeter Glock.

Without hesitation, Tom exploded past Agent LeBlanc towards the man holding the light and in less than two seconds had him on the ground with a knee in his back and a gun aimed at his head.

"Identify yourself," he barked into the prone man's ear.

"Don't shoot. Don't shoot. I was just going to the can and heard you guys out here in the dark. Identify yourselves."

By now Malcolm had arrived at their side. Agents LeBlanc and Archibald, hunched over in shooter's stance, covering the path from both directions. Malcolm turned off the spotlight and took a small LED light from his pocket. He shined the light in the man's face forcing him to squint.

"Where's your campsite and how many are in it?" he said. His voice was low but authoritative. He left no room for discussion.

The man pulled an arm out from under his body. "Right there." He pointed at a 9x12 family-sized blue tent about thirty feet away. "I'm here with my wife and kids."

Two small, wide eyes stared out the tent door when Malcolm flashed his light in that direction.

Tom eased his knee from the man's back and holstered his pistol. He produced his FBI credentials and held them in front of Malcolm's light. "FBI," he said. "How long have you and your family been here?"

The man was still shaken from the attack. "This afternoon. What's going on?"

Tom got up, reached down and took the man's arm and pulled him to his feet. "Go into your tent, stay there and don't say a word. We'll want to talk to you in a few minutes."

The man hesitated. Malcolm pointed.

"Now."

The man scooted over to his tent and slipped inside. He could be heard talking to his family in a low, excited voice.

Malcolm reached down and picked up the man's spotlight. "This may come in handy," he said.

LeBlanc joined Tom and Malcolm. "Just a toy," he said. "We'll show you a real light when this show gets underway. So far, I haven't seen any other signs of movement." He looked at the glowing hands of his watch. "At least we have our hearts pumping now. Our boy should be coming down that road at any minute."

A faint glow could be seen slowly coming their way. All four men melted into the underbrush. The two agents in the tent slipped outside and lay down, blending into the duff covering the ground. They waited.

After a few minutes, the rental car came into sight. The driver strained to read the campsite numbers in the dark. His headlights barely illuminated the ground-level posts offering directions to the newly arrived. The campground operators expected people to arrive during daylight hours, not the backend of the night.

When the car finally came parallel to the designated spot, it stopped. The driver quietly eased out the door, conscious that everyone around him was sleeping, or so he thought. Using an inadequate flashlight, he looked around the raised pad designed for a tent. To his left, he spotted a metal container designed to hold hot ashes from campers' barbecues. The people in charge of the National Forest always let their fear of forest fires define their priorities. Preventing fires rated near the top of the list.

Leaving his car running and the door open, the man headed towards the disposal unit. He raised the cover and peeked inside before slipping a pair of green neoprene gloves onto his hands. He had come prepared to dig in the black ashes. He pulled a plastic-wrapped package from its hiding place, brushed off the loose ash and pulled the Ziploc top apart. He withdrew a stack of bills, letting the wrapper drop to the ground. Even in the overcast darkness, the FBI agents could see the smile on his face reflected from the car's interior light.

He removed his gloves. They joined the plastic bag on the ground as he let the edges of the bills slip through his thumb, doing a quick count. He pocketed the money and headed back to his vehicle

Tom lay about fifty feet away in the wet grass, LeBlanc about ten feet from him. The agents from the tent had worked their way up to the back of the car.

"OK," Tom said in a low whisper. "Take him."

Maurice keyed his walkie-talkie. "Now."

The four local agents all sprang into action. As promised, the two agents from the tent carried lights that turned night into day, blinding the photographer. Before he could even call out in surprise, he found himself slammed into his car with his hands pinned behind his back.

He kicked back at the agent holding him and caught him on the shin. As a reward, he was quickly crashed face down into the dirt. The weight of the agent landing on top of him expelled all the air from his lungs and any more thoughts of resistance from his mind.

"FBI, you're under arrest," the covering agent hissed into his ear.

"Holy shit, you've got him."

Tom turned to see the camper and his young son standing behind him.

"Get back into your tent." Tom pointed as he spoke in a low, urgent whisper. He didn't want to wake the entire campground.

The man and boy held their ground. "Is this one of the terrorists?" The thought of terrorism appeared to be on everyone's radar. "He doesn't look like a terrorist to me. Are you sure you have the right man?"

Anger flashed in Tom's eyes. Malcolm quickly stepped between the two men.

"Here, take your flashlight and get back into your tent. There may be more criminals around. We don't want you caught in the line of fire."

"What? The line of fire?"

The threat of danger spurred the man to action. He crouched down, put his hand on his son's shoulder and pushed him down into a crouch as well. His eyes darted around in the darkness. "Are you serious?"

"Get back into your tent," Malcolm said, "and get your family on the floor." Like Tom, his voice brokered no argument. The two agents' eyes met and shared a brief look of frustration. Malcolm pointed again and the intruders duck-walked back to the safety of their accommodations. His wife and daughter could be seen standing outside in the reflected glare of the bright spotlights.

Malcolm and Tom moved up to the lights and stood behind them. The vantage point gave them a good view of proceedings but shielded them from being seen. One of the agents emptied the suspect's pockets onto the hood of his car. Besides the money he had just picked up, his pockets were nearly empty. A handkerchief, some lens tissues, a package of Tums and a credit card with no name or number. The card's chip discreetly held all the information. They found no wallet or other form of identification.

"What the hell is this all about?" The indignation in the suspect's voice suggested he wasn't going to roll over and cooperate. "Where is he going with my laptop?"

One of the agents had immediately snatched the computer from the car as soon as the lights had come on. As instructed, he didn't do anything but hold it.

Tom remembered the previously captured computer had run a hard-drive scrubbing program triggered by a retina scan of the people trying to operate it. He was taking no chances. No one would open this computer until it was safe and sound in an FBI laboratory. Their intent was to open the case and secure the hard drive before opening the cover. It would be decrypted to see what information it would give up.

"You can't take my computer. I'm an American citizen. I know my rights." The man's voice was getting louder.

"Detect any sign of an accent?" Tom asked Malcolm.

Malcolm shook his head. "Midwest, maybe."

Tom nodded in agreement. "Take him to Petersen," he said to Maurice. "Charge him with speeding and unsafe use of an automobile. I don't think he had any intention of staying here."

Confusion filled the Colorado agent's face. "Speeding? Are you serious?"

"It'll do for now," Tom said. "I think we will come up with a few more charges once we start talking with him."

The now-cuffed man squinted into the blinding spotlights, trying to see who was making the decision. "I want a lawyer," he said.

"That's your right," Tom said. "Call one. Give me his number, I'll call him for you or I'll gladly appoint somebody to represent your interests." The tone of his voice suggested the latter suggestion might be a stretch of the truth.

The man glared in the direction of the voice he could hear coming from behind the bright light. He seemed to consider the offer. "Don't bother. I haven't done anything wrong. I don't need a lawyer."

"There you go," Tom said as he smiled to himself. The words were music to his ears.

◀53▶

"GOOD MORNING. I'M Special Agent Thomas Burke. This is the chief of staff of the state of Georgia, Malcolm Truex." Tom paused and studied the reactions of the man sitting in front of him. He remained stoic. Then in a slow drawl, he said: "Special Agent? I don't think you have any power in this park. Special means you have limited powers."

"You're right about that, Matlock. And when you committed a crime in Michigan and crossed state lines and committed crimes in Colorado, those limited powers kicked in. We'd like to ask you some questions."

The man shrugged then shifted his gaze to Malcolm. "You're a long way from Georgia. I doubt that you have much jurisdiction in Colorado."

"I've been seconded to the Federal Bureau of Investigation to assist in the investigation of the school bombings taking place across the country." He smiled. "Don't worry; I'm here with the president's blessing. I can bust your ass with the same power as the rest of the FBI." The claim was only a slight stretch of the truth. Some president, not necessarily the current one, had in the past given the FBI the ability to bring in outside expert help. Malcolm's appointment took advantage of this old ruling.

The man's smile quivered slightly and then took on its former lustre. "Now why would you want to bust my ass? I am just a freelance photographer shooting some of nature's beauty in a state park. Or at least I was until your storm troopers snatched me out of my car and dragged me off down here.

"Of course, I know your buddy was there." He flicked his thumb towards Tom. "I recognize his voice. The big cheese. Barking orders to everyone."

Malcolm sat down at the table ignoring those comments. He had a single sheet of paper in front of him which he studied for several seconds before looking up. "You've been involved in at least fifteen insurance cases where you just happened to be at the right place at the right time to capture incriminating film footage." He glanced at the paper again. "You have sold at least five videos to the pseudo-news shows depicting police violence for which we understand you were well paid." Malcolm looked up at the man sitting across the table struggling to remain neutral at the accusations. "I see no circumstances where anyone paid you for nature pictures." Malcolm continued. "So let's cut the bullshit."

"Hey, I'm a lucky guy. I happened to be in the right place at the right time." The man smirked at the two FBI agents.

Tom yanked back a chair beside Malcolm and sat down, slamming a briefcase on the table in front of him. He flicked it open.

"I'm going to save all of us a lot of time," he said, absolutely no humour in his voice. "We know who you are and what you are doing in Colorado and, you will appreciate this, we have photographic evidence to back up what I'm going to tell you."

Tom took a picture of the photographer filming a column of flames shooting into the air. The light from the fire created a perfect silhouette of the man. Agent Spears had put together a photographic folder for Tom from his agent's surveillance photos along with all the appropriate documentation.

"This is you," he slid the picture across the table and tapped the time code in the bottom right corner, "at twenty seconds after three this morning."

The smile faded from the man's face.

Malcolm held up a hand. "Let me, Tom," he said in a pleasant voice. They were establishing who would play good cop and who would be bad cop early in the interview. It had been a while since they played this role together, but they easily slipped back into their previous comfort zones. "We don't want to intimidate the poor man. We simply want to learn what he knows." His gaze shifted across the table. "I'm sure you're willing to cooperate with our investigation." A smile lit up Malcolm's face. "Right?"

The man returned Malcolm's smile with a nervous smile of his own. "I'm not here to cause any trouble," he said. "As I said, I'm just a freelance photographer who happened to be in the right place at the right time to catch some shots of a school blowing up. I didn't plant any bombs or anything. I don't know anything about any of that." He held up his hands in a defensive display.

Tom slammed his fist onto the table. "Cut the bullshit. We both know you're involved in this up to your eyeballs. Right now it's a question of us conducting this interview or us turning you over to Homeland Security who will charge you with treason." Tom paused for a few seconds to let those words sink in. "The penalty for treason in this country is execution. You decide." He glanced over at Malcolm. "What do they use here in Colorado, Malcolm, lethal injection?"

All the blood drained from the man's face. "Let's not talk stupid here." His voice had lost all of its former arrogance. "I didn't kill anybody."

"You're the one being stupid," Tom interrupted. "But, there's no law against stupidity in this country. Treason, that's another matter."

"Let's dial back the rhetoric a little," Malcolm said, the voice of reason. "We have a few simple questions for you to answer. Is that going to be a problem?"

The man shook his head in short back and forth movements, relief evident. "No. Not a problem at all. Go ahead and ask me anything. I have nothing to hide."

"Let's keep it simple," Malcolm said. "Who hired you?"

The man's face turned ashen. "I don't know. Honestly, I don't know."

"You've got to do better than that. Are you being paid?"

The man nodded.

"Good, so who pays you?"

"I was contacted by email. I advertise on the Internet. The deep web. Do you know what that is? Of course you do." The words tumbled out of the man's mouth faster than school kids going to recess. "I was given an address of a park in Kalamazoo. I work out of Michigan. In a garbage can in an isolated part of the park, I found a computer, the address of a school, a list of instructions and an envelope of money. There was a promise of more to come."

"So you knew the school was going to be blown up in Kalamazoo?" Tom asked, leaning closer to the man.

"No, not really."

"Come on. Everyone in the country knows about the school bombings. What did you think was going to happen at that school at three in the morning that required a videographer?" Malcolm looked away in disgust. "I'm trying to help you out here, man. Don't treat us like idiots. My patience level is extremely low right now." He glanced at Tom and then back to the photographer, a look of disgust on his face. "Special Agent Burke is right. Homeland Security can have you as far as I'm concerned."

Malcolm got up from the table and headed towards the door.

"Wait." The man held up a hand. Malcolm was supposed to be on his side. "OK, so maybe I did suspect something. But nobody has been hurt by these bombings. We all know that."

Malcolm paused, started to turn back when there was a knock at the door.

Tom twisted in his chair, irritated at the knocking. He gave Malcolm a flick of his head. Malcolm walked across the room and looked through the window. Agent Spears stood there, a message pad in his hand.

"Sorry to interrupt, but this is important," he mouthed through the glass. He held up the pad. He had scrawled URGENT across the page.

Malcolm opened the door, took the message, studied it briefly, and turned to Tom. The fatigue that had been dragging him down disappeared. "Holy shit, Tom, you'd better have a look at this."

In two steps he crossed the room, extending the message pad to his partner. Tom read the message, paused, and read it again. "For god's sake, Malcolm, what is your boy up to now?" He looked at his prisoner across the table. "Don't move," he said and followed Malcolm and Agent Spears out the door.

Once outside the room, Agent Spears took Tom's arm. "I'm not exactly sure what's going on back in Georgia, but Agent Desmond sounded panicky. I think he has lost total control of the situation out there."

"Kevin never loses control," Tom said. "What did he say?"

"Just like the message says, the National Guard has been activated and are attacking a location in the Okefenokee Swamp as we speak. My assistant is getting the details, but I thought I'd better inform you of this at once. It seems a little over the top from what I know of the situation. I find it hard to believe they would take this kind of action without input from you. Kevin has already ordered a helicopter to take him to the scene."

Tom glared at Malcolm. "You don't know the governor of

Georgia very well. He's a loose cannon when his handler leaves him alone. Get hold of him, Malcolm. Find out what the hell is going on."

Malcolm dug out his cellphone and punched in a couple of numbers. He had the governor on speed dial. He waited impatiently for the governor to pick up.

"He must have come up with some crucial information," he said to Tom.

Malcolm held up a finger to stop him before Tom could answer.

Malcolm put the finger in one ear as he tried to make out what the governor was saying. The sounds of a helicopter engine drowned out his words. After several futile attempts to exchange information, he clicked off the phone and turned to Tom.

"Let's get over to the communication centre. Cellphone reception is too poor to hold a meaningful conversation. He's either in an OH58 Kiowa Warrior from the 1-1169th General Support Aviation Battalion in Savannah or a CH47F Chinook from Hunter Army Airfield. Those are the usual culprits when we activate the Georgia National Guard. I'll call The Adjutant General, Arthur Monahan. Even the governor can't use the Guard without TAG approval."

Tom turned to Agent Spears. "Send a couple of agents to finish interviewing the photographer. I want a complete timeline from when his bosses first contacted him until now. I want to know how he gets his clients, where he advertises, what he had for breakfast for the past week. I want everything there is to know about him."

"Malcolm," Agent Spears held up his hand to slow Malcolm down before he hurried away. "You had a call from your office." He consulted his notepad. "Joe Fisher. He said not to interrupt your interrogation, but you should call him as soon as you can." The agent stared into Malcolm's eyes.

"He claims he has taken over your office."

"Of course he has." Malcolm punched numbers into his cellphone as he started down the hallway. Tom hurried behind him. Events had spiralled out of control, and they had to catch up.

◄54►

GOVERNOR PETER WESTON peered down from the co-pilot seat of the Kiowa Warrior helicopter. As Commander-in-chief of the Georgia National Guard, he felt this was the proper place for him to lead this attack. To his left flew a partially loaded CH-47F transport helicopter with twenty-five fully armed guardsmen on board and a couple of embedded members of the media. One of the journalists was Rod Sanderson from New York Daily News.

Beneath him, the Okefenokee Swamp started to come into view.

Two hours before, all hell had broken loose as he surreptitiously monitored the computers of the extortionists/terrorists. He had yet to declare which he believed they were. They had dispatched coded emails to addresses all over the state. With the help of the two FBI agents assigned by Tom, and Joe Fisher, who had arrived early that morning, they had quickly decoded the first three messages. The information contained therein proved to be identical. The rest could wait until later.

The bombing in Colorado Springs had not gone as the bombers had planned. They suspected there was a leak in their organization. They were all to meet immediately at their headquarters. Diligent searching by Joe Fisher in the innards of the compromised computer came up with the GPS coordinates of that address.

The governor called up a Google map, plugged in the numbers and come up with a destination.

"The Okefenokee Swamp. We got them," the governor

declared to the three men. "This is the break we've been working for. Let's assemble a task force and take them down."

The agents shared his enthusiasm but not his plan.

"We have to contact Agent Burke," one of them said. "We'll bring him up to speed and work out a plan of attack."

"Burke is running around playing super-agent in Colorado. We don't have time to consult with him. We have to strike while the iron is hot." The governor sounded like he would broker no arguments.

The agents were equally adamant. "This is no time to go off half-cocked. We have to follow procedures. Let me call Kevin Desmond. He's running things in Agent Burke's absence."

"No, young man," the governor said, "I'm running things. You do know this is the governor's mansion you're in."

Joe Fisher had silently watched the by-play. He held out his hands in front of himself, palms down. "Let's everyone calm down and take a deep breath," he said. "It's going to take time for all these people to gather at their headquarters. We want to wait until they have all assembled."

"No," the governor said. "If they think we've compromised them, they may take off as soon as they all get there. We must be ready. If we lose them now, there's no telling when we will get an opportunity like this again. It's time to act. This intel is time sensitive."

He punched a button on his phone and waited for his secretary to respond. "Jennifer, get me TAG on the line."

"TAG?" one of the agents asked. His area of expertise was computer software.

"The Adjutant General," Joe said. "He's activating the National Guard."

"General," the governor said in his executive voice.

"We're ready. I have the co-ordinates."

The governor listened for a few minutes. "Sounds good," he said. "Pick me up in five minutes. I'll be ready."

He stood up and walked around his desk. "I'm sorry, gentlemen, it's time to leave. There is only room for one on the helicopter that's coming to get me. You guys do what you have to do." He turned to Malcolm's computer expert, "Joe, thanks for coming, but this saga is coming to an end. We appreciated your help."

He crowded the three men towards the door of his office. In the distance, the sounds of a helicopter's rotors could be heard beating through the air.

Joe reached out and shook the governor's hand. "Always glad to be of assistance," he said. Joe headed out the door and hustled down the corridor to Malcolm's office.

"Governor, you can't call in the Guard. The investigation is an FBI matter." The FBI agent made one more futile attempt to slow down the governor.

The governor gave the man an impatient look. "Do you think these guys could be terrorists?"

"That's quite possible but..."

The governor interrupted. "If you're familiar with the constitution you know that gives me the power to do what I'm doing. Now, good day gentlemen."

By now they had reached the door of the governor's office. He ushered them through and closed it again. The two men looked at each other, shrugged, and then reluctantly left the building. They had been there all night. It was time to make their report to their bosses.

The governor rubbed his bleary eyes. He had been hunched over a computer screen for much too long. It was time to get out of the office and to finally take real action. He grabbed a brown leather jacket from his closet, slipped it on and followed the agents out of the building.

Within minutes a military helicopter landed in a parking

lot beside the governor's mansion. Ducking his head, he ran up and pulled open the door. The man in the pilot's seat had two stars on the collar of his shirt.

"General Monahan?" The governor looked surprised. "I didn't expect to see you leading the mission."

"Gotta keep my hours up," the general said. He laughed. "And why would I miss the biggest thing that's happened in this state since the Civil War. When you called last night with your plan, I asked myself: 'Which pilot could I trust flying the governor of the state into a potentially dangerous zone.' Several names came to mind, but considering the risk, I thought I best do it personally."

"I appreciate that, General, but there should be no risk. We are only going to observe from the air." He pointed his thumb out the window. "Those men in that chopper are the boots on the ground."

"Well, Governor, that's how it looks on paper. My years of experience tell me things don't always go as planned, especially when the hostiles are a completely unknown entity. Have you decided if they are foreign terrorists or homegrown extortionists yet?" The general turned to face the governor sitting two feet away. "Or even worse, homegrown terrorists."

"The jury is still out on that. The fact that the money should come from the fast-food industry confuses the issue. All we know for sure is we are dealing with a group of fanatics, and we must stop them." The governor reached out and gave the general a friendly punch on the leg. "In a few minutes, we will have all the answers."

The general nodded in agreement and then focused his attention of the instruments in front of him. He flicked a switch on the radio, sending out an audible clicking noise. The Chinook pulled up beside them, the pilot focussing all his attention on the general. Monahan gave a big circular motion with his hand. "Our surveillance pictures are over an hour old," the general said to the governor. "I'll have these guys hang back here while we get the latest intel."

The pilot of the Chinook gave a thumbs-up through his window and turned his craft into a circling pattern. The general brought his machine around so that he was approaching the target zone from the east. With the rising sun directly behind them, they would be less visible from the ground.

The governor pointed at the helicopter sitting outside a hastily constructed fibreglass building. Through the binoculars, he could see the crest of the Okefenokee Swamp Park with the big green alligator snapping at him painted on the side of the machine.

"Does the park have its own fleet of helicopters?"

"Not that I know of," the general answered. "But it would be a great cover for the extortionists to fly around without arousing suspicion. The entrance to the park is over by Fargo on the western side. If they made their approaches from the north, park officials might not even be aware of them. A huge, vacant swamp extends that way for several miles.

There's a company in Savannah that rents a similar chopper, without the logo of course. I've used them. Rentals are unbelievably easy. A fifteen-minute shakedown flight and the proper licences are all it takes to get airborne."

"There are two mud-spattered SUVs down there as well with the logo on the sides. Again, they probably approach from a less travelled part of the park."

As they watched, a door of the building opened and a man carrying a large cardboard box exited. He carried the box over to the helicopter and set it down beside three similar boxes.

"Looks like they might be abandoning the place," the general said.

"That was my fear. As soon as the leader suspected he

was exposed, he pulled up stakes and is headed to new territory. There's a clearing about a half-mile down that road where the Chinook can set down. The troops can be on top of them in about five minutes. We can track anyone who flees from up here."

"OK," the general said. "It's not eloquent, but it should work. A chopper and two vehicles, how many people do you think we're dealing with?"

"Not more than we can handle, General. The men on the Chinook are all battle-hardened veterans as I requested?"

"The best of the best, Governor. Major Ron Smith served with me in Iraq. I have absolute faith in his ability to lead. As a bonus, they all have kids in school. They want to see this cleaned up as much as anyone before school starts next week."

"Don't we all. Give the order, General. Let's end this once and for all."

The general again keyed the radio, this time giving three distinct clicks. He climbed higher into the sky where they could watch the whole scene but not be as noticeable from the ground. They hovered over the intended landing area. In two minutes the Chinook appeared below them. Hanging out the side of the machine, a news photographer captured the scene below them.

The general keyed the mike again. This time he spoke. "Give 'em hell, boys. Try to take them alive, but remember you're number one."

"I'm going to give Malcolm a call," the governor said. "He put his life on hold for the past week while he worked on this. Too bad he can't be here to see it wrapped up."

He punched some numbers into his cellphone and started to bring the instrument to his ear. All of a sudden all hell broke loose on the ground below them.

◀55▶

"MALCOLM TRUEX'S OFFICE."

"Are you sure, Margaret? I hear we have an interloper setting up camp there."

Margaret hesitated. "I found him here when I came in. He said it would be all right with you, Malcolm. He was very insistent."

"I bet he was. Put him on the line."

Joe Fisher had left the door to Malcolm's office open and heard Margaret's part of the conversation. He punched a button on the phone as soon as the red light flashed.

"Malcolm, things are happening fast around here, too fast."

"Slow down, Joe. What's happening too fast?"

"The governor has activated the National Guard, supposedly because of a flurry of emails sent out by the terrorists, or whatever they are."

"So I've heard."

"What you haven't heard is that the Guards were standing by fully ready to go. He had a helicopter picking him up on the front lawn in less than five minutes. We both know things don't happen that quickly."

"On the front lawn?"

"Well, maybe not on the front lawn, but you know what I mean. When the governor gave the order, they were standing by. I've been here since four this morning. He didn't talk to TAG in that time, so he made the preparations some time ago."

There was a period of silence on the phone while

Malcolm contemplated this information.

"He was as surprised as hell when that school went up in flames," Joe said. "Me too, for that matter. I thought you were out there to prevent that."

"It's not what you think," Malcolm said. "We'll talk about that later. He must have alerted the Guard as soon as he connected with the terrorists' computer. He's not a man who sits around and twiddles his thumbs. When it's time to act, he acts."

"I know the governor's impulsive, Malcolm, but TAG is supposed to be the voice of reason. I'm telling you that helicopter had to be sitting on a runway idling very close to here when he made the call."

"Yeah, well General Monahan sometimes thinks he's the reincarnation of General Patton. He and the governor probably both agree with the quote 'A good plan violently executed now is better than a perfect plan executed next week.'"

"And what about you, Malcolm? Do you agree with that?"

A few more seconds of silence before Malcolm answered. "I'm not there, Joe. I can't comment on the situation that is unfolding in Georgia."

Now it was Joe's turn to be silent. "Why aren't you here, Malcolm? What the hell are you doing running around doing trifling work in Colorado when the important action is here in Georgia?"

Malcolm was taken aback by the attack from his friend. "We've captured the videographer, Joe. We were interviewing him when the call came in about the attack." He could almost hear the cringing in his voice. Maybe Joe was right. He should have stayed in Georgia and kept a watchful eye on the governor.

"How are you making out with the computers?" Malcolm asked, changing the subject. "Finding anything useful?"

"I've transferred the contents of the terrorists' computer to an external hard drive. I'm going through it now. It's got all their plans, the schools, the choice of explosives. I'm still digging to find out their true ideology. There has been nothing political in any of the files I've accessed yet, but there's a lot more stuff to examine."

By now Malcolm and Tom had reached the communication office at the air base. A uniformed airman stood outside the door awaiting their arrival.

Malcolm stopped before the airman could usher them into the room. "Tom, get hold of Kevin and tell him to get the details about the other bombs from Joe. Dispatch bomb squads right away to dismantle these devices. That's more important than him chasing the National Guard into the swamp and having a confrontation with the governor."

Tom looked aghast. "You want me to leave that idiot in charge? I can't do that, Malcolm."

Malcolm put on his best conciliatory face. "General Monahan is in charge of the operation, Tom. He's no political hack. He earned his stars in combat. He doesn't just talk the talk; he has already walked the walk.

"I know you are not a fan of the governor, but let me remind you of one important fact about him that you already know. He only has the very best people around him. As an Independent governor, he owes no allegiance to any political party. There are no pork barrel appointments on his staff."

Tom looked at his friend. "Have you discussed this with the governor?"

Malcolm was taken aback by the tone of the agent's voice. "We have discussed every scenario we could think of. Haven't you?"

"Of course we have, but it's our operation. The FBI is running this show, Malcolm."

Malcolm held up his hands as if warding off an attack.

"It is what it is, Tom. Right now, like it or not, the governor appears to be leading a group of Guardsmen into an attack on these terrorists. We may not like it." He shook his head. "Scratch that. We don't like it. But it is happening, and we have to live with it."

Before the fuming Tom could answer, they reached the communications room. Malcolm entered first.

A sergeant removed his earphones and turned to greet them. He looked frustrated. "I'm in contact with the Air National Guard in Georgia," he said, "but they are having a problem connecting with their assets in the air. I think it's a new recruit doing this for the first time. "I'm trying to guess what kind of equipment he has and am talking him through the procedures."

"Sign off with him," Malcolm said. "Call Hunter Army Airfield in Savannah. If I know the governor, this will be an army operation."

"You knew he was planning on doing this." Tom kicked a chair, causing everyone in the room to jump. His voice carried his frustrations from the hallway into the room with him. "I should have left you home. It's my fault. I brought the only voice of reason in that mansion with me."

Malcolm looked at the staring faces. "Calm down, Tom. Don't underestimate Peter. He's not as incompetent as you think." Malcolm hoped that using the governor's name rather than position might confuse the listeners in the room about whom they were talking. He still had his loyalties to the man.

"I've contacted Hunter," the sergeant said, breaking the tension in the room.

Malcolm jumped at the opportunity. "Have them patch me through to the governor's helicopter."

"Sorry," the sergeant said. "The mission is running silent. They are maintaining radio silence."

"Let me talk to Hunter," Malcolm said and slid into a

chair beside the radioman.

"This is Captain Malcolm Truex of the Georgia National Guard." He gave his regimental number. "Patch me through to the governor at once."

"I'm sorry, sir," a voice came back to him. "My orders are to maintain radio silence."

Malcolm banged his fist on the desk in front of him. "I'm overriding those orders, soldier. I'm the governor's chief of staff, and I'm telling you to patch me through to him."

There was a moment of silence in the room while everyone stopped what they were doing to see how this confrontation was going to play out.

Finally, the voice came back from Georgia with its slow drawl, "Again, I'm sorry, Captain, but my orders come from *General* Monahan. We are to maintain radio silence."

Malcolm banged the desk with both fists this time. He looked back at the FBI agent. "Any ideas, Tom?"

Tom looked equally frustrated, but could only shrug his shoulders in defeat.

The voice from Georgia filled the room again. "Wait, Captain. The general just broke radio silence. I'll contact him for you."

The radio room in Colorado filled with the static roar of a helicopter engine covering the muffled sound of an explosion. They were listening to an open mike.

"Holy hell," an excited voice said. "They blew themselves up."

"Jesus," another voice said. "Why would they do that? They were preparing to evacuate."

"That's the governor," Malcolm said. "Let me talk to him, soldier."

◀56▶

RAY TUTTY AND Paul Johnson stood behind Barbara Bishop's chair studying her computer screen.

"I don't understand this," Ray said. "There was a school explosion last night, and yet someone is buying up all of our stocks that are available. The price has gone up a couple of cents. Every other day since this started there was a big selloff every morning."

"This is the British Exchange we are looking at," Barbara said "It looks like the same group of buyers that had ended up cashing in on the bargains all week. I still can't track who they are, but today they didn't force the prices down. It doesn't make sense. They are grabbing up all the stocks they can get hold of at current prices. It's been over two hours now. New York will be opening in a couple of hours. We have to decide what we are going to do when that happens."

Paul walked over to the side counter and made himself a coffee. "Anyone want some fuel for their brains?" he asked. He sat in one of the office chairs and sipped his brew.

"I don't own a lot of our British shares," he said. "When New York opens, that's a different matter. It's hard to believe prices would drop here if they are rising in London. Stable prices or rising prices shouldn't be a concern to us." He took another sip of coffee.

"Stop stalling, Paul," Ray said, "what's your point?"

Paul ignored Ray and looked at Barbara. "Are there enough shares out there for someone to try a hostile takeover of the company?"

Barbara shook her head. "There's more than enough shares in this room to prevent that. They could make themselves a major player at stockholder meetings, but could never outvote the three of us."

"I didn't think so. Why would anyone buy stocks at a time like this? Until this school bombing thing plays out, if I weren't a vice-president, I wouldn't be investing in this company."

"That's not a concern right now," Ray said. "We're going to crush those terrorist sons of bitches. They will never take us down, and we will never pay them." Colour started to rise in his face.

"Calm down, Ray," Barbara said. She looked at Paul. "For an aggressive investor, volatile times are an opportunity to make a lot of money. Risk versus reward. Despite the rhetoric, Ray is right. We will come out of this bruised but not beaten. Once this fiasco ends, we will be as strong as ever."

Before Paul could respond, Barbara's phone rang. She answered, listened, and looked surprised. "Ray," she said, "the governor would like you to make yourself available for a press conference at the mansion right away."

"Is that Malcolm?" Paul said. "Let met talk to him."

Barbara shook her head. "No, it's Jennifer, the governor's executive assistant." She smiled at Paul. "You weren't invited, just Ray." She turned her attention back to Ray. "She's waiting for an answer."

"I don't jump every time that pinhead speaks. Who the hell does he think he is?"

"He'll be there," Barbara said. "Can you tell me what this is about?"

She listened some more and then said goodbye and hung up.

"She doesn't know what's up. The governor insisted that you be there for an important announcement. She found a note on her desk when she came in this morning to call you and arrange for your attendance. Incidentally, he's not at the mansion either. Jennifer hasn't seen him yet today. You have some time to clean yourself up."

"I'm not invited?" Paul asked. He gave Ray and inquisitive look.

"No." Barbara laughed. "She didn't mention you either way. I'm pretty sure you can tag along."

Paul gave Barbara a thumbs-up. "Right. I'll tag along." The smile on his face was replaced with a look of concern. "I still haven't heard from Malcolm. Something big must be happening. I can't imagine the governor calling a press conference to announce more of the same. Even he doesn't love the spotlight that much. Get Malcolm on the phone for me, will you?"

Barbara gave Paul an icy stare. "Break your dialling finger, did you? News break. We don't even dial anymore. We just punch buttons."

Paul faked a shocked look at the response. "I'm being polite. We're in your office. I didn't want to presume I could use your phone." He then reached into his pocket and withdrew his cellphone. Malcolm was on speed dial.

◀57▶

AS THE FLAMES from the explosion shot skyward, the general and the governor could hear Malcolm yelling on the radio.

"It's for you," the general said.

"Have the chopper sit down near the building and get those soldiers deployed," the governor said to the general. "We want to capture anyone who comes running out of that burning mess and put them out if they are on fire."

The general looked over at the governor, then down at the ground. Even the boxes by the helicopter on the ground were in flames. The alligator logo had melted into a pool of plastic on the ground. The paint was bubbling on the SUVs.

The governor followed the general's line of sight. "But not too close as to put them at risk," he added.

He keyed the mike. "Malcolm, this is not a good time. We've found the bombers' headquarters, and it appears to have blown up, not sure why. I'm going to have to get back to you." He flicked off the connection.

General Monahan brought his helicopter down to the level of the Chinook. "Major, find a safe place to land and have the men spread out. Watch for survivors."

Once the larger helicopter was safely on the ground, the general brought the Warrior down behind it. The two men disembarked and stared at the burning building. The news camera swung from the fire to the governor. A reporter stuck a microphone in the governor's face.

"Any comment, Governor? Was this the terrorist stronghold? Do you think they blew themselves up?"

"Somebody blew something up," the governor said, "but it's too early to speculate. This location is the school bombers' headquarters. We have irrefutable intelligence to confirm that. General Monahan was leading a force of the Georgia National Guard to capture and contain them."

The governor brushed the microphone aside and made his way closer to the site of destruction. He smiled as he walked away. That sound bite should lead off all the newscasts in the country until he could arrange a full-fledged news conference.

The explosion had flattened the fibreglass building. The remains of the roof lay in a heap amidst the flames, feeding the fire. The general's admonition about looking for survivors proved to be unnecessary. No one could survive this conflagration.

The pilot of the Chinook led a small task force into the intense heat intent on rescuing the extortionist's helicopter. They crawled on their bellies with reflective survival blankets fastened to their backs. They were still fifty feet away when the fuel tanks exploded into a ball of sky-seeking flame, throwing the chopper into the air before dropping it onto its side. Those soldiers nearest the explosion buried their heads in the dirt before squirming backwards away from this new menace of flames. Several bursts of gunfire shattered the air.

"Stand down," the general ordered, his voice carrying above all the noises of battle.

Blushing red faces distinguished those who had panicked and fired their weapons. They realized it was only a buildup of heat that caused the explosion. Suddenly the two SUVs' tanks erupted in flames as well, adding to the twisted scraps of flaming metal scarring the landscape.

"Move the men back, Major," the general barked. This was no time to be taking stupid casualties because of carelessness.

"General, there is nothing more we can do here," the governor said. "Have the guards secure the area until we can get a forensic team in. Even they won't be able to do anything until everything cools down."

General Monahan passed on the order, and then he and the governor mounted their transportation. Two of the embedded reporters came running over to stop them.

"Governor, are you leaving us here? We've got to get this footage back to our newsrooms." The looks on their faces suggested the big news part of the story had ended at this location.

"That's not our concern right now," the general said. He reached for the button to start up the helicopter. The governor reached out a hand to stop him.

"The people have a right to know that we've stopped these bombers, General. There have been millions of lost hours of sleep in the past week. Why don't we send these newsmen out in the Chinook and have it bring a forensic team back? We don't want to clutter up the area with a bunch of our air assets. We don't have that many of them."

The general gave the governor a knowing smile. "Of course, Governor. We should get these pictures out while it is still news." He signalled the major and made the arrangements for the ferrying service.

◀58▶

CAMERAS FROM ALL the major networks swung their lenses up over the roof of the governor's mansion as the jackhammer sound of the helicopter rotors announced the arrival of the governor back from the Okefenokee Swamp. Threatening storm clouds darkened the background, making it more difficult to pick up the incoming chopper. With the mansion in the foreground and the helicopter in the rear of the shot, there was no doubting the location of the news conference.

General Monahan took in the sight of all the satellite trucks and manoeuvred his aircraft a safe distance from the hubbub of confusion. He looked over at the governor.

"I guess word has gotten out, Peter," he said to the smiling governor beside him.

The use of his first name caught the governor off guard. Although the two men had been friends for some years, it was unusual for the general to use it. They were both quite comfortable using governor and general in everyday conversation. He briefly studied the general and wondered if he should read anything into the familiar use, decided against it and reached down to open the door and face the host of reporters coming across the parking lot. He stepped out and stood beside General Monahan while all the cameras captured the two men together.

Herb Solstace, the governor's security chief, appeared out of nowhere and cut off the charging reporters.

"This is a news conference," he said in his loud, booming voice, "not a free-for-all." He pointed towards the arranged chairs at the front of the mansion. "Sit over there, and we will take your questions."

Herb turned towards the governor as he approached from behind him. He pulled a couple of typed pages from the inside of his jacket and passed them to the governor. "Malcolm emailed you some remarks. Here's a summary. I've loaded the full text into the teleprompter. It should be your opening statement. He's on his way back from Colorado."

Herb grabbed the governor's upper arm and looked him straight in the eye. "Malcolm begged me to tell you to stick to the script. Things are in too much flux right now to be striking out on your own."

"Thanks, Herb," the governor said as he took the pages. "You know I will." He quickly scanned the top one and smiled. He had finally talked to Malcolm while he was flying back from the swamp and brought him up to speed on the rapidly unfolding events. At the time, he requested some talking points for the press conference. Malcolm had come through.

Herb reached out a hand to the general. "Good morning, General. I've got a bone to pick with you. We have security protocols for keeping an eye on this guy." He indicated the governor with his thumb. The governor had fallen behind as he read Malcolm's notes. "You can't come swooping in out of the night sky and be whisking him away, regardless of what he tells you." He grinned. "I'm telling you this because he doesn't listen to me, but hopefully you will."

The general thumped Herb on the shoulder. "Sorry, Herb. I'll keep that in mind for the future."

"Has Ray Tutty arrived yet?" The governor asked as he caught up to the men walking ahead of him.

"Oh, yeah, he's here," Herb said. "He's been waiting for over half-an-hour. You would think it had been all morning. I've told him nothing, although he has pretty much guessed that something big has happened."

"Beyond big, Herb. We're passing on a good news story."

"Should we bring Ray up-to-date before the news conference?"

The governor shook his head. "Ray catches on quickly. He will grasp the situation after I make my opening remarks. I want him here more to present a united front than to be making any major pronouncements. We have been in this together from the start. He should be here at the end."

◀59▶

THE GOVERNOR BOUNDED up the stairs of the mansion and stood in front of the middle of three microphones placed on the top step. General Monahan followed him at a more dignified pace and stopped at the first microphone. The governor signalled Ray Tutty to join them at the remaining mke.

The chatter ceased as all eyes turned to the three men. There was a full contingent of media on hand. More than could be accommodated in the mansion's usual press room. All the networks, as well as several of the cable stations, had responded to the invitation. Satellite trucks formed the backdrop for the reporters. This event would be broadcast live across the nation. Morning talk show hosts were going to have an unexpected day off.

"Good morning, ladies and gentlemen." The governor paused. His next words would be the lead story for the rest of the day.

"Our schools are once again safe. Our forces have neutralized the bombers."

He waited as a buzz shot through the crowd, a few whistles pierced the air. Some reporters pulled cellphones from their pockets. They wanted to make sure their editors had grasped the importance of this press conference and had the appropriate people standing by to do the recap after the conference ended.

Cameras could be heard clicking like hobnailed boots on pavement as still photographers captured this moment of freedom from future threats. The governor held his pose until the hubbub died down.

"With me on stage today are General Arthur Monahan, The Adjutant General of the Georgia National Guard." He indicated the general who stood with the military erectness expected of someone in his position. Then a slow smile spread across the general's face, and he raised his hand with a thumbs-up gesture. The reporters responded with smiles of their own.

The governor turned towards Ray Tutty. "I'm sure after this last stressful week you are all familiar with Ray Tutty, the president and CEO of BurgerCircus. Ray has been working in unison with my office on this matter from the start, and we appreciate the long hours he has put in."

Ray acknowledged the governor, a slight look of surprise on his face at the inclusive remarks.

Herb Solstace stood with Paul Johnson against the mansion doors under the parapet covering the main entrance, about fifteen feet behind the principals. "Is that teleprompter turned on? One sentence in and already he has struck out on his own."

The seated reporters started yelling questions at the governor who held up his hands for silence. "Please," he said. "You know the procedure. I have a prepared statement describing the information that is available. I should point out that this is an ongoing operation and is still unfolding as we speak. I will take questions after the statement, but because of the volatility of the situation, there is information that can't be released at this time. I ask you to use common sense with your questions." He paused and looked over the assembled members of the press. "What I'm saying is that in the interest of time, don't ask stupid questions. I am not going to reveal any information that would compromise the nature of the work being carried out in the field and put our assets at risk. We do have a limited amount of time for this press conference." He looked up at the dark clouds gathering above the reporters. Their eyes followed. Unlike the governor, they were exposed to the elements. "Don't waste it."

The reporters looked at each other. Those from away weren't used to being rebuked in this manner. The locals had heard it all before.

The governor glanced down at the teleprompter.

"Early this morning, General Monahan led a contingent of the National Guard to a site, that for the time being will remain undisclosed, and contained the terrorists who have been blowing up our nation's schools. At the time we had irrefutable information about this location as the terrorists' headquarters. There is no doubt in our minds that these were the people involved. As I said at the beginning, they have been neutralized."

A smile spread across the governor's face as he turned to look at a large screen set up at the back of the steps.

Film footage from the nose camera of the Kiowa Warrior lit up the screen displaying the seconds before the explosion and the complete destruction of the headquarters' building. The reporters sat back in their seats as the screen suddenly changed from near jungle greenery to bright reds and oranges as flames shot high into the air from the lone building on the ground. The screen went blank.

"We expect no further action from this terrorist cell."

The reporters broke out into spontaneous cheers and whistles before whispers filled the air as they speculated about the location of the attack.

The governor held up his hands again and received the silence he sought.

"We don't know at this time if the bombers intentionally killed themselves or if somehow their ordinance accidentally exploded. The site is still too hot to investigate. The National Guard did not engage the enemy and are not responsible for their deaths. We are securing the scene while we await the arrival of a forensic crew from the FBI to thoroughly examine the destruction. Until that is complete, no information will be given about the location. A small contingent of embedded reporters was on the Chinook helicopter with the guardsmen and their film and news stories will be shared with all of you."

Again the governor looked at the teleprompter.

"On another front, a school appeared to have been blown up in Colorado Springs early this morning. I'm sure you all watched, as I did, as it happened. This was, in fact, a ruse."

The governor stopped, a surprised look on his face. He glanced back at Herb Solstace standing by the window. Herb gave a shrug of his shoulders.

The governor went back to the teleprompter with renewed interest.

"An army demolition crew dismantled the bomb early last evening and what you saw were pyrotechnics set off by the soldiers from Fort Carson. It was an impressive display and gave us a chance to get our ducks in a row to enable us to make the attack on their headquarters later in the morning. My thanks go out to the men and women at Fort Carson for such a convincing job.

"At the same time, we were able to capture and hold one of the men involved in the explosion. We have him in custody, and he is alive."

The governor studied the last sentence. Was Malcolm taking digs at him in the middle of a press conference?

A murmur went through the crowd and heads could be seen nodding.

"As we speak, the remaining bombs in various locations around the country are being defused and dismantled from the information gathered in our investigation. If it has not already happened the threat will soon be completely contained.

"Gentlemen and ladies, those are the facts as we know them. Although they seem brief, I will again point out that this is an action in progress. I will entertain a few questions, a few intelligent questions."

Hands shot up all over the mezzanine. Questions filled the air.

The governor pointed to a man in the second row.

"Jeremy Ronstadt, Atlanta Herald. Governor, you refer to these people as terrorists. Do you have proof of that?"

The governor briefly studied the man before answering. "I have had maybe ten hours sleep in the last week, Jeremy. The sleep I did have hardly counted because the quality was so poor. Exploding schools filled my dreams; I woke at the slightest noise. I know several people in the state experienced the same thing. They contacted my office daily to see what I was doing about it if anything. I am glad to say they can see this morning we were indeed doing something about it. Tonight they can sleep in peace." A brief period of silence followed to let that fact sink in. "What about you, Jeremy? How did you sleep this past week?"

"Like you, Governor. Poorly."

"Well, Jeremy. That's the classic definition of terrorism. They put terror into the lives of citizens all across this country, disrupted our normal patterns of life. Now whether they are foreign terrorists or domestic terrorists, we don't know. We had hoped to answer that question this morning when we captured them. Now, unfortunately, we will have to wait and see."

He pointed to a lady dressed in a smart business suit sitting in the front row.

"Mary Small, CNN. Governor, what was the source of your information about where to find these bombers and how did you know about the Colorado Springs bombing?"

The governor glared down at the reporter aiming a microphone at him. He looked around the room. "Next question."

A few hands started to come down, went back up and then dropped into the laps of their owners. They reconsidered the quality of their questions. No one wanted to be on the receiving end of that wilting stare.

"Barry Jones, International Press. How certain are you that you have contained the threat, Governor?"

"We are absolutely certain we have contained this cell." The governor allowed a broad grin to fill his face. "But that is a fair question, Barry. Our intel to date suggests this group was acting on its own. We have the best experts in the field scouring chatter and other electronic communications to see if we can link these men to any other groups. As you know, no recognized terrorist group stepped forward to claim ownership of these attacks on our way of life. We continue to monitor the situation closely. At this point, we are leaning towards this being the work of extortionists. Strictly a money grab."

He nodded at a lady in the middle of the crowd waving a bright red hat in the air.

"Sandra Hill, Business News. Besides our way of life, there was a major attack on our fast-food industry, especially BurgerCircus. Mr. Tutty, how much did your company lose in the last week in sales?"

Ray snapped to attention. He had not expected to be included in the questions even though he had a microphone in front of him. His thoughts had drifted off to the image of the exploding building housing the men who had caused him so much trouble during the last week, something he had advocated for from the beginning. He sought to regroup. The question, he deduced, had something to do with lost revenue. She wanted to know how much profit the company had bled in the past week. So did he.

"What is important here today, as the governor said, is that we have finally brought this attack on our country and way of life to a halt. The overriding factor from the beginning was that we never give in to terrorism. BurgerCircus and the other fast-food companies held fast to that belief and whether or not it affected our revenue stream did not factor into our decisions. We stuck together and defeated this scourge."

"Good answer," Herb whispered to Paul. "Do you suppose he has any idea what the question was?"

Sandra remained standing. "My question is how much money did you lose during the week. Besides the destruction of schools, these terrorists attacked our economy. Businesses suffered all over the country. Yours stood in the forefront; I wonder how much you lost."

"Sandra," the governor intervened, "Ray has worked with me all week solving this problem of catching these bombers. The day-to-day minutia of running his company has taken a back seat to these concerns in the same way that the day-to-day operation of running the state was passed on to other people. Maybe in time, these figures will become available, but they are not the subject of this news conference."

"Governor, if I may." Ray held up a finger. He didn't need anyone, especially Governor Weston, speaking for him. "We did not let the attacks on our company force us from our normal way of doing business. BurgerCircus has been operating in the same way it always does despite some organized blockages of our premises by supporters of the bombers. I will repeat as you have heard me say several times this week: We cannot give in to terrorists. When they attack, it is important we do not let them alter our way of life. We find, contain and crush them. As for any loss we may have incurred, the company will absorb those and none of our employees or customers will suffer in any way."

"Thank you, Ray, well said." The governor turned back to the crowd and looked at his watch. "Any further questions?"

The lady in the front row jumped to her feet without being acknowledged.

"Mary Small, CNN."

"Think carefully, Mary," the governor warned.

"I have a question for General Monahan. General, is the army in charge of the disarming of the bombs still in the schools?

The general stepped up to his mike. "The FBI is overseeing this phase of the operation. As I understand it, the closest assets available to each site handle is being called in, whether it be military or police. Speed is of the essence. Every agency in the country is working in concert like a well-oiled machine acting on information supplied by Governor Weston."

"A supplementary question, if I may. What are the locations of those schools and what steps are being taken to look out for the people in the surrounding houses?"

"Mary," the governor said in an admonishing tone. "All necessary steps are being taken, including keeping the locations on a need-to-know basis. We don't want curiosity-seekers adding to the challenge of neutralizing these bombs. The safety of all concerned is at the forefront of the operation."

"General Monahan says you supplied the information, Governor. Where did you get it?"

"Same answer as before, Mary."

The governor looked at this watch. Herb started to walk forward as the governor said: "I'm sorry folks, that's all the time we have at the moment. There will be further details as more information becomes available. We should have a more comprehensive update by noon and will meet again at that time."

He turned to Ray Tutty and reached out for a handshake. Ray stepped forward, took the extended hand,

and the two men turned in unison to face the snapping cameras.

A voice came from a man jumping from a taxi in the driveway.

"Rod Sanderson, New York Daily News. I'm sorry, Governor, I was a little late in arriving. This news conference came together quite quickly. I hope I'm not repeating any previously asked questions."

The governor looked over the heads of the other reporters to the man pulling up at the back of the crowd. "No problem, Rod. Things are moving quickly this morning. I will take one more question."

Rod worked his way up through the throng of reporters and stood in the center aisle. The news cameras swung his way.

"No offence, Governor, but why was this attack led by the governor of Georgia with the Georgia National Guard and not federal troops?"

Governor Weston exchanged glances with General Monahan. " Rod, the guardsmen were led by General Monahan."

"But you were in the lead helicopter?"

"As governor, I am the Commander-in-Chief. I felt it was my duty to be present when we took these bombers down. These attacks were the greatest domestic threat we have had in this country since we ran out the British in 1784."

"Right. I'll be sure to include that in my story. My question, Governor, is specifically, why were you organizing the attack and not the president?"

The question seemed to catch the governor off guard. He slowly walked back to his microphone as he gathered his thoughts.

"As we all know, this is an election year. The president is running for re-election in a couple of months. I can only assume he has other things on his mind."

"Are you saying the president doesn't consider these bombings of national importance?"

"Rod, I'm not privy to what the president thinks. He has his priorities; I have mine. Stopping these bombings has been topmost on my mind ever since that school in Alexandra went up in a column of flames. I have thrown the full force of the state of Georgia behind this effort. My chief-of-staff is in Colorado, as we speak, interrogating the bomber involved in this morning's explosion there."

"Governor, did you pass your intel that led to this attack, wherever it took place, on to the president?" Rod smiled as both he and the governor knew he had just returned from the swamp on the Chinook helicopter ferrying the press.

"Members of the FBI are involved, Rod. The investigation is a joint operation between my office and the federal police force. Agents were present in my office when General Monahan picked me up this morning. Tom Burke, the agent-in-charge, is working hand-in-hand with Malcolm Truex, my chief. He was involved with the arrest in Colorado. Those are the feds, Rod."

"And yet, you organized the attack."

"Timing was critical, Rod. I had the information. I acted on it." He looked away from the New York reporter. "Thank you all for coming."

Rod held the floor. "I have one more follow-up question, if I may."

The governor scowled at the reporter. "One more, Rod. The investigation is still active. I have things to do."

"I only have one, Governor." He paused as all eyes turned towards him. "Are you going to run for the presidency of the United States of America?"

◀60▶

MALCOLM TRUEX AND Tom Burke stared intently at the small screen television on the bulkhead of the Lear 75 as it cruised high above the golden cornfields of Oklahoma. As soon as Tom found out what was taking place back in Georgia, he had hustled Malcolm on board the jet and set out for home. With a cruising speed of 535 mph, the trip would take a little less than three hours. *How much damage could Peter Weston do in that time?* Tom wondered.

"A press conference already?" he said. "Isn't that rushing things?"

The live image of the governor walking up the steps of the Georgia mansion filled the screen. Throngs of eager reporters filled the driveway in front of the building.

"Relax, Tom. Those papers in his hands are the notes I sent to him. All he as to do is follow them. It is important to get the truth out there before the rumour-mongers start writing their script of events. Once that happens, you can never reel their imaginary tales back in."

"I don't like it, Malcolm. We don't even know the real story ourselves yet."

"We know more than the conspiracy theorists do. Joe Fisher is delving into the contents of their hacked computer. Your boys should crack the hard drive on that photographer's laptop soon. I agree with the governor on this one. Besides we are not revealing any information about the bombers other than we have contained them."

The camera pulled back from the governor and picked up Ray Tutty walking across the broad landing to a microphone. He stood there awkwardly until the camera panned over to General Monahan.

"What kind of sideshow is this turning into?" Tom asked. "What's Tutty doing there?"

Malcolm's look expressed similar surprise. He recovered quickly.

"Ray has been involved since day one. It was BurgerCircus who the bombers expected to pay." His gaze switched to the FBI agent beside him. "In fact, he came on board before you did as I recall."

"Only as a mouthpiece, and with the governor on stage, we don't need another one of those."

"Shh," Malcolm said. "The moment of truth is upon us." He crossed the fingers on both hands. "Please, Peter, follow the script as I wrote it."

"Our schools are once again safe. We have neutralized the bombers." The words rang out from the television.

"So far, so good," Malcolm said. "That should make people across the country feel safe. I know I do."

"The press is eating it up," Tom said, pointing to the cheering members of the press corps. "Either that or they're happy to have a sound bite they can use. Good work."

Malcolm waited for the governor to start speaking again. When the introductions concluded, the governor started laying down the ground rules for questions.

"Did you write that?" Tom asked. "Some of these characters are right out to lunch with the questions they ask."

Malcolm chuckled. "Those aren't my exact words, but the governor and I have discussed making similar announcements before every press conference. He does this quite often if he is going to be holding back information. It sounds better than 'no comment' or 'I can't divulge that information at this time.' Those statements make him look like he is hiding something. This pronouncement puts the onus on the press to ask responsible questions. Instead of getting a reputation of asking the hard questions, you become known as the one who wastes valuable time. Everyone is on a deadline."

"Early this morning..." the governor started.

Malcolm's face lit up. "He's on script." He and Tom listened.

The switch to the helicopter's camera viewpoint caught both men off-guard. The sudden eruption of flames filling the screen brought exclamations from their throats.

Tom spoke first. "That gives a definite meaning to the expression 'to be neutralized.' Did you know that was coming?"

"Not at all. He never mentioned having filmed the sortie."

"It's probably standard operating procedure for the military. Things can get chaotic fast in these types of operations. Relying on people's memories when everything is going south isn't too reliable."

The governor moved on to the Colorado Springs school explosion. Tom noticed the surprised look on the governor's face when he got to the part about it being faked.

"You didn't tell him we didn't blow up the school?" he asked Malcolm. "Why not?"

Malcolm shrugged. "Didn't get a chance. He was going on about his operation, filling me in on the gory details, and didn't ask about ours. Next thing I knew, I was given the task of writing the copy for this news conference, and he hung up on me. It was too much hassle to call him back."

Malcolm waited for the governor to reach the line about the photographer being captured alive. He detected the slight reaction in the governor's voice. The governor had caught the jibe.

As the governor read the part about securing the remaining schools, Tom involuntarily showed his agreement with his nodding head.

"Joe Fisher contacted Kevin with this information about the remaining bombs. That ties up a lot of loose ends. We still don't know if we have everyone captured."

Malcolm agreed. "Time will tell, but I do think we have all the bombs that were already out there contained and by the looks of that explosion, their remaining product seems to have gone up in one hell of a big bang."

His attention returned to the tiny screen. "Here comes the fun part. I gave him notes to guide his answers on the obvious questions, but what the press will ask is a crap shoot."

They waited.

"What's a terrorist?" Malcolm said. "Good question. We expected that."

They listened to the governor's long drawn-out answer.

"Good, good," Tom said. "Explained the concept without revealing our lack of knowledge of who we're dealing with. 'Tonight they can sleep in peace.' I like that. I hate to admit it, but he is pretty good at this stuff."

"CNN. OK, here we go," Malcolm said.

"Don't answer that," Tom yelled at the screen as Mary Small reeled off her question. When the governor moved on, he shot a fist into the air. " Ignored her. Perfect response."

Malcolm shook his head as he watched. "You have to wonder if those people are that stupid. You might wonder if criminals pay those talking heads to gather intelligence for them."

They watched quietly. The governor seemed to be handling the free-wheeling questions quite well. Even "Bomb-the-Bastards" Ray Tutty held his own. As for General Monahan, after everything he had gone through during his career, facing the press was like talking to a kindergarten class. No one there would be shooting at him, not with real bullets anyway.

"OK, that didn't go so bad," Tom said as the governor wrapped up the questions.

"He's in his element in front of the people," Malcolm said. "I've never seen him tongue-tied by the press. If he doesn't know an answer, he admits that. He never fakes it."

"Right," Tom said. "Always tells the truth."

Malcolm smiled. "He chooses his words wisely." His attention snapped back to the television as Rod Sanderson's face came into view.

"This could get interesting. Rod never throws softball questions at these press conferences. Wonder what brought him running?"

Tom had drifted over to the small galley on the jet. He came back with two coffees and resumed his seat. "I knew this had gone too smoothly." He passed Malcolm a cup.

He listened to the first question. "That's a question that's been on my mind since we got that phone call in Colorado. Why is the Georgian governor leading this foray into the swamp?"

"Shush." Malcolm held up his hand. He wanted to hear this answer as much as Tom. Even though he and the governor had discussed the possibility of bringing in the Guard, it was never at the top of the list as the first choice of action. It was more like Plan B or C or even D.

They watched the back-and-forth between the astute politician and the equally shrewd reporter. Both men had brought their A-game to this debate.

When the governor took his shot at the president, Tom cringed. This president served as his boss. His action had been to assign Tom to handle the case, although there may have been a few intermediaries between the two men. Before he had a chance to comment, Rod Sanderson fired his SCUD missile at the heart of the governor. "Are you going to run for the presidency of the United States of America?"

In Atlanta, the eyes of all present turned to the governor for a response.

Aboard the Lear 75, Tom and Malcolm faced each other. The moment of truth had arrived. Their attention shifted back to the images on the bulkhead. The cameraman zoomed in on a tight shot of the governor's head.

A smile slowly crept across the governor's face. "That's twice this week I've been asked this question by you ladies and gentlemen of the press." He paused and looked back and forth across the crowd before locking eyes with Rod Sanderson.

"Are you so dissatisfied with the incumbent that you would latch on to anyone to take his place?" He held up his hand to stifle any answer that might be forthcoming. "The last time you asked this question, my answer was that I couldn't do any worse. Maybe I should upgrade that to I think I can do a whole lot better. That comes as no surprise to any of you. I have made my views of the current administration well-known over the last several months, indeed for the past four years." Again he paused. All eyes were on him. Pens were poised. Cameras were at the ready waiting to capture his announcement.

"The fact is, as you all should know, the time for having one's name on the ballot is long past. Every state puts out its own ballot, has its own rules. None of those rules allows anybody to get onto the ballot at this late date." He held his arms out to his sides, palms up and shrugged.

Mary Small jumped up from her seat in the front row. "There's always a write-in ballot." She sounded sincere.

"Thank you, Mary, for your vote of support. Never in the history of this fine, beautiful country, has the president ever been elected by a write-in campaign." He laughed and turned to Ray Tutty. "Ray here could be my vice-president. With his business acumen and my innate ability to get things done, we could make this country great again.

Maybe in four years time."

The governor started towards General Monahan, hand extended. It was time to wrap this up.

Rod Sanderson still stood in the centre aisle of the press section. "Governor, would you admit that it was your efforts that brought us to eliminating these bombers today? Your absolute refusal to give up brought the matter to a close?"

The governor stopped. He stepped behind the general's microphone, not going back to centre stage. "I would like to take credit for what you just said, Rod, but there were many people working as hard as I was, with the same dedication. My chief-of-staff, Malcolm Truex, FBI Special Agent Tom Burke, who is running this show, and hundreds of others all across the country who have vigorously chased down leads as we managed to uncover them, have worked equally as hard as I have in bringing these criminals down. I was fortunate to get the lucky break that brought it to an end. I am not going to say any more about it because it is still an ongoing operation."

Rod held his ground. "But it was you who uncovered the breakthrough?"

The governor smiled at the reporter but said nothing. After a few seconds, he put his hand on the general's shoulder and turned him towards the main entrance of the mansion. He reached out his other hand to Ray Tutty indicating he should follow. Together they disappeared into the building.

Back in the Lear, Tom looked at Malcolm. "Did he just kick off his campaign for the presidency, a write-in campaign?"

Malcolm looked dumbfounded. He wanted to deny that possibility, but he couldn't do it, not with any conviction in his voice.

◀61▶

BARBARA BISHOP LOOKED up from her computer as Ray and Paul entered the office. She reached out and clicked one of the function keys. Suddenly the room filled with the military strains of Hail Columbia from speakers mounted in the corners of the room.

"Very funny," Ray said. "Shut it off."

"My apologies, Mr. Vice-president," Barbara said with a mocking deferential voice. "You'll have to get used to people playing this every time you walk into a room."

"OK, so you watched the news conference. What did you think?"

" I didn't watch the press conference." The tone of Barbara's voice changed to one of true sincerity. "I've had about twenty calls asking if you are seriously contemplating a run for the vice-presidency." She hesitated. "I lied. I did watch the press conference; just not live. After about ten calls, I found it online and watched it there. Ray, they extended some serious offers of support. People like you who think the current administration is a joke."

"Whoa, whoa, whoa." Paul stepped forward, shaking his hands in the air in a stop sign motion. "Don't be filling his head with ideas like that. He can hardly stand being in the same room as Governor Weston. They would never make a political team."

"That was before I got to know the man," Ray said. "Now that I've worked with him up close and personal, he's not the dick I thought he was. He's a hard worker, and he has tenacity. Things I admire in people."

"No he doesn't," Paul started to say then changed his mind. "Yes, he is those things, but the two of you are like oil and water. You don't mix. Besides, you heard him; he is not running. Write-in ballots don't work."

"They could with the right people running a serious campaign. In the past, the people trying to get on the ballot that way were right-or left-wing nuts. Serious contenders have never given it a shot."

"Ray," Paul reached out, put a hand on his shoulder and looked him straight in the eye. "You are not a serious contender. You don't know anything about politics. Grab a coffee and let's see what's happening to our stock this morning. Catching those bombers has to have helped our position. Even you standing on that stage looking vice-presidential must have been worth a nickel or two."

He gave Ray a punch on the arm. He looked over at Barbara. She had a full cup of coffee beside her although Paul was willing to bet it had long ago turned cold.

"Fresh coffee?" he asked. "I'm making it."

She shook her head. "I don't disagree with you, Paul," Barbara said, "but some of these people who called this morning have big organizations behind them. They seemed to have warmed up to the idea of a Weston-Tutty ticket pretty quickly. Hell, Ray has a big organization behind him. BurgerCircus outlets cover every corner of the country and all the empty spaces in between. We all know his employees love him. There is no denying that."

"Ray's a great CEO," Paul said. "That's true. You love him. I tolerate him." He smiled in an attempt to ease some of the tension building in the room. "But running a major company is not like running the country. At BurgerCircus, if he makes a decision and can convince you it's a good idea, it happens.

"As an Indepentent president, Peter Weston is going to have both Congress and the Senate trying to undermine everything he proposes. Nothing will be good enough, because the better his ideas, the more it will destabilize the two-party system. They've got too much invested in the status quo to cooperate with anything he does. Even if the two of them got elected, as good as they might be, they would accomplish nothing worthwhile in the country." He shrugged. "It's the way of the world."

"Aren't you a picture of optimism this morning," Barbara said. "Aren't you the one with the innovative, new ideas, always trying to rock the establishment? Free coffee. Who thought that would work? Not me. Not Ray, even though he backed you." She held up a report from her desk. "Our coffee sales are up all day, even when they are paying. We can make this work."

"Of course there will be resistance at first," Ray said. "All we have to do is convince these old bastards we are there for the long term. If they stand in our way during the first four years, they will be swept out with the trash during the next election when we bring our slate of candidates along with us. It will start with the mid-term elections and spread like wildfire. Self-interest will win out. They will vote for us when they think their seats are on the line. Both parties."

Paul shook his head. "You're both crazy. An Indepentent presidency won't work in the real world. Just because the governor invited you on stage with him, shook your hand in front of the nation, and let you spout the party line, his party line: 'We don't negotiate with terrorists,' doesn't mean you are a team."

A ding sounded from Barbara's computer. She focused her attention on the screen. "Our stock went up another ten dollars." She looked at the clock and noticed the news had been broadcasting for five minutes. She knew the school bombing story led off every newscast in the country. At every new cycle, there was a rush of activity on the stock exchange.

"You boys are raking in the dough this morning." Her smile flashed on and then off her face. "Seeing Ray stand up to the bombers increases the people's confidence in the company. You say he was spouting the party line. I think he inspired people. He showed we don't have to lie down and take it. I think that confidence could transfer to votes."

"What are you doing, Barbara, looking to become Secretary of State, Madam Secretary?" Paul's face showed no hint of a smile. "You're supposed to be the voice of reason in this office. That's why we pay you the big bucks, to keep this guy under control." He pointed his thumb at Ray.

"Speaking of big bucks, what is our most active investor up to this morning? Is he buying or selling?"

"I've been trying to track him. I think he is doing the same as you two are: Watching the price of the stock go up and his net worth along with it. As near as I can tell, he is doing nothing."

Ray had been standing quietly while his two fellow executives snipped at each other. He walked over to the side counter and made himself a coffee, took a sip and looked at Paul.

"I think we can make this work. Of course, you would be left behind. Someone would have to run this company. You're the only choice to take over. Vice-president of the country is a full-time job if you do it right."

"You're talking crazy. You're talking like you've already won. Even if you and the governor tried this, it would be like running up a mountain backwards. You're not going to win. This country has a firmly entrenched two-party system. People still vote the way their grandfathers voted for no other reason than they always vote that way. Entire districts vote that way. Hitler could get elected if he ran for the right party."

Ray took a sip of his coffee, smiled and sat down beside Barbara to look at the stock market figures. He then turned his attention to Paul again.

"Not everyone votes for the same party every time, Paul. Governments change. We would have to capture that swing vote." He held up a finger. "That's a foregone conclusion. Did you know that less than sixty per cent of eligible voters cast their ballots in the last election? The remaining forty per cent is our target constituency. We will offer them something refreshing and new to get them off their backsides and out to vote." He held up a second finger. "Those two groups will give us our victory." He shook his two fingers at Paul displaying the victory sign.

"Two quotes come to mind from Winston Churchill. 'It's not enough that we do our best; sometimes we have to do what's required.'"

He paused to let that one sink in and then continued. "I like things to happen; and if they don't happen, I like to make them happen."

He stood up again, his body energized. His eyes sparkled with enthusiasm. "We can make this happen, Paul. This past week made me realize there is more to life than making money. Eventually, you have to give back. The country is in a terrible mess, and I sincerely believe that I could help to make it great again. Set up a meeting with the governor. We have to strike while the iron is hot."

"Another quote from Churchill?" Paul made no attempt to hide his sarcasm.

"Probably not, more likely from the 1500s, but I'm sure Churchill would agree with the idea. But if you want more quotes, some other Brit summed it up quite well: 'All that is necessary for the triumph of evil is that good men do nothing.'" Ray held up his two fingers again. "Victory, Paul. Victory. We're going to make America great again. That could be our campaign slogan. Call the governor."

Paul shot Barbara another exasperated look. "Let's think this thing over before we get too carried away. I don't think Edmond Burke planned to take on the two-party system in the U.S. when he said that."

"Carpe diem, Paul. Seize the day." Barbara laughed and turned back to her computer screen.

"OK," Paul said. "Here's the deal. Let's say the planets all properly align, and this thing did come together. Do you even know what the vice-president does? Hell, do you even know who he is?"

"He's the vice-president, just like you. He does all the heavy lifting."

Paul shook his head. "Not even close. He sits around and waits for the president to die. Nominally, he is the president of the senate, but he only gets to vote if there is a tie. It's a ceremonial position as long as the president is alive. You, my friend, would not survive a week doing it."

"There must be more to it than that."

"No there isn't. We choose vice-presidents because they can bring in votes the president wouldn't normally get. You might do that."

Ray looked to Barbara for support. She kept studying her computer screen.

Paul walked over to the window and stood staring into space with his back to the room for a full minute. Then he turned to Ray with a new look of optimism on his face.

"You could land some votes for the governor. He would need every one of them. He needs a vice-president from some other part of the country who could bring him more. If you're getting offers, I'm sure the governor is."

"So you want me to back him and then disappear?"

"No. Back Peter and if he wins become part of his cabinet. Secretary of the Treasury, perhaps or maybe Commerce. No, he owes you big time, go for the Treasury. You could make a difference there. Get it all spelled out in advance. You'd be fifth in line to become president. If we are going to do this thing, let's do it right."

Barbara looked up from her computer. "Secretary of the Treasury. That would be perfect. You've certainly complained enough about them in the past. Holding that post would give you a chance to do it your way. But, having said that, I don't think he could get elected without you. It would have to be VP or nothing."

Paul gave her a withering stare. She ignored him.

"You'd need a theme song," Barbara continued. "I'm thinking *Money* by the Beatles. That would fit you to a T." Again she hit a key on her computer, and again *Hail Columbia* filled the room. "Unfortunately, you're stuck with this. A ticket of you and Weston together could capture a lot of the female votes, say the middle-aged and over demographic. They are the ones who vote. You're both handsome dudes, and that's all it takes in some quarters to get elected."

◀62▶

AS MALCOLM TRUEX and Tom Burke rushed through the Atlanta International Airport, a man, carrying bundles of newspapers, nearly knocked them off their feet.

"Sorry, man," the newsie said. "Got to get these papers out. Biggest story to hit the front page since we shot Osama Bin Laden."

Malcolm's eyes widened as he captured the glowing headline: *Bombers Annihilated.* In smaller type, the subhead read: *Governor Beats Bombers at Their Own Game.* Under that could be seen the top of a colour picture of flames shooting into the air.

"Oh shit," Malcolm said as he pulled a dollar bill from his money clip. "Give me one of those." He pulled out another bill. "Make it two." He passed a paper to Tom who stood there in grim silence shaking his head.

Finally, he looked at Malcolm. "That attention-grabbing whore. I should never have left him here alone. And look at this." He pointed to a single column sidebar story on the right-hand side of the page. "Write-in Campaign for President?"

Malcolm glanced at the article. "Come on now, Tom. The governor never said that. He dismissed the idea as impractical."

"And yet here it is in the newspaper."

Malcolm quickly scanned the portion above the fold. "Maybe it's you who should run. He did say you were in charge when asked about federal involvement."

"He may have mouthed the words, Malcolm, but I didn't

feel the love."

The men folded their papers and resumed their rushed trip along the corridor. Robert Pettala, Malcolm's driver, waited for them on the concourse outside. Malcolm wanted to get a first-hand account of what had transpired at the press conference, both before and after the cameras were activated. Robert acted as his eyes and ears when Malcolm found himself out of range.

As they stepped outside the airport, the thickening clouds that had been threatening all morning started to sprinkle water on their heads. They sought cover under their newspapers and hustled over to the waiting car where Robert held both side doors open. Malcolm jumped into the front, Tom in the back.

"Back to the mansion," Malcolm said. He looked back at Tom for confirmation.

Tom nodded consent. "Might as well find out who fed us all this intelligence. I'd like to be looking the governor in the eye as he explains how everything came together so quickly."

"Quickly doesn't do it justice," Robert said. "It felt like someone opened all the doors at the zoo and emptied the cage." He looked at Malcolm. "At least the doors to the monkey cages."

Malcolm noticed the puffiness around his driver's eyes. "Were you up all night? Why did he have you involved?"

"Not all night. He called me around three. I had to go pick up Joe Fisher and bring him to the mansion."

"Why you? Why didn't he send his driver?"

"The official limo was designated to transport General Monahan."

"The general was there at three o'clock in the morning?"

"Joe Fisher, General Monahan and his aide, two FBI agents, his personal cook keeping everyone fed, Herb Solstace. I tell you it was a zoo. Did you see the press conference on TV? He carefully orchestrated that. It didn't suddenly fall together."

"You were there when this all came down?"

"Off and on, when I wasn't running errands and making phone calls."

Tom leaned forward over the back seat. "So when did they know they were going to attack the bombers' hideout?"

Robert glanced into the rearview mirror. "Sometime after the school was blown skyward. That's when all hell broke loose. Before the school went up in flames, or so we thought, everyone was geared up to announce the arrest of the man in Colorado Springs and the prevention of the bombing of another school. That was the breakthrough story.

"As I said, all the doors to the monkey cages were left open. When the school went kaboom, all the doors at the zoo sprung open at once.

"The general had already left to make preparations for having the Guard on standby in case they were needed. They were going to be here for the press conference to show how close we were to a breakthrough."

"You mean the advance preparations were not for the destruction of the hideout?"

"Hell, no. The governor was as surprised as anyone when that bomb exploded. He thought you were there to head it off. As I said, everything was set to make the big announcement about how the bombing had been prevented.

"Next thing we knew, the roof of the school is floating through the air in a ball of flames. Great job, I might add. You convinced everyone something had gone terribly wrong. Then there was a sudden flurry of emails from the bombers' computer. Everyone started running around like a chicken with its head cut off except Joe Fisher. He had already uploaded the contents of the bombers' computer onto an external hard drive that he had disconnected from the Internet.

"When the bombers started calling everyone into headquarters, Joe went on that hard drive and dug out their location in the swamp. Once he had the information on a stand-alone computer, he didn't have to worry about alerting anyone. He had a steady stream of data scrolling on two screens, fingers dancing across the keyboard. Bingo, just like that he had the location. Man, that guy knows his stuff."

Robert focussed his attention on his driving as the traffic started to pick up in the downtown core.

"That's when things really started happening. The governor called the general and told him there had been a change in plans." Robert turned to look at Tom. "Your boys almost had a conniption, told him he couldn't do that without consulting with you." Robert shrugged. "You know the rest."

Tom tapped Malcolm on the shoulder. Malcolm turned to look at the backseat passenger.

"Tell me again how I'm the one running the show," Tom said.

Malcolm started to comment, but closed his mouth and faced forward. All three men remained silent, lost in their thoughts.

◀63▶

THE GOVERNOR HELD up his hand as Malcolm and Tom stepped through his office door. His other hand held a phone to his ear; a smile lit his face from ear to ear. He motioned the two men to sit while he listened. Finally, he thanked the caller and promised to keep in touch.

"Thank God, you're back," he said to Malcolm. "This whole thing has taken on a life of its own." He turned to Tom. "Great job in Colorado, Tom. You had me fooled. A fake explosion proved much better than no explosion at all. When it was revealed to be us taking over the bombers' agenda and beating them at their own game, it made us look totally in control of the situation."

Tom smiled in spite of himself. "Thank you, Governor. The army has to get most of the credit for that manoeuvre."

"The army? Didn't you sign off on it?"

"Their idea. I agreed to run with it."

"Right. That's what leaders do. Again, good job."

Tom's look ranged between satisfaction and confusion. It was nice to be recognized, but what was the governor's motive? Tom had no love for politicians.

The governor turned his attention back to Malcolm. He indicated the phone with one hand. "That was Governor Morrissey from Montana on the phone. You remember him from our trip out there last year."

The governor paused for Malcolm to acknowledge the meeting.

"He thinks it's time to have new blood in this upcoming presidential race. If I'm going to run, he can get me on the ballot in Montana if we act right away. They haven't printed the ballots yet, and he thinks a write-in ballot would be too cumbersome. No pressure, but he might be interested in running for vice-president on an Independent ticket. We have to keep that last part on the down-low until we make a decision. He doesn't want to cut his ties with the party unnecessarily."

Malcolm sat there shaking his head while the governor talked. "No, Governor. A move like that would be a mistake."

"You're right. It's too soon to be picking a vice-president. There's so much to do before we get to that stage."

"No, Governor. The whole idea is wrong. Write-in ballots don't work. Don't waste your capital on a losing prospect. Four more years of this government and you won't even have to run. They'll be handing you the presidency."

The governor's face changed to one of dismay. "Jennifer," he called out to his executive assistant. She immediately appeared in the doorway. "Tell Malcolm what you've been doing since the press conference ended."

Her body sagged. *Don't drag me into the middle of this conflict,* she thought. She had been with the governor since his days as mayor of Bakers Siding, but at the same time, she knew how much Malcolm brought to the office.

"The phone has been ringing off the hook with offers of support," she said. "Serious offers. Governors, members of Congress, big money people. They all want to see the current administration thrown out, but don't see anyone suitable to take their place." She paused. "Until now. As a team, you two represent hope for the country."

"As a team, Malcolm," the governor said. "I don't want to do this without you."

The implication hung in the air.

"What do you think, Tom? Is this the time for a change?"

Tom measured his words carefully. He didn't think Peter

Weston should be anywhere near the presidency. At the same time, he could see him riding this wave of popularity to the Oval Office.

"That's a political question, Governor. My position with the FBI demands that I avoid politics at all times. That includes the appearance of being involved with politics. I'm sure you understand if I abstain from answering."

Malcolm looked at his former partner. He knew exactly where the man stood. "Speaking of politics..." He let the sentence fade.

"I understand your position, Tom. That's part of the problem with this country. Everyone is afraid to say what they think. I've had calls from California, Florida, Texas, all offering support but wanting to stay off the record until there is an official announcement. If they commit and I don't run, they will feel hung out to dry. I say if they feel that strongly that we should kick the incumbent out on his ass, speak up. Everyone knows where I stand on the matter."

He held his hands out in front of him, palms up. "As much as I would like to debate this matter with you two and bring you around to my way of thinking, we have more serious concerns on our hands right now. I notice the rain is starting to fall. That should cool down the fire at the bombers' headquarters and allow the forensic guys to start their investigation. We have to interrogate the bomber you guys caught in Colorado. Did you get a chance to interview him at all?"

Malcolm nodded. "He's just a photographer. I don't think he knows much. The Colorado FBI has taken over the interrogation. They will keep us up to date.

"More importantly we have sent his laptop back to Langley for the experts to try to crack. There may be some valuable information on it."

"Langley?" the governor said. "Joe Fisher is in your

office hacking into the headquarters computer. He may have more luck than the FBI guys. I knew his skills topped the lists of IT techs, but seeing him in action boggled my mind. You were wise to bring him in, Malcolm. I came third in the Google Code Jam a few years back. Joe entered twice and won both times."

"Yeah," Malcolm said. "That happened during his nerd phase. He doesn't talk about it anymore."

All three men looked at Tom's pocket as his cellphone chirped a tune. "Speaking of Langley," he said, as he answered. "Special Agent Thomas Burke."

Tom listened. Responded with a few grunts every so often, then turned to the governor. "Did you say Fisher is here?"

"Took over Malcolm's office." The governor pointed down the hall.

Tom smiled, phone still to his ear, left the governor's office and turned in the direction indicated.

"You had to lead the charge?" Malcolm asked when Tom was out of sight. "Couldn't you simply have let the FBI do their thing?'

The governor leaned back in his chair from the force of the attack. "Time dictated our course of action. The National Guard were on standby. Their choppers were fuelled and ready to fly. If we had waited, we might have missed capturing them. No, that's not true. We would have missed them. I tell you, Malcolm, they were packed and ready to run."

Malcolm shook his head. "You didn't capture them, Governor. They're all dead."

The governor turned to his computer monitor. "Let me show you the video from the Kiowa Warrior nose cam. I think they were minutes away from evacuating and something went horribly wrong. I think they intended to blow the place up as soon as they left."

Both men watched as the image grew larger as the helicopter moved closer to the encampment. Suddenly flames lit up the screen. The governor hit the pause button.

"See that?"

"The place blew sky-high. I saw it at the press conference."

"No, look at how it blew up."

Malcolm studied the screen more closely. The governor drew a circle on the screen with his finger.

"The entire perimeter is in flames. It imploded from there." He let the pictures advance a few more frames. Flames enveloped the entire building, blowing in, not out.

"Their intention, as soon as they had vacated, was to destroy all the evidence and leave no trace behind them. Somehow it detonated early."

"Or," Malcolm said, "they committed suicide."

"No, I don't think so. We could see the men on the ground loading the vehicles as we approached. The Chinook flew high enough to be hidden from the ground by the clouds. We didn't appear to present a threat at that point. They planned to get out of Dodge, and somehow the detonator got triggered prematurely. I'd bet my life on that."

Malcolm continued to concentrate on the screen. "Tom's boys might be able to answer that question. There's not much left to investigate."

Tom knocked lightly at the office door and stepped inside.

"Fisher is talking geek to the techs at Langley. With his help, they've already gained access to the laptop's hard drive. He had already cracked a password file on the bomber's computer. What's the use of having sixteen-character passwords if you have to write them down to remember them?"

Malcolm noticed the slip of paper in Tom's hand. "Do you have something for us?"

Tom nodded. He passed the paper to Malcolm. "The photographer's Facebook page. Claims his name is Ahmed Al-Ja'fari."

He looked at Malcolm. "You talked to him. He sure as hell is an American. Do you think he converted to Islam and became a home-grown terrorist?"

Malcolm looked from the paper to Tom's face. "Not this morning, he wasn't. This morning he claimed to be simply a photographer chasing the American dream. Maybe some days he has delusions of grandeur." He moved over to the governor's desk. "Let's have a look and see what the page says."

"Dammit," the governor said. "I knew they had to be terrorists, frightening the people like that. There had to be more motive than money."

Tom looked over Malcolm's shoulder at the Facebook page. He scanned down as Malcolm looked through the messages on the screen.

"The usual anti-American rhetoric. Nothing new."

Malcolm scrolled back to the top of the page. "Look at the language. It's stilted. This crap didn't come from the man we talked to in Colorado. The whole thing is fake."

"Fake?" said the governor. He moved in for a closer look. "Can we bring him back here and interrogate him? Get to the bottom of this thing ourselves?"

"I texted this new information to the agents currently conducting the interrogation," Tom said. "We'll see what they think."

A ding sounded from Tom's pocket. He pulled out his cellphone and looked at the screen. "That was quick. Let's see what they have to say."

The expression on Tom's face underwent a radical change. He looked up at the other two men, barely suppressing his rage.

"Sons of bitches," Tom said. "Homeland Security has

stepped in. They have taken over the investigation. Foreign threats don't come under the FBI's jurisdiction."

Malcolm could not hide his surprise. "They've got him already? That was fast."

Tom nodded. "I don't think the president took kindly to the insinuations made by the governor at his morning press conference. He jumped at the chance to take you out of future inquiries." Tom addressed the last comment to Peter Weston. "You can be sure Homeland Security won't share any information with the FBI, and by extension, you are now out of the loop."

"But we captured the son of a bitch. We did all the work." The governor got up and walked over to the window of his office. The rain created splashes when it struck the ground.

"I promised the press we would have a follow-up press conference when we got new information. I intend to do that." He indicated the rain with his hand. "It will have to be an inside venue."

"You don't want to do that, Governor. Homeland Security doesn't do press conferences."

"Well, I do. The takedown happened in Georgia. What happens in Georgia falls under my jurisdiction. I'm not going to be obstructed by that asshole of a president because he doesn't want me talking to the press."

"Do we have anything new to offer them?" Malcolm looked pensive. "They don't want to hear a rehash of what they already know."

"Malcolm," Tom said. "Are you listening to me? It's Homeland Security's case now. We're out of it. I'm supposed to report to—" he looked down at his phone, "—a Gerald Kennedy and pass over my notes. Let me assure you, these guys don't play well with others."

"I hear you, Tom." The governor moved closer to the FBI agent and stared directly into his face. "They want to cover everything up. Claim it's all wrapped up and not give any details, or even pretend it didn't happen. We need to reassure the people that we've caught these guys. They want to know who they are. They want to believe it can never happen again. In three days, they will send their kids back to school. They have to feel it's safe to do that. Turning off all the information and going silent won't give anyone a feeling of security. We can't pretend the last week didn't happen."

Malcolm turned to face the governor. "You can't talk about anything taking place from this point on. We can report on what we did during our investigation, including our belief that this is a pure extortion plot and that the cameraman is no more a foreign terrorist than Tom is. It's all about the money and has nothing to do with foreign governments or insurgents. If the president wants to challenge us, it will be up to him to make a statement."

Tom stood waving his hands in front of Malcolm. "Stop, Malcolm. I know you're frustrated. So am I. But we can't do any of what you are saying. I report to Kennedy, and I'm out of it. So are you. You have been working for the FBI, remember. Governor, you don't want to tangle with the Patriot Act. It gives these guys unbelievable power, even against you."

The governor ignored Tom's implied threat. "Malcolm, why don't you believe they are terrorists? Look at this Facebook page. This guy is a terrorist regardless of where he was born or where he lives. Look: 'Death to American Infidels.' How much more proof to you need?"

"This is hokum, Governor. It is designed to throw our investigation off-track if one of them gets caught. We go off looking for political motives where none exist, and our whole inquiry loses focus. I've looked into this guy's eyes. He had no causes in mind, no ambitions to overthrow any governments. All I saw was the desire to make money any way he could."

"Maybe you're right. We'll see what comes out of the explosion site in the swamp. With this rain, the Feds should be examining it by now."

Tom looked down at the floor as if lost in thought. "Governor, you're out of the loop. Your people are not examining the site. The FBI are. Anything found during their search will be passed on to Homeland Security, not you."

The governor smiled. "Is that so? Maybe we'll let the people decide. Despite the support I was receiving, I thought a write-in ballot was too far-fetched to think about seriously. I'm not so sure now. Let's give the country back to the people."

Malcolm snapped around and stared at the smiling face beside him. "That's not what I suggested, Governor. That idea is absurd."

◀64▶

THE PRESIDENT OF the United States stepped towards the microphone as the last notes of *Hail to the Chief* faded away.

"I wish to make a brief statement regarding the take-down of what has become known as the school bombing terrorists, after which I will announce my campaign agenda for the next three days as we make a cross-country tour."

The buzz in the room increased in intensity.

"Excuse me, Mr. President." One of the front-row reporters held up his hand. "I thought you circulated your schedule for the next three days last week. I have already booked flights and hotels to New York, California and Florida."

The president looked back over his shoulder at his press secretary, Harold White, who stepped forward. "No problem," he assured the reporter. "Those are the states we will visit. There might be a variation in the cities. Some of the governors we had planned on campaigning with have a conflict in their schedules. We are working to resolve these issues. We'll give you more details after the statement."

Harold White stepped back and the president resumed his position behind the mike.

"Are these governors refusing to campaign with you?" The question came from the back of the room.

"Of course not," the president said. "There's a conflict. We can't control everyday events. Things happen when you are running a state the size of California."

Again Harold White stepped forward. "We will discuss

this after the statement."

The president scowled at the man and cleared his throat.

"Does this have anything to do with the announcement made by Governor Peter Weston this morning?" All eyes turned to the reporter. "Rod Sanderson, New York Daily News. There is talk of a write-in campaign to elect the governor in the upcoming presidential election in November."

The president scoffed at the idea. "Write-in campaigns don't work. Hell, we can hardly get people to mark an X. They won't be writing a whole name."

A collective gasp filled the room. Harold White rolled his eyes.

"There's always a first time," Rod Sanderson said. "Especially if there is a big enough demand for a change."

Harold stepped forward again. "Ladies and gentlemen, the president is about to make a statement." Harold's red face belied the controlled timbre in his voice. His eyes burned into the eyes of the assembled press before settling on Rod Sanderson. "Please hold your questions until the appropriate time. One more outburst and we may remove you from the room, Mr. Sanderson. You, of all people, should know better."

The reporters furtively glanced around the room to see if anyone would challenge the threat. None did. Rod Sanderson made a zip-his-mouth gesture, turned an imaginary key and tossed it away.

The president clutched the sides of the podium He glanced down at his notes.

"Early this morning the National Guard, acting on evidence gleaned by the FBI and others, conducted a raid on an encampment in the Okefenokee Swamp in rural Georgia." He read with a stilted voice. "The buildings involved at one time housed park equipment, but have for some time been unused.

"These were believed to be the leaders of the terrorist group harassing the nation, demanding money and blowing up schools. The Guard has neutralized them.

"At the same time, Special Agent Tom Burke led an FBI raid in the Cheyenne National Forest in Colorado and captured the remainder of the terrorists. At this time, we believe we have taken the entire cell into custody, and the threat to our schools no longer exists.

"A Facebook page suggests ties to overseas extremists. All the captured terrorists have been turned over to Homeland Security who will now assume the lead role in the investigation. As such, Homeland Security will filter any further news releases on this matter taking, into consideration the effect they have on national security.

"This concludes my statement on this matter. We will entertain no further questions until Homeland Security resolves all outstanding issues."

The president looked back at his press secretary for confirmation of the facts as presented. Harold nodded and gave him a go-ahead look.

"There are handouts on the new schedule for campaign events in the upcoming days. These are self-explanatory. The press office will handle any further questions.

"Thank you for coming, and God bless America."

As a unit, all those on stage turned and started towards the exit behind them.

Rod Sanderson jumped to his feet. "What kind of bullshit is this? The nation has been held hostage by these bombers for a week, and you are going to dismiss it with a one-minute statement? Where were these terrorists from? Who funded them? How many were captured? The people have a right to know these answers."

The president had almost made it to the exit door. Harold had a tight grip on his arm and kept pushing towards the opening. With a yank of his arm, the president freed himself and glared at the man trying to restrain him. He walked back to the podium and squared his shoulders.

"I would like to answer your questions on this matter, Rod, but national security is at stake. Those are good questions and deserve answers." He looked at Harold. "We will pass this information along when it becomes available, and we are sure we eliminated all the risks. Nothing trumps the need to keep our nation safe and secure."

"Are you saying, Mr. President, the threat still exists?"

"There are always threats, Rod. The American people have to remain vigilant against attacks on our great nation every day."

"That's bull—," Rod paused. "That's rhetoric, Mr. President. Is there still an impending threat to our schools? They open in three days."

Harold crowded in beside the president, fighting to get control of the microphone.

"My, my, Rod, you do get around. Didn't I see you grilling Governor Weston a couple of hours ago? Are you building up or burning up your Air Miles?"

"I follow the story wherever it takes me, Mr. Secretary. My task is to find the truth and report it as it exists, not as our politicians would like to pretend it exists. My question stands. Are our schools still in jeopardy?"

"Homeland Security has taken over the file. That's all I can tell you, but I will sleep soundly in my bed tonight."

"The president reported that the National Guard conducted the raid this morning. Wouldn't it be more accurate to say the Georgia National Guard conducted the raid?"

The president elbowed his way back behind the microphone.

"There is only one National Guard. You would think you people in the press corps would know that. The event took place in Georgia. Obviously, members of the Guard from that state took part."

"So, you ordered the attack that killed all those people?"

The question caught the president off-guard. Again the press secretary stepped forward. "We do not openly discuss operational details of ongoing operations."

The other members of the press gallery looked back at Rod. No one dared interrupt the back and forth with questions of their own.

"My information suggests Governor Weston led the attack personally."

Uncontrollable rage took over the president. "Peter Weston is an asshole and publicity seeker. This was a military operation and would have been led by—" he quickly looked down at his notes for a name "—Major Ron Smith."

The press secretary tried to regain his position behind the mike.

"I believe General Arthur Monahan served as the ranking military person on the scene," Rod said before Harold could correct the president.

The president clutched the podium and held his ground. "Was he? And how would you know that? Were you there?" His frustration had reached the boiling point.

Again, like spectators at a tennis match, all eyes swung back to Rod Sanderson.

"As a matter of fact, Mr. President, I was." Gasps of surprise emanated from around the room. "I was part of the embedded press corps. Surely you read my stories before coming out this morning?"

Harold's shoulders dropped. He turned and signalled two Secret Service agents to come forward. "The president is feeling unwell. This conference has come to a close. Address any further questions to my office."

Together the three men escorted the president off the stage, leaving a stunned group of reporters in their wake.

◀65▶

"DO YOU KNOW what is missing on these computers?" Joe Fisher asked Malcolm Truex. "Clutter." The question turned out to be rhetorical. "I have the hard drives from both the headquarters computer and the laptop you confiscated in Colorado. I had done a complete download before the Homeland Security types took over.

"The information on both confirms they belong to the same organization. The laptop incontrovertibly links your boy in Colorado to the bombings. Partitions on the laptop isolated some of the data from the user unless he had been supplied with the proper codes to access it. Information was doled out on a need-to-know basis."

Malcolm watched the screen as Fisher scrolled through various menus, occasionally stopping to study the data.

"What do you think is missing?"

"The clutter." Joe turned to Malcolm's desktop computer shoved to the side of the work area. "May I?" His fingers danced across the keyboard. "I've already cracked your password code. I'll show you how to create a real one." The smirk morphed into a smile.

"Here is the official government stuff. I didn't look at that. These are files that contain high scores, standings, etc. from games you've played. Metadata—data about data. It accumulates.

"Does the governor know he pays you to play Yahtzee with people all over the country? You've got ten games on the go. You're not even that good."

Malcolm's face reddened. "I glance at it a couple of times

a day. So shoot me. What else?"

"Here are deleted pictures, emails, files, things you think you've cleaned up but still exist if you know where to look. Garbage."

Joe pointed at the two external hard drives connected to his computer. "Nothing of this nature exists on these drives. It's not natural. I think they are contrived."

"Really," Malcolm said. "I feel the same way about the supposed Facebook page of the photographer we arrested. It's as phoney as a three-dollar bill."

Joe Fisher shook his head. "No this isn't phoney. Everything is accurate. It has all the schools that the bombers intended to blow up. We gave a list to the FBI to investigate. They found bombs at all of them; the location of their headquarters is exactly where it said it would be. All true. Somehow it doesn't feel right. They conducted their broadcasts on the Internet. They should have picked up some junk."

"You think they are feeding us this information? Why? Who?"

Joe shook his forefinger in Malcolm's direction. "That, my friend, is the sixty-four thousand dollar question or, I guess, the one hundred million dollar question. Someone went to a lot of trouble to set these guys up. Just to kill them? There are easier ways to do that.

"Bad publicity for the fast-food restaurants? Again, there are easier ways to do that."

"Here's the big thing," Malcolm said. "No money changed hands. Ray Tutty and his compatriots refused to pay. Instead of bad publicity, Ray came out looking like a hero. 'We don't negotiate with terrorists.' His mantra resonated with most of the people. In fact, now that it's over, it will resonate with everyone. We've stood up to the bad guys on our turf and won."

"Folk legend stuff. There were no real winners. How

many schools were damaged or destroyed?"

"Seven. One here in Georgia, one in Texas, one in Montana, one in New York and one in Michigan. In California, it was a dud, as was the one in Colorado."

"The one in Colorado can't be described as a dud. You had decommissioned it before it went off."

"No, it was a dud. The C4 proved ineffective when tested in the lab at Fort Collins. It wouldn't have exploded."

Joe sat quietly as if deep in thought.

"What?" Malcolm asked. "You think that is significant?"

"So even if the team we sent in were bumbling idiots, they wouldn't have been hurt?"

"We sent in a crack demolition team, the best of the best."

"Let's say it's interesting. It was in a heavily populated area. Is there any truth to the rumour the school in Alexandra was slated for demolition next year?"

"Rod Sanderson brought that up at one of the press conferences. I never had the opportunity to check it out." Malcolm gave a slight, gruff laugh. "I had other things on my mind."

Joe kept his serious demeanour. "You don't anymore. Check it out and let me know what you discover."

The smile dropped from Malcolm's face. "You think it's significant?"

"Let me know what you find. I know this is your office, but get lost. I've got work to do. Get my information and take the rest of the day off. You've earned it."

"Tell that to the governor."

"I can't. The governor has left the building. I saw his car leave about five minutes after Tom Burke left. You're free to go home."

Malcolm walked over to the window overlooking the driveway of the mansion. Splattered droplets of rain created parallel rivers running from top to bottom.

"Strange, I thought he planned to hold another press conference."

"Maybe he's looking for a larger venue, somewhere dry. He can't have this one in the parking lot."

"Maybe, but he has people who do that. What's he up to now?"

Joe looked up from his computer screen. "I don't know. I don't care. I have work to do. Get out of here. Get me that information I asked for."

Malcolm stared at him momentarily. "I'll get Robert to look into that for you."

"Robert? Your chauffeur? I'm serious about this."

"Robert is also my researcher. The governor runs a tight ship. We multitask."

Joe started to respond, but Malcolm's phone gave a distinctive chirp.

"It's the governor," Malcolm said and stepped into his reception area.

"Are you still at the Capitol?" the governor asked without any preamble.

"Yes, coordinating with Joe."

"It's been a hectic morning. Have you had breakfast yet? I'm ordering chicken and waffles at the Sun Dial. You should be able to be here in less than ten minutes. Are you in?"

Malcolm's circadian rhythms had been so out of whack for the last week that meal times seemed to be haphazard at best. The mention of breakfast made him realize that he was hungry.

"I'm on my way."

Malcolm knew the governor had more on his mind than breakfast. He would not waste time on the phone discussing it. Whatever it was could wait ten minutes.

◀66▶

"DEREK SAUNDERS IS on his way over. He sounds pissed about something."

Barbara Bishop stood in the doorway of Ray's office.

Ray looked up. "He's always pissed about something. He should be pleased this school bombing thing is over. His restaurants would never be able to afford to contribute to a fund to pay off the bombers, not that that would ever have happened."

"Maybe he found out you're running to be vice-president and he's a Republican."

Ray scowled. "Don't say that so dismissively. The governor is still dealing with the aftermath of this morning's events, tying up loose ends." He got up and walked around to the front of his desk. "The more I think about this idea, the better idea I think it is. It's time to shake up the old system. Politicians have forgotten what serving our country is about. They think it's them. It's not. It's the people."

"Practising your stump speeches already. That one has a nice ring to it. Wait until Malcolm Truex punches it up a bit. It will be a winner."

Ray produced an uncharacteristic shy smile. The idea continued to grow on him. Then his usual smile returned. He pointed at Barbara. "I was thinking about taking you along with me to Washington, but it might be best for you to stay here with Paul. He will need your guidance. I don't."

The door to the outer office slammed open. Both turned towards the sound. Derek Saunders charged across the outer office and through the door. Without breaking his pace, he slammed a fist into Ray Tutty's face. Ray crashed against his desk and folded up onto the floor.

"What the hell?" He glared at his competitor restaurateur. "Have you lost your ever-loving mind?"

Barbara stepped between the two men as Ray slowly made his way to feet. "Security," she called out as loud as her voice would allow. "Someone come in here. Call 9-1-1."

A uniformed chauffeur showed up almost at once. He looked at the red welt on Ray's face and grabbed Derek Saunders from behind, pinning his arms to his side, then, quickly and efficiently took him to a sitting position on the floor. A set of handcuffs materialized out of thin air and appeared equally as fast on Derek's wrists. Chauffeur did not adequately denote this man's job description.

Ray held up a hand. "Don't call the cops yet."

He sat back on the edge of his desk while rubbing the side of his face.

"Have you lost your mind, Derek? Why shouldn't I have you charged with assault, you dumb bastard?"

Derek tried to struggle to his feet. He realized this was futile. A heavy hand rested firmly on the top of his head, pushing down slightly. A knee pressed firmly into the centre of his back. The more he struggled, the heavier the hand. He soon realized sitting still was in his best interest.

"Let me up, dammit." He tried to look back over his shoulder. The pressure on his head remained constant. "I'm calm. I'm not going to hit anybody else. I want to talk to this scumbag, Tutty. He owes me an explanation, and I want to hear it face to face, not from some flunky who is working for him, spouting the company line."

Ray gave a nod to the chauffeur who grasped Derek's shoulders and in one quick move had him.

Ray stepped forward. "Let's hear it, Derek, and it had better be good."

Derek could smell the hazelnut flavoured coffee on Ray's

breath. He tried to step back, but the chauffeur blocked him. Instead, he leaned towards Ray.

"You're trying to wriggle out from under your offer to buy my company, you thieving son of a bitch."

A look of confusion filled Ray's face. He shook his head slowly back and forth. "I have no idea what you're talking about. Buying your company has been the farthest thing from my mind for this past week." He sat back on the edge of the desk. "You do know we've been dealing with a volatile situation?"

"Damn right I know, and you've been trying to sneak in under the radar and buy up shares of my company cheap, a lot of shares."

Ray looked over at Barbara. She shrugged and shook her head. "No, I haven't."

"Well someone has; if it wasn't you, you have a competitor in taking over my company. Someone has been gobbling up thousands of shares every time the price drops, and this past week the price has been like a yo-yo every day."

"Uncuff him," Ray said and walked behind his desk. "Sit down Derek and explain this to me." He looked at Barbara. "Get Paul in here. I want to know what the hell is going on."

"There's nothing to explain. Someone is trying to do a hostile takeover of my business. Are you surprised that my first thought goes to you?"

"Frankly, yes. We already have a friendly takeover in the works. Why would I screw that up?"

"Because you saw a chance to save money."

Ray scowled. "Derek, the only reason I wanted your company was to enable me to service some smaller communities where a BurgerCircus didn't make economic sense. A few bucks a share either way has no bearing on this deal. Once I take over the share price will skyrocket." He paused. "But now you've got me worried."

◀67▶

MALCOLM STEPPED FROM the elevator on the 71st level of the Westin Peachtree Plaza and looked out across the city from 723 feet in the air. He never tired of this view. In his periphery, he noticed the governor waving to get his attention. He walked over to the table and sat down.

"I've ordered your waffles," the governor said.

A waiter appeared with a glass of water and a flagon of coffee.

"I'll take the coffee," Malcolm said with a smile. "It's time to recharge the batteries."

The waiter filled Malcolm's cup and topped up the governor's.

"Your order will be along shortly," he said and hustled over to another table.

"Malcolm, you're not going to like what I have to say, so let's get right into it."

Malcolm nodded. "You want to run for president."

The governor's face flashed a brief look of surprise before returning to neutral. "It's time, Malcolm. This is our best opportunity, and it will only come once. The odds of electing an Indepentent candidate compare favourably to those of a snowball in hell. I know that."

"No, Governor, they are not even that good."

Peter Weston smiled. "If ever there is going to be an opportunity, this is it. The incumbent is a bumbling idiot. The other side can't seem to come up with a credible candidate even though that person would be a shoo-in winner. They shot themselves in the foot big-time at their national convention.

"And, here is the big point. With only two months to go until the election, we don't need a huge bankroll to make it happen."

"We might not need a lot of money, but we do need some money. More than we have on hand."

"I know, Malcolm. You may be surprised at this, but, without even officially throwing in our hat, we are getting several offers of funding. Mostly small amounts, I admit, but there are a couple of substantial anonymous donors. They will mail in their cheques as soon as we declare. The people are ready for a change."

Peter looked out the window at the changing cityscape below, avoiding Malcolm's harsh gaze. Then he looked back with renewed determination on his face.

"Malcolm, this is our only chance. We have to hit the news cycle hard. We have to keep this school bombing thing in the press as long as possible. The president wasn't part of the solution. The current administration is going to try to bury this as quickly as they can. They don't accept domestic terrorism. It makes the president look unloved. They are doing their best to blame this on foreign nationalists who want to destroy our way of life based on the homepage of the guy you captured in Colorado. Homeland is not buying that for all the reasons you don't.

"Malcolm, the people have a right to know what is going on, a right to know who was terrorizing them. We can't let these attacks be covered up. We have to stand up for the everyday American. If we gain some free exposure along the way, so be it. We'll take anything we can get. We're fighting on a shoestring, but we are fighting for a just cause."

The governor returned his gaze to the window again, seemingly trying to build up for another round of arguments from Malcolm.

"You're right, Peter."

The governor spun around in his chair. "I'm right?" He studied Malcolm. "I know I am. It's you I'm trying to convince."

Malcolm smiled grimly. "In four more years, under this administration, the America we know will be a relic of history. This president is totally under the control of his handlers, and the sad part is, we have no idea who those handlers are. But, the one thing we do know, their interests are not the country's interest. They are totally self-centered."

Now Malcolm paused and looked out over the cityscape as the restaurant slowly revolved. He looked back at the governor. "All this money you say is coming. There can't be any strings attached. That's the way we've always run our campaigns, and we can't have any anonymous donors. It's against the rules, and it's against everything we believe in. Those people will have to step forward and be recognized."

Peter Weston shook his head. "That's a problem, Malcolm. It's not going to happen."

"There's no other way. Make it happen, or we'll proceed without them."

"What if they give the money to me, no strings attached, and I self-fund the campaign?"

Again Malcolm shook his head. "They could form Super PACs. They would act independently of our campaign but with the same end in mind. We are on the federal stage, so technically we could do that. The optics might turn off the voters. They are looking for a new way of doing things, not more of the same in a different suit. Everything has to be out in the open."

Peter swirled the coffee in his cup and watched it spin for several beats before looking at Malcolm again.

"Leave it with me. I'll make it work. These men are patriots. All they are looking for is the return of honest government."

"Peter, we're talking millions of dollars to fund a campaign."

"The time is right, Malcolm. If we're ever going to have a chance to run for the presidency without selling our souls to some outsider, now is the time."

Malcolm paused as the waiter arrived with a steaming plate of waffles, drowning in blueberry sauce and surrounded by peaches, all capped with a generous helping of cream. He took a forkful and savoured the flavour. The governor sat and waited, not interrupting the silence between them.

Finally, Malcolm looked up. His eyes burned into those of the governor. "We would have to put together one hell of a team."

The governor nodded. "One super hell of a team."

"And I'm sure you have some names in mind."

The governor smiled a broad smile. "Of course I do. Some are obvious. Some you will have to have an open mind to accept. We will run a unique campaign. Most of it is going to happen on daytime and late-night talk shows. People pay more attention to the fake news shows these days than they do to the real ones."

Malcolm shook his head. "It's important that we control the message. We can't sell out to the cheap laugh. We're talking about the highest office in the country. We already have a clown filling that position. We have to offer a serious alternative to overcome the pull of party politics. He could be a sexual predator, and some people will still vote the party line. We have to bring in enough new votes to overcome those people who have their heads buried in the sand."

"Or firmly up their asses."

Malcolm smiled. "See. That's what I mean. We can't be going for the cheap laugh even if what you're saying is true. We have to convert some of those people to squeak by in some states. How are yourskills as a proctologist?"

"I agree with you, Malcolm. You'll handle the serious shows. We don't have enough time to have you lurk in the background. You'll have to be front and centre beside me. I'll be my usual charismatic self on the less formal appearances. I've always wanted to meet Ellen. Together we'll be unbeatable." The governor paused and became silent for several minutes while Malcolm devoured the rest of his waffles. He studied the man sitting opposite him.

"I thought you would fight me on this, Malcolm. I had a whole list of arguments to lay on you. I'm surprised you acquiesced so quickly."

Malcolm laughed. "Peter, I did fight you on this. I pointed out all the reasons not to do it. I argued with you at every turn, to no avail. At some point, arguing becomes useless. You are going to carry through with this; my job is to make sure we do it right. I may not agree, but I can do everything in my power to make sure we win. We will only get one shot at this. Winning is the only option."

◀68▶

PAUL JOHNSON KNOCKED on the door leading to Ray Tutty's office and walked in without waiting for an acknowledgement.

"What's up?" He looked at the serious frowns on everyone's face. "Did someone die?"

Ray pointed towards a chair. "Sit down. According to Derek, someone is trying to undercut our deal to take over his company."

Paul laughed a gruff laugh. "No offence, Derek, but why would anyone besides us want your company? It's a living example of mediocrity in action."

Derek turned on Paul, fire flashing in his eyes. "Don't be such a pompous ass. It may not be BurgerCircus, but it's not that bad."

"Yeah, man, it is. I've been working on the changes that are going to take place right away when we take over. We have to turn it around quickly before it becomes associated with our brand. It's going to work for our purposes, but, as I said, I can't see anyone else wanting to buy into it."

Barbara looked up from her computer. "Derek is right about someone buying up shares. In the past week when our stock was on the roller-coaster ride, someone was buying and selling ours and making great profits from the fluxing prices. At the same time, someone was buying up Derek's shares at their low points and hanging on to them. They stand to make a considerable profit when we announce our takeover."

"This smells of insider trading," Paul said. "Who knew

about our takeover plans, Derek?"

"Who knew? It was at best an open secret. Several people knew we were in negotiations. If it hadn't been for this school bombing fiasco, nobody would have cared. It would have been business as usual." Derek looked over at the coffee bar in the corner of Ray's office. "I need a coffee. Any objections?"

"No, go ahead," Paul said. "We give it away for free."

Ray walked over to the office window and studied the view of downtown Atlanta. Finally, he turned and looked at the others. "The question we have to answer is: Is someone trying to take over Derek's restaurants or are they simply looking to cash in on our deal?

"The former could be a problem. We are too deeply invested in our expansion plans to change course now. This intruder could drive prices up to make the whole deal uneconomical.

"If they are just trying to make money then it doesn't make a hill of beans of difference to us as long as they sell their shares. We don't care who we buy them from. It shouldn't matter to you either, Derek, as long as you weren't selling your shares when the price went down. The adage is 'buy low, sell high.' You do understand that, don't you?"

"Go to hell," Derek said. There was a slight tremble in his lower lip. "With this extortion threat, we didn't know how low the prices were going to go. It's good business practice to protect yourself."

Paul took a couple of steps towards Derek. "How many shares are we talking about here? Are you still the principal shareholder?" He looked over at Barbara. "Are we dealing with the right person here?"

She shrugged.

He looked back at Derek. All signs of the earlier humour had left him. "Are you trying to screw us over? Don't. Our offer is more than generous. If you're trying some backdoor effort to increase our offer, let me tell you right now, it's not going to happen."

The venom in Paul's voice startled Derek. This was a new side of the man with whom he had been negotiating for the past several weeks. He held up his hands.

"It's not me, Paul. I want this deal to go through as smoothly as possible. You know that."

"I thought that," Paul said. "I'll know it when the share transfer is complete. Now that these bombers are dead and we can get back to normal, let's finish the deal." The usual radiant smile came back onto Paul's face. "Before long, we'll be involved in an election campaign and struggling to get Ray elected as vice-president."

Derek looked from Paul to Ray and back to Paul. "Vice-president of what?"

Paul laughed. "Haven't you heard? Ray's turned over a new leaf. He's going to do for America what he did for BurgerCircus. He's going into politics."

A smile flickered onto Derek's face and just as quickly off again before turning into a look of confusion. "The candidates are all picked. The conventions were months ago."

"Not all picked. Ray and Peter Weston are running as Independents. Don't spend all that money we are going to give you. We will want some back as a political contribution to our campaign."

Derek looked at him with disbelief. "You're having fun with me, right?" Then his face took on a more serious demeanour. "That's not the worst idea I've heard. Hell, you can't screw things over any more than the current administration. Governor Weston has turned Georgia around in the last six years." He looked over at Ray. "And you're no slouch either. When is the official announcement going to be made?"

◀69▶

MALCOLM AND THE governor ran up the stairs of the mansion and into the building.

"Joe Fisher is camped in my office," Malcolm said. "I'll check in with him, and then we'll get the ball rolling on our announcement. You already have a news conference scheduled to provide an update on this morning's takedown of the extortionists. You know the first question will be about you running for president. What's your plan? Are you going to be coy or is this the big moment?"

"All the media will be there. It would be counter-productive to deny it and then try to get them together for another press conference and admit that we are running. We should play it by ear. If they ask, we announce. If no one asks, we'll bring it up at the end, although that would be a little less dramatic."

Malcolm laughed. "If Rod Sanderson is there, you know that will be the first question out of his mouth. When we win, he will be taking credit for getting you into the race."

Malcolm turned serious. "What about Ray Tutty? Is he a part of the team or was that simply banter earlier today?"

"Get settled and come to my office," the governor said. "We have a lot to discuss before we go public. I don't want to do it here in the hallway."

Joe Fisher looked up as Malcolm entered. "Where's my information about the schools?"

"Schools?" Awareness appeared in his eyes. "Robert's looking into it for you. It was less than an hour ago that you asked. Exercise some patience."

"OK, this is me being patient. I want information on all the schools that were blown up. Can Robert get that as well?"

"I'm sure he can, but that will take a little longer. What's the relevance of all this information?"

"Not sure. Might be important, might not. Get it."

Malcolm shrugged. "Have you learned anything new?" He indicated the computer.

"Still working on it. Exercise some patience." Joe gave him a sardonic grin. "It's like I said. Everything is too perfect. I'm still trying to dig deeper. The governor is back. Chat with him. I hear he's running for president."

"Where..." Malcolm started to ask, but let it drop. Joe Fisher seemed to have his sources for everything.

Peter Weston looked up as Malcolm walked into his office. He had several sheets of paper on his desk and was sorting them into various piles.

"Offers of support," he said as a means of explanation.

He held up one pile. "The time is right. Go for it." He held up the second pile. "I'll give you my support in any way I can." He held us the third pile and gave it a little shake. "The cheque is in the mail. Run that bastard out of office and the country.

"It's coming together, Malcolm. There are some very generous pledges of support here."

"That's good. We'll need every penny of it to make this work. But, as much as we need the money, we have to get an organization in place all across the country. We need boots on the ground to get out the vote. We needed it yesterday. Time is short, too short."

The governor nodded. "I know that. Remember Governor Morrissey from Montana offered to throw his name in the hat for VP. I'd be in the east; he could cover the west. He's a good man, popular in his state."

Malcolm shook his head. "Not popular enough. We need

someone who will carry more than one state. Montana only has three seats in the Electoral College. Hardly even a drop in the bucket. We need someone with universal appeal across the country."

"As you keep telling me, a write-in vote has as much chance as a snowball in hell. Not a lot of people want to risk cutting their party ties to jump on the bandwagon. It will be political suicide if we lose."

"My point exactly. We need a non-politician."

"A non-politician for vice-president? Malcolm, you're crazy. Maybe we could look at the candidates defeated in the primaries. One of them may be pissed off at the party enough to take the leap."

Again Malcolm shook his head. "No, Peter. You were right with your first choice. We have to talk Ray Tutty into getting on board."

"Tutty?" The governor looked shocked. "Tutty?" he repeated. "He's big money. I hate everything he stands for. He had a purpose; he served it."

Malcolm marvelled at how the governor could create the impression that he and the CEO of BurgerCircus were such good friends when he stood before a TV audience or the press and in private despise the man.

"No, Peter, he still has a purpose to serve. He can win this election for us. As I said earlier, most of the diehard party-liners are not going to change their votes for anyone, especially an Independent candidate. We have to get out the forty per cent of the people who don't vote now. Most of them, as you know, are the young people. The people who work for BurgerCircus, have played ball on one of the sports teams sponsored by BurgerCircus, the people who eat at BurgerCircus or, perhaps most importantly, went to school on a BurgerCircus scholarship."

Malcolm paused to let those numbers sink in. "That's a big number of new voters, but with a little luck, they will bring their families along with them. The parents who didn't have to pay for their kid's college, the uncles and aunts who cheered in the stands at the stadiums and ball fields around the country, and as fickle as it may seem, the people who like a good burger and cup of coffee."

Malcolm was pacing now. Excitement built in his voice. "The other thing about these people, the big thing about these people, they are not all in one state. They represent every part the country. Add these voices to the voices already disenchanted with the current administration, and we could have enough votes to snatch this election from the established parties. Peter, this is going to be a battle, but it is a battle we can win if we use every resource at our disposal. Ray Tutty is one resource we want to capitalize on, like it or not."

"Get serious, Malcolm. He runs a fast-food joint. What does he know about politics?"

"He's the CEO of the largest fast-food company in the country. He started flipping burgers like hundreds of kids out there now. He worked himself up to be the top dog. Remember your speech earlier this week. He is the perfect example of the American Dream. Everyone has that dream. Everyone thinks it could happen to them. Ray is an inspiration to all those people. Nobody resents him. They want to be like him. Sorry to say this, Governor, but he will be more popular than you out on the stumps."

"Don't go putting your words into my mouth, Malcolm. OK, I may have said them, but you are the one who wrote the speech."

"And you delivered it so well because you know that every word is true. Call Ray. Get him on board right now."

◄70►

RAY TUTTY RETURNED the phone to its carriage. The others knew the call came from the governor based on the side of the conversation they could hear. They studied Ray, who sat in his chair staring out into the room. His demeanour betrayed the seriousness of the question the governor had asked. He looked calm but contemplative.

"It's official," he said. "The governor wants me to be his running mate for a bid at the presidency. I know we've discussed it in theory, but now it's real. He'd like an answer sooner rather than later. He has a news conference scheduled for later today about the capture of the bombers and will make the announcement then."

Barbara and Paul exchanged quick glances. They had advised Ray on major decisions before, but nothing like this.

"You've got to do it," Paul said. "You are the right man at the right time. The country can't take four more years of incompetence. I know I was against it before, but the more I think about it, the more the idea grows on me."

Barbara nodded and then pushed the button on her computer to play *Hail Columbia* again. "Your biggest challenge will be to slip into the role of number two. We must establish areas of responsibility before we sign on. Peter Weston is a politician. You're all business. Your union is not a marriage made in heaven, but we can meld it into a powerful force that no one can beat."

She looked at Paul and laughed. "If we could teach a guppy to talk, it could beat this incumbent. The other party is counting on that fact to win. Their candidate is not much better than a talking guppy, except that she is afraid to talk. That's not to say it won't be an uphill climb. No Independent has ever captured the White House. Get ready for the ride of your lives, gentlemen. We're about to make history."

Paul walked across the office and opened a cupboard door. He took down a bottle of Canadian whisky and poured three glasses. "A toast to the future," he said as he passed each of the others a glass. "Life will never be the same."

"True," Barbara said and downed her drink. "Now get on the phone and call the governor back. We need to set up a meeting."

Ray took a sip of his drink and set the glass down. "I don't want to appear too eager. I should wait a bit."

"Ray, the election is in two months. We don't have a second to waste. We are eager. There is so much to do and so little time. Come on, grab that phone."

Thirty minutes later, Ray, Paul and Barbara were meeting with Malcolm and Peter in Ray's office. Malcolm had suggested they not hold the meeting in the governor's mansion. From here on in, optics would be everything. As their campaign gained strength, every move they made would be scrutinized by their opponents. Malcolm didn't want to give them any freebies.

Within minutes of the hand-shaking and congratulations, the two alpha males started butting heads.

"It's too early in the scheme of things to be defining the vice-president's responsibilities after the election," Peter insisted. "We have to get elected first."

"I'm not giving up my role at BurgerCircus to become someone's puppet," Ray shot back. "I've seen too many do-nothing VPs. I'm not going to be one of them. Let's set out the ground rules right now, or I'm out."

The two men glared at each other, neither willing to back down. This start did not bode well for future success.

Barbara stepped forward. "Gentlemen, gentlemen," she said in a soothing voice. "We have work to do and not a whole lot of time. Let's agree that in the past, many vice-presidents took a low-key, backseat role in governing. Ray doesn't fit that mould. His expertise is business and finance. Let's agree here and now that Ray takes a prominent role in those areas. BurgerCircus is a worldwide company. Ray has contacts in many countries around the world, some right up to the highest level. Again, let's not waste that resource. Governor, you may not want to hear this, but he has more experience in foreign affairs than you. Let's agree to utilize that expertise."

She looked from one man to the other. "Good, that's straightened out. Now we have to plan a strategy to get elected, or these points are moot."

"Do we have a list of all the employees that worked for the company while Ray was climbing to the CEO post?" Paul asked.

Barbara tapped a few keys on her computer. A list of names and email addresses started scrolling by. It took a couple of minutes to load fully.

"Let me divide them by state and create a map," she said.

Malcolm and Peter exchanged a surprised look. The entire country looked like it was suffering from an outbreak of the measles as the red dots filled every state. Ray Tutty would be having a lot more say in things than they had realized. He brought much more than name-recognition to the table. Malcolm felt for the first time that they had a serious chance of winning.

"I can't guarantee all those people will vote for me," Ray said. "But we have very few disgruntled employees. Those few that are, we make every effort to resolve their issues."

He winked at Barbara. They had set up this program before the political people had arrived. He knew what kind of impression it would make on people whose lives revolved around polls. The governor might publicly proclaim he didn't believe in polls, but Ray knew the owners of the state's largest survey company. BurgerCircus shared their services along with the existing administration among others.

An hour later, the fledgeling team had an operational map on paper. Malcolm had put together an announcement in the form of an answer to a question from the press. Smiles drifted into the serious discussions, and the former animosity melted into a thing from the past.

Malcolm looked up from reading the proposed announcement. "Barbara, gentlemen, our lives are about to take a severe turn in the road. Hang on and let's enjoy the ride."

The others held up their coffee cups. "Hear, hear," they said in unison.

◀71▶

MALCOLM AND THE governor returned to the mansion with both an emboldened and deferential attitude change. The idea that they could succeed had gone up several notches in their thinking. The realization that Ray Tutty brought a lot more to the table than they had initially believed caused them to rethink their battle plan.

The original idea required them to push the capture of the school boomers constantly into the faces of the voters. They would continue to do this. The country had dodged a bullet, and Governor Weston had led the charge, not the sitting president. It was imperative they hammer that point home.

Creating a video of the various schools being blown up and concluding with the much more violent explosion of the extortionists' compound would be the drawing point of their talk-show appearances. Malcolm knew that, if done right, the video would quickly go viral on social media. The key aspect of this plan was to tie the governor's role in making this happen and his leadership throughout the torturous week of threats together.

He would be seen as a man of action while the president would be seen to be only interested in his re-election. The president's belief that the only form of real terrorism came from offshore would bite him in the ass. This plan would work on several levels, not the least of which would be capturing the youth vote—18-21, "old enough to fight, old enough to vote" as the 26th Amendment put it. These young people formed a large part of the forty-odd per cent of non-voters.

The plan had been to build their campaign around this platform. But now, seeing the potential support Ray Tutty could bring to the cause required second thoughts of their basic premise.

The governor had turned the state of Georgia around in the last six years and made it much more productive. But honestly, who, outside of Georgians, cared about this? Ray had taken a third placed fast-food chain and made it a worldwide leader in the business. In the process, he had acquired a huge amount of wealth. He exemplified the American Dream, and now he was about to ascend to the second highest position in the country, the vice-president. If he could do it, so could you, would be the message. That was the crux of the American dream.

As great a selling point as that would be, the big thing he brought to the table was all the people he had helped along the way. Ray understood that the success of the company came from the success of the employees. He had gone out of his way to help them succeed, and now the chickens would come home to roost. They would reward him, not only with their votes and if possible the votes of their friends and families, but more to the point, they would be boots on the ground throughout the country.

These would be the previous "why-bother-to-vote" demographic. Those who believed voting only changed one old white man in a suit for another old white man in a suit. With Ray on the ticket, this would not be the case. They would have a face they could identify. Malcolm would make sure the team capitalized on that fact. Right now he had a press conference to organize. He looked out the window. The rain showed no signs of letting up.

◄72►

AT 4 O'CLOCK Eastern time, Peter Weston once more stood on a stage in front of the press. This time he was down the street from the governor's mansion in McElreath Hall at the Atlanta History Center. The venue held 400 people and the press had filled most of the seats. The rain outside swept through the gardens surrounding the ancient building and pounded on the large windows creating an almost war-like atmosphere with its rat-a-tat-tat sound.

"This morning I promised you more information as it became available regarding the horrific bombings of our public schools for the past week. Bombs exploded in Georgia, Texas, California, Montana, New York, Michigan, and Colorado, where we captured one of the extortionists.

"This investigation has been taken over by Homeland Security." He paused and looked around the room at the expectant faces.

"I don't have to tell you, people of the press, that Homeland does not play well with others."

A smattering of laughter rippled through the crowd of reporters.

"They have cut off all access to information about the events of this morning and taken all our files from the past week. Consequently, the investigation led by the state of Georgia and with the full assistance of the FBI has been shut down and Homeland has told us we are to make no further comments on the matter. Anything we say, we've been told, could be a threat to national security."

A rumble of groans filled the hall.

"Are we here for nothing?" someone asked.

"The people have a right to know," another said.

The governor looked over to Malcolm standing slightly off stage and smiled. Malcolm insisted someone would make this point.

"That is exactly what I believe," the governor said, raising his voice above the dissent. "The people of this great country have been put through a week of hell. They, we, have a right to know who led this attack and why.

"Speculation suggested the person captured in Colorado had ISIS leanings. Experts in this field have pretty much disproved this theory. It was a hoax designed to lead us away from the true perpetrators of these crimes. We now believe they were domestic terrorists and as you all know, our president only believes in terrorism that originates outside our country."

The room darkened slightly, and a screen descended behind the governor. The image of the school in Georgia going up in a ball of fire filled the screen, followed in quick succession by the schools in Texas, California, Montana, New York, Michigan and Colorado. The video dropped to slow motion. The nose of a Kiowa helicopter fluttered in and out of the picture of a building surrounded by trees. The camera oscillated in a slow, smooth arc, capturing a wider field of view.

"The Okefenokee Swamp," one of the reporters said, breaking the mortuary-like silence in the room. Murmurs of agreement came from several others.

The screen suddenly turned red and yellow as flames climbed into the air in the eerie slow-motion image. As dramatic as the other pictures had been, this one overshadowed them all. It went on for several seconds before settling into a massive ground-based fireball.

The building reappeared and blew up again, this time in real time. It then froze on the final image of destruction.

The governor stood on stage, his back to the people, looking at the screen. He slowly started shaking his head as he turned to face them.

"It was indeed one hell of a week."

The usually boisterous press corps sat in solemn silence.

"Florida was scheduled for tomorrow. The bomb squad from the Dade County Police Department decommissioned an explosive device late this morning based on the information we provided them. Downtown Miami was the planned site. It's hard to believe it could have exploded without a serious loss of life.

"To date, no one has died. We speculate the bombers were going to up the ante in Miami. Take off the gloves, so to speak. An explosion there would have kicked off the start of week two of their attack on our society. We are only speculating, but it appears people would die. Also, tomorrow would have been the first day of school in Florida. The governor there had a serious decision to make, as did the governors in every state in the nation. Should they let the kids go back to school? Fortunately, we didn't have to make that determination."

He looked back at the screen. "The extortionists have been neutralized."

"Governor, I thought Homeland said there was to be no further comment. Are you taking on the federal government with this dissent?"

"Everything you just saw has been on TV and in the newspapers several times over. It is in the public domain. It would be an attack on your First Amendment rights to try to restrict it now."

A reporter half way up the aisle stood up. "Is this your first volley of an attack on the sitting president?"

The governor shielded his eyes from the light shining upon him. "Rod Sanderson? I thought as much.

"Yes, Rod, it is my intention to overthrow the government of the United States." The governor paused to let that message sink in. "But I will do it at the ballot box. Myself," he held out his hand to the left side of the stage where a man walked into the spotlights, "and Ray Tutty, you all know Ray after this week of hell, intend to run for the presidency of the United States on an Independent ticket."

No one in the room expressed surprise.

◀73▶

FOR THE FIRST month, the two old-line parties ignored Peter and Ray's campaign. Why would they bother with them? Write-in votes didn't work. In early October, the incumbent realized he might be losing votes he needed to this upstart duo. He had no fear of the Independents winning, but he needed every vote he could get to hold off the other old-line party. The election had become a horse race.

Pollsters could see the trend developing. They were the first to understand that something important and almost as ground-breaking as the American Revolution itself had descended on the country. An Independent party had taken the lead in the polls with a little over two weeks to go. Would this be a repeat of the Georgian gubernatorial election six years previously?

Peter and Ray did not run a flashy campaign. They stuck to the basics, capitalized as much as possible on TV talk and news shows to get their faces in front of the public at no cost to themselves. Every time there was an update on the school bombings, they made sure they were called in as experts. These breakthroughs were few and far between. Mohammad Alzabar, the money courier at the National Forest in Colorado had been captured and turned over to Homeland Security. He was a dead end. His role was less significant than the photographer's. He knew his part in the scenario, the money drop, and nothing else.

As the second Tuesday in November drew ever closer, they had to open the spending taps to make sure every corner of the nation got their message. Those voters who only watched sports or soaps could carry the balance of power. New advertising targeted them. The time for change had descended upon America. It could only happen if everyone exercised their constitutional right to vote. No one could be standing on the sidelines at this crucial phase of the country's existence. Failure to vote would be a vote for the status quo.

Despite this outpouring of advertising dollars, Malcolm noticed, they always had that extra few bucks when they needed it to push into an area where their support was lagging. Money, although always tight, seldom seemed to be an issue.

His first thought suggested Ray was coughing up the required funds. Ray was definitely in this thing to win. There existed no limit on how much of his own money he could dump into the coffers. Malcolm talked to Ray on a daily basis. Ray made no indication that he had become an unlimited bankroll for the win.

Although nothing prevented Ray from spending his money, this was not an investment that had any upside if they did not win the presidency. It was money down the drain for the losers. No payoff, no recovery. Ray wanted to win, but he was still a shrewd businessman. Malcolm was skeptical that Ray was the source.

◀74▶

PAUL JOHNSON AND Joe Fisher stared at a map spread out on Joe's desk. Joe's office, at the back of their campaign headquarters on the first floor of the BurgerCircus office tower, formed the nerve centre of this presidential run. A glass partition cut off the area from the rest of the open room. Several computers lined the walls. Stored in their data banks were the names of every potential party supporter. On election day, each would be tracked to make sure he or she had indeed shown up to vote in their respective states. If not, they would be getting phone calls, offered rides, cajoled to do their civic duty. All parties would be doing this. The most successful at this persuasion game could well be the overall winner.

"Paul, I don't believe in coincidences," Joe said. "I also know that humans like to find patterns where they don't exist. Having said that, I have found something interesting."

Paul looked closer at the map. Nothing jumped out at him. "Go on," he encouraged.

Joe pointed to a series of stars drawn on the map in red ink. "These are the bombing sites from August. These little numbers are the number of Electoral College seats each state has. I was studying those when I noticed something out of the ordinary."

Paul tried to see the correlation between the two. "Son of a bitch," he said. "Outside of Montana, these are all big number states. Georgia has 16, California has 55, Texas has 38, Michigan has 16, New York has 29, Colorado drops off at only 9."

Joe tapped the map. "We prevented the bomb from blowing up in Florida, but it has 29 as well." He looked at Paul. "What do you think?"

"You don't believe in coincidences. Colorado and Montana seem to break the pattern. The bombers were simply targeting areas of high population to make the most impact."

Joe was about to respond when Malcolm Truex tapped on Joe's door and walked in. "Glad you're both here," he said. "We may have a problem."

He placed a folder of papers on top of the map.

"I fear someone might be breaking the rules regarding the size of donations a company could offer a candidate. There's unaccounted money showing up in our war chest."

Paul laughed. "We'll take all the money we can get. Who knew it cost so much to run an election campaign? Those other two parties' spending must be into the billions by now. They've been at it for over a year."

"I agree," Malcolm said, "We don't want to turn any funding away. I have two main concerns. If someone is making illegal donations, it could blow us out of the water if discovered this late in the game. Elections are fickle; anything could destroy us.

"If it is some anonymous donor, what do they expect in return for the much-needed financial support?"

He looked at Paul. "Is Ray slipping a few spare million into the pot without telling us?"

Paul denied knowledge of any extra funding. "Ray does not want to appear to be trying to buy his way into the White House. I noticed the surprise funding. I thought Peter was putting up the extra funds."

Malcolm laughed at that suggestion. "I'm surprised Peter is not getting his meals from food banks. He hasn't got that kind of money."

"Someone has," Paul said. "Now that we have become a

serious threat, we will be under more severe scrutiny. We had better find the source of this money before it bites us in the ass. The donations could be a dirty trick from one of the other parties. Ten million well invested if the information comes out a couple of days before the polls close. If we look like we're cheating, that could be a game changer in a race this tight."

Malcolm looked at Joe. "Can you look into this? We want Peter and Ray to keep their focus on the big prize. It's too late in the campaign for distractions, and I'm not sure either of them understands federal funding regulations."

"We can't have you distracted at this crucial point, either," Paul said. "You're getting almost as much television time as the other two. Some people must think you work for CNN or Fox News; you're there so often."

"Our candidates provide the charisma; I provide the meat and potatoes of our plan of governing. It's not exciting, but it is leaps and bounds ahead of what any other parties are offering. It gives the voters something they can talk about around the water cooler; it keeps the pundits on point with our platform."

"It's also keeping you in the public eye, smart, intelligent chief-of-staff, former FBI, tough on crime. It all helps."

A little colour crept into Malcolm's face. "Anything for the cause."

Paul smirked. "Time is short. I'll liaise with you, Joe. There's no sense wasting time tracking down information I have at my fingertips. We'd better get on this right away."

"Sure," Joe said. He looked at stacks of papers on a nearby table. "I had run out of things to do anyway. No offence but I work better alone. Paul, you get me started, and I'll call you if I need your help." He indicated the stack of papers. "I'll give you a list of things I had planned to do this week. Deal with them."

◄75►

JOE FISHER LOOKED up from his computer as Paul Johnson and Ray Tutty walked into his office. All the blinds were closed, creating a low-light atmosphere. Several operating screens crowded the tables scattered around the room.

Dark circles gave his eyes a sunken look. Several days of facial hair adorned his usually clean-shaven face. His hair looked damp and clean, suggesting he had showered for this meeting.

Joe held up a finger and reached for his phone. "Malcolm, we're ready," he said and hung up.

Seconds later, Malcolm walked in, a tray of coffee in one hand, a box of doughnuts in the other. He sat in one of the easy chairs placed in a circle near Joe's desk. The others joined him.

Two computer screens formed part of the circle. Joe hit a key on one of them, and a slight hum filled the room.

"Are we here for the latest polling updates?" Ray asked. "We don't have time for that."

Joe gave him a solemn stare.

"Gentlemen, what we are about to discuss today cannot leave this room. I need your word on this."

"Come on, Joe," Ray said. "We can't swear about something we know nothing about."

"We are going to have the most serious discussion you have ever had in your lives. It stays with us."

"If you are telling us we can't discuss this with anyone outside this room," Paul said, "then we need to add two more people to the group. Barbara plays a key role in every decision we make. She should be here."

"Barbara?" Joe asked. "The cute chick from upstairs?"

Paul rolled his eyes. "You would be dead if she heard you say that. She's Ray's executive assistant and much, much more. She needs to be here."

"Peter obviously should be here," Malcolm said. "He is the candidate."

"The governor is campaigning in Texas. He has been deliberately left out for reasons that will become apparent," Joe said. He looked at Paul. "Call Barbara. Tell her to hurry."

Paul took his phone from his pocket. "I have no signal."

"That hum," Joe said, "is electrical interference for any electronic device in this room except my computers. Call me paranoid, but we can't risk anyone eavesdropping on this discussion."

"OK," Ray said. "This is getting spooky. What the hell is going on?"

"Step outside and call Barbara," Joe told Paul. "The rest of you talk among yourselves. We'll start when we are all here."

Minutes later, Barbara walked into the room. She had a confused look on her face. "No one told me about a meeting."

"It was a need-to-know basis," Joe said as he dragged another chair into the circle. "Have a seat."

The others looked at him in anticipation of a great revelation. Joe did not have a reputation for pranks and tricks and never wasted his own time.

"Last week," he started, "Malcolm presented a problem with our contributions. It looked serious, and with Paul's help, I got started right away. It was much trickier than I had anticipated.

"It seems there are several unaccounted for donations

showing up in our war chest. This money could be a potential problem. With Paul's help, I discovered it ran into millions of dollars. With further searching on my own, it turned out to be tens of millions of dollars.

"I asked myself: who has that kind of money to throw around?" He looked at Ray. "Immediately, I thought of you."

"You thought wrong, pal," Ray said. "I might have that kind of money, but it is nothing you can get your hands on, not several million."

Joe nodded. "I know. Further research showed that every time a large donation came in, someone sold a huge block of BurgerCircus shares. It made no sense that it would be you. You can pour as much of your money into the campaign as you want. You have already done that. There would be no reason for secrecy. I tried to trace the source of the funding. I checked out other large shareholders of BurgerCircus. No one is in the same league as you three.

"That's when it got interesting. The funds came from six offshore accounts. No matter how hard I tried, I could not figure out who was behind this. The strange thing, though, was that even though there were six separate accounts, all the money ended up coming into the campaign bank account in the same way. This pattern led me to believe there was only one person behind the whole charade."

"I noticed those sales," Barbara said. "I knew nothing about the money going to the election campaign, so I dismissed it as someone cashing out their investments over a period of time so as to not to drive the stock price down."

"Makes sense," Joe said. "Anyway, I wasn't making any progress with this. I found no link to anyone at BurgerCircus. Given enough time, I could probably track the person down, but time is at a premium. The election is only a little over a week away. I moved on."

He took a drink of coffee and remained silent for several

seconds. "There are only two real benefactors of our election, Ray and Peter. Well, three, if you count the nation as a whole. Getting rid of the current administration is not an area where we can have any form of failure. The current administration must be booted out, no ifs, ands or buts."

Nods of approval circled the room.

"I moved on to Peter. We've been friends, or at least acquaintances, for years. He's not poor, but I know he doesn't have that kind of money. If he was involved, the funds had to be coming from an outside source. Why were they so covert unless they had already spent their limit on donations? Then I asked myself, did the money supplier hope to buy future concessions from the government? Let's face it, the president, by the stroke of a pen, can make or break any company. We are now talking billions of dollars, not millions. A great return on an investment.

"I decided to see who Peter had been talking with lately. The day of the explosion seemed to make a good initial starting point. I could move forward or backward from there depending on where the investigation led. I called up his phone records for that day."

"You what?" Malcolm said. "Peter has a secure government phone for his personal use. It's the highest level of encryption. Not even you can access those calls."

Joe allowed himself his first smile since the meeting began. "Right."

He tapped a few keys on his laptop, and one of the screens beside him came to life. "If I could tap into his calls, it might look something like this." A list of phone numbers and times appeared. He turned to Malcolm. "The first one is an incoming call from you. About fifteen seconds."

Malcolm nodded. "The connection was too poor to talk."

"Note the second one. Outgoing, two seconds long."

Joe stood up and clasped his hand in front of his chin like a child saying his nightly prayers. He stood quietly before looking intently at each person seated in the circle.

"This is the point of no return. When you arrived, I told you nothing said here could leave this room." He paused, a pensive look on his face. "Now is the time to leave, if you don't think you can do that regardless of what I'm about to say."

Malcolm looked at the others. "We're all in this together, Joe. What did you find out?"

Joe looked around the room. The others stoically stared at him. He struck another computer key. The familiar picture of the nose of the Kiowa helicopter appeared and advanced to the point of the explosion. They had all seen this video several times in the last two months. Joe stopped the video and backed it up a few frames. He picked a laser pointer from his desk.

"Look at the times," he said and pointed to the bottoms of the respective screens. One said 0721, the other 1221.

"What are we looking at?" Ray asked. "They are five hours apart."

Joe shook his head. "The phone is Eastern Time; the video is GMT, Greenwich Mean Time. They are identical."

An icy silence settled over the room. "What are you saying, Joe?" Malcolm asked. "Are you saying the governor blew up that building?" He shook his head in disbelief. "That is what you are saying. There has to be some other explanation."

"It gets worse, Malcolm," Joe said. "I'm sorry."

Again his fingers flicked over the keyboard. The screen turned blue with a white line through the centre. Joe typed again. A slight tone sounded, and the white line flickered.

"I just pinged the phone number. There is not much juice left in the battery, but I did get a signal." He hit another key. A set of coordinates printed on the screen with a Google map picture in the background. "It has to be a sat phone. That is the Okefenokee Swamp."

Malcolm leaned back in his chair, rubbing his face with both hands. "I can't accept this. It can't be true."

"As near as I can figure, the phone did its task and must have somehow been blown clear by the explosion. One chance in a million but that's the only explanation."

"No, this can't be true." Malcolm leaned forward. "I'll call Tom Burke. We'll get the FBI to go in and find it."

"No." Joe slapped his desk, causing the others to jump. "Nothing said in this room can leave. We tell no one about this."

The others all started speaking at once. Joe held up his hand for silence.

"We have to inform the FBI," Paul said, "or Homeland. Someone."

"No one." Joe's voice took on a stringent tone. "The fate of the nation is on the line here. This is much bigger than all of us. You must see that."

Again, the room fell silent as those words sunk in.

"Are you suggesting we go on with the election as if nothing has happened?" Barbara shook her head. "You just accused the man of mass murder, and now you want to make him president. What kind of sick bastard are you?"

"A lot sicker than you think. I've given this matter a lot of thought. I've lost a lot of sleep. There is only one solution."

◀76▶

SEVERAL HUNDRED MILES to the north in Washington, an equally important discussion was in progress. The president's re-election team crowded around a table in a small room in the West Wing. Like Peter Weston, the president was not a part of this meeting.

"This whole campaign is a failure. We're losing to a write-in candidate. How did things get so screwed up?"

"I said right from the beginning we needed a new candidate. The last four years have been a disaster. The guy has the IQ of a half-eaten banana."

"In the beginning, that was a good point. We had an agenda. We manipulated him into making things happen. Check your bank accounts. It's not that much of a disaster."

"It is now if we don't win, and things are not looking good."

"There's nothing we can do in the time remaining to improve his image. We need dirt on Governor Weston. We need to tarnish his image."

"Good luck with that. The man's a national hero. To hear people talk, he single-handedly took down what he refers to as the domestic terrorists. Why did we let the president deny that domestic terrorism exists? Why couldn't he be tough on crime?"

"Because our backers don't want the feds nosing around in their world."

"Gentlemen, this discussion is going nowhere. We need decisive action."

"Decisive? As in shoot the son of a bitch?"

"For god's sake man, we're in the White House. They bug every one of these rooms."

"All I'm saying is that something has to happen and soon."

"This is going nowhere. Talk to your people. Come up with some good ideas. We'll meet back here late this afternoon. At that point, we need concrete plans."

Presidential press secretary Harold White remained sitting as the others filed out. He lowered his head to avoid looking at them. He had said nothing during the meeting, just listened and observed. He was not really a part of this inner circle.

He shook his head. *No wonder we're in trouble*, he thought, *if this is the brain trust running the campaign.*

◀77▶

JOE FISHER'S OFFICE felt as if something had sucked all of the air from it. Malcolm, Ray, Paul and Barbara tried their best to reconcile the accusation made by Joe Fisher with the man they knew Peter Weston to be, or thought they knew.

"I agree with Malcolm," Ray finally said. "There has to be some other explanation."

"Trust me, people, I found this as hard to believe as you," Joe said. "I have done everything possible to disprove my findings. The evidence is overwhelming. There is more than this simple phone call."

He held up a sheaf of handwritten papers. "It is all right here. You can read this later, but nothing leaves this room. For now, take my word for it. We have to move on."

"Move on to where?" Barbara asked. "I cannot condone making a killer president. End of discussion."

She crossed her arms and sat back in her chair. Her look indicated nothing would change her mind.

"We're on the same page, Barbara," Joe said. "But this is the beginning of the discussion, not the end. We all agree that the current regime must not be allowed to continue. They are slowly destroying the country. The president is an idiot, and the people pulling strings behind him are criminals. The people agree with us. Not for nothing are we leading the polls at this late date."

"Release this information and see how quickly that drops to zero," Barbara said. "Are you suggesting he was behind the whole school-bombing fiasco?"

"It's all here in this report. I've hacked Peter's personal computer. Not the one at the mansion, the one at his house. As I have said several times now, this information cannot leave this room." Joe held up his report. "This will be shredded as soon as this meeting ends. There are no other copies."

Ray shook his head. "I'm sorry, Joe. I'm afraid I'm like the apostle Thomas. I have to stick my hand in the wound. Show me the evidence now. Let me come to my own conclusions." He looked at the others. "Don't you agree?"

Joe held up one hand. With the other, he pushed a button on his phone, sparking it to life. He glanced at the time. "It's a little early for lunch, but who among us is on an ordinary schedule? I'll order some food while you people study this report. I'll keep it light; you may not want to eat when you've finished reading it."

Joe's prophecy proved to be true. The trays of fruits and vegetables were mostly untouched an hour later when everyone had scrutinized the report. They had drained the coffee urn.

Malcolm got up and started pacing the room. He thought better on his feet. "OK, Joe. You are the only one who has had time to absorb this revelation. What do you propose? You wouldn't have called this meeting without having a plan."

"The plan is simple, Malcolm. We need a new candidate."

"With a week to go? You're living in la-la land. Jesus Christ himself couldn't pull off a victory in just a week."

"No, but someone who has been campaigning for two months might have a chance. It is a write-in vote we've been advocating. Peter's name is not on any ballot."

Joe looked over at Ray. "We could move you up a slot. You have a huge base of support. In all honesty, without you, this campaign would not have stood a chance of succeeding. You are charismatic. You bring the BurgerCircus constituency with you. That was crucial. Your 'we don't negotiate with terrorists' slogan carried the day back when schools were blowing up all over the place."

Ray shook his head. "I'm flattered. Having a CEO of a major corporation may carry the day for vice-presidency, but I think the people would balk at putting him in charge. I truly believe it would become a losing cause."

Barbara couldn't contain the surprised look on her face. "Look who has matured over the last two months. I thought you would jump at this opportunity. I do agree with you.

"We can't bring in an outsider at this late date. That only leaves one other choice. Malcolm, you have been campaigning as hard as both of these other two guys. Not only that, you have been the one delivering the serious message of what we plan to do when we win. It's not going to be easy, but we must convince the people to make you the write-in candidate."

"Like Ray, I'm flattered—"

Before Malcolm could decline, Paul jumped into the discussion. "Joe made one very important point. We must defeat the current government. That is the one thing that brought us together for the last two months. Nothing has changed. It's time to suck it up and step into the fray. I agree with Ray about his chances. Malcolm, you have no options. We are not asking, we are telling you. You are the new candidate for president. You've got the experience. We all know you were the power behind the throne in Georgia. The time has come to don the crown."

"Settled," Ray said before Malcolm could respond. "Now, for the big problem. If we aren't going to release Joe's findings, and I agree we can't, how do we get rid of Peter? It has to happen in a way that doesn't take the campaign down with it. I don't think he will step aside and endorse you, Malcolm. He's too hungry for the presidency." He looked at Paul. "I've told you all along we can't trust the guy."

"Sure you did," Paul said. He looked at Joe. "I'm sure you have a plan."

Joe let out a long sigh. "Barbara called me a sick bastard. She may have been right. Peter has to disappear."

"Kidnap him?" Barbara asked. "And what, hide him for eight years?"

Joe ignored the interruption. "I am only going to suggest this because the fate of the whole nation is on the line. Our goal is to save the country from collapsing in on itself due to incompetent leadership. No, it's worse than incompetence, it's criminal. We are in a war whether we realize it or not. Wars have casualties."

"No," all four of them said in unison.

Joe sat down and crossed his hands in front of his chest. He looked down and studied them for a full minute before looking up. The others were too stunned from his suggestion to say anything.

"We all know that Georgia is a death penalty state. If I presented this report to the authorities, Peter would be found guilty of mass murder. Execution is the punishment for this type of crime." He paused. "If we wait for the case to crawl through the courts, we get four more years of incompetence. If we expedite proceedings, America prospers again. Look on it as a patriotic duty."

"That may not be true," Malcolm said. "His defence would say he was fighting terrorism. He could get off."

"I understand your resistance, Malcolm. I do," Joe said in a quiet voice. "The simple truth is that Peter was maximizing his profits by eliminating his partners. If they were terrorists, so was he. They weren't, neither was he. It was all about money and power."

Joe looked over at Ray. "He targeted BurgerCircus for two reasons. He thought he could manipulate your stock prices in his favour. By controlling the flow of information, he kept the stock values on a roller-coaster. He knew when to buy and when to sell. He made a fortune."

"And the other reason?" Ray asked.

"Initially, he didn't like you, Ray. In fact he hated you. Somewhere along the line you dissed him."

Ray grunted. "I remember. He crashed one of my parties and tried to turn it into a fund-raiser. I threw him out."

Joe nodded. "That would do it. He was, however, pragmatic. He saw your value to the campaign and made the most of it. None of that changes the fact that he was a criminal."

The electronic hum in the room seemed to grow louder. No one moved. No one spoke.

Finally, Barbara asked: "How would it happen?"

"If we all agree, it has to be unanimous, the how is not important. What is important is that we be immediately ready to jump into action. A little over a week is not much time. On the other hand, a short space of time may work in our favour. There will be no time for the changeover from Peter to Malcolm to fall out of the news cycle's top position. That sounds crass, I know. We will need all the breaks we can get.

"Are we all in favour?"

◀78▶

JOE FISHER SCANNED the building crowd at the Buccaneer Stadium in Corpus Christi, Texas. Peter Weston's campaign rallies drew bigger and bigger crowds with every stop. Today a stadium with a capacity of 18,000 would be the venue. They might not fill it, but they would come close. The election rhetoric between Peter and the incumbent had become laced with more and more vitriol as voting day drew nearer. The crowds ate it up. They could see history was being rewritten and wanted to be a part of the process.

A large stage had been built at one end of the football field. Two large television screens flanked both sides of the podium, giving everyone a close-up view of the candidate. Peter had spared no expense.

Joe found a spot on the fifty-yard line and waited. Like most people in the milling throng, he wore a Corpus Christi Hooks baseball cap to fight off the glare from the sun. The temperature had climbed to seventy-three degrees and continued rising. The beak hid most of his face from the news cameras set up to cover the event. He had trimmed his upstart growth of facial hair to resemble a beard and added a blond wig under his hat. Unlike the days in early September when they had to beg the media to attend their rallies, the coverage now extended across the nation on every nightly newscast, both cable and network. Today, they would get more than they bargained for.

Joe had made a reservation at the Red Roof Inn a couple of blocks away even before his meeting with the others. His plan called for a specific room at that location, a top floor room. He had been fortunate enough to land it.

The last several hours saw him scurrying around the southern states. As soon as the meeting had ended, he scooted back to his home in Florida to pick up some necessary supplies. From there, he grabbed a flight to Corpus Christi and booked into the hotel under a false name. This subterfuge was merely a precaution. He would later hack the hotel's computer and remove all traces of this booking.

He hustled up to his room and threw open the curtains. If he leaned out slightly, he could see the workers outlined by bright lights putting the final touches on the stage 1800 feet away at Buccaneer Stadium. He heaved a sigh of relief.

He unpacked an unassembled rifle from his luggage, put it together, and mounted a laser sight. The rifle barrel had some camouflage colours designed to make it less noticeable and not able to reflect light. From another case, he retrieved a remote controlled device to operate the trigger mechanism and attached it to the rifle. He unfolded a metal stand and took it over to the ledge of the open window. He carefully lined it up to face the stadium and fastened it securely in place with suction clips. The clips would each connect to the front of the rifle barrel with wire.

He picked up the rifle and noticed his hands were starting to sweat. He wiped them on his pants and sat on the edge of the bed. It was not like this was his first time handling a rifle. He had been a Ranger when he served his military stint. He didn't necessarily believe in conscription. He did believe everyone should spend some time serving their country in the military. It gave them a better understanding of the price required to send forces around the world to defend our way of life. Not the financial price, the personal price.

This assault would be different. Joe knew the intended

target. That didn't change his resolve. He was still defending his country from its enemies. This time the enemies were from within.

He got up and walked to the window. Being careful not to be seen from the street below, he looked through the telescopic sight. In the distance, he could see the podium where Peter Weston would be speaking the next morning. His plan would work. The fine-tuning would come at 6:30 a.m. when the first light of false dawn would allow him to accurately adjust his aim.

From a third case, he gingerly removed a tiny plastic bag of grey powder with two wires sticking out. It held a mixture of rust and aluminum known as thermite, with a magnesium fuse. He placed this bag onto the remote stand for the rifle and taped it in place. He placed the rifle on the stand and attached the wires to the remote unit. Although the rifle itself was untraceable, he did not want anyone to be able to examine the remote control unit. It was proprietary to him, and although no one could trace the parts, someone knowledgeable in the field could associate the design with him.

The thermite, when triggered, would burn hot enough to not only destroy the remote unit but cause the rifle to separate from the stand and fall out the window, taking the stand with it when it toppled forward. On the ground below, a tall hedge of red roses covered the side of the building. The rifle assembly should land behind the flowers. It might take months before anyone discovered the rifle. Not burning down the hotel in the process would be the tricky part.

The window covering would be raised, and a special blanket, designed to look like a hotel window would cover the rifle. With luck, when it went out the window with the other items it would float down and cover everything. The backside of the blanket was a light green. If it landed properly, that would be strictly serendipity; everything would be hidden.

Joe had had his first decent night's sleep in a week. He sprang out of bed at 6:15 and started to make final arrangements. He sighted the rifle to a spot eight inches above the podium. Peter usually grabbed both sides of the stand and remained firmly behind it. Joe placed the blanket carefully over the entire ensemble, making sure the barrel was clear and the laser was unobstructed.

He stopped in for a continental breakfast before checking out. He sent his luggage to the airport in a taxi and walked the half-mile by road to the stadium.

A representative from the local BurgerCircus was warming up the crowd with tales of working with Ray Tutty in the early days as they built the franchise into the mega-operation it had become.

"I remember Ray working with one kid for over an hour just to teach him how to flip a burger the right way. It wasn't that the kid couldn't flip a burger, it was that he wasn't doing it the right way. To Ray, if a job was worth doing," he looked around the crowd, and they joined in as he finished the line, "it's worth doing right." Then they cheered wildly for themselves.

The rep held up his hands. "There is another man, also from Georgia, who believes and lives that saying. In six years, he has taken the small state of Georgia from being the rump of the nation to be one of the most productive per capita in the country." A ripple of applause ran through the audience. "Now, he wants to do the same thing for the entire country." Wild cheers emanated from all parts of the stadium. "And you can make that happen." More cheers. "Texas has thirty-eight electoral seats. Let's put them where they will do the most good." The stadium went wild.

Joe was astounded by the crowd's reaction. He knew support had been growing in leaps and bounds. He plotted the changes daily on his computer charts. This experience was the first time he had been in the field and got to feel the emotion of the crowd. He found that he was cheering along with everyone else, and this was only the warm-up act.

Suddenly, the music of Queen boomed out of the speakers with *We are the Champions*. The excitement in the crowd became palatable as they spontaneously started clapping and singing along. Unknown to Joe, this same reaction had been shown on television many times in the last few days.

Peter did not keep them waiting. He bounded out onto the stage, a picture of youthful energy. Cheering that had been loud reached a crescendo. Joe whistled and shouted along with the rest. Not to do so would make him stand out like a tomato in a cucumber patch. Peter stormed back and forth across the stage pointing at people and giving the thumbs-up sign. He stopped at the podium and waited for the cheering to subside.

"Thank you, fine people of Corpus Christi and people of Texas for that rousing welcome." The speakers were up a couple of notches. The crowd cheered again. Joe could see that this speech would take a while. Loud whistles and clapping would punctuate every statement. There were no dissenters in this crowd.

"I am here to welcome you as well. I want to welcome you to a new era for our country. I want to welcome you to a new beginning. I hate clichés as much as the next guy, but the time has come for out with old and in with the new."

And so it went for another fifteen minutes. Peter set out his new image of things to come, and the people responded with rousing support. Then the mood of the speech changed.

"It's important to understand what I intend to do for you. Equally important is to realize how little the current administration has done. I hate to give the man the title of president. Puppet is more appropriate. The people pulling his strings are lining their own pockets with your money. Not just your tax dollars; that would be bad enough. They are changing the rules on how we do things in such a way that they will be making money at your expense for years to come, long after we throw this administration to the curb. Not only your money but your children's money and your grandchildren's money.

"We can't sit back and expect others to do the heavy lifting for us. Next week, you must do your civic duty and exercise your right to vote, your right to rid the country of these vermin. It will take every vote we can get to overcome that mindless majority that votes the party line because their father did and their grandfather before him. They vote without thinking of the consequences. You," Peter pointed at the crowd. "You and you." He pointed to both bleachers and the football field. "You are the ones who can make change happen. It will require more effort than marking a simple X, and it should. We are changing the world. You have to write my name on the ballot. You must do that."

Peter stepped to the side of the stage and looked up at the monitor.

Joe had gotten so caught up in the speech that he thought he had missed his chance. He thought Peter was wrapping up the rally. That was not the case.

Both screens lit up with the exploding schools. Joe flinched. It was much more dramatic on a fifty-foot screen than on a twenty-two-inch computer monitor. As it came to a close, Peter returned to the podium, holding the image on the extortionists' compound exploding. "We all remember that hellish week in August."

The crowd had become subdued. A few obscenities could be heard among them acknowledging that they remembered. The image of Peter filled the screen again.

"Your puppet president twiddled is thumbs while our centres of learning burned, while the future of our kids went up in smoke. You all remember the little town near Laredo right here in Texas. Their school, up in smoke. I don't want to blow my own horn, but I could not stand by and do nothing. With the help of Ray Tutty and Malcolm Truex, I took the bull by the horns and tracked down those vile criminals. While the president slept, we dealt with them."

Oh, Peter, you lying hypocrite, Joe thought. He took off his sunglasses and put on a pair that would detect infrared rays. Immediately, a red dot popped onto Peter's chest. He waited for Peter to position it over his heart.

Peter, you could have done so much if you had just done it by the books.

"I brought the extortionists to justice." Peter's voice thundered throughout the stadium and into the surrounding streets.

Joe pushed a button on the remote in his jacket pocket. He didn't even hear the shot above the enthusiastic cheering filling the stadium. A bloom of red appeared on the white shirt over Peter's heart. He staggered backwards, a look of confusion on his face. Two recently appointed Secret Service men rushed from the side of the stage.

Some of the crowd were still cheering. Others stood in shock as they watched Peter fall out of the picture on the monitor. The monitor operator saw the life drain from Peter's eyes the second the bullet tore into his chest. He knew he was missing his chance to immortalize this moment for years to come, but he didn't follow Peter's body to the floor. Instead, he focused his camera on a giant backstage picture of Peter and Ray. Even presidential hopefuls deserved to die with dignity.

Then all hell broke loose.

◀79▶

"THE PRESIDENT SAYS," CNN talk show host Sean McNeil pointed out to Malcolm, "your campaign is 'the biggest threat to this country since the attack on Pearl Harbor and the people must put it down.'"

Malcolm chuckled. He had finagled a full half-hour on this morning news and opinion show. With so little time remaining in the contest, this was a major coup of free airtime.

"You are a threat to democracy and the American way of life," Sean continued.

"There is a party that represents a threat to the American way of life in this election," Malcolm said. "Unfortunately, they are now in power. If he sees us as a threat, perhaps he should read the Gettysburg Address where President Lincoln refers to 'government of the people, by the people, for the people.' Our president seems to confuse 'the people' with the so-called one per centers, the wealthy elite."

Sean scanned his notes. "He uses Italy as an example of what can go wrong when the two-party system breaks down. There has not been a majority government there since the end of the Second World War. He says nothing gets accomplished."

"It may seem that way," Malcolm agreed, "but in this..."

A high-pitched tone sounded on the set. A red and yellow banner with the words "BREAKING NEWS" scrolled across the screen. A producer rushed out and handed Sean a sheet of paper,

"This just in," Sean started to read and then came to an abrupt halt. His face blanched. He looked at Malcolm and then back at the producer, who shrugged.

"What is it?" Malcolm asked, concern in his voice.

The senior producer came out of the control room. He removed Malcolm's lapel mic and escorted him off the set and back into his office.

Sean cleared his throat and read: "Governor Peter Weston, independent presidential candidate, has been shot at a rally in Corpus Christi, Texas before an estimated crowd of 20,000 people. Sources on the ground, say the governor was wrapping up his speech in front of the wildly supportive crowd when he collapsed on the stage with an apparent gunshot wound to the chest. Secret Service agents, recently assigned to Weston, rushed him to a nearby SUV and whisked him away to the hospital. We have no further details at this time."

The camera cut away to Texas where the police on the scene were being overwhelmed by the shocked crowd. Some crowded towards the stage; others threw themselves onto the ground; while the majority started clamouring for the exits. A uniformed officer ran to the microphone. He appealed to everyone to keep calm and remain in their seats. Either no one heard him, or no one cared what he had to say.

Joe Fisher ducked behind the bleachers and hopped a low fence. Luck was with him. A taxi had dropped off a fare on Upper River Road. He grabbed the cab and headed for the airport. His cell phone rang a few minutes into the trip. He looked at the call display.

Sorry to do this to you, old buddy, but sometimes in the fog of war, you have to look to the greater good.

"Are you near a TV?" he asked before Malcolm could

speak. "It looks like someone beat us to it."

"What?" Malcolm asked.

"Peter has been shot in Corpus Christi. It's all over the television."

"I know. I'm on television. I'm at CNN."

Joe hesitated for a few beats. "That's perfect. Make the announcement." He paused again. "That didn't come out right, I'm sorry. Still, we can't miss this golden opportunity to start the campaign. Serendipity is on our side."

Forty minutes later, Joe was at the airport, checked in and ready to go. The flying time back to Atlanta would be two and one-half hours. He hoped to slip in unnoticed. All electronic traces of his visit had been scrubbed from any computer databases before he exited the plane.

Malcolm called Ray Tutty and filled him in on his conversation with Joe. Ray told him to go for it. He composed himself and asked the producer, "Can I make a statement?"

The producer's eyes lit up. He was fighting the urge to ask for that very thing. "I'll get you miked up," he said.

Malcolm took a seat facing Sean who looked surprised to see him back. The scene on the monitor changed from the milling crowd at Buccaneer Stadium to a shot outside of Corpus Christi Medical Center. The actual shooting had been shown several times already. A reporter stood there ready to make a report.

"Mary Sergeant has an update from outside the Corpus Christi Medical Center," Sean said. "Mary?"

Mary looked into the camera, sadness written all over her face. "We've been told that Governor Weston did not survive. He was declared dead on arrival by the medical team here at Corpus Christi Medical Center. First indications are that a single gunshot wound to the chest was immediately fatal. That's all they are saying at this time. Back to you, Sean."

This information came as no surprise to either Sean or Malcolm. They had been tipped off by a reporter covering the event at the stadium that Peter was dead before his back touched the stage. They held this information back while they waited for official confirmation.

"I'm sorry for your loss," Sean said to Malcolm when they were back on the air. "I know your relationship with the governor goes back a long way."

Malcolm nodded his head to acknowledge the sentiment.

"I know this may be the last thing on your mind right now, but what will this do to your campaign. Everything seemed to be turning in your favour."

"Sean, the governor did not enter this contest because of any great desire to become president. We have made massive improvements in the state of Georgia, both economic and cultural. There were still things we want to do.

"Much of our effort was being thwarted by the inept and may I say, corrupt government in Washington. Peter realized—we all realized—that we had to clean up that mess before we could make any real progress. The school bombings are a case in point. The president had his head in the sand. His re-election was his top priority. Peter Weston stepped up to the plate in the president's absence and took those criminals down.

"After a great deal of soul searching and discussion, a group of us—the governor, myself, Ray Tutty, and several other patriotic Americans—realized only one solution existed. Peter stepped up once more and threw his name into the hat. We all knew the odds were overwhelmingly against us, but we had to do what was best for the good of the country as a whole."

Malcolm paused and looked into the lens of the camera.

"Peter Weston's assassination has changed nothing. We can only do what Peter, Governor Weston, was trying to do. We must defeat this current incompetent government.

"Ray Tutty and I discussed the matter minutes ago and agreed we can't quit the fight now. Peter would insist we continue." Malcolm's stoic resolve seemed to shake a little. His eyes became moist. He took a deep breath, swallowed and continued speaking. "With this in mind, Ray will continue his fight for vice president and I take the lead and go for the presidency."

Sean couldn't hide his surprise. "You, Malcolm?"

"I believe everything Peter believed, and that most of the American people believe, according to the polls. If we quit now, the bad guys win."

"Bad guys? Are you suggesting the president had anything to do with Peter's death?"

Malcolm held up his hands and shook his head.

"No, Sean. It's too early for that. As you know, I'm a former FBI agent. Those years in the agency taught me you don't accuse someone first and then look for evidence of their guilt. You gather all the facts and see where those facts take you. Finding Peter's killers will become an important part of our mandate."

"So you're not accusing the president or his administration."

"No, not at this time. Some, however, might apply the Duck Test."

"Duck Test?" Sean raised his eyes inquisitively.

"Walks like a duck, swims like a duck, quacks like a duck ..." Malcolm let his voice trail off. "As you said earlier in the hour, the president said we must be put down."

"Ouch," Sean said. "Did I say that?"

Malcolm rolled his eyes. "With a little over a week to

go until Election Day, we will have a lot to overcome. You were surprised that I would put my name forward. I understand your concern. Despite my years working behind the scenes, I don't have name recognition across the country. That will be a serious problem in a write-in vote."

"You've spent a lot of time here on CNN pushing forward your platform. A lot of people must recognize you by now."

"True, Sean, but not everyone watches CNN, except for right now. Spectacular events make you the go-to channel."

"We do our best to get people on the ground as quickly as possible. Today, we were already there."

"To be accepted as a write-in candidate, I have to register in several states. To do that, I need varying amounts of signatures from registered voters, up to forty thousand in Oklahoma. Starting tomorrow, we'll have forms at BurgerCircus outlets where people can sign up. We've already done if for Peter. Now we have to do it again for me and in the next couple of days."

"You do have a favourable name for a write-in candidate." Sean hesitated, not sure if he should continue. With the death of Peter Weston only minutes before, this may not be a good time to be making light of the situation.

"Favourable?"

"True-X."

Malcolm laughed in spite of his attempts not to. "I like that. Can I use it?"

"Fill your boots," Sean said, feeling pleased with his little witticism.

Little did he realize how popular the phrase would become.

◀80▶

THE PRESIDENT STEPPED up to the podium at the hastily called press conference. He wore a freshly-pressed suit, his hair was combed, but his face carried the weight of the ages on it.

"I'm going to make this short," he said. "An unholy act took place hours ago in Corpus Christ, Texas, an act that we can't tolerate in America, won't tolerate in America. We will unleash the full force of the law on the perpetrators of this vile crime.

"It is well known that Governor Weston and I butted heads over several issues. I extend my condolences to his family. God bless America."

The president turned to walk off the stage when the questions erupted from all over the room. The loudest asked: "Do you have any leads? Who do you suspect?"

The president ignored the questions and kept walking towards the exit.

"It has been suggested that your administration has the most to gain from this assassination. I am not accusing you of having any part of this, but do you think it was your followers that carried out despicable act?"

The president's face took on a brilliant red hue as he turned to face the questioners.

"I will not dignify that slanderous insinuation with an answer."

"Again, Mr. President, I am not suggesting you were personally involved, but your biggest competition has been eliminated. It can only help you chances of winning. What about your re-election team? Could one of them be involved?"

Harold White, the president's press secretary, rushed forward. These were the questions he had feared. *What had those idiots trying to get the president re-elected done? Would a serious investigation lead back to the president?*

"Rod Sanderson." Harold pointed a finger at the reporter. "I might have known. These insinuations are inappropriate even disguised as questions. A man has been murdered. We will investigate and find and punish those responsible."

"You were second in the polls and slipping fast. Do you feel relief now that Peter Weston is out of the running?"

"We all know polls can be slanted by the questions asked. Voting day will be the true test, and the president looks forward to that challenge. He will be vindicated by the majority of votes he obtains."

"Malcolm Truex has stepped into Weston's slot. Should he be worried for his life?"

"True-X," Harold scoffed. "It will take more than a catchy phrase to propel some unknown to the highest office in the land. We protect all candidates, even those who don't have a chance. This news conference is over."

Harold grabbed the president by the elbow and escorted him off the stage.

Rod Sanderson turned to the other reporters. "To paraphrase Shakespeare, I think they protest too much."

◀81▶

THE FINAL WEEK of the campaign kept everyone at Malcolm and Ray's headquarters hopping. They received thousands of signatures more than they needed to make the write-in votes stick if they could get them. The subject of the apathy of the voters raised its ugly head at every meeting. A major change of thought had to wake up the voters to get them out to the polls.

A few billboards appeared in the major cities around the country. "Make your vote count. Mark the True-X." Efforts were made to get these signs included on the news programs of every network. The novelty of the slogan made it newsworthy. CNN loved it. It was their idea. They couldn't show it too often.

Every time the president or vice-president appeared on a news show, updates about the governor's assassination were requested. There were no answers. Every unanswered question raised the spectre of the administration's involvement. Social media and the Twitter universe were having a field day with wild speculation. Conspiracy theories abounded everywhere. Malcolm and Ray kept climbing in the polls.

Joe Fisher's fallen rifle remained undiscovered. He pondered the risks involved in going back to Corpus Christi and retrieving the only possible piece of evidence that existed. He decided to wait until after the election.

As Election Day approached, both Malcolm and Ray felt the increasing pressure for them to appear in public. Although neither admitted it, both feared for their lives.

There was no proof that the president's cronies had assassinated Peter Weston, but Joe claimed someone had beat him to it. If that were true, and they had no reason to disbelieve him, they both wore targets on their chests.

Barbara was the first to put it into words.

"You can't be putting yourselves at risk anymore. There is more than enough demand from the networks to keep you both in the public eye and safely in the confines of a television studio. I forbid you to do otherwise."

Ray laughed. He looked at Paul. "You realize that in three days it will be you that has to take all this abuse. I'll be safely in the White House; she will be your executive assistant back at BurgerCircus."

"No," Paul said. "She will be a vice-president, like you, but unlike you, she will have so much on her plate that she will leave me alone."

Malcolm listened to this byplay and looked relaxed for the first time in weeks. "That's not true. My vice-president is not going to get a free ride. I have an agenda for you that will make you wish you were back at BurgerCircus. Bring a suitcase with you to the West Wing on January 21st and be prepared to live out of it for the next eight years.

"In the meantime, which of these news and late-night shows are going to give us the most bang for our buck?"

"I have a list," Barbara said. She hit a key on her computer. "I've downloaded your schedules to your phones."

Sean Rhyno — Morning commentary

In other news:

Many of you are wondering who this Johnny-come-lately candidate for the presidency, Malcolm Truex, is. Where did he come from? What does he stand for? Those of you who are regular viewers of CNN should have a good understanding of the answers to these questions. He was the chief-of-staff of the late Georgia governor, Peter Westin, Independent presidential candidate, until Westin was brutally shot to death while campaigning in Texas last week. Truex had spent the last two months explaining Westin's platform on any news show that would talk to him, including mine. he has shown a very intimate knowledge of the party platform.

As a former agent with the FBI he became an invaluable part of the investigation of the school bombings that rocked the nation last August. Initial he was the Georgian liaison to the FBI, but soon became as deeply involved as any of the other agents. You may recall he took part in the only actual arrest of one of the extortionists.

We at CNN are not endorsing Truex as a candidate. We stay above politics. We believe that voters should be informed in order to make a vote that counts. This is simply equal time with the other front-runners. You will recall we profiled them in July after their respective conventions.

Please do your civic duty on Tuesday and get out and vote for the candidate of your choice.

◀82▶

ON TUESDAY NIGHT, Malcolm, Ray, Paul, Barbara and Joe gathered in Ray's office on the top floor of the BurgerCircus building to await the results of the vote. A big-screen TV brought CNN into the room with them. Joe sat at the computer.

He had written a program to analyze and make predictions as the early reports filtered in from their workers across the country. Some states didn't allow write-in votes. He ignored those. Others would re-elect the current party in power if they ran a monkey on a stick as a candidate. He recorded those votes but didn't waste computer resources examining them.

He knew where they had to win and dumped most of their resources in those states. Two of them, California and Florida, always seemed to bring up the rear with their results. It would be a long night.

Several party workers were doing the same thing on the first floor at campaign headquarters. Spirits were high. Most of these people had never been this intimately involved in an election before. They didn't understand what kind of odds they were bucking. Whiteboards covered all the walls with small maps on them, representing the fifty states. As results poured in from across the country, a team stood by to record and update them. A running total of Electoral College seats won was displayed on a seventy-two-inch screen at one end of the room and connected to Joe's computer.

The trend developed early. Record numbers responded

to the "Mark the True-X" campaign. Voter turnout numbers were in the high eighties and low nineties. Not since the election of Abraham Lincoln in 1860 and the controversial vote of 1876 had eighty per cent of the people turned out to vote.

When California went his way, Malcolm had a twenty-eight seat lead, not a landslide but unprecedented for a write-in candidate. Only Florida had yet to report with its twenty-nine seats. The popular vote numbers were through the roof in Malcolm's favour. Where he won, he swept the state; where he lost, the races were photo finishes.

At 4 a.m. Malcolm leaned over Joe's shoulder and studied the numbers on the screen. "Come on, Joe, make a prediction. You've been right all night."

"Sorry, bud. Too close to call. Over thirty per cent of the population of Florida is over sixty. At that age you become set in your ways." He turned to face Malcolm. "Now if that school had blown up, things might be different. A fiery explosion gets people's attention." He gave Malcolm a light tap on the shoulder. "Relax."

"I hope it's not like 2000," Ray said. "I couldn't take this being dragged out for days."

Barbara opened one eye from where she lay on the couch. "Wake me when it's over. I don't care anymore."

Numbers started to scroll on Joe's computer. Music filled the room—Hail to the Chief. Barbara leapt to her feet.

"Is that it? Did we win?"

"Do we have champagne in that bar fridge?" Joe asked.

Paul grabbed Malcolm's hand and pumped it up and down. "No time for champagne up here. We have to get to the first floor."

He handed Malcolm and Ray a sheet of paper each. "Here are your acceptance speeches. Don't go off script." He looked into Ray's eyes. "Especially you. This is no time to gloat."

"How wrong you are, Paul. Now is exactly the time to gloat." Ray grabbed Malcolm by the shoulders and gave him a bear crushing hug. Let the party begin."

Television cameras from all the networks had taken up positions along a back wall of the headquarters. As the votes poured in, skepticism had disappeared among the top TV executives. They ordered their senior talking heads to Atlanta.

Ray ran into the room ahead of the others and up to the hastily added podium. He addressed the excited throng gathered in front of him. "Ladies and gentlemen, America, your new president." He pointed to Malcolm as he entered the room.

Workers, who minutes before had been struggling to stay awake, their voices worn out from intermittent cheering throughout the night as the results surged first one way and then the other, came alive again. The room filled with applause. Despite the late hour, no one had left.

Tears streamed down Malcolm's face as he mounted the makeshift stage. He seized Ray's hand and held it high in the air.

"We did it," he said. "We did it."

Malcolm's face became solemn. "This is where I am supposed to congratulate the losers on what a great campaign they ran. I won't. America, we have a new government that believes in honesty and truth. We are going to start with that right now. They ran a campaign of smut and lies, a dirty campaign. You, my fellow Americans, saw through their deception. You fought for a better America, and you are the winners here tonight. I thank you for that."

Paul could see his speech sticking out of Malcolm's jacket pocket. He smiled inwardly. He should have known better.

Malcolm turned to stare directly into the closest camera.

Instantly, a tight close-up shot filled the monitor.

"Congressmen, Senators, take note of the popular vote. If you choose obstructionism as your way of governing for the next four years, your political careers will be cut short. We hope for, and the people demand, bipartisan representation. Remember why you are here—to govern this great country and make it even better. The time of feathering your own nests has ended. Remember that when you report to the Capitol tomorrow. To those of you who have overthrown incumbents, Ray and I welcome you to our team."

Now Malcolm smiled at the cheering group of workers. The camera faded back to catch the entire room. Malcolm took Paul's speech from his pocket and acknowledged Paul standing in the front row. He opened the paper and lay it on the podium.

"I want to thank all of you who worked so hard to make this happen, not just those in this room, but across the nation. I thank all of you voters who took a chance on something different, those of you who voted for the first time, those of you who voted again after a long absence. This is your victory as well."

The crowd in the room shouted approval. Malcolm let them continue for a few minutes.

He put his hand on Ray's shoulder. "We will not disappoint you."

Ray stepped up to the mike. He pretty much followed Paul's words, but the delivery was his own. Once again the crowd became fired up. Ray looked at his watch.

"Let's go home everybody and get some well-deserved sleep. You have earned it. Tomorrow is a new day for our nation. Let's be well-rested and ready to tackle the world."

He and Malcolm walked off the stage arm in arm. They went directly to the elevator and back to the top floor. They left Paul and Barbara to field questions from the media. Joe slipped into his office. He left the lights out. He settled into an easy chair, closed his eyes and fell immediately asleep.

The sun broke on the horizon and sent bright shards of light into Ray's office. Malcolm raised a glass of champagne and toasted Ray. Both men had removed their ties and taken off their jackets. They sat quietly for several minutes. Realization of what had taken place started to settle on them. A formidable task stretched out in front of them.

Malcolm looked over at his new vice-president. "Holy shit, Ray. What have we done?"

Ray smiled. "We're living Peter Weston's dream."

◀Epilogue▶

JOE TOOK A final look around Malcolm's old office at the governor's mansion. His work here was completed, for now. His packed suitcases sat by the door in anticipation of a trip back to his condo in Florida, perhaps with a side trip to Corpus Christi.

"You can't go yet, Joe," Malcolm said. He was sitting on the edge of his old desk. "I have a couple more questions."

"Some things are better left as they are, Mr. President— sleeping dogs, how they get the caramel into a Caramilk bar, and Peter Weston's sordid secrets."

"Tell me more about the money. Where did it come from? How did it work?"

Joe walked over to the window and looked out at the fountain in the middle of the circular driveway. Malcolm waited for him to speak.

"I have to know, Joe."

"No, Malcolm. You don't." He paused, then slipped into one of the more comfortable chairs in Malcolm's office. "But, I don't want you nosing around on your own."

After a short period of silence while Joe stared out the window at the blue sky overhead, he continued.

"You have to understand that Peter really wanted to be president. For the prestige, for the power, or did he think he would be able to make a difference. I don't know."

"I worked with him every day for several years. I know how much he wanted it."

"No, I don't think you do, Malcolm. Anyway, he took every cent he could get his hands on and with as much of a

442

margin as he could obtain from his broker, he bought stocks of BurgerCircus. He then dragged them into the news by making them the main target of his band of extortionists. He knew Tutty wouldn't pay. That was crucial to his plan.

"Almost immediately, the stock shares took a dive. He sold all his shares as the price started going down. He re-bought them at the bottom of the dip plus more. He did this every day for five days.

"The key to the plan was his ability to force the fluctuations in prices by controlling the news cycle. He knew when to buy and when to sell."

Malcolm joined Joe at the window. "That seems like a lot of money in a short time."

"It is. I did the math. It didn't quite add up. Somewhere through the week, he started buying shares of another company, a lesser fast-food place. Their values rode the same roller coaster as BurgerCircus. Peter bought on the bottom of the cycle but didn't resell them. He accumulated a huge portfolio of their shares. BurgerCircus bought out the company about a week after the bombing ended at an inflated price. I checked to make sure Ray wasn't involved. The deal had been in the works for months. Peter made a killing."

"Derek Saunders' company," Malcolm said. "I heard them discussing the takeover at one of our early meetings at Ray's estate. Peter must have heard them, too."

"Peter milked the system until he had raised enough money to make his run for the top job. He killed off any witnesses who knew anything of value, his partners in the scheme. A few people are still out there somewhere. They knew their little portion of the task, nothing more. He didn't see them as a threat. They don't know Peter was involved.

"In fact, none of the partners knew they were dealing with the governor of Georgia. They all thought it was about the money. We know how convincing Peter could be. The put up a bundle of cash to fund the scheme and expected to get millions in return.

"They didn't arrive at the compound on that fateful morning. They had spent the night there. The flurry of emails and instructions we decoded was all showmanship. Peter played us all, even me."

Joe put a hand on Malcolm's shoulder.

"Malcolm, he spent months planning this right under your nose. His only shortcoming came with the cameraman in Colorado. The plan called for him to be an Islamic terrorist. You and Tom saw right through that and Peter abandoned it right away. That proved to be serendipitous. Since he wasn't a foreign terrorist, the president didn't get involved, much to his detriment. Peter raked in all the credit."

Malcolm stepped back.

"What about the money still in those accounts? Does it sit there forever?"

"No. Peter didn't do the buying and selling himself. He was too busy keeping all the balls in the air. He worked through an accomplice. That person will receive a windfall."

"So, we have a threat out there that could blow up in our faces?"

"Not likely. To blow the whistle on us, he would have to admit his involvement in the whole scheme, including the murders in the swamp. I think he'll happily take his money and quietly drift in the background. The funds that ended up in the campaign chest belonged to Peter. The donations were legal."

He paused and held up a finger towards Malcolm. "But don't get too vigorous in your search for his killer. We don't want any of this to come to light."

Joe shrugged. "That's it, my friend. You know what I know. Now forget about it and save the country from destruction. The fates have stepped in and dropped the world on your shoulders. Prove that you're better than Atlas."

Malcolm shook his head. "Atlas was tasked with holding up the sky to keep it from crashing into the earth, a more formidable job. When I start to falter, you will be my first call."

"You've got my number, pal." Joe grabbed a suitcase in each hand and walked out the door.

Malcolm took one last look around the office that had dominated his life for the last six years. "This was the frying pan. Now let's try the fire."

ABOUT THE AUTHOR

Art Burton lives in Latties Brook, Nova Scotia, Canada with his wife, Flame and dog, Charley.

He took an early retirement from The Halifax Herald at the end of 2002 where he had been a printer for 26 years before joining the IT Department. When he left the hustle and bustle of life in the big city for the more relaxed, laid-back lifestyle of rural Nova Scotia, he decided it was time to move up from printing to writing.

He has written six mystery novels as well as two books of related-short stories about the hobos who passed through Central Nova Scotia during the Great Depression.

For more information on these books, visit his web page at artburton.ca.